HARLEM REDUX

A NOVEL

Persia Walker

SIMON & SCHUSTER

NEW YORK   LONDON   TORONTO   SYDNEY   SINGAPORE

SIMON & SCHUSTER
Rockefeller Center
1230 Avenue of the Americas
New York, NY 10020

This work was previously published,
in slightly different form, by iUniverse.com, Inc.
SIMON & SCHUSTER and colophon are
registered trademarks of Simon & Schuster, Inc.

For information about special discounts for bulk purchases,
please contact Simon & Schuster Special Sales:
1-800-456-6798 or business@simonandschuster.com

Designed by Jan Pisciotta

Manufactured in the United States of America
10 9 8 7 6 5 4 3 2 1

Library of Congress Cataloging-in-Publication Data

Walker, Persia.
    Harlem redux : a novel / Persia Walker.
        p. cm.
    1. Harlem (New York, N.Y.)—Fiction. 2. Harlem Renaissance—Fiction. 3. African
Americans—Fiction. I. Title.

PS3623.A438 H37 2002
813'.6—dc21   2002017551

ISBN 0-7432-2497-3

Acknowledgments

This work owes a profound debt to the writers of the Harlem Renaissance . . . Countee Cullen, Rudolph Fisher, Langston Hughes, Zora Neale Hurston, James Weldon Johnson, Nella Larsen, Claude McKay, Vivian Morris, and Wallace Thurman, among others. Their short stories, novels, memoirs, essays, and articles fired my imagination. Their writings were windows against which I pressed my nose, eager as a child, to spend many pleasurable hours viewing their world.

Thanks also to historians David Levering Lewis, Carl T. Rowan, Michel Fabre, Tyler Stovall, Steven Watson, and Lionel C. Bascom. Their informative, perceptive, and very enjoyable works on the Harlem Renaissance provided a wealth of information—more than I, with my skills, could do justice to. For whatever insufficiencies this text might contain, debit them to me, not my sources.

A special round of applause for Julie Castiglia, my agent, for her determination and steady guidance, and for Andrea Mullins at Simon & Schuster for making the editing process a genuine pleasure. Between these two dynamos, I was well taken care of.

My heartfelt gratitude to Debbie Geiss-Haug, Sonia Ehrt, Michelle Bonnardot, Michelle Moore, Kathy Raymond, Dina Treu, Gabriele Heblik-Hochholzer, and Professor Charles James. And a special thanks to Henry Ferretti. They've been steadfast friends, forgiving unreturned phone calls, missed get-togethers, and general unavailability. Without their humor, patience, encouragement, and feedback, this novel might never have been completed.

Most of all, I want to thank my Mom, for her love and faith, and my little troopers, Tyler and Jordan, for so generously sharing their Mom with David and Annie, Gem and Lilian, Nella, Rachel, and Sweet.

Persia Walker
Munich, Germany
November 9, 2001

To Mom, Tyler, and Jordan

Prologue

The room was dark, except for one silvery ray of moonlight. An icy wind slipped in through the open window, swept around the room, and caressed her with chilling fingertips. She came to with a start. The darkness shocked her. The silence told her she was alone. How long had she lain there?

Her hands had been folded across her chest. She felt throbbing spurts of warm liquid spilling onto her breasts, drenching the soft cotton of her night-gown. And she sensed the approach of that final darkness. The urge to close her eyes, to give in, was overwhelming. The room seemed to revolve. Slowly. Her eyelids drooped. An inner voice asked:

Are you really going to lie there . . . and bleed to death?

Her eyes snapped open.

No.

At first, her hands seemed mercifully numb. But within minutes, the pain had grown more pronounced. Soon, it was agonizingly refined. The tortured nerve endings in her slashed wrists screamed with voices that echoed inside her, quickening and clarifying her thoughts.

I have to get help.

She tried to move her legs, but they were like logs, heavy and inert.

Find another way.

Pressing her elbows to her side, she twisted her upper torso and rocked back and forth. Her body rolled once, twice, then over the edge. The bed was high; the fall was hard. She landed with a heavy thump and for a moment lay stunned. Her heart pounded; her thoughts struggled for clarity.

There was no way she could use her hands. They were half-dead clumps of flesh. But her legs had been jolted back to life. Elbows still pressed to her side, she rolled over onto her chest, drew her knees up under her, then pushed herself up with her elbows. Leaning on the mattress to brace herself, she could stand.

The effort cost her. She sagged against a bedpost. Trying to hold on, she threw her forearms around the carved wooden beam. Her limp hands dangled, dripping their warm liquid. Cold sweat slipped down from her forehead and upper lips.

The darkness crept nearer.

Time had played a trick on her. She wasn't in the house on Strivers' Row, but elsewhere. The air didn't smell of jasmine and tobacco, but of the sea. She was in the Hamptons, in Nella's house. There came the sound of a life-and-death struggle, a gunshot. She again saw a pair of dead, staring eyes.

"No," she whispered. "No. I won't let you do this."

She held on and the darkness receded. She knew where she was. She could make out the shapes of furniture by the moonlight—could even see her own shadow as she clung to the bedpost. But she felt seasick, as if she were clinging to the mast of a swaying boat. Her stomach heaved and she bent over, vomiting on herself and the bed. She clung to the bedpost as another wave of dizziness passed over her, then straightened up with a moan. Wiping her mouth with the back of her forearm, she smeared her face with blood.

Time's running out.

She could make it to the bedroom door.

Fifteen steps. That's all it would take.

But she hesitated. She did not know what—or more accurately, who—might be waiting for her on the other side. In a bizarre way, her bedroom meant safety. She heard a thump. Her heart lurched. Was it a footstep in the hallway—or just the house settling on its foundation? She swallowed and took a deep breath. She would have to make it down the stairs, creeping along with the help of the banister, then make it into the parlor before she could reach the telephone. If she fainted along the way, on the steps or at the parlor entrance, then . . .

No, not the door.

What then?

An icy breeze stroked her cheek.

The open window. Get to it. Scream. Call out—that's the way to go.

She counted backward from three, focusing her energy. At zero, she let go of the bedpost and took a step toward the window. Her legs were weak and shaky. Her knees trembled, but they didn't buckle. She took another tottering step. And another. That window had never seemed so far away; her body never so unwilling.

She was nearly across the room when it happened.

She tripped over the hem of her gown and toppled forward. Her head hit the corner of an antique linen chest. A sharp pain lanced through her skull and the moonlight, dim as it was, grew dimmer.

No, not now. Please, not now.

But her vision blurred and the light grew duskier. She lifted her head a wobbly inch or two, her eyelids drooped and her head sagged to the floor.

She might have drifted away permanently if it hadn't been for the wailing scream of a racing police siren. The sound expanded in the air, ballooned inside her head, until it seemed to explode inside her skull. She lay blinking in the dark, telling herself it was all a bad dream. But the cold floor under her face was real. So was the blood that had congealed and crusted on her face and arms and chest. She was awake and she had to get going. She didn't know how much blood she'd lost, but she assumed she'd lost a great deal. If she passed out again, she wouldn't wake up.

She was too weak to stand again, so she half-crawled, half-dragged herself across the floor. An eternity passed before she reached the base of that window. She rested, panting, and looked up.

The casement sill was little more than a yard above her head, but it might as well have been a mile. Her head throbbed. Her heart knocked. She wanted to sit and be still.

Get to that windowsill. Find the strength.

Curling up, she leaned one shoulder against the wall and inched her way up. It was taking forever. She was swimming up from way down deep. She held her breath, struggling against a vicious, relentless, downward pull. Clear droplets of agony slipped down from her temples. Would she ever reach the surface?

Then she was up. Fully upright. She leaned into a blast of frigid air. It cut to the bone, but it felt good. So very good! To be standing. To be at the window. To *still* be alive.

Pushing aside a porcelain vase on the windowsill, she flopped down on the narrow ledge and looked out. The small dark street seemed empty.

No! There has to be someone. Please, Lord, let there be someone. Help me this once, damn it. I'm begging you, begging you to help me. Now!

She noticed a light shining in a second-floor window across the way.

"Help! Help!" she screamed, but the wind, merry and malicious, kissed the words from her mouth and whipped them away. "Pleeease! *Some*body! *Any*body! HELP MEEEE!"

Again the wind, ever careless and cruel, swallowed the sounds of her pleading, took them so fast she barely heard them herself.

She pushed herself to hang out the window. Down the street to her left was a man walking his Doberman. He was stooped with age and bundled against the cold; his cap jammed down over his ears.

"Hey, mister! Mister, please! Up here! Send help! Please, mister, *please!*"

The man did not respond but the dog paused, perked up his ears, and howled. The wind that swept her words away served up the dog's mournful wails with mocking efficiency.

"*Please! I don't wanna die! I DON'T WANNA DIE!*"

The dog barked harder, louder, belting agitated yowls that rode the hellish gusts of wind up and down the street. Hope pulsed through her. The Doberman pulled on his leash, strained in her direction. The dog's owner yanked him back. He cuffed him on the nose. And dragged him off down the street. Away from her.

"*NO!!!*"

Her elbow touched the vase. She turned without thinking and gave it a shove that sent it plunging out the window. She watched it turn and tumble as if in slow motion, saw it crash and explode into minute pieces. She looked down. Had they heard?

They were gone. So quickly. Gone. As though they'd never been there.

Her legs gave out. She crumpled to the floor, her outstretched arms smearing trails of blood on the wall. Her head sagged.

"Oh, God . . . no," she wept. "Don't let this happen. This can't happen."

Then she felt the curtains. Made of lightweight silk, they billowed about her face, as familiar, as gentle, cool, and caressing as a loved one's touch. She closed her eyes. An eerie calm crept over her. Odd, how the pain was receding. If only she could rest. Sleep.

No! She wanted to live, to hold on. She loved life. She refused to let it slip away. Not like this. Not while she was young. Not when she finally . . . had nearly everything . . .

But the darkness was getting hard to fight. She had never felt so tired. Her inhalations grew fainter. Her eyes slid shut. From behind her closed eyelids, she saw her inner lights fade individually, felt herself float away, bit by precious bit, as her blood-starved organs shut down, one after another. She was about to die and she knew it. Summoning her strength, she raised her face to bathe it in the moonlight. She held it there with stubborn determination for several exquisite seconds. Then her last inner light faded and with a moan she slumped down, a bloody but still beautiful corpse gazing blindly at the bleak night sky.

1

The Lost Son Returns

Lilian's older brother had been away for years, but he had altered little, at least on the surface. He was thirty-five. Silver already touched his temples, but his hair was otherwise still dark and thick. Quite tall and lean, he had an oval face and clear olive skin with a strong fine profile. He had retained the lustrous dark eyes that had melted many a feminine resistance. Time had magnified their eloquence. Maturity had deepened them and experience saddened them. He was aware of his effect on women, but he tended toward solitude, and though he enjoyed female company, he always feared that in the end, a woman would ask for more than he could give. Or worse, that he would give all he had, then see her pull away in disappointment and leave him.

Well-built and poised, David McKay had a reputation for dressing well with tasteful understatement. His clothes were of excellent quality, but close inspection would have shown them to be worn. There were no holes or tatters, hanging threads or missing buttons, but the clothes, like the man, gave off an intangible air of fatigue. Even so, he was usually the handsomest man in any crowd. That day, his dark gray cashmere coat was buttoned high against the early spring chill. He wore his fedora tipped low to one side, just enough to cast a shadow, but not enough to hide the sad gleam in his eye.

Like his sister, David preferred to stay out of the limelight. But his air of quiet distinction was noticeable to even the most casual observer. It was all the more evident that chilly March Thursday because of the mute pain in his eyes. The early evening's dusky skies emphasized his pallor. Sorrow had grayed his complexion. Tension had cut furrows into his handsome face. He was bone-weary. From shock, grief, and lack of sleep. His sister was dead and buried some three weeks, but he had only learned of it the day before.

He had forgotten much of the past twenty-four hours. The last moment he did recall was when he got that note while eating lunch at his desk in Philadelphia, that telegram summoning him home. He had an excellent memory. It could be useful, but there were times when it absorbed information he would have rather forgotten. The words to that telegram, for example, would remain etched in his memory until the day he died. It had turned his world upside down. When he left his law office to head home and pack, he was as disoriented as a man who suddenly finds himself walking on the ceiling.

Lilian was a part of him. It was nearly impossible to accept that she was gone. He swung between anguish and numbness. His mind struggled to accept her death even as his heart rejected it. Her presence hovered in the air about him, a gentle warmth that carried a hint of the light powdery perfume she wore. Whenever he looked at a crowd, he thought he saw her face.

It had never occurred to him that Lilian might die. He had not seen her in four years, but he had always been able to visualize her writing poetry at her desk or reading a newspaper before the parlor fireplace. Those images had comforted him. He had summoned them in times of doubt. Lilian: stable, dependable, clearheaded, and never changing. Whether she agreed with his life choices or not, she had been there for him.

It wasn't only her death that stunned him; there was the manner of it: The telegram said she had committed suicide. When had Lilian's life become so unbearable that death seemed to offer the only relief? And why?

She had mailed him a letter on the first of every month for some two years, starting in January 1923. Her letters had never reflected dissatisfaction with her life. They were always warm, colorful missives, filled with innocuous but witty gossip or news about her writing career. Her letters had arrived with efficient regularity until a year ago, in March 1925, and then ended abruptly. He told himself now that he should have become worried at her sudden silence. He should have made inquiries. That last letter had begged him to return home. He hadn't answered it.

Now he longed for one more chance to hug her, to tell her how proud he was of her, to confess and explain the unexplainable. But he would never have an opportunity to do that—never. And that stunned him.

Struggling to confront the inescapable, he tried in vain to reconcile the immense contradiction between her dramatic death and her deep devotion to discretion during life. She was a proud, gentle woman, known for her exquisite discipline, delicate tastes, and exceptionally even temperament. Were someone to ever write her life story, a most likely title would be *Pride of Place*. She was a reclusive person, raised with a deeply ingrained awareness of her responsibilities toward her family, her class, and her race—in that order. A conscientious conformist, she strove to keep her name synonymous with propriety, refinement, and perfect manners. She scrupulously guarded her privacy and avoided contact with anyone whose behavior might attract inappropriate attention. It was a horrible irony that the most private of all acts—the act of dying—had made her the source of tabloid scandal.

He had lost all sense of time during the train ride from Philadelphia. Fear had lengthened the trip into an eternity. And fear had shortened it, propelling him toward his destination much too quickly. He had gotten hold of a copy of the *New York Times,* but neither the latest corruption tales involving the Democratic Party machine at Tammany Hall nor the political circus of the Sacco-Vanzetti case could distract him. His terrorized mind fought to stave off the coming appointment with his very personal reality. A vague protective hope that some terrible mistake had been made rode with him, kept him company the entire way, but this false friend abandoned him the moment his train pulled into Manhattan.

That was less than an hour ago. Now he stood on the doorstep of his family home on Harlem's elegant Strivers' Row, deeply disoriented, his one suitcase at his side, and it seemed that the family maid was the only person there to greet him. But the sight of her loved and familiar face warmed him.

Annie Williams's wizened face lit up when she saw him. Her hands went to her cheeks and her dark eyes widened in surprise.

"Mr. David? Is it you? Is it really you?"

David gave a barely perceptible nod and the whisper of a smile. He sensed her astonishment melt into joy, momentarily eclipsing her grief, and felt the knot in his chest loosen. God, how he'd missed her. She'd been there as long as he could remember. His eyes went over her. She was ginger-brown, like her favorite spice, a thin, wiry woman of strength surprising in someone her size and age. She was in her late fifties. Most of the time, she appeared younger, but mourning for Lilian had taken its toll. Her eyes were sunken and ringed by circles of dark gray.

He wrapped his strong arms around her in a hug. Her soft breath buffeted his ears as she whispered gratitude to God for having answered her prayers. Finally, she stepped back, swiped at her tearful eyes with her apron, and took a good look at him.

"Where you been, Mr. David? We sure did miss you. Coulda used you 'round here."

"Movement business," he said, glancing away.

"It was so horrible when you didn't come back. We thought you was dead and gone. Nobody seemed t'know nothin'. Them Movement people even offered a reward. But they just gotta lot a kooks writin' in. Nothin' worthwhile. 'Magine, Miss Lilian knowin' where you was all the time. I ain't faultin' her for not sayin' nothin'—I'm sure she had her reasons, but—"

He managed a small smile and looked at her. "I asked her to be discreet."

"Well then, I guess I can't say nothin'—but it sure woulda lifted a coupla hearts t'know you was all right."

She ushered him into the house. Until that moment, he'd wondered if he would actually manage to set foot in it again, but with her to welcome him it wasn't so difficult.

I'm acting like a child, he thought.

And like a child, he let her ease off his coat. She brushed her hand over it and hung it in the vestibule closet.

"I was goin' through Miss Lilian's things after the fun'ral. That's when I found your address. I wish I'da known where you was before. Maybe it woulda made a diff'rence. Then again, maybe not. I just know I sure is glad you here. I'm so glad you come back."

Her eyes went over him devotedly. It had been years since he'd seen so much love for him in anyone's face. He walked into her arms. They held one another again and it was hard to tell who was comforting whom.

In her own way, Annie had helped raise him and his twin sisters, Lilian and Gem. She'd seen them through their first loves and first heartaches. She'd rejoiced with them when they won school prizes and comforted them when they lost. He knew that she was as proud of the McKay children as she would've been of her own. As she hugged him, her flat, spade-like hands patted him on the back.

Like I'm a child, he thought. *And I'm glad of her comfort, like a child. All these years of living away, and the moment I return here, I'm—*

"C'mon, Mr. David. Let me fix you somethin' t'eat."

He nodded and followed her as she led him down the corridor. She moved with unfamiliar slowness, as though the weight of her years were bricks on her back. Her left shoulder was a tad bit higher than the other from a slight curvature of the spine he hadn't noticed before, and she walked with a slightly perceptible limp. He did not remember her being so frail, so worn.

What else had changed? He cocked an ear. He didn't know what he was listening for, but he knew what he heard:

Emptiness. No sounds of life, of love or laughter. Just a roaring emptiness that fills every nook and cranny. A hollow silence that echoes every thought, every heartbeat.

He looked around, at the paintings on the walls, the flower-bedecked tables that lined the hallway. All seemed familiar, yet remote. His eyes knew what to expect, but none of the sights seemed to touch his heart. He was detached and distant and it reassured him to feel that way.

This is like a place I only dreamed of.

But then his gaze fell on the dark gleaming door to the left of the library. This was the door that had guarded the heart of the house. This was the door that had haunted his childhood dreams and even now—

His breath caught; his shoulders rode up. He counted his steps and kept his eyes straight ahead. The hallway seemed to twist and lengthen. It was taking an eternity to cross that door. Every footfall echoed in the thudding of his heartbeat. Finally, they were past the door, beyond it. The hallway snapped back into shape. He exhaled.

They entered the kitchen. It was warm and comforting, familiar in its rich mixture of smells. His joints were stiff after the long train ride. He eased himself down into a chair at the kitchen table and let his tired eyes drift over the spotless room: up to the clock on the wall, down to the gas stove, the enameled sink and the refrigerator. His breathing slowed.

How many meals have been prepared in here . . .

This kitchen was Annie's domain. She'd made it her own, made it a place for more than just physical nourishment. Annie's kitchen was a source of warmth, a place for truthful conversations. It was a place to break down and weep or bust out with a big laugh, to be temporarily free from concern about what was or was not becoming in a colored family of status. Never before had he been so intensely aware of the role Annie's kitchen had played in his life. Never before had he so envied the boy he'd been.

She moved about the room, singing softly to herself. He watched her go about boiling water and heating something in a pot on the stove. Nothing more was said as the contents of the pot simmered. In a short time, she placed a cup of black coffee and a deep bowl of rich vegetable soup before him. She went to the pantry and fetched him bread and butter. He ate in silence. For a while, the only sound was the clink of his spoon scraping against the side of his bowl.

She poured herself a cup of coffee and sat down at the table across from him. He felt her eyes dwell on him with affection. He could imagine what she thought she saw: a good man possessed of a kind and compassionate nature, a man who performed brave deeds. He could imagine her talking to her friends. He could just hear her describing how it was before he went away.

"Always so nicely dressed in his deb'nair British suits. Never a hair outta place, shirts perfectly pressed, razor-sharp crease in his pants, black shoes so shiny you could see your face in 'em. 'Fine David McKay,' the young ladies used t'call 'im. Them girls

was crazy 'bout my David, with his soft hair. But David never had no time for any of 'em. He was too busy studyin'. Wanted to be a lawyer. That's what he done, too. After he come back from the war, he went off to Howard University an' got hisself a fine ed'-cation. Then he got a job with the Movement. They sent 'im on down south. He went t'get t'the truth b'hind them lynchin's. It's dang'rous work, goin' down t'them there hot spots. Those ol' crackers would just as soon lynch a colored man as look at 'im. That was back in '22. There sure was a lot t'keep a colored lawyer busy back then. Still is. Sad to say, there still is."

David thought about a little town in Georgia and his brief sense of well-being vanished. A chill touched his soul. He'd virtually disappeared after joining the Movement. He had kept his whereabouts secret from all but Lilian. He looked at Annie. Had she read his letters? No, it wasn't likely. She was inquisitive, but she could be trusted to respect private matters. Furthermore, he'd been careful to keep his letters lean.

Finishing his soup, he laid his spoon and napkin neatly to one side. Silence permeated the room, thick and waiting. His mind was filled with questions. So many questions. They mobbed his mind like grief-stricken relatives clamoring around an accident scene, all seeking the impossible, the essentially unattainable—an explanation, an answer, a satisfying solution to that one question survivors are always driven to ask: Why?

"What happened?" he asked. "What brought her down?"

Annie wrapped her hands around her coffee cup. It was old and chipped. He realized with a start that the cup was the one he'd given her as a Christmas present when he was ten years old. He'd spent all of his first allowance on it.

"I don't know if I can give you the answers you need, Mr. David. I seen a lot in this house, and I got my thoughts. But they's just the notions of an old woman."

He'd never known her to lie or bite her tongue when the truth needed telling. "It's me, Annie. Whatever you want to say, however you want to say it, just go ahead."

She looked away, out the window, where a couple walked past pushing a baby carriage. The young husband said something and his wife gave a high-pitched giggle. Inside the kitchen, it was quiet, so quiet that David could hear the sound of his own breathing. He waited. He could be patient. As a lawyer, he'd learned to be patient. Her eyes swung back to his. *Do you really want to know?* she seemed to ask.

Yes, he thought. *I want to know.* "I need to know," he said.

Her roughened hands trembled. "Well . . . a lot's done happened since you been gone, Mr. David . . . an awful lot." Her words pierced him.

"Go on," he whispered, his voice suddenly hoarse and tight and unwilling.

"I don't know where to start. It's hard when I think back on all I seen and heard." Her voice trailed off. "Miss Gem come back for a while—"

"*Gem* is here?"

"No, she gone. Been gone. She didn't stay long. Just long enough t'try t'cause trouble." An expression of disapproval flitted across her face. "Anyway, she left again after a few months. And ain't nobody heard nothin' from her since Miss Lilian died."

"Does she know?"

"She should. I sent a tel'gram. She never sent no answer. Never showed her face. I don't know what t'make of it. Nobody does."

He had his own opinions on the matter, but he kept them to himself. "Go on."

"Well, that young Miss Rachel—you know she was gone for a while—well, she come back, too."

His heart gave a little twist. He kept his face unmoved.

"And then . . . as for Miss Lilian . . ." Annie paused.

"Yes?"

"She got ill. Her mind went. And ain't none of the doctors knowed how t'help her." Annie folded her hands together. "But I'm gettin' ahead of myself. The biggest change, the one I'd better begin with, is how Miss Lilian up and got married."

David's eyelids raised involuntarily, then lowered like shutters yanked down over a dark window. *Married.* He shivered and wondered at his own reaction. Surely news of a marriage was to be welcomed.

It was also to be shared.

Why didn't she tell me? She never once wrote a word about it, not even dropped a hint. All those letters of pretended openness. By saying nothing, she lied.

He was suddenly furious. And instantly ashamed. How could he be angry with the dead?

"I wondered if she'd written and told you," Annie said. "Didn't think she had. She didn't tell nobody."

"You mean she eloped?"

"It'll be exactly two years ago next month. She kissed him in March, married him in April. Knowed him for one month. Met him at a fancy-dress dinner them civil rights folks at *Black Arrow* magazine had down at the Civic Club. You musta heard 'bout it."

Yes . . . The dinner had caused a lot of talk. It was widely written about in the Negro press. The dinner introduced the cream of Harlem's black literary crop to influential white publishers. It was held at the Civic Club because the Fifth Avenue restaurant was the only classy New York club that admitted patrons regardless of color or gender. It was the perfect meeting place for distinguished black intellectuals and eminent white liberals. As a writer and editor at the *Black Arrow,* Lilian would have been there.

He loosened his collar. What kind of man had finally elicited Lilian's love? She had made female friends quickly and maintained them easily, but men she had kept at a cool distance.

"So who was the lucky guy?"

"His name is Sweet, Mr. Jameson Sweet. He's gone on business. He'll be back Sunday. Maybe you know him? He works for the Movement, too."

A light flickered in David's deep-set eyes. Regret, anxiety, and fear rumbled like freight trains through his chest. He had known he was taking a risk in returning, but the danger was closer to home than he had anticipated. He felt Annie watching him, her eyes quick with intuitive intelligence, and forced himself to remain calm. He must take care. She was as gentle as a dove, but as sly as a fox.

"Mr. David, I got your old room waitin' for you," she was saying softly. "I gave it a good goin' over when I knew you was comin'."

"No, it's better if I stay in a hotel."

"This is your home."

Not anymore, he wanted to say. "It's better if I go. I can't stay long, no way—"

"Oh, but you got t'stay."

He gazed at her. "No, Annie. I've got business down in Philadelphia—"

"You got business here, too. *Fam'ly business.*"

"Annie—"

"Miss Lilian's gone and Miss Gem's 'cross the ocean. I'm just an ol' woman and I got no say. You the only one left t'set things straight."

His eyes narrowed. "Set what straight?"

She measured her words. "Mr. David, you and I, we both know . . . well, we both know that things ain't always the way they seem." She looked at him as though that explained it all.

It didn't. As far as he was concerned, it most definitely didn't. "Yes . . . and?"

Her expression became somewhat impatient. "Mr. David, I'll put it as simple as I can. More than one fox got into this chicken coop while you was gone."

"You mean Lilian's husband—"

"I mean he's sittin' pretty in this here house, *real* pretty."

A pause, then: "Just what kind of man is he?"

"A hard man, a determined man. And he ain't the sharin' kind." She reached across the table and laid a firm hand on his wrist. "Now Miss Lilian never meant for this here house to pass outta the fam'ly. You know that."

What she said was true. This beautiful house had been his father's pride, the crowning glory of a lifetime. A stately, turn-of-the-century Italianate building on tree-lined 139th Street, it boasted twelve rooms, casement windows, and iron filigreed balconies. Set on Strivers' Row, with its air of manicured exclusivity, the house was a monument to Augustus McKay's real estate acumen. It was a coveted symbol of the McKay family's status among Harlem's elite—and a lightning rod for the hate and envy of others.

"Mr. David, you can't be willin' t'give up your daddy's house—just like that." Annie snapped her fingers. "You can't be."

He gazed steadily at her for a long time. She meant well, but she didn't know. How could she? He had forfeited the right to call the house his home. He was in no moral position to reclaim his birthright. He doubted he ever would be. The small jaw muscles on either side of his face began to bunch. He had but one question.

"Did he hurt her?"

"Things . . . like I said . . . ain't always the way they seem."

He considered the matter. "I'll stay until I've talked to Sweet. Maybe he and I can reach some agreement."

She leaned toward him, her eyes burning. "Mr. David, it's time for you t'take your place. Here. You got a point t'make. Make it now. Later might be too late."

She led him up the stairway, humming a spiritual as she climbed. She moved slowly, but he moved even slower. His suitcase seemed to grow heavier with every step.

Part of him was relieved. He had been waiting for this summons for a long time. The night before, he had dreamed that by returning home, he would be walking into a trap, that his family, Strivers' Row, Harlem—they were all bundled together—would swallow him, smother him. He had seen mocking phantoms, knowing smiles, and pointing fingers. Tossing and turning, he had entangled himself in his bedcovers, ripping the sheets as he struggled to break free. When he'd finally jerked upright, he was panting and disoriented, drenched in cold sweat. He'd stared blindly into the dark, his

agitated heartbeat thudding in his ears. He had known he couldn't run forever. Known he would be summoned back. Someday. Somehow.

"It's so nice t'have you back, Mr. David." Annie swung open his bedroom
door and led him into the room. "I freshened it up for you real nice."

She offered to unpack his bag for him, but he shook his head. He
watched tensely as she bustled about, plumping pillows that had already been
plumped, smoothing a bedspread that had already been smoothed. Then she
glided past him with a warm smile and was gone, drawing the door closed
behind her, leaving him alone with his ghosts.

He understood what people meant when they spoke of time standing
still. The room seemed to be exactly as he had left it. Even the extra pair of
navy blue socks he had laid out but forgotten on the dresser top was still
there. He left his suitcase by the door, crossed the room, and yanked his
closet door open. It too was as he had left it: empty, except for an old black
suit and his army uniform. He stroked the lapels of the army greatcoat and
fingered a cuff.

It had been seven long years since the war. Since the Hell Fighters
marched up Fifth Avenue. Since the city had given a dinner in their honor.

*Damn, we were so proud then, so proud. And so hopeful. To think of all the
dreams we dreamt . . .*

Faces of the men he'd known flashed before him. Joshua Lewis, Ritchie
Conway, Bobby Raymond . . . He'd lost contact with all of them. He would
have liked to believe that most had fared well, but from what he'd seen since
returning in 1919, he doubted it. A week after coming back, his best friend,
Daniel Jefferson, had died while still in uniform, and it was an American
mob, not a German soldier, that killed him. Danny had had the temerity to
tell a white woman in Alabama that he was a man who had fought for his
country and deserved better than to be called "boy." He was dead within
the hour.

The war over there was nothing—nothing compared to the one over here.

David fingered his medal, still pinned to the front of his jacket. He had
won the French Croix de Guerre for facing down a German raiding party
on his own.

Medals are for heroes, he thought, *heroes* . . . and dropped his hand from the
medal as though it suddenly burned him.

His eyes moved to the black jacket. June 1921. His father: an old man,
propped up by thick pillows, dying from tuberculosis; an old man with a
grasp of iron and a will of steel.

"You go finish up at Howard. Be somebody. Make a difference and fight the good fight. And always, always protect your sisters."

Then there was his father's funeral service at Saint Philip's Episcopal. As befitting a man of Augustus McKay's social and financial stature, the service was weighty, dignified. An impressive convoy of expensive cars accompanied his coffin to the cemetery. Afterward, there was a small gathering at the house "for the right people."

When the last guest was gone, David and Lilian huddled near one another on the parlor sofa, sharing a pot of tea, relieved at the quiet. Gem flounced into the room, gay even in funereal black. She saw her brother and sister sitting together and was instantly jealous.

"Plotting, plotting. Something nifty, I hope?"

David gave her a look that silenced her immediately. She actually flinched. He was hard hit by his father's death and showed it. He and his father had never gotten along. Whether David could admit it or not, there had been several times when he had wished his father dead. But once the old man was gone, David missed him. Gem, however, was quick to push her grief aside, assuming she felt any. Her mind was on one matter and one matter only: money. She suggested that Lilian and David buy out her share of the house. She was sure they would agree, and they did. It was the first and last time the three of them agreed to anything with alacrity. Gem took her money and vanished within days. David and Lilian supposed that Gem had gone west, since she had mentioned Los Angeles, but they couldn't be sure. Indeed, they didn't much care.

The day we laid Daddy in the ground marked the last day we stood in the same room together. Not that we planned it that way. Not that we would've ever guessed it would turn out that way.

He and Lilian returned to their respective universities: He to Howard law in Washington, D.C.; she to study French literature as a Cornell undergraduate in Ithaca, New York. She would earn a Phi Beta Kappa key. Whether or not their chauvinist father had wanted to admit it, Lilian was the family brain. Gem had had the talent to develop into a gifted and memorable if radical poet, but she had dissipated her ability. After two years of cutting the rug and doing the bumpty-bump, dancing her semesters away, she'd quit her studies at the University of Southern California.

But if Gem failed to live up to Daddy's hopes, then so did I.

Standing in his room that March evening, he felt a familiar surge of shame. Yes, he had kept his promise to Augustus, but it had been to the letter—not in the spirit—of the old man's wishes. Over the past four years, he'd wandered far from his father's mansion. Could he find his way back? He had no choice. He had to, if he was to understand Lilian's death and regain control of his father's house.

David closed the closet door. He went to the window, parted the curtains, and looked out. The street seemed deserted, except for an old man walking his Doberman. David stood there thoughtfully for a minute or two, then let the curtain drop, went to the door, and left. A few steps to the right and down the corridor and he was in front of the master bedroom. He put his hand on the doorknob, but then hesitated. This was the room in which it had happened. He dreaded the sight of it. Yet he felt compelled to view it. Perhaps standing in this room would help him accept the reality of her death . . . of her *suicide.* He twisted the knob very gently and slowly pushed the door open.

The strong smell of fresh paint rushed out from the closed room, stinging his nostrils. Catching his breath, he paused on the threshold. He didn't know what he had expected to feel, but it wasn't the odd sensation that overcame him. He felt as though he were standing before a museum diorama set up to replicate Lilian's room. This subdued, muted place could not be real. It lacked the familiarity, the homeyness of Lilian's room. It could not be the genuine article. *But it is,* he told himself.

In the cold light of that March evening, the room was dim. Lilian's combs, brushes, and hand mirror were laid out on the dressing table. Her hairpins were neatly aligned on a little mirrored tray. Delicate perfume bottles by Lalique were arranged to one side. The bed's counterpane was obviously new, as were the curtains at the windows. On the night table next to her bed lay her Bible, closed but with strips of red, yellow, and blue ribbon inside it to hold her place. Family photographs of their parents and of her with Gem and himself were artfully arranged atop the chest of drawers opposite the foot of her bed. A sad smile touched his lips. Even a picture of a stray puppy Lilian had adopted as a child was there.

He let his eyes drift over the dresser top once more and frowned. Something was missing. At first he didn't know what it was. Then it hit him. All those photographs of Lilian and the family, but not one of her husband. Why not? Why, if she'd loved him—if they'd had a good marriage—were there no photos of him on display with the others in her room?

"Mr. Jameson moved out after it happened," said a voice behind him. David turned. It was Annie. "He took another room," she said.

David nodded. He could understand that. He certainly wouldn't have wanted to continue to sleep in a room in which his wife had bled to death. He took a few steps into the room. Annie followed him, and they paused at the foot of the four-poster bed.

"Is this where she did it?"

She nodded. "Mr. Jameson had a new mattress brought in." She gave a little shudder and hugged herself. Her gaze went to the base of the windowsill. "Sometimes . . . sometimes I ask the Lord why I had t'be the one t'find her. But I s'pose it was better me than someone who didn't love her. I was there when she came into the world. It was only right that I be there when she left it."

Bending down, David brushed his fingertips over the new counterpane. A pale ivory, it would have pleased Lilian. He turned to Annie. "Tell me about it . . . about how it was when you found her."

Annie paused, then said: "She suffered a bad death, Mr. David, a real bad death. They say you shouldn't never touch nothin', so I left the knife right there on the bed where it was, but I did close her eyes. And I laid a blanket over her. Then I called the police. And sat down in the room t'keep that last wait with her. I thought about all the years gone by and the thousands of kind things Miss Lilian done for me. I'da never imagined her goin' like that. She was such a lovely young woman, so very sweet. She was a lady, a real fine lady."

David's gaze went again to the photos. "That, she was . . ."

"Them cops sure took their sweet time comin'. It was just the death of another colored woman t'them. They didn't know nothin' 'bout how wonderful Miss Lilian was. And they wouldna cared. Me, I didn't mind the wait. I didn't like seein' her that way, but I knew it was likely the last time I'd see her at all."

"The funeral . . . was it nice?"

"Oh, yeah." She smiled. "It was somethin' t'see. And so many people showed up, so many. They had t'close the doors t'Saint Philip's t'keep the peace. But that was t'be expected. Seein' as how your family is so known and all, that was just t'be expected."

"I wonder . . . how many of those people actually cared about her."

She was thoughtful. "You know how people can be, Mr. David. You know how they can be. Lotsa folks who didn't have no time for her when she was sick, and lotsa others who never knowed her—well, they all just had t'come . . . just had t'come an' see when that sweet child died."

2

Harlem on My Mind

David paused on his doorstep, pulled his hat down lower, and wrapped his coat tighter. He would take a walk. To stretch his legs. To see how Harlem had changed. And to forget what Annie had told him. *A lot's done happened since you been gone.* He shuddered and forced his thoughts in another direction. His gaze traveled up and down the street, registering the familiar homes of his neighbors. After a minute, he turned up his collar, went down the front steps, and started toward Seventh Avenue.

It was a curious sensation to be back. There was, above all, a sense of unreality; that sense, once more, of time having stood still. The trees appeared a mite bigger, but nothing else on the block had changed. It was still serene and immaculate. No matter the weather or the light, the trim, neat houses of Strivers' Row looked regal and well-to-do. As they should. After all, they were designed for the affluent. That the homes should land in the hands of blacks was a development that David H. King Jr., the original builder, had probably never foreseen.

When King commissioned New York star architect Stanford White to design the series of houses in 1891, King envisioned homes for wealthy white families. At first, that's what they were, homes for white millionaires, such as the first Randolph Hearst. But a depression hit Harlem's inflated real estate market in 1904 and opened the way to black residency. By 1920, a good number of New York's most prominent blacks—the Rev. Dr. Adam Clayton Powell Sr., James C. Thomas, Charles W. Anderson, and others—had moved to Harlem. Already by 1914, even modestly affluent blacks could afford to buy Harlem real estate. By 1917, white brokers were begging for white investor interest in Harlem by advertising how cheap property had become. And by 1920, superb properties such as the King Model Houses had begun to pass into the hands of black professionals. As black families moved in, white ones moved out. The houses along what would be known as "Strivers' Row" went for a song.

"A twelve-room house. Fit for a king. For nine thousand dollars," Augustus beamed in announcing his purchase. "Nine thousand dollars. It was worth it."

The McKays were the sixth family to arrive. Dentist Charles H. Roberts and Dr. Louis T. Wright, Harlem Hospital's first black doctor and later its chief of surgery, soon became the McKays' neighbors. Then there was Vertner W. Tandy, widely recognized as the first black architect to be licensed in New York State, and Lieutenant Samuel J. Battle, Manhattan's first black police lieutenant. Eventually, Strivers' Row would become a popular address for black theatrical stars: composer Eubie Blake, orchestra leaders Fletcher Henderson and Noble Sissle.

Back courtyards, gardens, and fountains connected by an interior alleyway ran the length of the block. The houses on the north side of 139th Street, including the McKay house, were neo-Renaissance, made of thin, reddish Roman brick. The pale cream-colored houses running along the south side were neo-Georgian. All displayed the same spare but expert use of classical details. All were set back from the pavement to emphasize privacy. And all had rear entrances that kept the unsightly business of housekeeping where it belonged—out of sight.

The residents of Strivers' Row were a proud lot. They strove for excellence; hence the street's nickname. They kept their trees neatly tended and their hedges closely clipped. Entrance railings and balustrades were painted, windows and front steps washed, brass doorknobs and knockers polished.

Over time, the Row had become a tiny oasis of spacious ease and prosperity surrounded by a desert of danger, despair, and decay. When David stepped around the corner of 139th Street and Seventh Avenue, he entered a world of poverty, of rotting garbage and ragged children. The juxtaposition of rich and poor never failed to give him a jolt.

Seventh Avenue, that broad thoroughfare that slashes through the heart of Harlem, was well peopled even that cold evening. Tall trees with thick trunks spread their gnarled branches over the wide dark street. Beige and brick-brown tenement buildings, four and five stories tall, rose up on either side like mammoth shadows in the evening light.

He headed downtown, taking long, even strides, doing his best to appear at ease. He walked neither quickly nor slowly. His expression was neither curious nor indifferent. His eyes examined everything but dwelled on nothing. He saw a world of cracked pavements and battered trash cans. He passed rows of dilapidated buildings and he knew, without having to enter them, what they looked like inside: Dark, dirty hallways. Broken windows. Rusted pipes. No heat. No hot water. Rats and roaches, ticks and water bugs. Many of the folks who lived in those buildings slept ten to a room.

Most of black Harlem's residents had originally fled Georgia, the Carolinas, Virginia, and other points south, seeking jobs and safety from the pervasive threat of the lynch man's noose. They'd come north, dreaming of the Promised Land, and ended up living a nightmare. Some people could barely afford "hot beds," mattresses they switched off with other shift workers. Many couldn't even find jobs. Harlem's biggest department stores depended on blacks as customers but refused to consider them for hire.

Seeing the myriad ebony, brown, sepia, and amber faces that now peopled Harlem's streets, it was odd to think that not so long ago, Harlem was white. Only about thirty years earlier, in the late 1800s, it was Russian and Polish Jews fleeing the pogroms of Eastern Europe who had given Harlem its color. Even as recently as fifteen years earlier, Russian Jews had dominated the census figures. Then, there were the Italians—the area from Third Avenue to the East River was "Harlem's Little Italy"—and the Irish, the Germans, the English, the Hungarians, the Czechs, and others coming from the Austro-Hungarian Empire. Harlem did have a smattering of Native Americans and a small but stable black population—the descendants of freed slaves—but by and large, the neighborhood's complexion was pink.

All that had changed, seemingly in the blink of an eye, and Harlem was now indelibly brown. Years later, people would forget that Harlem was ever white. Those few who remembered would sometimes still wonder what had happened.

King's decision to build the homes on what would become Strivers' Row was part of a turn-of-the-century construction boom in Harlem. The anticipated building of new subway lines into Harlem had turned the neighborhood into a target for speculators. Developers snapped up the remaining farmlands, marshes, garbage dumps, and empty lots that still constituted a good part of the area. Between 1898 and 1904, brownstones rose up on every corner. But by 1905, the party was over. There were too many apartments and too few renters. Even after the Lenox Avenue subway was completed, high rents discouraged the anticipated influx of new residents. The real estate market broke and people panicked. They needed tenants and needed them badly.

Meanwhile, downtown in mid-Manhattan's miserable Tenderloin district, the construction of Pennsylvania Station was destroying the area's few all-

Negro blocks. Colored families being forced out of their homes wondered: Where to next?

In stepped Philip Payton Jr., a Negro real estate broker. His Afro-American Realty Company brought the white owners of Harlem and the colored families of the Tenderloin together. White owners might not have been thrilled to rent to blacks, but they preferred it to ruin. Some decided to take any Negro tenant who would pay the high rents being demanded. Hundreds, then thousands of blacks moved to Harlem. The neighborhood swelled with poor people burdened with inflated rents they couldn't afford and grand apartments they couldn't maintain.

David had spent more than half his life in the rat-infested Tenderloin and clearly remembered his family's move to Harlem when he was nineteen. He understood the hope that Harlem had represented to New York City's black residents. It was their chance to build a community—a respectable, decent community. Now, as he gazed at the tenements around him, he wondered how far that dream had been realized.

Harlem's residents were caught between low salaries and high rents, yet many people saw it as the largest, most dynamic black enclave in the United States. And in fact, the community was alive with success stories and colorful characters: bootleggers and racketeers, literati and blue bloods, barefoot prophets and uniformed liberators.

As David waited for a streetlight to change, his gaze drifted over the street life around him. There were so many half-forgotten, familiar sights. Mamas tired after a long week's work dragged toddlers with one hand and hugged grocery bags with the other. Tail-wagging dogs strained against leashes to gain the nearest fire hydrant. Stray cats with scarred faces and ripped ears huddled alongside the entrances to alleyways. Hip young men with cool ambition in their eyes hustled by. Others, with deadened dreams, sat on stoops or leaned languidly against street lamps. Street vendors hawked toys, perfume, dresses, stockings, and watches. Their goods spread out on torn blankets, they proudly displayed a profusion of glittery items one might desire, but would never use. And an abundance of dreary items one could use, but would never desire.

He'd been away a long time. What he saw was both familiar and foreign. Part of him was baffled and bewildered. But another part, a deeper part, understood and accepted, without doubt or dismay. He walked for hours. Nostalgia slowly drew his unwilling soul into her lonely embrace. These were the streets he'd roamed, the alleys where he and his friends had played. He remembered the days when 134th Street was the northern boundary of

Negro Harlem, when a black man knew never to cross Lenox Avenue, no Negroes lived on or near Seventh, and none dared to appear unarmed on Irish Eighth. He remembered so much, but realized he'd forgotten even more. This was indeed his town, but it was no longer his home.

What he needed, he decided, was a drink. What about Jolene's? It was a lap joint, not far away. Back in his first days home after the war, when he and his friends wanted a break from the cabarets, wanted something a little dingier, dirtier, and down-to-earth, they would hit Jolene's. Gem had sung there sometimes, living out her fantasy of being a torch singer.

Jolene's was a dive on the edge of Harlem's "low-down" district, on 135th and Fifth. It was run through the back door of a grocery store. A body could stroll into that store any night until five in the morning to find Birdie Williams perched on his stool behind the counter. Signs in the window advertised five-pound bags of sugar for twenty-two cents, half a pound of bacon for a dime, and three cans of dog food for thirteen cents. You could also buy a bottle of Pepsi for a nickel, but if you were a regular or knew the right words, Birdie would let you go downstairs, where you could get happy with some hootch. If you thought you could get in because you were a Somebody, then you were wrong. Birdie kept a sling razor ready just to show you how wrong you could be.

When David pushed open the door to the store that night, he found Birdie cleaning his fingernails with the tip of a nasty-looking blade. Birdie looked up and saw David, and a surprised grin spread over his broad face.

"Well, hot damn!" Birdie jumped up and came around the counter. He pumped David's hand and slapped him on the back. "Man, oh man, I ain't seen you since Hannibal was a child. Where the hell you been?"

"Layin' low. Takin' it easy."

"Shit, I heard you got lost down—"

"That was just talk, man. Just talk."

Birdie perched on the edge of the counter. "Sorry t'hear 'bout your sister. Was a damn shame."

"Thanks."

"Stayin' long?"

"Just visitin'."

David glanced around. He saw nothing but two bags of sugar and a lonesome can of dog food, the sum total of Birdie's efforts at pretending to run a legitimate operation.

"So who's playin' tonight?"

"Sweet Lips and his boys. We had Ethel in last night."

"Seriously. I seen your face before."

"He got a sister," Jolene said. He was looking evil again. "You know her. Gem—"

"You Gem's brother?"

David nodded.

"Well, if that ain't a monkey's uncle. She used to come in here. Liked to sing a song or two."

"Yeah . . . But that was years ago."

"Not that long. She was in here last year. Lookin' mighty fine, too. She's back in Paris, I hear."

"Paris?"

Stella smiled. "You ain't heard nothin' from her, huh? I dig that. Well, I don't know if you're interested, but I was talkin' t'Shug the other day—"

"Shug?"

"Shug Ryan. He blows a pretty mean sax. Shug and Gem used t'hang out in Montmartre. He just come back from over there. He mighta seen her."

David wasn't sure he wanted to talk to Shug, but he asked anyway: "Where can I find him?"

"Hell if I know." She shrugged, turned to Jolene, and put her glass down on the bar. "Set me up, babe." Then she glanced at David's empty glass and his sad eyes and smiled. To Jolene, she said: "Gimme the bottle. My friend here and I, we gonna make a night of it."

David saw the look on Jolene's face and Stella saw it, too. David didn't want a fight, but he was too tired and wrung out to care. Stella laughed and flung an arm around Jolene's meaty shoulder, then planted a kiss on his scarred cheek.

"Don't make no trouble," she whispered, "or I'm gonna be gone with the morning light."

Jolene did as he was told.

It was past four in the morning when David left Jolene's, melancholy and drunk. As the lively sounds of Jolene's faded behind him, images of Lilian's room returned. And that curious sensation it had given him of a museum exhibit—staged, detached, sanitized—gripped him once more. He shivered. How he dreaded going back to that house.

A lot's done happened since you been gone.

Stella had invited him to enjoy her hospitality, but while expressing his appreciation, he'd refused. Now, he wondered if that had been wise.

My life, he thought, *is just a series of missed opportunities.*

He only hoped that he'd walked enough, drank enough, smoked enough reefer to exhaust himself. He wanted to sleep like a rock. *No, like a dead man,* he thought, and chuckled at his morbid humor. He made his way back to Strivers' Row. After letting himself in, he managed to hang up his coat and was about to climb the stairs to his room when his gaze fell on the door, *that* door, the one next to the library. He stared at it, like a moth drawn to a flame. One moment, he was standing by the newel post; the next, he was facing the door. His hands hung at his side, balled into fists. Beads of perspiration sprung up on his forehead. His right hand went out. He touched the doorknob . . . then hesitated. What would he find behind this door? Indeed, after all these years, what in the world was he looking for? Reconciliation? Peace?

He gripped the knob and twisted it.

It wouldn't budge.

He blinked, confused. Then, taking a deep breath, he gripped it harder, jiggled it and tried to turn it again.

It held fast.

He fell back, baffled. He didn't remember the door ever being locked. Running a hand through his hair, he tried to clear his thoughts.

But, of course. I locked that door the day Daddy died. It's been closed ever since.

He closed his eyes. Suddenly, he was so tired. Here in this empty house, this house that was so full of ghosts and memories, how would he ever find rest? As in a daze, he spread his hands over the door panel and leaned his face against it. The polished dark wood felt cool and smooth. He let his mind drift back . . . back through the years to the times when he and his sisters had been summoned to this office, to one particular afternoon in which he alone had been called.

"You're my heir and I expect great things! Great achievements!"

Images from that afternoon flew toward him like slivers of a splintered mirror. He spun around and pressed his back against the door.

"You've been given an edge in life. What've you done with it?"

"I've done my best."

"Your best? Well, your best could've been better!"

David clapped his hands over his ears, but the words echoed inside his head. It had been five years since his father's death. *Five* years. Why hadn't the old man's voice died with him? Why did it live on to haunt him?

You've been given an edge, an edge . . . Your best could've been better!

He tore away from the door with a cry and stumbled toward the stairs.

On the third step, his strength left him and he sank down. He lay crumpled on the step, weeping with dry wretched sobs.

A lot's done happened, done happened, done happened . . .

A lot's done happened since you been gone . . .

He drew himself up, staggered up the stairs, down the hallway, and into his room. He sagged down onto his bed, still fully clothed, and closed his eyes, exhausted.

But sleep eluded him.

He lay awake, his eyes burning in the dark, and the voices followed him. They came from either side, chanting in a rhythm that threatened to drive him insane.

And always protect . . . always protect . . . always protect your sisters . . .

And always (she suffered) . . . and always (she suffered) . . .

(and always) She suffered a bad death . . . a bad death.

With a groan, he turned over and punched the pillow. In the morning, he'd ask Annie to tell him the full story of what had gone on in the house.

3

Annie's Tale

"For a good part, the story of Miss Lilian is the story of Miss Gem. You never could mention one without the other. Diff'rent as day and night, but just as connected. Lookin' back, I sometimes wonder whether Miss Gem's return marked the beginnin' of Miss Lilian's end."

Annie placed cream and sugar on the kitchen table, but David decided not to use them. He needed coffee and he needed it black. His head hurt and his eyes were bleary. He hadn't been able to touch the grits, biscuits, and sausages she'd made. He'd called himself seven kinds of fool upon waking. Going to Jolene's had seemed like a good idea last night, but he was sure he'd never do it again. The price in pain was too damn high.

She took a seat opposite him, added a little cream to her coffee, and stirred it with an even rhythm. Her voice, as quiet as a coming storm, slowly filled the room.

"Lotsa folks say the trouble started when Miss Gem went back t'Europe. I say it began a lot sooner: the moment she arrived. From the day that girl stepped foot in this house 'til the day she left, she ain't meant nothin' but trouble. Miss Gem come back for a purpose. I could see that the minute she walked in the door. She had that look in her eye. That look, if you know what I mean. I don't know what she done all 'em years in Paris, but whatever it was, it sure left her lookin' lean and hungry."

Lean and hungry, David repeated to himself. *Gem was always hungry. Somehow, we all were. Funny about that. Or maybe not so funny when you think about it. That we should be as rich as any colored family needs to be, yet still hungry.*

"It was Halloween," Annie was saying. "Miss Lilian got t'the door before me. She didn't even bother t'ask who it was. She was expectin' a bunch of kids, some trick-or-treaters, I guess. When she saw who it was, she lost her voice. Couldn't find nothin' t'say.

"Miss Gem stood there like a ghost that ev'rybody's put out of their

28

minds, even if they ain't quite forgotten about it. The wind was at her back—whippin her hair up, like a black cloud. She'd been gone five years—*five years*—but didn't look a day older. Maybe she was a bit thinner, but she still had that smooth, creamy skin. And she had this sable coat, thrown over her shoulders. Wore it like a queen, she did. Rich and sophist'cated—like a Eur'-pean. Miss Gem knew she was somethin' t'look at. *Knew* it. It was in the way she held herself: just so. And in the way she looked down at Miss Lilian.

"Y'know it's hard t'b'lieve that they started out as iden'ical twins. I ain't never seen two women given the same material work so hard t'do somethin' diff'rent with it. 'Course, Miss Lilian was lovely in her way, too. It's just that her way weren't Miss Gem's way."

No . . . it wasn't, thought David. Lilian also had the slight but shapely build of a dancer and the paradoxical air of being fragile yet strong. She too had the oval face, fawn-colored complexion, and lustrous chestnut hair typical of her family. But Lilian downplayed her looks. Her full lips were sweet and generous, but she was puritan in outlook. She rarely put on makeup. She wore her long hair in a tight bun. And she treated clothes as a pragmatic matter: Fashion was a secondary indulgence. Her outfits were neat, tailored suits; her perfume, clean and light.

"Well, Miss Gem was alookin' at Miss Lillian like a lion on the hunt. Miss Gem threw her head back and laughed. You know how she likes t'flash them pretty teeth. Then she teased Miss Lilian. Said: 'Cat got your tongue, sister dear?'

"Miss Lilian asked Miss Gem, just as cool as you please, 'What're you doing here?' Miss Gem didn't like that. She got this funny look on her face and said, 'It's wonderful t'see you too, dear. It's wonderful t'see you, too.' She took Miss Lilian's face in her hands and kissed her twice, once on each cheek. Lawd, Lawd! You woulda thought Miss Lilian was bein' clawed, the way she yanked her face back. She looked down at Miss Gem's suitcases—two large ones standin' on the doorstep—and Miss Gem caught her.

"'You'd better make up your mind fast,' she said. 'The neighbors'll start talkin' if they see me standin' here like this.'

"Well, that did it. You could see Miss Lilian didn't like it, not one bit, but she stepped aside and made for Miss Gem t'come in.

"'You ain't changed a bit,' Miss Gem said. 'Still a fool for appearances.'

"Then she put her hand on her hip and strutted on by. Miss Lilian asked Miss Gem what time her ship had got in, but I think she really wanted t'ask Miss Gem when her ship was *leavin'*. Either way, Miss Gem ignored her. Just gave a little wave of her hand. She stood under the light of the vestibule chand'lier. She coulda been an actress standin' in the spotlight. Her face glowed; her eyes sparkled. Miss Gem always did have a flair for the dramatic. She just stood there, quiet-like, lookin' 'round. Then she whispered somethin' 'bout not much havin' changed. Turned t'me, told me it was good t'see me. Then she gimme them little pecks on the cheek them Eur'peans pass for kisses. I know they treat the help different over there, but Miss Gem knew she was back in Harlem, where a smart colored woman don't try t'lord it over the help."

David smiled at that. Gem knew better than to strut in front of Annie. If anybody in the house could yank Gem's chain it was this old woman. He raised his cup to his lips and took a sip of coffee, enjoying its bitterness. "Did Gem say exactly where she was all those years?"

"Miss Lilian tried t'ask her, but Miss Gem just waved her away again. Said she'd tell her all 'bout it later; she just wanted t'enjoy bein' home at first. Said she was dyin' t'look 'round. Wanted t'know if her old room was the same. But she didn't even wait for Miss Lilian's answer. Miss Gem went t'the foot of the stairs and looked up. She pushed her coat off her shoulders, just let that beautiful coat land in a heap at her feet, then she run on up the stairs, never once lookin' back. Left me and Miss Lilian standin' down here with her luggage on the doorstep, like we was bellhops or somethin'.

"Miss Lilian turned t'me and told me t'clean up the downstairs thorough. She grabbed my arm, led me t'the parlor, cluckin' like a worried hen, and pointed out stuff she wanted put away. It didn't take long t'see what she was up to: clearin' out all signs of a man in the house. That's all it was.

"I said t'Miss Lilian: 'You can't keep Mr. Jameson a secret. When you gonna tell her?'

"Her jaw got tense and that look come on her face—you know the one I mean—sort of pained and worried. 'Not now,' she said.

"'You got t'tell her sometime,' I said.

"She shook her head. 'Maybe Gem won't stay that long,' she said. 'She might leave before he gets back.' Then, she gimme a hug and told me she'd take the luggage upstairs herself.

"Miss Lilian put off tellin' Miss Gem about Mr. Jameson for as long as she could. And that was only 'bout a week. She got away with it that long 'cause Mr. Jameson was outta town. Miss Lilian was real careful 'bout not lettin' Miss Gem into her bedroom neither, where she coulda seen signs of him. But by-and-by, Miss Lilian lost hope that Miss Gem was back for a quick visit. I don't know where she thought Miss Gem might go, seein' as how Miss Gem didn't know nobody in Harlem no more. She'd been away too long.

"Now cain't no woman hide the fact that she got a man livin' with her. 'Specially when ev'rybody up an' down the street know 'bout it. I don't know who that sister of yours thought she was foolin'. But even if nobody hadna said nothin', Miss Gem woulda figured it out all by herself. That woman's got the nose of a cat. She can smell a man hangin' round like an alley cat can smell a rat.

"Well, Miss Gem had me and Miss Lilian runnin' 'round, servin' her like she was the Queen of Sheba. One night she come back 'round four o'clock in the mornin', hissy as a snake. She'd been hangin' out at Hayne's Oriental and somebody'd asked her what she thought of her sister's new husband. Nat'rally, she ain't knowed nothin' but nothin' 'bout what they was talkin' 'bout. So, they laid it on thick. I ain't never seen nobody as angry as Miss Gem at that time of mornin'.

"Well, she woke Miss Lilian. Me, too, for that matter. I was in my room, but I could hear 'em. I reckon the neighbors heard 'em too, the way they was carryin' on. Miss Gem told Miss Lilian she was a fool.

"'Don't you realize he married you for your money?' she said.

"Miss Lilian said she didn't care.

"'Well, you'd better start,' Miss Gem said. 'Ev'rybody's laughin' at you. Ev'rybody knows he ain't no good.'

"Miss Lilian asked Miss Gem, since when did she care what ev'rybody says. 'You never cared before,' Miss Lilian said. 'And for once I don't care neither. Ev'rybody thinks they know he doesn't love me. *I* know for certain he does.'

"Then they sorta got quiet. Dropped their voices like. And I'm glad they did, 'cause I didn't wanna get involved no way. I don't have no trouble stayin' outta other people's business. Not that anybody ever asked my opinion. But I'll tell you somethin': Layin' in the dark that night, I got a sense of fore-bodin', the likes of which I ain't never had b'fore. It sat like a rock, here in my chest."

She wedged her fist tight up under her bosom. "It was fright'nin' t'lay in bed and list'n t'them voices. Voices that sounded like the folk they b'longed to was dead. Voices that made you think of ghosts. Ghosts that kept on fightin' into the grave."

David shifted uncomfortably. He was a lawyer and lawyers like facts. He didn't like superstition and any reference to it unsettled him. But what unsettled him more, if he were honest, was the way her words echoed inside him. He was frightened all of a sudden, and he wasn't quite sure why.

"What happened next was written on the wall," she said. "Anybody with eyes t'see woulda known what was comin'.'' She picked up her cup and ran a finger over the nicks on its rim. "Mr. Jameson come home the next day. Miss Lilian was out runnin' errands. Miss Gem come downstairs lookin' for Miss Lilian and found Miss Lilian's husband instead. He was in the parlor, sortin' his mail. Miss Gem stopped short in the parlor doorway. She was wearin' a frock, red like cherries. I seen her. We'd just got some new flowers for the vest'bule and I was standin' there fixin' 'em. I must say she looked very pretty that day, very pretty standin' there. She was watchin' Mr. Jameson, waitin' for him t'see her.

"He was sittin' at your daddy's old writin' desk. He didn't notice her at first 'cause he was concentratin' on a letter. Had his pipe in his mouth. That man smokes a nice pipe. Uses fine tobacco. Actu'ly, Mr. Jameson's pretty fine hisself. I got t'give the devil his due. He's the kinda man ev'ry Mama warns her girlchile 'bout.

"Well, I could see Miss Gem just lickin' her lips. She cleared her throat— real delicate-like but loud 'nough for him t'hear. Mr. Jameson looked up, said hello, and went back t'his mail. Then he swung his head back 'round again. His eyes liked to pop right outta his head.

"'Lilian, what have you done to yourself?' he said.

"Miss Gem gave him time t'take in every pretty detail. Then she sort of floated on in and gave him her hand. Introduced herself, real lady-like. Said it was 'So nice t'meet him.' Just as sweet as she could be.

"Now, I must say, Mr. Jameson's got the manners of a gentleman. He stood up quick as lightnin'. And Miss Gem, she broke into a smile as wide as the Mississippi.

"'I *like* tall men,' she said, real soft-like. 'You remind me of Daddy.'

"'Do I, now?'

"'Yes, you do.'

"They shook hands for a second too long, if you know what I mean. Then the front door slammed and they jumped apart. Miss Lilian come in. Fresh as a June breeze. Cheeks all rosy. She was a-glowin'. Didn't have no idea of what was comin' at her. But when she saw them two together, she got right pale. Her face got all pinched. She tried t'act like it was all right, made a big show of huggin' and kissin' him. Miss Gem stood by, patient-like, her arms folded cross her chest. Her 'spression was pleasant and polite. Miss Lilian wrapped her arms 'round Mr. Jameson's waist. She said she was happy he and Miss Gem had fin'ly met. But she didn't sound happy. And she told Miss Gem it was nice of her t'keep Mr. Jameson comp'ny while she was out. Miss Gem said it was no trouble, no trouble at all.''

Annie rose from the table and went to the stove. She picked up the cof-feepot. "You want some more?" she asked him.

"No." He shook his head. "I've barely touched what I've got." He let her pour herself a cup, then asked: "So, did Miss Gem try to . . ." He paused, searching for the words. "Try to, you know . . ."

Annie nodded and her lips tensed. That look of knowledge and disap-proval once more flitted across her face. She brought her cup to the table and eased back down onto her chair. "Once she'd met him, Miss Gem was real polite t'Mr. Jameson. She didn't show nothin' of her true feelin's. Nothin' happened: no fireworks, no nothin'. Miss Lilian let out a breath of relief. That was one naive chile. I coulda told her it was the quiet b'fore the storm. Miss Gem was just bidin' her time.

"Oh, she was proper and correct when Miss Lilian was round, but the moment Miss Lilian was outta sight . . . Hmmm-hm! Miss Gem used t'follow Mr. Jameson 'round with her eyes whene'er they was in a room t'gether. She'd say li'l cuttin' things at the dinner table and look over at Mr. Jameson like they was sharin' a secret. She'd find a way t'touch him, get close t'him, ev'ry time she saw him. She'd brush up 'gainst his shoulder if they happen t'come in a room at the same time. She had somethin' in mind all right.

"Miss Lilian saw what was goin' on, but she wouldn't let it get t'her. She did say somethin' t'me. Once. We was in the kitchen. She wanted t'know 'bout supplies for a dinner party she was plannin'. I don't right recall how we got on the subject. Maybe I asked her 'bout the seatin'. Anyway, she said t'make sure Miss Gem's place at the table was as far down from Mr. Jameson's as possible. She musta caught my look, 'cause she turned her eyes away sorta embarrassed. Then, she said, 'I know there's nothin' t'worry 'bout, Annie. Gem's tryin' t'rile me. She wants t'prove that my man's no good. But we not gonna play her game. He's not 'bout t'give her the satisfaction, and neither am I.'

"Miss Lilian tried t'sound brave, but her voice shook. She weren't nowhere near as confident as she made out t'be. She knew Miss Gem wasn't one t'give up easy. Now I know lots of women woulda put their sister outta the house. But Miss Lilian wasn't like that. I don't b'lieve it ever crossed her mind. Still, there was a lotta talk goin' round. Some people said Miss Lilian was a fool. Said she'd invited the fox into the chicken coup, and was workin' hard on keepin' it there. But Miss Lilian said her marriage was her business. And she was *not* gonna let the gossips get their way."

"Why didn't Sweet do something to set Gem straight? Say something?"

"Well, actu'ly, he did. I gotta say he tried. It was 'bout a month later, in late November. Miss Lilian went to a lit'rary conference in Chicago. Mr. Jameson drove her t'the train station.

"That mornin', I washed the windows, startin' with the downstairs, and worked my way up t'the second floor. It got t'be 'round lunchtime. I was heatin' up some chowder—I love me some soup, 'specially in the winter-time—and the doorbell rang. It was Miss Gem. She'd gone out and forgot-ten her key. I let her in. She went on in t'the parlor. I went back t'the kitchen. I was breakin' my last cracker over my soup when I looked up t'check the time, and I sees Mr. Jameson's car pullin' up t'the house. I let Mr. Jameson in, then came on back in here, finished eatin', and did the dishes real quick. The wash was next, so I headed upstairs t'get the used linen and dirty clothes. I had t'go past the parlor. Them doors weren't shut all the way. I couldn't help hearin'. Mr. Jameson had joined Miss Gem in the parlor. Now Mr. David, I ain't never eavesdropped before. Ain't never spied on nobody. But that day, somethin' told me t'go on and do it. Soon as I saw them two was in there t'gether, I put my eye t'the crack in the door and had me a good look-see.

"Miss Gem had found herself some bootleg liquor and was curled up on the sofa with a glass of it. Mr. Jameson was leanin' up 'gainst the fireplace mantel. He was tellin' her that Miss Lilian had missed her at breakfast. Miss Gem shrugged like she didn't care and said she'd see her sister when she got back. Mr. Jameson didn't like that attitude, didn't like it at all. But he didn't say nothin', just took out his cigarette case and lit a Lucky Strike. He smoked for a li'l while, all the time studyin' Miss Gem. Finally, he turned round and tapped his ashes in the fireplace. Then he gave Miss Gem somethin' t'think 'bout.

" 'I'm only going to say this one time,' he said. 'And one time only. I won't let *anyone* make my Lilian unhappy. I don't intend to make her unhappy myself. She's one of a kind.'

" 'She certainly is,' said Miss Gem.

" 'I bless the day she married me.'

" 'I'm sure you do.'

"Mr. Jameson liked that answer even less, but he let it go. Miss Gem, she grabbed her drink from where she'd put it on the floor and swung her legs down off the sofa. She sallied on over t'the table where she'd stashed her bot-tle, poured herself another drink, and made one for him, too. Then she sort of sidled on over t'him and pressed the glass in his hands.

"Why wasn't he smokin' his pipe, she wanted to know. Said she liked his pipe. Told him he prob'ly only smoked it t'impress women. Well, Mr. Jameson told her that if that was the case, then she'd best take note he wasn't interested in smokin' his pipe 'round *her.* Miss Gem gave a little laugh and scolded him for bein' so direct. Anyway, she said, the only reason he wanted Miss Lilian was the money her daddy left her. She told Mr. Jameson that he and Miss Lilian didn't have nothin' in common. Said that *even if he did* want her sister, there weren't no reason why he shouldn't want her more.

"Mr. Jameson took a long, hard look at her. Said she must take him for a fool, but he was gonna have t'disappoint her. He loved Miss Lilian, he said.

"'You mean you love her money,' Miss Gem said.

"Mr. Jameson got angry. Said he didn't care what she thought, but she'd better get one thing straight: Couldn't nothin' happen—not between her and him, not between him and Miss Lilian—if he didn't say so. He was her sister's husband and she'd better get used t'it.

"Then he told her that he understood if she was jealous. Said she had reason t'be, since Miss Lilian had 'out-classed' her and all. Miss Gem got so angry, she threw her glass at him. Mr. Jameson stepped aside and the glass broke at his feet. He laughed at her. Well, Miss Gem couldn't take that. She went crazy, tried t'hit him, but he caught her.

"'Don't,' he told her. 'Don't ever do that.'

"He never raised his voice, but you knew he meant business. She told him she didn't never let nobody laugh at her. He lowered her arm and kissed her wrist, real gentle-like. Then he asked, 'Is that better?' Well, it musta been 'cause she got her lazy smile back. She leaned into him. He stroked her face. He cupped her cheeks. Then his grip got tighter. He squeezed so tight it hurt t'see. She tried t'pull away, but he yanked her back. Then he kissed her. Well, I'm callin' it that, but what he done ain't had nothin' t'do with no affection. She fought him—leastways, at first she did. Pounded him on the chest and such. But then she started t'give in. Started t'put her arms around him. And the minute she did that, he let her go. Pushed her away. She fell back, hit the mantelpiece. Mr. David, there was tears in her eyes. That man actually made Miss Gem cry. He got t'her. Looked at her with 'bout as much feelin' as a butcher's got for a cut of meat. Said the only kinda lovin' he'd ever have for someone like her would be hard and quick—when he wanted it and how he wanted it."

"For *'someone like her'?*"

"Sure 'nough. She swore t'him that he'd regret it. He shrugged. Said maybe he would—maybe he wouldn't."

Annie sipped her coffee and was silent, thoughtful. "The strange thing of it is, after a while I got the feelin' Miss Gem genuinely cared for him. It started as a game. Just t'spite Miss Lilian. But then Miss Gem fell for him. Fell hard. She changed after he put her down like that. She started treatin' Miss Lilian with more respect. No more of them sly looks at him.

"It was just after that, that Miss Gem and Miss Lilian started spendin' more time together. They'd go on shoppin' trips. Come back laughin' and gigglin' like they was schoolgirls. I wondered what Miss Gem was up to. Later on, I started to think that maybe she was poisonin' Miss Lilian 'gainst Mr. Jameson."

"Why'd you think that?"

Annie looked at him. "'Cause of what happened later."

And just what was that? David wondered. He could try to get Annie to clarify her statement, but why rush her? He'd find out soon enough what she meant. Pressing his fingertips to his eyebrows, he massaged the muscles over the bridge of his nose. Poisoning Lilian against her husband would be something Gem would do. If she couldn't have Sweet, then she'd take away the woman he really wanted—and ruin Lilian's feelings for the man she'd finally found. David looked at Annie and his eyes hurt.

"What then?"

"Miss Gem went out and got herself a man of her own, a West Indian guy. Ev'rybody in the neighborhood was talkin' 'bout it. They said he was a gangster. Well, you never know now, do you? She brought him 'round here a coupla times. Seemed like a nice 'nough fellah. Li'l bit older. Quiet. Good t'look at. But smooth. Maybe too smooth, when I think 'bout it.

"Ev'rythin' seemed so nice for a while. Miss Gem and Miss Lilian was gettin' along. Miss Gem was goin' out all the time with her fellah. Miss Lilian was busy with her poetry readin's. Then, it all fell apart.

"Miss Lilian took ill. Got the tremors. Her hands would start t'shakin'. She got so she could barely hold a cup. She started complainin' 'bout her eyes, too. Said her vision was gettin' blurry. One minute ev'rythin' would be fine and clear. The next, she was as blind as a bat in a ray of sunshine. Mr. Jameson took her t'the doctor, but the doctor said he couldn't find nothin'. Told Miss Lilian it was her nerves. She was workin' too hard, he said. She'd been takin' on extra work since her boss left and she was writin' poems, book reviews, and the like. Doctor said she'd have t'cut back, go t'bed and get some rest.

"Well, she tried. But it didn't do no good. She'd start havin' nightmares the minute her head hit the pillow. Sometimes, she'd wake up screamin', babblin' 'bout voices in the dark. Mr. Jameson, he told the doctor t'give her a sleepin' potion. But them spells come on her so sudden, nobody knew what t'do. And they'd go way quick as they come. One minute, she could see; the next she couldn't. One minute, she was sittin' at her desk, typin' away; the next, her hands were shakin' so bad she couldn't hit the keys. And her heart—she said it'd beat so hard, she thought it was 'bout t'jump outta her chest.

"We was all desp'rate, tryin' t'find ways t'help her. We was so busy with Miss Lilian, wasn't none of us payin' no attention t'Miss Gem. She seemed fine enough with her fellah. But then somethin' went wrong there, too. Folks say he jilted her. I don't know 'bout *that*. I ain't heard nothin' 'bout them s'posed t'be gettin' married. But he sure 'nough dropped her. They had a big blowup. Right out in public. Ev'rybody was talkin' 'bout it. She left town right after that. Said she'd had enough of New York. At least, that's what Miss Lilian said. She the one went out there and talked t'Miss Gem. Nobody else did."

"When was that?"

"Last year. 'Round this time. Strange how Miss Gem took off: Not a word t'nobody. Gone. Into thin air, much the way she came." Annie felt around in her apron pocket, pulled out a small white handkerchief, and blew her nose softly. "After Miss Gem left, Miss Lilian started drinkin'. Havin' blackouts. Sometimes she'd lose track of hours. Didn't have no idea where she'd been or what she'd been doin'. Leastways, she *said* she didn't know. But *I* knew. She'd go places when Mr. Jameson wasn't home; come home late at night. I smelled smoke on her clothes and liquor on her breath.

"God forgive me if I'm wrong—but I think it was Miss Gem who got Miss Lilian started down that road. She's the one taught Miss Lilian 'bout smokin' and drinkin'. T'this day, I wonder why Miss Lilian listened."

Maybe, he thought, *just maybe Lilian thought she was missing out on life.* He didn't know why he thought that, but something inside him told him it was so.

Bitterness touched Annie's face. "She dropped all her old friends; got right secr'tive. And she tried t'fire me. Me, of all people. After all I'd done for her. After she'd promised me a place 'til my dyin' day. Well, she had t'bring me back a week later. Miss Lilian didn't say nothin' 'bout why she'd changed her mind. But *he* told me the new girl had burnt a hole in his best shirt. Said he liked a smooth-runnin' house. He was the one told her t'fetch me back. She didn't want t'do it, but he forced her to."

David's dismay deepened.

She sighed. The tightness around her eyes softened. "It was sad, so sad, how Miss Lilian changed t'ward the end. Forgettin' things and all. Her hair turned white. She was scared of her own shadow. She'd have fits. Tear all her clothes outta her closet. One time she couldn't find a frock she wanted. Mr. Jameson suggested she wear somethin' else. She got so angry she grabbed the shears off her desk, started rippin' her clothes up. Said she hated her clothes; hated her life. Then she looked at *him*. Ran at him with the shears. He caught her just in time. Shook her. Her eyes cleared and she broke down. Started weepin' like a baby."

David was by nature a silent man, so he had listened to Annie's account for the most part without interrupting. Now he continued to regard her for some time without speaking. The more she told him, the less he understood. The babble of inner voices seeking answers had only intensified, their questions multiplied. A sliver of pain darted through his head. He rubbed his temples. He was so terribly hung over. He turned his gaze to the window. Vaguely, he noted a rumble of thunder in the distance, like the faint rolling of drums. It was hard to believe what he was hearing about Lilian.

"But what caused it all?"

"Coulda been Miss Gem's up-and-going like that. Mr. Jameson sure didn't seem t'know what t'do. He said nobody, but nobody, could figure it out. Not none of the doctors, anyway."

"Was she taking medicine?"

"Yes, but I don't r'member no names. Just somethin' t'calm her nerves."

The rain fell suddenly. Fat drops beat a hard ratta-tat-tat against the windowpanes. The only light in the kitchen came from the soft pearl gray of the storm clouds outside. They could have been sitting in a small, shadowed cave.

Inwardly, he shuddered. *Lilian, dear Lilian. How was it possible?* Leaning on the table, he rubbed his eyes. *A lot's done happened since you been gone.* He groaned. *Yes, it had.*

Some two years ago, in April 1924, Lilian had impetuously married a virtual stranger, moving with amazing alacrity. That same year, Gem returned. She was at the house for roughly five months, before suddenly, inexplicably, taking off again. Lilian had written him for a whole year without once mentioning either her new husband or Gem's return. She had lied to him by omission, and betrayed Annie's trust by trying to fire her.

That wasn't Lilian's way. It wasn't her way at all.

He'd been so grateful for the bits of news she was sending him that he hadn't noticed what she was leaving out.

Now that's a lie.

The truth was, he'd sensed that something was wrong. Sensed it. And when the letters stopped, he could've asked why—

But I was too busy hiding my own damn secret.

He raised his head. Now he knew that Lilian had had her secrets, too.

But why hide her marriage and Gem's return? Why not write and say she was ill? It was unlike her to be so secretive. Perhaps she didn't want me to worry.

That would have been like her: self-sacrificing, determined to resolve her problems alone. Only Lilian had remained loyal to herself, to her home, to their father's vision of what it meant to be a McKay. Only she had really tried. He had more in common with Gem than he wanted to admit. They'd both become wanderers. Both had rejected their upbringing and tried to reinvent themselves.

But he was ashamed of his new identity. He lived in a personal hell of his own creation—and from what Annie said, he suspected that Gem did, too.

He could imagine Lilian's shock when she opened the door and found Gem standing on the family doorstep. They hadn't heard anything from Gem since December of '21, when she'd sent a postcard from Paris after six months of silence. At the time, they'd wondered whether she was paving the way toward asking for more funds, but as far as he knew, nothing more had been heard from her. Not before that Halloween night.

Gem's return meant that her money was gone. She had set sail for home and the one sure touch for easy cash. But someone had gotten to the till before her: a watchful husband. Gem might have figured that it would be difficult to manipulate Lilian, but easy to seduce Sweet. She had never had to do more than crook her finger to make a man come running. But Sweet was different. He had refused to budge. For once, Lilian had it all: the man and the money.

Sister Gem was down on her luck. Is that why she hightailed it back to Europe?

Perhaps. But it was unlike Gem to give up easily. Especially when it came to men and money. He would've expected her to make another play for Sweet. Instead, she had reconciled with Lilian. That was surprising.

But then she left, although she knew that Lilian was ill. Now that was not surprising, not surprising at all. And her silence since Lilian's death, it fit her pattern also.

He resented Gem's absence, but he was relieved by it, too. He preferred to handle this matter alone. She might have been able to help him, but he doubted she would have been willing to. She might have been the only one, other than Annie and Sweet, who could help him understand why Lilian had died. But Gem knew how to set his teeth on edge and enjoyed doing so. She was fickle and unreliable, two qualities he despised. She had an easy charm he found suspect. She had never once thought about pleasing anyone but herself. And she had nothing but contempt for her family.

Had Lilian given Gem money to go away? Not exactly paid her off, but . . . Gem must've gotten the money from someone. From whom else, but Lilian?

"I wasn't in the house when she did it," Annie was saying. "She told me she was goin' t'stay with friends for the weekend. Said she'd be back Monday afternoon. That's when Mr. Jameson was s'posed t'be back, too. So I went and visited my nephew. I'll wish t'the day I die that I'd stayed here. She musta done it sittin' on her bed. The mattress was soaked. Blood ev'rywhere. On the walls, the bed canopy, the floor. Pools of blood. Dried hard, dried black. I don't remember much more. She was wearin' a white gown, I think. Or it had been white. And she was sittin' under the window, lookin' up t'Heaven. Her eyes, those beautiful sweet eyes, was wide open. And she had these deep cuts, one in each wrist. I'll never forget that. All it took was them two wounds, just them two wounds and Miss Lilian's life poured out."

4

Lilian's Grave

She was buried in a municipal cemetery at least an hour's drive away in Brooklyn, amid a sea of white and gray headstones. Standing at Lilian's graveside, David gazed out over the memorial park. *She was never fond of Brooklyn,* he thought. *Except for Coney Island, she had no use for the place. That she should end up here . . . Of all places, here . . .*

"It was the only place Mr. Jameson could find for her," Annie had told him. "It's a shame Miss Lilian couldna been buried in consecrated ground, closer t'home."

It's a shame she's here at all.

Crouching down by the grave, he reached out to touch the hard mound of earth. Slowly, his hands balled into fists. It was such a struggle to believe that Lilian—gentle, proud, and deeply religious—would take her own life. *What brought you down, little sister? What brought you down?*

A breeze, unseasonably warm and gentle, caressed his hair. His nostrils caught a faint whiff of perfume, lightly sweet and powdery. He imagined he heard her voice.

Remember me, she seemed to say. *Forget what others tell you. Remember me, as you knew me.*

He'd been five years old when Lilian was born. From the moment he laid eyes on her, he'd given her his heart. His parents were touched and amused, but perplexed by his singular affection for Lilian. She was a twin. Why did he love her more than Gem, who was as sweet and huggable as her sister? How could he, as small as he was, even tell the two tiny girls apart? He shrugged— he didn't know. He simply never mistook one for the other.

Snatches of memories floated to the surface of his mind. Images of life with Lilian: holding her up in the shallow end of the public swimming pool as she splashed about; stealing chocolate chip cookies for her from Annie's

41

kitchen; standing side by side at their mother's graveside. They had been so close. How could he have let four years go by without seeing her?

The last time he *had* seen her, she had been conscientiously teaching English to bored high school students. It was her way of living up to their parents' edict of giving back to the community. He had visited her classroom one day and, quite honestly, found her a tedious, uninspiring teacher. He had come away wondering whom he should feel sorrier for, Lilian or her students. He thought her effort misdirected, but he admired her for it just the same. During summer breaks, Lilian would escape to Provence. She had friends there who rented her a small cottage. She wrote during those summers, but she seemed to have given up any hopes of a serious literary career. Then her situation changed.

From Lilian's letters, he knew that she had met Helga Bennett during one of those summers in southern France. Bennett was just launching the *Black Arrow,* which was to be not only a literary journal, but also the official voice of the Movement. Bennett was so impressed with Lilian that she invited her to join the staff. She became Lilian's mentor, but was herself inspired by Lilian's enthusiasm and vision. They both dreamed of a day when Harlem artists would receive the same recognition, prizes, and contracts that white writers did. Lilian wanted to read books about her people, written by her people. By that she meant books about well-bred, refined colored people. There was, she said, enough being written about the downside of Negro life, about the crime and the poverty. Someone had to tell the story of the educated colored people, too. Someone had to speak up for the Negroes who were doctors, lawyers, philosophers, professors.

"We live as a minority within a minority," she once wrote him. "It's time our voice was heard. That would advance the cause of the entire race."

By the time of her death, Lilian was a senior staffer at the *Black Arrow* and making her own mark as an author. The Nubian Art Players had performed her unstructured play, *Shadowlands,* the year before. She had written one novel and was working on another when death claimed her. Her first book, *Lucifer's Parlor,* was a social statement about Irish and Negro life in the Tenderloin. Her second work, *Lyrics of a Blackbird,* dealt with betrayal in a genteel Harlem family. Her first book was well received. He was confident that her second one would have been, too.

Someone had placed fresh roses near her headstone. The flowers were a pleasing soft shade of pink. He brushed them with his fingertips. The blooms were stiff in the cold air. They would discolor and shrivel soon. He closed his eyes. The pain in his head had become a steady pulse. There was again that breeze from nowhere. He blinked and looked up at the sky, but saw nothing there. No miraculous face in the clouds, not even a sudden ray of sunshine to ease the bleakness of the day. What had he hoped for? Leaning forward, he examined the farewell on Lilian's gravestone, mouthing the words.

"Lilian McKay Sweet, 1897–1926. To my Lilian, I will miss you."

He assumed that Lilian's husband had written the words. Sitting back on his heels, he wondered, *Who indeed was Jameson Sweet?*

5

The Book of Rachel

When David returned home, Annie was sitting at the kitchen table. She had a nearly empty bag of string beans on one side of her and a big pot of beans and water on the other. She grabbed up several beans from the bag, lined their ends up, and snapped their tips off with a smooth twist of her wrist—*blat-blat-blat*. She tossed the last of the beans into the pot and dropped the tips onto some newspaper sheets.

"How was it?" she asked, stopping her work to look at him.

"Fine. It's not a bad place, that cemetery. Just far from home."

She nodded. "Too far."

She shoved her chair back and stood up, wiping her hands on her apron. Then she rolled up the newspaper, put it into the bag, and set it aside for garbage.

"I'll just let these soak for a while," she said, putting the pot of beans on the stove. "Sit down. Rest your feet. You left without eatin' breakfast this mornin'. I just made some coffee and I baked a pie, apple, 'cause I knows that's your favorite."

"Oh, Annie, I—"

"It ain't no trouble. That's what I'm here for, t'take care you." She wiped up the table and motioned for him to take a seat. He did. She took down a plate and fork and poured him a cup of coffee. "Before I forget, Miss Rachel stopped by t'see you last night."

He bit back his surprise and forced a smile. "How'd she know I was back?"

"Oh, everybody know you back, Mr. David. Everybody know that." She fetched the pie, set it on the table before him, and served him a healthy slice. "Miss Rachel helped me nurse Miss Lilian when she was sick."

"Did she, now?" He picked up his fork. "What did she say last night?"

"That she wants to see you."

Keeping his face devoid of expression, he reached for his cup and took a sip. A question hovered on the tip of his tongue. "Did she ever marry?"

Annie looked at him. "No, Mr. David. She never did."

He flushed at the knowledge in her eyes. Mercifully, she left him, saying she had shopping to do. Alone, he drained the coffeepot. But, although it was delicious, he barely tasted the pie. One name echoed in his mind.

Rachel.

She lived in a tenement building on 130th Street, on Harlem's southern edge, in an area called "Darktown," presumably because it had been an area for black residency since the 1890s, when the rest of Harlem was still white. It was a crowded building. Most of the apartments were filled beyond capacity. She was the only resident who could afford the luxury of living in her apartment alone.

She sat on the couch near her parlor window, a small, delicately slim creature in a warm tailored frock. Flipping the pages of a thin photo album, she studied the photos one by one. Pictures of her and the McKay children: of her and Lilian; of her and David; of her, Lilian, and Gem. Studio photos taken over time, paid for by the McKays.

The friendship between the McKays and the Hamiltons went back some twenty years, when both were living in the Tenderloin. The two families had lived only blocks apart. They attended the same church and Rachel went to the same school as the McKay children. Rachel spent many afternoons after school playing with Gem and Lilian. Her mother worked. Mrs. McKay was at home. The arrangement was practical.

No one thought of long-range consequences.

Like the McKays, the Hamiltons started out poor. Unlike them, the Hamiltons stayed that way. While Augustus McKay, a waiter, sunk every extra dime he had into real estate, his buddy Bill Hamilton, a better-earning mortician, drank and gambled away his dollars. McKay's fortunes took a decided upswing in 1907 when the Pennsylvania Railroad purchased some of his Seventh Avenue property for more than one hundred thousand dollars. Three years later, in 1910, when the twins were fourteen and David nineteen, the McKays left the miserable, overcrowded Tenderloin and bought property on West 134th Street, joining other prominent blacks in Harlem. It took the Hamiltons, now consisting only of Rachel and her mother, another nine years to achieve the move uptown, and when they did, it was to squeeze into a grimy four-room apartment on West 130th

Street with four other families. By then, David was back from the war and
the McKays were on the move again, too—this time, into their home on
Strivers' Row. Over the next few years, the McKay property would rapidly
rise in value, and the building housing the Hamiltons would just as decid-
edly decline.

Despite the economic fissure dividing the McKays and the Hamiltons,
the friendship that began in the Tenderloin endured. Rachel remained one
of the few people outside the McKay family who could tell the twins apart.
For nine years, she doggedly made the trip uptown to visit Lilian. The instant
affection she'd felt for Lilian in the first grade deepened, as did the instant
antipathy she'd felt toward Gem. As for her feelings for David, they were
clear even to the blind.

Rachel closed the picture album with an air of finality and put it back on
her bookshelf. She looked at her clock. How would he react to her message?
Would he come by to see her? Going to her dresser, she eased out the top
drawer and dug out a hand mirror. She had spent the better part of the
morning preparing for his hoped-for visit. She had marcelled her hair and
put on her best dress. It was a cream creation called "champagne beige." She
had bought it from a "hot" man. People said hot men sold stolen goods.
Rachel neither asked nor cared. Like most Harlem women who bought
from hot men, she spent little mental energy on the ethics of buying possibly
pilfered merchandise. If she thought about it at all, she shrugged and said the
stores priced the clothes too high anyway, so if something "fell off the truck"
or was "rescued from a warehouse," it was a way of robbing the rich to give
to the poor. What she did know, and knew for sure, was that hot men
enabled her to dress well and inexpensively. Her earnings were meager as a
nurse at Harlem Hospital.

Rachel regarded what little she could see of herself in the mirror coolly,
looking for the person she imagined and hoped David would find. Her short
hair was groomed using Madame C. J. Walker's products. Her fingernails
were scrubbed and meticulously self-manicured.

Some Georgia plantation owner had passed down vivid green eyes. Otherwise, Rachel's dark-skinned African forebears had prevailed. Her charcoal
complexion unmistakably marked her as one of their own. She knew that
people often murmured that she would have been quite pretty if she were
not so black, but they raved over her eyes.

Rachel often wondered how an emblem of sexual and racial degradation
had become a badge of honor. It was perverse to idolize the legacy of a

white slave-owner's lust. But all rational analysis aside, Rachel loved her jade eyes, too. Her sooty complexion was another matter.

She knew the frustration that compelled some dark-skinned women to try to lighten their complexions. Her friends went from slathering their faces with bleaching creams to swallowing arsenic wafers. She scorned such solutions. She knew they weren't effective; her pride would've kept her from using them even if they were. Unlike her friends, Rachel didn't blindly worship light skin, but she did see the practical advantages of having it. If she caught herself wishing she'd been born with beige skin, it wasn't necessarily because she found it beautiful but convenient. "Whiter" meant "righter" in the world she knew.

Take the McKays. Their buttermilk beauty added much to their prestige. Even during the Tenderloin days, the McKays seemed set apart. They were admired and envied. Invitations to their home were rare and highly coveted. Everywhere they went, they were warmly received.

Once upon a time, she dreamed of becoming a McKay. She had loved David since they were children, but she'd never dared hope for his love in return. Four years ago, it seemed as though he had fallen in love with her. They'd met secretly. She'd given him her heart, her body. She'd trusted him completely. Then one day he had gone away, on Movement business, and failed to return.

Desperate, Rachel went to see an old West Indian conjure woman and paid her some hard-earned cash. The woman told her to take a pair of David's shoes and sprinkle a little "come on home powder" on top of the toes. If he'd gone south, then she should swing the shoes around and set them down with the toes pointing north.

"He'll be back in seven days, honey."

Rachel had a time getting a hold of David's bedroom slippers—that's all he'd left behind—but she managed to do it. She sprinkled the slippers generously and followed the conjure woman's instructions to the letter.

"But it didn't help. He didn't come back," Rachel complained, returning to the woman.

"Well, somebody somewhere is workin' mo' powerful magic than you."

The old woman chuckled and shut the door in her face. Rachel was nearly broke, but she cared little about the money. She wanted David back.

Now he was again in Harlem. She shook her head at her earlier foolish fantasies. She wouldn't make the same mistake twice. Life had taught her hard and bitter lessons. It simply didn't pay to be naive.

*   *   *

David climbed the steps to Rachel's building uneasily. As Lilian's best friend, she could probably help him, but would she be willing to? What had his disappearance meant to her? They had been young. He could barely remember the person he'd been when he'd last seen her. The life he'd led, the pain he'd felt and witnessed since then, had changed him irrevocably. Rachel represented a life he had been forced to leave behind. Surely, she must see that neither of them could take their love affair seriously. That it was better to consign it to the brief but intense passions of youth. That it was better not to ask whether it could have endured.

He carried a bouquet of pale pink roses, difficult to find that time of year and expensive. After a moment's hesitation, he rang her bell and went in the building's entrance. He found her second-floor apartment easily and had just raised his hand to knock when the door was yanked open. His breath caught at the sight of her. She had changed.

She was still very pretty, but so thin. Gray circles ringed her eyes and faint hollows touched her cheeks. The years had added an air of fragility. Something inside him fluttered and his vision of her reverted to what it once was. No longer was she the woman he had abandoned, with all the guilt that entailed. She was, first and foremost, a dear friend. And he had missed her. Suddenly, he was glad, very glad, that he had come. Her face broke into a heart-wrenching smile and she threw her slender arms around him.

"I'm so sorry about Lilian," she whispered.

Seated on her sofa, the two them shared a warm drink and homemade apple betty. Rachel had displayed his flowers prominently in a vase on her coffee table. Glancing around, David admired the soothing atmosphere of her apartment. She had chosen her furniture with an eye for comfort as well as beauty. He saw too that she had been influenced by his mother's tastes, but discerned that she had adapted them to fit her own personality. How could Rachel live so well on a nurse's salary? Smiling gently, he told her that he was glad to see her. He'd heard that she'd gone away.

"I had to come back," she said. "Two years ago. I had to. Just like you."

His smile faltered. "It's not the same. You came back because you wanted to. I returned because I had to. Lilian's death is the only reason I'm here."

He saw the flash of pain in her eyes and instantly regretted his words. She knew he had not come back because of her. No need to remind her. Once again, his eyes went over her. The bleakness in her gaze; the sag in her shoulders: What had happened to her? He started to ask, then stopped. If he inquired about her last four years, she might inquire about his.

She asked if he planned to move back into the house. Her voice was full of hopeful expectation, but when he shook his head, she seemed more relieved than disappointed. "So you'll be selling your half to Sweet?"

"I don't see why I should."

"But if you don't want to live there—"

"That house was Daddy's pride. I'm not giving it up."

"I see."

Did she? He'd never been able to fully read Rachel, nor she him.

She gazed down thoughtfully at her small, neat hands, which lay folded in her lap. "So how long *will* you be staying?"

"Not long."

She gave him a long, intent look. Behind her beautiful eyes battled pride and desire. "And there's no way you can move back?"

"No way at all. As soon as I'm done, I'm catching the first thing smokin'."

The forced casualness sounded false even to his own ears. Her face took on a set expression. He was reminded that Rachel had a firmness of character that was startling in one who looked so delicate. She could express herself in cool, precise terms when she wanted to. When she raised her chin, he knew what was coming.

"If Lilian's the *only* reason you're back, you might as well leave right now. You can't change what happened."

"I have to know why she did it."

"You never will—"

"I have to try to understand."

"Or try to ease your conscience?"

Her remark stung, as he knew it was meant to. He felt himself grow warm.

"Thank you," he said, "for putting it so succinctly."

Her expression softened. "I'm not judging you, but that don't mean I got to help you deny the truth neither."

"I'm not asking you to."

"Aren't you?"

He smiled grimly. "Perhaps you're right. But I didn't come here to talk about myself."

"Who then?"

"Lilian's husband." His eyes traced her lovely profile. "Do you know him?"

"He's a good man. Kind. Loyal." Her eyes flickered over him. "The kinda man a woman can depend on."

David's face grew taut. "So he loved her?"

She nodded.

"Treated her right?"

"You mean . . . did he treat her better than you treated me?"

Their eyes locked.

"You don't give a man a break, do you?"

"Only when he deserves one."

Utter silence.

"Rachel . . . I know I hurt you," he said huskily. "I never intended to."

"Then why did you?"

He regarded her with regret. How could he answer her? What could he say? As always, when words failed him, he found another way of communicating. Without thinking, he reached for her. He put his arms around her and hugged her. She resisted for a moment and then put her arms around him, too. They clung to one another. Her cheap perfume, acrid yet seductive, enveloped him. She had worn the same scent when he'd last seen her. He paused in his thoughts, remembering.

Life was much simpler then. We were both so hopeful.

"I'm sorry," he whispered. "More sorry than you'll ever know."

"But why? Why'd you stay away so long?"

"Don't ask," he said. "I can't answer."

She pulled away. He reached out to caress her cheek but she averted her face, then turned back to gaze at him with suspicion. Taking his left hand, she laid it on top of her own and studied it. She turned it this way and that, with the air of a gypsy fortune-teller. With her fingertips, she stroked his palm and traced a line along his fourth finger. She found no traces of a wedding ring, but still she asked: "Who is she?"

"I've stayed alone."

She searched his face with wide, clear eyes that not only sought the truth of his feelings, but also revealed her own. He had the momentary illusion that if he peered into her eyes, long enough, deeply enough, he would learn all there was to know about her. But then, he asked again about Lilian, and the illusion died. Rachel's face clouded over; her lovely eyes became dim.

"There's nothing to tell. Lilian just got sick. That's all. She just . . . got . . . sick."

"I can't accept that. There's more. There's got to be."

"David, I know you feel bad, but you can't start chasing demons. Listen," she said with a rush of feeling. "Sweet was always here for Lilian. She had herself a good man." A trace of bitterness crept into her tone. "It's okay if you were out there having a good time, baby, 'cause believe me, at the end, she didn't even know you were gone."

"You're not being fair," he said and felt like an idiot saying it.

"Well, neither are you."

Her eyes challenged him and he started to respond, but then something happened: He remembered how much he'd enjoyed her peppery temper. After a moment, he laughed gently and conceded. "You're right."

She looked at him. Then her anger faded as quickly as it had come. A smile came to her lips, too. "You hungry?"

He nodded.

"C'mon, then. Let's have lunch."

He helped her set the table and noticed the floral design on her china. It was familiar. "These were my mother's dishes. Her everyday service."

"I always liked them. After your daddy died, I asked about them. Lilian said I could have them. She didn't mind and Gem didn't care. Don't you remember?"

He didn't, but it mattered little. The dishes and the silverware she gave him to lay next to it conveyed a feeling of comfort. The tension between them eased. As she worked to prepare the meal, she exuded an air of serenity. She had the face of an ebony Madonna: gentle and sweet, but solemn. He noted the calming beauty of her dress. She seemed at peace with herself. He envied her.

The air of contentment that filled her kitchen as she cooked stayed with them. They left the topic that had brought him to see her and spoke of pleasant matters. She had seen a new exhibit of sculpture by Meta Warrick Fuller. Fuller's work was brilliant. Did he know that Fuller, a black woman, had actually studied in Paris with Rodin?

When given free rein to choose her topic, Rachel made a spirited conversationalist. Her inquisitive mind had refused to accept the limitations of her formal training and sought to expand itself. She was well read. Her knowledge of contemporary literature, philosophy, and art was more than adequate for intelligent discussion. She also had a spicy wit that cut through pretension and hypocrisy.

He looked at her laughing face and wondered, *What would've happened if I had returned?* But there was no point in thinking about it. Whatever chance they might have had was gone. His fall from grace when he decided to stay away four years ago would be nothing compared to the condemnation he would suffer if she knew *why* he had stayed away.

And was it wise to visit her, speak with her, sit in her kitchen and share her meal? His visit was meant to heal old wounds, not inflict new ones. He needed her forgiveness. For his sake, as well as hers. He would have to leave Harlem within twenty-four hours. The moment he clarified a few questions about Lilian's death and settled matters concerning the house with Sweet, he would board a train and speed back to the life he had built in Philadelphia.

That life was simple. It was lonely but not entirely dissatisfying. As a lawyer, he helped people. He lived modestly so he could afford destitute clients, those who might not have had a chance otherwise. He was extremely effective as a criminal defense attorney. In fact, he had made a name for himself, not as a defender of lost causes, but as an honest man who could make things happen.

His work had become his penance. Guilt drove him during the day and exhaustion put him to sleep at night. A successful court decision helped to assuage his shame, but never fully lifted it. Success also fueled his anxiety. He dreaded newspaper coverage that might bring him attention. So he always sought the small cases, the ones no one wanted to be bothered with. But too often, a case would take a twist that lent it unexpected significance. When this happened and reporters knocked on his door, he would bar himself in his small one-man office. He would think of home. He would dream of seeing Lilian and Rachel and Annie.

On Christmas Eve 1922, deeply homesick, he had written to Lilian and mailed the letter before he could change his mind. She had quickly answered. A correspondence gradually developed, sporadic and hesitant on his side, consistent and faithful on hers. After a few months, he suspected that she knew why he was staying away and what he was doing. In time, he became certain she did. But she never once criticized him nor did she pry. Her letters expressed love and gentle curiosity. Her tactful avoidance of issues that might have pained him convinced him that she understood and accepted his way.

Lilian was the only person with whom he had been honest, and that was because she had never forced him to lie. He could not expect that of Annie or Rachel. Their grief over Lilian's death and relief over his return had temporarily abated their inquisitiveness, but it would return if he stayed too long. He would have to leave in order to retain their respect and affection. He was convinced of it.

In the meantime, he meant to make the most of his short visit by finding out everything he could about Lilian's last months. Looking at Rachel, he thought he understood her reluctance to discuss Lilian's illness. It was, after all, an unpleasant subject. But surely she must understand his need to know what had happened.

"Lilian used to write me," he said, "telling me all the goings-on."

Rachel dabbed at the corner of her mouth with her napkin. "Did she mention me?"

"Once. She said you'd moved away."

"Is that all?"

He nodded.

Rachel picked at her food. "You know, Lilian and me . . . well, we sorta had a falling-out. It was more on her side, really. She dropped me. From one moment to the next."

"But you two were like a married couple."

"Yes, maybe. But Lilian did drop me. She threw her sticks in with Gem." Rachel gave a rueful little laugh.

David laid down his fork. "Actually, Annie did say something about that. But it's hard to believe."

"Well, believe it. Somehow, Gem got Lilian to trust her. It started with them going out all the time, shopping together. By the time Gem left, she could get Lilian to do just about whatever she wanted her to. Even quit her job."

David looked stunned. "But that job at the *Black Arrow* meant the world to her."

"Lilian said her doctor had told her to quit, too. But she didn't quit when *he* told her to. She quit when *Gem* told her to. Lilian said she could use the time to work on her book. Well, I didn't trust Gem. She never wanted to help nobody. So, I went to see Lilian. I tried to tell her that Gem was probably up to something, but Lilian wouldn't listen. It wasn't none of my business, she said. She wouldn't talk to me after that. Ignored me when she saw me at the poetry meetings."

If anyone other than Rachel had been telling him this, he wouldn't have believed her. But Rachel and Lilian had been like sisters for years. Rachel loved Lilian more than Gem ever loved her, and he knew Rachel would never lie. It hurt to think that Lilian had betrayed their friendship in favor of Gem. "Betray" was perhaps too harsh a word. Gem, after all, was Lilian's sister, her flesh and blood, and it was fine if Gem wanted to be close to Lilian, to repair their relationship. But she never should've done it at the cost of Lilian's friendship with Rachel. She never should've forced Lilian to make that choice. And Lilian should've refused to make it.

"Months went by when I didn't see her," Rachel said. "Then, in the fall, Sweet sent for me. Wanted me to help Annie nurse her, just 'til he found somebody regular. I got to admit, I wasn't too keen on going over there at first, seeing how she'd treated me, but then we'd been friends for so long . . . and Sweet was so worried. It scared me when I saw her. She wasn't the same, David. You wouldn't have recognized her."

"Annie said the doctors could never figure out what was wrong with her."

"They mentioned schizophrenia."

Schizophrenia. He turned that over. It was one explanation. "Okay, you say you didn't see her for months, but somebody else must've seen her, talked to her. You knew Lilian's other friends."

"I don't run in them circles. Rats and dicties don't mix. What's between the Hamiltons and the McKays is special."

"Yes, it is." He took her hands in his. "But what about the poetry meetings at the library? That was common ground."

"Lilian dropped out. Cut off everybody. The folks who saw her on the street said she was like ice. Told them she'd never liked their work. She said she'd had her fun with the literary crowd. Now she was into a better class of people. Turns out, she'd taken up with some rich ofay. You know the kind. A 'Negrotarian,' as Zora Neale would say."

David's dark eyes widened. Anthropologist Zora Neale Hurston had coined the term "Negrotarian." It reflected the cynicism of black artists who were mildly uneasy with or outright distrusted the motives of their white patrons. Some Negrotarians were devoted philanthropists; others merely sought the thrill of being trendy. Some were members of that spiritually Lost Generation—they stopped off in Harlem on their way to Paris. The more profit-oriented Negrotarians looked at blacks and saw green: They calculated money when investing in art, literature, and entertainment with fashionable African American themes.

"So, who was Lilian involved with?"

"A woman named Nella Harding. Ever heard of her?"

He thought for a moment. Then it came to him. But if that was the woman, then—

That must've been one odd friendship.

Nella Harding—the Nella Harding he was thinking about—was the kind of person to have attracted Gem . . . and repelled Lilian.

"What was Lilian doing with somebody like that?"

From Rachel's expression, David could tell that she thought him naive.

"Listen," she said, "a lot of Negro writers would like to ignore Nella, but she's got Mister Charlie's ear. She's got what they call '*in*fluence.' Big time. She can open doors with a phone call. Even someone like Lilian, who had money and connections, has to kneel before Mister Charlie, sometime. Don't you see? The jigs have got to try to use the Nellas of the world, but ain't none of us stupid. We all know that they're using us, too."

6

Nella's Party

Nella Harding's latest proud product was a prime example of what Rachel meant. *Ebony Eden* was supposedly based on Nella's experiences in Negro Harlem and it was a best-seller. Everyone was talking about it, but few would admit to having read it. The book's plot was simplistic and rudimentary: A cabaret singer falls in love with a jazz musician, only to see him constantly betray her with other women. One night, in a fit of drunken jealousy, she shoots her lover and his friend, and then turns the gun on herself.

Not a single critic, black or white, deemed the book to be of literary value. One newspaper dismissed it as "cheap romance, colored café-au-lait." But stores couldn't stock it fast enough to keep customers happy. One of New York's culturati had written a book, and what a book! It promised to tell all about a secret and deliciously sinful Negro world. Sales went over the top.

Blacks denounced Nella as a literary voyeur. Some accused her of having exploited the Harlemites who trusted her in order to swell her pocketbook. The more generous said Nella had tried to serve two masters at once: She had pandered to the lurid curiosity of her white readers and to the ethnic pride of her black ones.

David had read the book. His judicial mind noted that *Ebony Eden* did take in High Harlem, with its genteel brownstones and polished grammar. The book's characters were distilled caricatures of Harlem's more colorful figures. Nella even took a poke at her fellow whites: Her husband, Nikki, appeared thinly camouflaged as a white missionary who was "astounded to discover jungle bunnies" who debated contemporary German literature, were intimately acquainted with Dadaism, Kandinsky, and Bauhaus realism, and were multilingual and widely traveled. But David quickly perceived that what Nella viewed as positive in blacks was what she saw as "primitive," and that this is what she emphasized. Nella depicted a black world characterized by rapacious lust, primordial superstition, and impenetrable stupidity. David found the book worse than insulting—it was demeaning. He could understand, however, why white critics found it fascinating.

"As propaganda for the so-called 'New Negro,' the book speaks volumes," said one.

"Volumes of nonsense," said the Negro press. "For us colored, *Ebony Eden* is the equivalent of taking one small step forward and two giant steps back."

Despite the uproar over *Ebony Eden,* or in some corners because of it, Nella remained Harlem's most welcome "Nordic." With her decided gift for always being at the right place at the right time, her penetrating presence was hard to avoid. She and Nikki had become point men for fashionable white America's fascination with black Harlem. They regularly escorted wide-eyed visitors to speakeasies, rent parties, and cabarets. The Hardings liked having Harlem come to them, too. Their "mixed" parties—long, languid, liquored evenings where black artists mingled with white society—were the talk of the town. The Hardings were giving a bash at their house in the Hamptons that evening. When the operator put through David's call to Nella that day, she told him to join in.

"I'd prefer to speak to you alone," he said.

"So would everyone." She laughed. "Just come and we'll see what we can do."

As David stood before the Hardings' imposing front door that Saturday evening, unease weighed like bad cooking in his belly. He was running a risk by showing up at such a trendy gathering. Suppose someone from the Movement was there? There could be questions.

But he had to talk to Nella about Lilian. That overrode every other consideration.

Squaring his shoulders, he pressed the doorbell. A chime rang deep within the house. Within seconds, a butler opened the door and ushered him in with a gracious bow.

David stepped into a spacious entryway softly lit by clusters of small gilded sconces. There was a high, wide arch at the other end . . . waves of warmth from human bodies gathered together . . . voices raised in hilarity . . . the babble of excited chatter.

He took a deep breath.

The butler eased David out of his coat and led him through the archway to the salon. David paused on the threshold.

To have said the room was overdone would have been kind.

It was huge, at least three times as large as the McKays'. And whereas the McKays' was restrained, tranquil, and patrician, this one was grand, golden, and glittering. The walls were covered with brocaded ice-white silk framed by slender gilded moldings. The same silk hung in deep folds at the ceiling-high windows, and it was drawn back to reveal gold lining and a trim of gold braid. Padded sofas and fat cushions, all upholstered in white with gold brocade, were placed about the room. Small table lamps with diamond tears dripping from the shades provided soft highlights and shadows over other corners of the room. The white, the touches of gold, and the sparkling lamps made all the perfectly tailored tuxedos and perfectly styled frocks seem even more perfectly sophisticated.

One-quarter of the people wearing those tuxedos and frocks were well-heeled blacks, easily recognizable from the theater world. The rest were whites: socialites, local politicians, and Harlem club owners.

Negrotarians, thought David, *a whole room of them, gathered under Nella's roof.*

The Hardings had decorated their party with Negro artists who were the darlings of every critic's pen. The actress Selena Ashburn, who boasted that she could drink any man under the table, stood holding an empty flute glass in one hand and a plate of appetizers in the other. Roland Pierce, the fabled jazz musician, was talking to friends in one corner. The poet Julian Woodstock was telling a joke in another. His group also included the opera singer Sylvia Burroughs, composer Geoffrey Gerard, and Broadway comedian Fannie Howell.

No one from the Movement, thought David with relief. But then a little voice said: *No one you recognize.* He recalled that he'd had little chance to become acquainted with the New York office staff before being sent south.

David felt as set apart as a dead man walking among the living. So much vivacity . . . So much sparkling wit . . . It exhausted him to see it. The hum of happy voices irritated him. Anger flashed through him.

So many of them must've known her—

His sister had been dead three weeks and now these people were carrying on with asinine jocularity. As though nothing had happened. As though the world was still right. As though he weren't a man who was walking on the ceiling.

What was he doing here? How long would he have to hold out in this room of blinding, burnished, specious smiles? Not a single guest was standing alone. All stood in small conversational rings. There were no outcasts.

Every guest had been carefully chosen for his or her ability to fit in. Apparently, to stand alone, as he preferred to do, would be unforgivable.

But then his observant eye picked out several tense faces hidden behind the grins of forced glee. The Hardings had indulged in a certain malevolent sadism. They'd invited the most hated critics of several artists in the room—then mercilessly abandoned them to one another.

David became aware of a warm presence nearby.

He turned at the touch of fingertips on his elbow. A sweetly scented woman had materialized at his side. Their eyes locked. He had never seen eyes like hers: a deep sapphire blue, set under long, black lashes and slender plucked eyebrows. Captivating eyes, mesmerizing. But for all their wide-open charm, they held an unmistakable shrewdness. Despite their apparent warmth, they chilled him: a knowledgeable woman, but predatory. Her platinum-blond hair was done in finger waves that framed her face. It was a lovely face, like a doll's, but faint rings under her eyes and a certain hollowness to her cheeks hinted at an excessively indulgent life. Despite this, her hair still glistened and her ivory skin had a soft luster. Her lips, painted a deep burgundy, were the only points of intense color on her face, and they were moist and provocative. Her shimmering gown could have been liquefied gold, the way it flowed over her curves. She was, without doubt, one of the most alluring women in the room, but she left him cold. She smiled, flashing two rows of tiny polished teeth.

"I'm Nella. You must be David."

Her voice was husky. She was standing quite close to him. Her scent, a heady mixture of Chanel, gin, and cigarettes, enveloped him. He fell back a step. She extended her hand. Automatically, he took it. And she drew him to her. Her hand was small and soft.

Like a leopard's paw.

He had the acute sense that it was she who held him and not the other way around.

"Touched that you could make it," she purred. "I was very sorry to hear about Lilian. She was a lovely girl. I miss her."

"You knew her well?"

"Not really."

"But—"

"We'll discuss it later."

He examined her with astute eyes. She was the kind of person who amused herself by collecting people, throwing them into an arena, and watching them rip one another to shreds. Well, he had a reason for being at her house and it was not to perform like a slave in her personal Colosseum. She *would* speak to him. It might take time, but she would. Meanwhile, he would try to be as superficially sociable as the rest of her guests.

She lit herself a cigarette, grabbed herself a fresh glass of gin from a passing waiter, made sure David had a drink too, then settled them both on a corner sofa. She observed him over the rim of her crystal glass under suggestively half-closed eyes.

"I heard that you're marvelously attractive but utterly unapproachable. Does the description fit?"

"Admirably."

Her eyes twinkled. "You're a very serious man, aren't you? Don't you ever laugh?"

"When I have reason to."

"Yes, of course." She crossed her legs and became suitably serious. "You've been gone a long time, haven't you?"

"I wasn't here while Lilian was ill, no."

"And now you'd like to talk to people who knew her."

He nodded.

"Well, I can't help you," she said. "I didn't know her that well—certainly not well enough to explain why she did what she did." She paused. "I could tell you about Gem. Would that help?"

Why, he wondered, *was she claiming to know Gem, but not Lilian?* His answer was cautious. "Perhaps."

She studied him, curiosity beaming out of one eye, calculation out of the other. "But why should I tell you anything? What do I get out of it?"

"What do you want? Money?"

She threw her head back and laughed. "Nothing so simple."

Her jewel-like eyes glided over him. My, my, she was a live one. On a side table, he noticed a copy of *The Beautiful and the Damned,* F. Scott Fitzgerald's mood piece depicting the dissipated lives of a wealthy couple.

"You haven't introduced me to your husband," he said.

"He's out of town this week." She leaned closer to him. "Convenient, don't you think?"

"I suppose it depends . . . on what you have in mind."

Her bright eyes grew even brighter. "You just must come and see me. One day next week. I'll be at the Fifth Avenue address." She told him exactly where. "Come, darling. I'll give you everything you want. And more."

Yes, he was sure she would.

"That's a lovely offer, but I can't accept it. I'll be leaving town."

She pouted. "Must you?"

"Absolutely."

"How tiresome."

"So, we have to talk. Now." He put his glass down on the table nearby. "I wanted to ask you—"

Nella raised a hand and pointed. Her gaze had fixed on a point across the room. "There's someone I'd like you to meet."

He followed Nella's pointing finger and saw a large man cutting through the crowd toward them. Actually, it wasn't so much that he was cutting through the crowd as that it was parting before him.

People are moving to get out of his way, thought David.

The newcomer's robust figure was sleekly packaged in an expensive suit. His left hand was shoved into one pocket; his right held a short, fat cigar. He bore no resemblance to his newspaper photographs. The grainy newsprint had always conveyed the sense of a crude ruffian, but in life Adrian Snyder presented the image of the polished, successful businessman. He was in his early fifties. There was nothing to hint at ruthlessness, nothing to show that here was a man whose rivals tended to end up in the East River.

Nella cheerfully waved him over.

No one knew for certain how Adrian Snyder had made his fortune, neither the numbers runners under him nor the Feds who kept a covert eye and watched him. But no one seemed to doubt that Snyder was a major player in organized gambling. All agreed that he had impressive financial resources. His holdings included some of Harlem's best apartment buildings, a Long Island estate, and several thousand acres of prime New Jersey farmland. He was an influential and generous patron of small businesses and community efforts. His thriving operation at the Forest Club financed the Agamemnon awards given out by the *Black Arrow.* But, as David knew, not even Snyder's wealth could bridge the cleft of prejudice that divided American blacks from their West Indian counterparts. The intimate cliques of genteel Harlem excluded him. They coolly accepted his money but rejected his person. In turn, he viewed upper-crust Harlem with contempt. West Indian society had its own circle. Among his own, he was highly esteemed.

David and Nella stood. She made the introductions. Adrian smiled amiably at David and warmly extended his hand.

"Nella said she'd invited you. I'm glad to see that you've come."

David accepted the handshake, but he was taken aback at the man's en-

gaging familiarity. To the best of his knowledge he had never met him before. Snyder must've read David's expression.

"I knew your sister, Gem."

David understood. "So you're the one." He withdrew his hand.

"I see you've heard."

"Of course I have."

Nella stepped in with a mild pleasantry and the three of them chatted
awkwardly for several minutes.

"Oh, there are the Lunts!" she cried suddenly. "I've just got to go and
greet them." She laid a light hand on David's forearm. "You'll be all right,
won't you?" She glanced at Snyder and gave him a gay smile. "You'll take
care of him for me? No games with cement shoes now."

With that bad joke, she gave a mischievous giggle and scooted off. David
watched her go. Had she invited him there to meet Snyder? He turned back
to the gangster. Snyder's expression had changed. His demeanor of affability
was gone. His face was hard and drawn.

"We have to talk," said Snyder. "Come see me."

"I don't have time. I'm leaving tomorrow."

"Whatever you got to do, it can wait."

"I'm afraid it can't."

There was a pause.

"I'm not used to hearing the word 'no,'" said Snyder.

"Then perhaps it's time you learned."

"Do you know who I am? I mean *really* know?"

"You're a crook. A rich crook. And you don't mind spilling blood to get
your way."

"But that doesn't bother you, huh? You're not scared?"

"What bothers me is what happened between you and my sister."

"Humph. Funny you should say that, 'cause it's been bothering me too."

"It's a bit late to apologize, isn't it?"

The corners of Snyder's mouth curved in a brief, humorless smile.
"You've got a smart mouth. I hope you've got the brains to go with it." He
studied David, then said. "Come see me. I'm paying you the compliment
of inviting you, not ordering you." He paused and an unexpected gentle-
ness entered his eyes. "I'll even say please. For both our sakes, please change
your mind."

Before David could utter another word and assure him that he would not,
under any circumstances, change his mind, Snyder had turned and gone.
David watched him, thinking that Snyder moved swiftly for such a large man.

Selena Ashburn's brassy voice boomed across the room, commanding just about everyone's attention. "Who's serving? I need a drink, damn it, and some music. Roland, where *are* you?"

The tall, loose-jointed man with an easy grin broke away from a group in one corner. "Yo, Selena," he said. "Take it easy."

"Easy, my ass. I want some music, honey. Gimme the good stuff."

Roland Pierce chuckled. "Calm down, Mama. You's givin' me a fright. You know that Papa's here and he gonna do you right."

He ambled over to the piano and sat down. After first tickling a few treble keys experimentally, he slid into a medley of silken jazz. Conversational clusters broke up as people arranged themselves around the piano. Nella reappeared. She clutched David's arm possessively and sighed happily.

"Negro music is marvelous, simply marvelous! I adore spirituals and jazz and the way you people sing the blues. Two years ago, Nikki and I attended our first Negro Orphan League Ball. That was it. Since then, you people have taken up all my time. I hardly see any white people anymore. But I don't mind. I do so love to help whenever, however, I can."

David gave her a look. Nella had made a name for herself by writing columns in the white press about Negro music and the people behind it. Gospel, spirituals, jazz, the blues: She praised them all rhapsodically in review after review. She astutely mixed gossip, fact, and innuendo in a colorful and potent brew. Few readers could distinguish one element from another. Nella's articles had helped the careers of a few colored artists, but more than anyone else's, they had helped her own. David simply shook his head at her and remained tactfully silent.

Roland's performance started off an evening of apparently spontaneous entertainment. Someone cleared a space and Luella Hughes performed a solo from the latest work by the Black Orpheus Ballet Group. Her sleek and sinuous movements cast a hush over the gathering. Julian Woodstock inserted a melancholy note with a reading from his *Heaven's Trumpet*. And Sylvia Burroughs brought everyone to tears with a spiritual. Then the butler passed around a new round of drinks and Nella told Roland to pick up the pace while she turned down the lights. Roland's nimble fingers danced over the keys in a jaunty ragtime and the guests drifted back into conversation, well-lubricated by Nella's superior gin.

By then, David was also beginning to get a pleasant buzz. Nella had stepped briefly from his side. He let his gaze wander over the gathering. It happened to land on a cluster of faces nearby and his attention snapped into focus. Two men and one woman were engaged in a hefty discussion. Actually, only one man was doing most of the talking. He was tall and lean, of aristocratic bearing, with a handsome light brown face. He appeared to be in his late fifties. His head was balding, his forehead broad, his silver-flecked mustache and goatee meticulously groomed. His dark eyes revealed an incisive intelligence; his jaw suggested determination. Everything about his demeanor bespoke discipline and precision, concern and compassion; it also indicated intolerance, impatience, and absolute conviction in his own beliefs. David recognized him instantly: Byron Canfield was the author of the seminal work *The Color Line,* a collection of essays on the plight of black Americans. More to the point, he was a magisterial officer of the Movement.

David's thoughts raced. How could he have missed seeing Canfield before? The man must've arrived during the performances.

I've got to get of here. But no—that won't do. I haven't gotten Nella to talk. I'll simply have to stay clear of Canfield. Make use of the fact that although I know him, he doesn't know me.

He could at least move to the other side of the room.

He was about to do so when one of Canfield's comments caught his attention.

"What Nella thinks is good and what I, as a colored man, think is good, have nothing to do with one another."

"Don't dismiss the book so quickly," said the other man. "She's made white people aware of educated Negroes."

"Humph! She's made caricatures of us—rarefied versions of the 'noble savage.'"

"Give the woman her due. Her book deals with passing, segregation, the differences between DuBois and Booker T. In some ways, the book is deep."

"The book is trash. And she's a leech, a culture-sucking parasite."

"She talks about the shit we're doing to ourselves. Like how we light-skinned colored scorn white separatists, then turn around and cut against our own people. People are upset 'cause Nella hit dirt. She exposed family secrets."

"Well, it ain't her family. It's none of her business. And the more attention we give that damn book, the more people will buy it. Those fools demonstrating outside the publisher's office today—they did nothing but drive up sales. Idiots."

Remarkable, thought David. *If Canfield thinks so little of Nella and her work, then what's he doing here? It's like giving her the Movement's seal of approval.*

He felt Nella return to his side and turned to her. "By any chance, are you celebrating *Ebony Eden* tonight?"

She smiled. "You haven't read it?"

"I *have*—"

"But you don't like it?"

"There are . . . points with which I have difficulty."

She appeared to be tickled by his tact. His eyes flickered over to the little group that had been criticizing her book. She caught his glance and laughed. It was a practiced, pleasant, musical sound.

"Them. I don't mind them. The fact is, you people don't trust anything we whites write about you."

"The fact is, *we people* have good reason not to."

"Is that so?" She regarded him with faint disappointment, as though she had expected better judgment from him. "But if I don't write about Harlem, someone else will. And with a good deal less sensitivity."

"Are you so sure?"

She looked stunned. How could he question her commitment, her understanding of the issues at hand?

"Harlem is a field waiting to be harvested," she said. "It's ripe with fresh, untouched material. No one has written the ultimate gambling or rackets story. No one has unveiled the seductive secrets of cabaret life. Who has even bothered to inquire into how such a melting pot of diverse African tribes can coexist? No one. Nobody has taken a bite out of all the luscious and wild fruit that's for the taking in Harlem."

It was a nice little speech. How often had she delivered it? Quite often, if one could judge by how fluidly the words with their rather mercenary logic flowed over her tongue. He was impressed by her enthusiasm, but appalled at her insensitivity.

"Has it occurred to you that what you find exotic and captivating we might consider embarrassing, offensive?"

Like a spoiled child, she stamped her foot. "I don't care."

"Exactly. You don't. We do."

She put a hand on her hip and wagged a finger under his nose. "Instead of complaining, you Negro intellectuals had better hop to it. Harvest your own fields or ambitious whites will get to it before you do. They'll gather quickly, steal away silently, and sell your life stories right out from under you."

"Just as you did."

She opened her mouth, but nothing came out. Slowly, she closed it. A new respect for him came into her eyes. He'd got to her. She smiled, her indignation fading.

"Yes . . . just as I did."

He couldn't help but smile, too. She was amusing, in a way.

"I like you," she said. "You're honest. You have the nerve to tell me to my face what you think . . . unlike others." She looked over at the little group. Her expression became roguish. "Come, I'll introduce you."

Nella slipped her arm inside his, as if they had known each other for years, and David found himself propelled toward a meeting with Byron Canfield. He tried to ignore the sinking feeling in his stomach and worked to keep his expression bland.

"People," Nella called out lightly. "This is David McKay."

Three heads bobbed with sympathetic nods and stretched with empathetic smiles. The woman, a short, plump lady with neat gray hair, clutched David's hand, murmured words of condolence, then excused herself, muttering something about the lateness of the hour. Canfield shook David's hand firmly.

"My sympathies regarding your sister. I didn't know her personally, but I heard of her. From her husband. A marvelous trial attorney."

David didn't know whether to feel reassurance or panic. On the one hand, if Canfield knew Sweet, then that spoke for Sweet's legitimacy. On the other—

Before David could stop her, Nella had touched his shoulder and was saying with an odd sense of personal pride: "David here's a lawyer, too."

Canfield's inquisitive eyes flickered over him. "Really?" Something registered in Canfield's eyes, something that made David uneasy. Did Canfield know him—know *of* him? David wondered. He tensed for trouble, but none came. The conversation flowed on and David was relieved to see that he would not be the center of attention.

Having wondered how Nella had lured Canfield to her party, he now caught a hint of an explanation. Apparently, Canfield had written a negative review of *Ebony Eden*. The review had been given wide coverage and somewhat dulled the glimmer of Nella's success. She'd invited Canfield to her party to discuss the matter. Or so it seemed. David wondered whether Nella's indignation was simply a subterfuge. He remembered her words— that she didn't care what black people thought about her work—and he believed them. If that was true, then her sole purpose for inviting Canfield was to dupe people into believing that Canfield didn't think so badly of her book after all.

David had another thought and it made him queasy. Had she invited him to her party to bring him together with Canfield? Did she already know of his life in Philadelphia? Or was he being paranoid? Every now and then, he caught Canfield looking at him. When David met his gaze, Canfield would smile. But the smile never reached his eyes. They remained thoughtful.

If David hadn't been so preoccupied, he would've found it amusing to listen to Nella and Canfield dicker. It was clear that Canfield, despite his opinion about Nella and her book, felt complimented by her attentions. Naturally, however, he refused to change a word of what he had written. He did magnanimously offer to edit any of her future manuscripts for "verity of content and character." But Nella's smile froze on her face at the very thought of it. David, despite his unease, chuckled inwardly. It served her right.

For a moment, Nella's attention went to another of her guests in their little circle, and Canfield turned to David. "We're neighbors, you know."

"On Strivers' Row?"

"Moved there two years ago. Why don't you stop by tomorrow?"

"I'm sorry. I have a train to catch."

"You're leaving? Too bad." Canfield rubbed his chin. "Actually, I'm sure I've heard your name before. And it wasn't from Sweet." He paused, looking at David, his eyes speculative. There was something . . . something worth remembering, and he was on the verge of grasping it. David was about to make a distracting comment, when one of Canfield's eyebrows shot up. "Yes . . . of course. It was when you joined the Movement—some years ago. That's how I know your name. Everyone in the New York office was looking forward to working with you." Canfield's eyes narrowed. "Then you were sent out on a case and . . . and—why, you're the one who *disappeared*."

Canfield's voice carried, not across the room, but far enough to let others standing close know that something was wrong. Nearby conversation died. Nella's eyes, like those of her guests, went from Canfield to David and back again. David's heart skipped a beat. For a moment, words failed him.

"Where in the world have you been?" Canfield demanded.

The question, so directly put, was brutal. David had been dreading it for years. Now here it was, presented to him not in private, the least he could have hoped for, but before influential listeners—"inquisitors" was the word his mind supplied. He felt more than a little ill. Nella took a step away and to the side. He could see her out of the corner of his eye. A little smile played about her lips. Was this an ambush, after all? Did she know? But how could she? There was only one way to handle the situation. He adopted a pleasant, urbane expression and allowed a trace of amiable condescension to creep into his tone.

"I've been busy handling matters elsewhere."

"So, you didn't disappear?"

"Of course not."

"But no one in New York heard anything about your reassignment. I certainly would've heard something." Canfield paused. "Where did you say you've been working?"

"I didn't."

Canfield looked as though he'd been struck. He arched a heavy eyebrow and gazed at David with increasing displeasure. David met Canfield's gaze head-on.

"The Movement is large, complex," David said. "One hand doesn't always know what the other is doing. My responsibilities require me to move around a lot. You know how it is."

Canfield looked David up and down. He stroked his mustache. "No, in this case, I don't. Normally, we keep close tabs on our workers, for their own safety. And I usually know if—"

"Byron, don't be such a bore." Nella stepped to David's side and wrapped a proprietary arm around him. "I was just being polite, introducing you. But I've barely had a chance to speak to him myself. I certainly didn't bring him over here for you to grill him." She stroked David's collar. "Leave that up to me."

There was some uneasy laughter.

Canfield cracked a thin smile. "Yes . . . perhaps you're right. I think it's time for me to go." He offered David his hand. "It's been . . . shall we say . . . very interesting to meet you."

"Likewise," said David, shaking Canfield's hand.

Turning back to Nella, Canfield thanked her for her hospitality.

"You're not bailing out on me?" she said.

"I must. I have to go to the office tomorrow."

"Work even on a Sunday?"

Canfield glanced at David. "Calls to make. Questions to ask."

Nella shrugged, pointedly dismissing him. She turned away from the group, pulling David with her. "My, my, dear boy. You got the old goat going. Just what have you been up to?"

"Nothing interesting."

"But Canfield—"

"—is a bit overcurious."

"Well, so am I." Nella's eyes moved over him intensely, as though if she tried hard enough, she could see right through him. "You've got a story, dear boy, and I want to know it."

"You're mistaken."

She eyed him shrewdly. "Smart of you to leave tomorrow."

"Why?"

"Because if you stayed, Canfield would unearth every detail he could about you. And so would I."

His heart thumped heavily, but his smile stayed easy. "It would be a waste of your time."

7

Getting to Know the New Relation

Davidd rose early Sunday morning to the rhythmic drumming of raindrops against his bedroom window. He had slept like a man buried alive, kicking and clawing at the sheets. Now, rubbing his eyes, he threw aside the bedcovers and swung his legs out of bed. Staggering to the window, he drew apart the curtains. Dark bands of sooty clouds roamed the sky, trailing ragged tendrils as dirty as trampled cotton. Turning away from the window, he went to his washstand and poured cold water from a porcelain pitcher into a basin. He splashed his face once, twice, three times, the chilly drops splattering his bare chest and shoulders. Grabbing a towel, he dried himself, rubbing his skin with rough strokes. He happened to look up and caught sight of his reflection in the bureau mirror. The puckered skin of an angry scar slashed across his left shoulder. He stared at it and a mental trapdoor opened. For one horrid moment, he was falling, falling into a deep, dark place.

Jonah . . . Jonah, in the belly of the whale.

There had been only one time in his life when he'd been called upon to display not only physical but also moral and spiritual courage. And he had failed. Miserably. He had never forgiven himself. And he lived in constant fear that his failing would be discovered. Worse, he dreaded the possibility that he would be put to the test once more and his weakness revealed, but this time before an audience, in such a way as to ruin him. He touched the scar.

The war over there was nothing—nothing compared to the one over here . . .

He shuddered, wrenched his eyes away, and tossed his towel over a chair. Dressing quickly, he left his room. Annie stood at the foot of the stairs.

"Mr. Jameson's back," she said. "He's expecting you."

"I'm glad Annie found your address," said Sweet, his voice a rolling low timbre.

"I wish I could've been here sooner."

"We would've contacted you, but we didn't know how. Lilian said nothing."

She told me nothing about you either, David wanted to say. Had she ever planned on telling him? Or had she simply trusted that he would always stay away?

After breakfast, he'd told Annie that he was ready to meet "the mystery man." She started off down the hallway. He realized with growing consternation that she was heading for his father's office. She put one hand on the doorknob, turned to him, and raised the other. "Wait." Then she knocked lightly and went in. Fifteen seconds later, she reappeared. Seeing his expression, her forehead creased.

"Yes, he's in your father's office. I know it's a shock, but please try to get along with him. For now, you've got to try."

David smiled to be polite, but said nothing. Trying to get along with Jameson Sweet was neither his concern nor his intention.

The room he'd entered had a high ceiling but was dusky, deep, and narrow. Weighty tomes of encyclopedic volumes lined the walls on either side, as somber as soldiers guarding a path and pointing the way forward. Thick pile carpet covered the floor, absorbing the sound of every footfall. The air was bitter, stale, and still, tainted by the flat smell of old tobacco. He thought of his father and a sense of unspeakable regret rose within him. He had to force himself to put one foot in front of the other.

The room culminated in a rich mahogany desk set before a tall slender window. Thick drapes were drawn to block any outside light. A banker's lamp cast a soft amber glow over part of the desk. The weak light shied away from the man that sat behind it. Shadow obscured his face. For a moment, the room was filled with an unearthly quiet. Then Jameson Sweet leaned forward into the light, as stealthy as an animal emerging from its lair, and the two men took each other's measure.

Sweet's complexion was smooth, almost unnaturally even—*like a mask,* thought David—and the color of mahogany—*a tough, resilient wood.* Sweet's close-cropped hair was an inky black and meticulously cut. A refined sliver of a mustache graced his upper lip, as dignified and precise as the stroke of a master's paintbrush.

Like Gem, David was struck by Sweet's uneasy resemblance to Augustus. Physically, Sweet was as dark as Augustus was light. *But looks are irrelevant,* thought David. He could smell the rank odor of frustrated ambition. It had a bitter bite he'd learned to recognize among those who roam the halls of justice.

Sweet rose to his feet with grave dignity and came from around the desk. From his lush cashmere sweater to his tailored woolen pants, he was immaculately attired in black. He shook David's hand firmly and willingly. There was no apparent enmity in him. But his lizard-like eyes were cold. David sensed a hypnotist's gift for persuasion and an actor's skill at pretense. Here was a man who would not be lightly deceived or led into revealing more than he chose.

Sweet offered David a drink, which David declined. They then moved to the parlor, which held a sofa and a couple of armchairs, one of which was a deep royal blue. With its high, wing back, this particular chair was quite regal. When Augustus first had it brought in, the family gathered around and laughingly nicknamed it "Daddy's throne." Augustus had spent many hours in the spacious chair, staring into the flames of the fireplace, planning his investments. Lila had sat opposite him, reading, casting a thin shadow. Sweet now sped to sit on Augustus's "throne." David merely shook his head and took a seat on the couch opposite.

Annie had lit a fire in the fireplace and brought them coffee. Flickering flames threw devilish reflections on their faces. Sweet lit his pipe. He smoked contemplatively, his eyes on the flames, and David watched him.

"When did she fall ill?"

"Around February of last year."

"What kind of doctors did you take her to?"

"Every kind that I could think of."

"Psychiatrists?"

"She saw Dr. Hawthorne once a week for six months, then refused to go anymore."

"You couldn't change her mind?"

"She wanted drugs, not therapy. Drugs to make her sleep. Drugs to wake her up. At first, they helped, but soon the effect wore off. She started drinking. She thought she could hide it, but I know what drinking looks like. And smells like. She lost weight, went down to nothing. Her face got puffy. She was tired and sleepy, kept falling down. Kept seeing things, hearing voices."

David listened not only to what Sweet said, but how he said it. Sweet's voice was melodious, full of cadence and echo. It was the modulated voice of a natural orator, an invaluable commodity for a courtroom contender. Sweet had presence. His charm was calculated and purposeful. He had passion, the dark and dangerous kind. He was indeed the type of man to fall deeply in love, but would he have fallen in love with a shy, reserved woman like Lilian?

"She seemed to get better for a little while after Gem left—Gem's being here must've been too much for her—but the improvement didn't last. And then she was worse than ever. Hawthorne suggested that I put her away, but she begged me not to. I told the doctor to get us a nurse. I asked Rachel Hamilton to step in temporarily. We'd just arranged for someone permanent to take over when it happened. Annie found her. I was in Newark that weekend. When I got home that Monday, the police were here."

"Did she leave a note?"

Sweet rested his pipe on a large crystal ashtray. He took a wallet from his back pocket, and removed a folded square of white paper from it. This, he handed to David. The note was typed:

```
Tears and nightmares never persuade family and
friends of the depths of your despair. But death,
at a stroke, ends all doubt.
```

"They're the words of the French-Algerian philosopher Pierre Lorraine," said David. "But Lilian never liked Lorraine." He handed the slip of paper back to Sweet. "That weekend, why did you leave her here alone?"

"I didn't—Annie was here."

"But no nurse—not Rachel."

Sweet looked at David. "No."

"Why not?"

A pause. "This is beginning to sound like a cross-examination."

"I just want to know why she was left alone. A simple enough question."

"There was . . ." Sweet shifted in his chair. "Well, a mix-up. A very unfortunate mix-up. I left Lilian with Annie on Thursday. The nurse was supposed to come that Friday—but she didn't. Annie had planned to go visit family. She started to cancel when the nurse didn't show. But then Lilian told her to go ahead. Lilian said she'd be going to visit friends. She'd be gone all weekend, so it would be okay for Annie to leave. I'm sure Annie wouldn't have left the house otherwise. You can't blame the old woman. She's—"

"It wasn't Annie I was thinking about."

Sweet's dark eyes glittered. "You know, you have a helluva lotta nerve."

"You married my sister after knowing her for exactly one month."

"It was love at first sight."

"Love for her . . . or for this house and what her name might bring you?"

"I won't even dignify that with an answer."

"I didn't think you would."

"Look, I loved your sister. And yes, I love this house. I love it because we were happy here together."

"And now that she's gone, you intend to stay."

"I have a *right* to stay."

"Your 'right' came into question the day she died."

Sweet gave David a cool appraisal. Then he chuckled. "So that's what this is all about. You don't care about what happened to Lilian. You're the one who's only interested in the house. You stayed away all these years, waiting for your chance. Now she's gone and you want to take over."

"It *is* my family house."

"It was."

"It still is." David rose to his feet. "If you loved her, and I'd like to believe you did, then nothing can replace your loss. And it would be a double blow to lose the home you shared with her. But you must understand, she would've never wanted this house, our father's house, to pass out of the family."

"Like it or not, I *am* family. And legally, I own fifty percent of this place. But possession is nine-tenths of the law. Now I'm perfectly willing to purchase your half—"

"I'll never sell my share."

"And I'll neither sell nor give up mine."

"I advise you to reconsider."

"Are you threatening me?"

"I'm giving you good advice. I don't want a battle. I'm willing to give you the benefit of the doubt. I heard that you took good care of Lilian when she was ill and if that's true, then I'm grateful. But if it isn't, then trust me, I'll find out and you'll have hell to pay. So I suggest you leave. Now. Go while the going is good."

Sweet studied David. Then he leaned back in Augustus's armchair and situated himself comfortably.

"Get used to me, brother-in-law, get used to me. I'm here and I'm here to stay."

When David left the parlor, he intended to go back to his own room. Once upstairs, however, he found himself continuing down the hall to Lilian's room. Standing at the foot of her bed, he let his gaze pass over the dresser top again. He eyed the perfectly replaced wallpaper, the refurbished bed, and the well-scrubbed floor. His face was drawn, his eyes thoughtful. He needed to leave town, but having met Sweet he knew in his bones that there was more to Lilian's death than met the eye. Surely this room could tell him something.

He heard a cough behind him and spun around. It was Annie. He saw the worry, the fear and uncertainty in her eyes, and understood. He had said he would leave when he had spoken to Sweet. Now that he had, she wondered whether he was about to go. But like every natural diplomat, she knew better than to introduce the subject of her main concern.

"Mr. David, you shouldn't stay in this room by yourself," was all she said.

He gave a brief, gentle smile to reassure her. "I'm fine. I've been thinking about what you said, about how things aren't always the way they seem."

"And?" She came up to him.

"And I find it strange, very strange . . . that she chose to cut herself there, in the bed." He felt Annie's questioning gaze. "When people slash their wrists, they often do it in a bathtub filled with warm water. It contains the blood . . . and makes the dying faster."

He leaned against one of the bedposts. The surface felt cool and smooth.

"Even the bedpost was covered in blood," said Annie. "Bloody hand-prints, as though she'd grabbed it t'help her stand."

He looked at her. "Why would she struggle to get up after lying down to die?"

"I don't know. But she sure 'nough got up. There was a line of blood runnin' from here t'there." Annie pointed to a place about five footsteps away. "And on up t'the windowsill." She swung her arm in a low arc and pointed to the base of the window. "That's where I found her."

He studied the area. A ghostly ache swelled in his chest. Turning around, he let his gaze travel over the newly papered walls above the bed, over the new canopy, and then back over the trail that Annie had indicated on the floor.

"Tell me about the blood."

"The what?"

"The blood. Was it in spots? Close together?"

"It was everywhere. Like I said: Dried hard. Dried black."

"And what about on the floor? Was the blood in large splatters or—"

"Mr. David, what you wanna ask me somethin' like that for?"

"Bear with me. It's important."

She set her shoulders and still looked unhappy, but complied. "Well, the blood on the floor . . . It wasn't in spots. It was more spread out, smeared-like, in a wide line, like somethin' had been dragged—"

He nodded. It was the answer he'd expected. "And you say, it appeared that she'd been here alone?"

"Weren't no hint of nobody but her."

"No sign of a break-in?"

"None at all." Her forehead creased. "Why you ask, Mr. David?"

"Blood everywhere, you said. Usually, that means a struggle."

"You mean, like a robber?"

It wasn't at all what he meant, but he said nothing.

"A struggle . . ." She reflected. "But nothin' was missin. Nothin' 'ceptin' that vase."

"Which vase?"

"The one that used t'sit in the window." She pointed. "You r'member?"

"That little Japanese one? It was gone?"

"Smashed t'smithereens on the sidewalk. And there was blood on the windowsill."

He went to the window. Faint pink smears still showed on the sill. Or did he imagine them? Drawing his fingertips over the new coat of paint, he was thoughtful. He drew the curtains apart and peered out. It was a crisp, clear Sunday morning, and Strivers' Row was impressively still. The best of Harlem was undoubtedly gathered together in their finest finery a little ways over and down the road at Saint Philip's to worship. The street was empty, as it would've been that night.

That night. Who would've been out on the street that night?

David perched on the edge of the windowsill and stared out. He pictured the little vase, remembering its delicacy and beauty. He thought of the love and effort that must have gone into fashioning it. He recalled how his mother had treasured it, admired it, striven to protect it from the clumsy, the curious, the covetous. She had kept it sheltered here, within the heart of the house, where only the most trusted were allowed. How and why had the vase been ripped from its place?

He could imagine it in freefall. In his mind, he watched it tumble over and over, spin out of control, then crash against the concrete pavement. He saw its fragile beauty shatter. And he saw Lilian. Also fragile. Now also shattered. A chill, as sharp as a scalpel, pierced his core. He shivered. The vague notions that had been germinating in his mind for the past days became clear.

Conservative and cautious, the Lilian he knew wouldn't have married someone she barely knew. Sensible, sane, and solid, she wouldn't have slashed her wrists. Stoic, proud, and deeply religious, she would never have shamed her family name.

Not the Lilian he knew.

Annie had come up alongside him. She was staring out the window herself now. He turned to look at her.

"Do you believe my sister killed herself?"

Annie's gaze was fixed on the hard pavement three stories below. "As God as my witness, after I seen the way that sickness changed her, I b'lieve . . . I b'lieve she coulda."

"But you don't believe she did."

"No . . . I don't." With a sigh, she looked at him. "I could never help wonderin' why she dragged herself, used her last bit of strength, t'get t'this window."

"But you know the answer as well as I do."

Her eyes met his.

"She came to this window," he said, "to get help."

From her expression, he knew they'd reached the same conclusion.

To get help. Like pebbles piercing the surface of a still, deep pond, those three small words would cause ripples if applied to Lilian's death. They implied, in effect, that she had either regretted her decision to die or that the decision itself had been someone else's to begin with.

"So, you're gonna stay?"

"Yes," he said and his voice was tired. "I'm going to stay."

She exhaled with relief. "I'm glad, Mr. David, so glad. Things is gonna get better with you here. I know they'll be just fine."

Her sweet words brought a bitter taste to his mouth.

You don't know me, he wanted to say. *You don't know what I've been doing. If you did, you'd turn your back on me. You'd help me pack my bags yourself.*

8

Rachel and the McKays

A few blocks away, Rachel was thinking about how small her apartment was and how much she would've loved to move. Her thoughts skipped nimbly to the McKay house, as they often did at such times, and in her mind's eye she could see their beautiful parlor—

Big enough to hold a wedding in.

And the spacious upstairs bedrooms—

Why go away on a honeymoon?

The house was wonderful, of course, nearly perfect, but as every woman knows, there's always room for improvement.

First things first. If it were up to me, I'd change them old paintings in Lilian's room, throw out the—

She happened to glance out her bedroom window and her daydreams about redecorating were for the moment forgotten. A young girl, about seven or eight, was jumping rope across the street. The child's feet kept getting entangled in the rope, but she refused to give up. She would patiently unwrap the rope from around her ankles and start jumping again. She did this repeatedly and Rachel watched, fascinated. If there was one thing she admired, it was determination.

She's just like me. One day she's going to be Somebody.

Rachel leaned on the windowsill. A sad smile played about her lips.

Isabelle would've still been too young to skip and jump like that. But in a few years, she would've been able to . . . she would've been, if she'd lived.

She blinked and wiped the sudden tears away, staring through blurry eyes at the child across the street.

Go on, girl, she whispered. *Go on. Don't never give up.*

Rachel knew the meaning of perseverance. She recalled the days when she'd travel from the Tenderloin to visit the McKays after school. How she'd struggled to imitate the family's effortless grace. How she'd striven to emulate its sedate gentility. All to no avail. She had learned the hard way just how complex and uncompromising the African American elite could be in its membership requirements. If you could not certify pedigree and demonstrate connections, your presence was condoned but you were given to understand in subtle and polite ways that you would not be—*could not be*—considered a member.

Her clothes, for example, had always made her stick out like a sore thumb. Lilian had offered to share her clothes with her, but Rachel was too proud to take them. And so she'd worn the same clothes to school, day in and day out, for nearly two years: a pale blue shirt, in some places held together with pins; a long gray skirt; thick black stockings that were pulled down and tucked under at the toe; and black brogues that had seen much, much better days. Some of the girls at school had tried to taunt her, but Rachel had a fury in her that caused them to step back. She wasn't interested in impressing *them*. It was the McKays she wanted to impress. It was their world she yearned to be part of. And if it hadn't been for her no-good father, she would've been.

When he died, I didn't care. I was just glad me and Mama were free of him.

And when they moved, *finally* moved, uptown, she'd rejoiced, thinking she had it made.

But that was foolish, now, wasn't it?

One afternoon—it was right before Christmas—she'd gone over to the McKays'. It was 1920, the first Christmas after Lila McKay's death, and Rachel was twenty-three. Lilian had told her to come by to pick up some presents. Rachel had gone to the front door, as usual, and rung the bell. Annie opened it promptly.

"Hi!" Rachel fixed a bright smile on her face, although she didn't particularly like Annie. Never had and didn't even know why. "Miss Lila told me to stop by," she said, wondering why Annie just didn't step aside and let her in, as she always had.

"I see, miss. Well, you'll have to go round by the back side."

Rachel looked dumbstruck. She hadn't heard right. She couldn't have. "'Scuse me?"

"I said, you'll have to—"

"I heard what you said. You don't understand. I never use the back way. Why, I'm not a serv—"

"I know, miss." Annie's tone was restrained but firm and it was starting to get on Rachel's nerves. "Most times, there ain't no problem with you comin' in this way. But t'day Mr. Augustus's got comp'ny." Her eyes dwelled on Rachel, as if to repeat: *Comp'ny. It's pretty clear what that means, ain't it?*

Rachel felt herself grow smaller and smaller. And her face grow hotter. She was furious to find tears coming into her eyes. Blinking rapidly, she brushed them away.

"You let me in!" she cried, balling up her puny hands into impotent fists. She saw the pity in Annie's eyes and that made her angrier. "Let me in, I said!"

Annie sighed. "C'mon 'round back, miss. Don't stand out here in the cold no more. Miss Lilian's waitin' for you and I got t'get back t'my pie."

Rachel stared at her a second longer, then dropped her fists, defeated. "You can tell Daddy McKay that he'll rot in hell before I walk through *his* servants' entrance."

Annie smiled, unperturbed. "You want me t'tell him that, miss. D'you *really* want me to?"

Rachel wanted to smack her. She almost did, but some residue of common sense took hold. "Why d'you stick up for him?" she cried. "You know that he's . . . he's . . . that he's evil."

Annie's eyes widened just a tad. It wasn't much of a reaction, but it was something. Rachel pulled her thin coat tighter around her, whirled, and stomped away. At the end of the block, something made her pause and look back. Annie was still standing in the doorway, watching her.

Two days later, Lilian, Gem, and David showed up at Rachel's door, with presents for her and her mother.

"I'm very sorry," Lilian said. "I didn't know Daddy had told Annie to do that."

And what would you have done if you had *known?* thought Rachel. *Probably nothin'.* But she saw the look on Lilian's face and knew her friend's apology was genuine. And so she relented, at least until Gem opened her mouth. Gem took one of the assorted candies they'd brought Rachel's mother, one of the choicest ones in fact, and popped it into her mouth. She was home from college, and it looked like the only subject she was studying out in California was how to wear makeup.

"Look," said Gem, giving her fingertips a quick lick, "you have to understand. Daddy had guests. Some very important people. We just couldn't let you in. Not by the front door. It would've been unseemly. After all, *we* are people of consequence. You're not."

Rachel's anger surged back. Her mother had set a teapot on the table and for one crazy moment, Rachel was sorely tempted to grab it and bash Gem over the head with it. She almost reached for it when she caught David's expression. He'd been silent so far throughout the visit. He was looking at her now with amusement. There was affection and mischief and yes, admiration too. His eyes went to Gem and then back to her and she understood.

Don't take her so seriously. None of us do.

But that was easy for him to say. He was Gem's older brother. He was one of those "people of consequence." Rachel knew at that moment that she disliked Gem because deep in her heart, whether she wanted to admit it or not, she believed that what Gem said was true.

"You're too tied up with them McKays," Rachel's mother told her later. Minnie regarded her only child with sad exasperation. "You should be proud to be a Hamilton. We ain't rich, but we's a fine family, too. We just as good as them McKays. What you wanna be one of them dicties for, anyway? Most of them rich, light-skinned colored folk don't even know what side of the bridge they standin' on. Don't know if they's black or white. 'Least you know who you is, honey. That's important. It's about the most important thing there is. It's one thing you got over any dicty any day."

A *dicty*. Yes, the McKays were dicties. But she was infatuated with them.

Rachel adored her mother, but she'd chosen Mrs. McKay as her role model. Lila McKay had been both dark and beautiful. She'd married a successful light-skinned man. She'd been cultured and gracious. Lila had lived barely eight months after moving into her new Strivers' Row home, but before her death she'd completed its decoration. In a burst of activity, she sought out beautiful pieces from the Americas, Asia, and Europe to create an atmosphere of harmony and comfort. Mixing antique and modern with a sure hand, she'd created a luscious home.

Rachel was back at the McKay house as soon as the Christmas and New Year's holidays were over, as soon as the McKays' circle of parties ended and the rounds of important guests slowed down, as soon as the imperative for her to enter by the servants' gate was lifted. And sometimes, to make up for the disastrous holidays, she was now allowed to sleep over.

Her stays at the McKay house were tantamount to visits to a small but lovely mansion. She loved how the tiered chandelier in the McKays' entryway twinkled overhead; how the polished wooden banisters of the curving stairway gleamed softly; how the smell of fresh cut flowers sweetened the air. She never ceased to wonder at the walls of delicate Japanese prints with their soft pastel colors and the fine ink drawings by French masters. She hesitated to step on the beautiful Aubusson rugs that adorned the parquet floors, but joyfully curled her toes in the deep pile cream-colored carpet that covered the parlor floor. She sank happily into the deep chairs that furnished the library and let her eyes rove eagerly over the endless shelves laden with dark leather-bound books. When not there, she dreamed of the large airy rooms, of the massive soft beds with their long, tapering posts.

She'd lie on her narrow cot at home wondering how it would be to live permanently in such plenty. Her contact with the McKays taught her to love nice possessions at an early age. Over time, her desire would grow into a craving.

"Honey, if you ain't careful, your love of pretty things'll be your downfall," her mother would tell her. "People like us, we can't afford such fine things."

"Yes, Mama," she'd say and keep on dreaming. Most of her earnings now went toward clothes, books, and furnishings. She would've liked to wear frocks and furs from Bendel's and Revillon Frères, but this was patently beyond her. Some looks she could approximate, but others she knew better than to even try. She preferred to do without rather than settle for the embarrassment of a cheap copy.

She turned away from the window and surveyed her neat little bedroom. She thought of Annie and David and Sweet.

All of them sitting in that huge house not so far away—while here I am, stuck in this little cage.

The image flashed through her mind of her living in this "cage," forced to struggle until the last of her youth was gone, until nothing was left of her strength and she was an old crone, dying, forgotten, and bitter.

Oh, how long? she cried. *How long before things go well enough for me to get out of here?*

9

Sweet's Rear Guard

Some five months earlier, on the night of October 10, 1925, a mob armed with pistols and baseball bats had charged the home of a young black Chicago physician. Boston Richards had just bought the house, which was in a white neighborhood. As the mob rushed forward, he opened fire and a white man died. Dr. Richards was caught and charged with first-degree murder. But he was lucky. He wasn't summarily lynched, as he would've been elsewhere. Instead, he was jailed and tried in what became highly publicized proceedings.

Six weeks of heated courtroom drama came to a grinding halt when Richards' lawyer had a stroke and collapsed during an argument with the presiding judge. The Movement took up the matter. The case files, dozens of them, landed on Byron Canfield's desk in January. To contemporary eyes, Richards' innocence might seem obvious. But in 1925, no black was ever justified in raising a hand, much less a weapon, against a white. Canfield knew that to beat the odds and win an acquittal he'd need the assistance of the best legal mind the Movement could offer. If he'd stayed in New York four years earlier, David McKay would've come to mind. Now it was Jameson Sweet.

Months of working on the case had brought Canfield and Sweet a bond that surpassed mutual respect. Long hours of sweating over law books and plotting strategy can teach a man a lot about how his colleague thinks. Canfield decided that Sweet was one of the best legal gamesmen he'd ever known.

He could've been my son, he thought.

He and Emma had never had children. When young, she hadn't wanted to have any. An image of their barren marriage bed flashed across his mind. He sighed. He'd once loved her. God, how he'd loved her! But that was then. What it meant to love was a faint memory. It was no more relevant to his current state of mind than a faded rose pressed between the pages of a forgotten diary.

He removed his coat from the vestibule closet and took his hat down from the shelf. She came out of the living room just then and paused with one foot on the stair.

"You're going out?" she asked.

Her voice held a trace of disappointment and that surprised him.

Perhaps there is something left.

He shrugged into his coat, buttoning it up and adjusting the collar. He looked at her round familiar face and for a moment felt regret.

"Just down the street. I have to see Sweet." He yanked down a cuff.

"Right now?"

"Right now. He's in trouble."

She said nothing more and he turned away from the look on her face. It was a vague, haunted expression that arose whenever he mentioned Sweet's name. A mixture of resentment, jealousy, and longing—as though she'd been reminded of the children she'd refused to have.

Canfield stepped out of his house and looked up the street. A few doors away, Sweet had just left the McKay house. The two men met midway down the block and after a few moments of discussion decided to walk along Lenox Avenue.

Canfield studied Sweet. The young lawyer had been preoccupied lately. He hadn't been making mistakes, but his work wasn't as exact as it used to be. Of course, with Lilian's illness and now the sudden reappearance of her brother, it was to be expected.

"This is about McKay, isn't it?"

Sweet glanced at him. "You've met him?"

"At Nella Harding's last night."

"He does get around, doesn't he?" Sweet clamped his pipe between his teeth. "So what did you think of him?"

"Something's very wrong there—"

"He's a troublemaker. He stayed away while Lilian was alive, didn't show his face while she was ill; now he comes and wants to play the hero."

"In what way?"

"Well, he just about accused me of killing her."

"He didn't! He wouldn't have!"

"Oh, but he did. He didn't come right out and say it, mind you. He didn't have to."

Canfield shook his head. "His own guilty conscience, that's what's behind it."

"Definitely. Didn't do anything for his sister before, so he's angry at the person who did. But if that's all there was to it, I wouldn't be bothering you."

"Well, what is it then?"

"He wants the house."

Canfield stopped and stared at Sweet, then shook his head. "Actually, I'm not that surprised. Irresponsibility and greed tend to go together." They began walking again. "But there's more than just run-of-the-mill greed at work here. Four years ago, David McKay left on Movement business and disappeared. God only knows what he's been up to. It would be horrible if he's done something that would destroy the credibility and efficiency we've worked so hard to build."

"I know the name of a man down in Philly. He's done some work for the Movement. He's good, *real* good. If there's anything worth knowing, he'll find it. I think we should contact him—for the sake of the Movement, of course."

Canfield glanced at Sweet. Something in Sweet's tone bothered him, gave rise to a slight unease. After a moment's consideration, he dismissed the feeling. "You're right, of course. We should do something."

"So I have your backing?"

Again, Canfield found himself hesitating and wondered why. Was it because he disliked the idea of investigating a fellow lawyer? Or was it because he disliked the idea of investigating a fellow race man even more?

"Well?" said Sweet.

Canfield looked at this young lawyer he so admired, feeling that glimmer of unease, but seeing nothing in Sweet's eyes to justify it. "All right," he said, "Do it."

10

Gem's Indelicate Tales

David was relieved to see that Sweet had left the parlor. He sank into his father's armchair, made a tepee of his fingertips, and stared into the crackling flames.

If what he suspected was true, then Lilian had been murdered. It didn't take a leap of the imagination to land on the most likely suspect. But it would take a great deal of imagination to ferret out the full truth of the matter and find proof, legal proof, of a crime. He didn't have much time. He'd been back in town only two days and already two people were suspicious of him: Nella and Canfield. It could be a matter of days before they found him out. He had to move fast. But where should he begin?

The doorbell rang, interrupting his thoughts. He heard Annie answer, then the soft tones of another woman. Rachel. Seconds later, Annie showed Rachel into the parlor, then left and shut the door behind her. David rose at the sight of her. He put on a smile. He wasn't in the mood for company, but it would be wrong not to greet her. Furthermore, she did look comely, fresh and crisp in her nurse's uniform.

"My, my. What a surprise. Your patients must love to see you coming."

"Hush your mouth," she said, but her eyes twinkled at the compliment. She handed him his leather gloves. "You left these at my place. I was hoping to get them here before you left."

"Well, that was nice of you, but I'm not going anywhere."

"You're not?"

"Not for a while."

She looked at him for an explanation, but he gave her none. Instead, he invited her to coffee. She agreed, saying she had an hour before her shift started. Once settled, he reminded her that she'd told him that Gem seemed to exert a strange influence over Lilian. How could that be? Their relationship certainly hadn't started out that way. No, she agreed, it hadn't. And she herself was bewildered by how it had changed. Because it was a big change, she said, and she told him about an evening in which she, Gem, Lilian, and Sweet had gone out together.

"Lilian had some tickets for the Harlem Symphony. Fletcher Henderson was playing. The place was packed. We were all in a good mood. Afterward, somebody suggested we check out Happy Rhone's place over on 143rd. Lilian didn't want to go. But Gem pushed for it."

He'd heard of Arthur "Happy" Rhone's. It was closed now, but at the time it was the place to go if you wanted to see and be seen. It was known as "the millionaires' club," and it was posh. The interior was a sleek and sophisticated ebony-on-ivory. It was the place where Hollywood met Harlem, a name-droppers' paradise, where Nobodies and Somebodies swung to the same smooth sax.

"It's not the kind of place Lilian would've liked," he said.

"She hated it. Said it was stuck-up and snooty. Well, it was, but it was fun."

Rachel told how the four of them lucked out and got a table with a good view of the floor show. But none of them watched it. They were too busy listening to Gem. She held them spellbound with risqué, bawdy stories about her life in Paris. She had an endless supply of tales that she felt just had to be told. David could almost hear Gem, chattering like a magpie.

"There was this silly man who claimed to be a Russian count. He could've been. Nobody, absolutely nobody gave a damn. But I thought I'd give him a turn. He had money, after all, and lots of it. For my birthday, he took me to the Château de Madrid. Very exclusive. Just outside Paris. But they wouldn't let him in. I was perfectly dressed, but he—well, Russians, you know."

Gem rolled her eyes. "You won't believe this: He went 'round by the kitchen and got hold of a waiter. He bribed the man to swap clothes with him. That's how we got in. He danced the tango with me in a waiter's dinner jacket. Not one of those hoity-toity so much as sniffed the difference."

She chuckled, delighted at her wit. "We ate caviar—nasty, nasty stuff—and drank champagne 'til three in the morning. Then we went for a swim in a pond in the forest. I think it was breakfast time when we finally collapsed in bed. We were tired, but not too tired to, well . . . shall we say . . . enjoy one last tango."

She softly exhaled. Her shadowy eyes slithered in Sweet's direction, lingered a moment, then slid over to Lilian. Sweet's eyes glittered. Lilian's face was pale, very pale. Gem raised her glass to her lips, hiding a satisfied smile.

Then she went on recounting tale after tale of merry mischief and creative self-indulgence. She told of parties that began on Wednesdays and ran on into the weekend. She described a world of manic gaiety, one in which people threw champagne bottles out of windows, ran half-naked through the streets, and danced on car tops past dawn. Rhapsodizing over a supper party she attended, Gem said the champagne punch was made from fifty bottles of brut, and gallons of whiskey, Cointreau, and gin.

"Then there was the Four Arts Ball. It's a huge, wild thing given every June by art students in Paris. Thousands of people in costume—if you want to call it that. People don't really wear much more than body paint, a loincloth, and maybe some feathers on their heads. I went to one ball at the Porte d'Auteuil with a rich kid from Minnesota. Everyone was supposed to dress up like an Incan. Robby—that was his name—rubbed himself down with red ocher and strung three dead pigeons around his neck."

Sweet leaned forward. "And what did you wear?"

"Something exquisitely fashionable and stylishly simple . . . bare breasts and a turquoise wig."

Sweet smiled faintly. Lilian gagged. She grabbed her glass of water, tried to drink it, and sloshed water over her chest. She jumped up so violently that her chair toppled over. Her eyes were wet; her shoulders hunched. She hugged her purse to her chest as though it were a shield.

"I have to go," she gasped, then fled the room. Sweet went after her.

"Lord help the person who's got something Gem wants," Rachel said. "That woman would scare the Devil himself if he got in her way."

Indeed, thought David. Gem had been mercilessly clever. She had chosen a public place, with a private audience, to reveal her own rebellious morality, to tantalize Sweet and embarrass Lilian with suggestive tales. Had Sweet really remained immune to Gem's charms?

"But Gem didn't stop there," Rachel said. "First, she went after Lilian's marriage to Sweet, then she went after her friendship with me. She made out like there was something between Sweet and me or that I wished there was. See, I knew Sweet before Lilian did. We grew up on the same block. His family moved there after you guys left. Lilian knew that I'd met Sweet before, but I'd never told her that we'd known each other as kids. It was a long time ago and it wasn't worth mentioning. But Gem used it. Twisted it around. Put it in Lilian's head that I liked Sweet."

"Surely Lilian didn't believe her."

"No, but that was just the beginning."

David could well imagine. He knew Gem's methods. *What a waste of human energy.*

Rachel said she had to leave. He showed her to the door. At the last moment, she stood on tiptoe and brushed her lips against his cheek. He was surprised, but pleased. She took his hand.

"Walk me to work, why don't you?"

"All right."

As he turned to get his coat from the closet, he had the feeling that he was being watched. He glanced over his shoulder and saw Annie, standing at the foot of the stairs. Guilt gripped him. He didn't know why. "I'm just going to walk her to the hospital," he said, wondering why he felt bound to explain.

Annie nodded, but said nothing. Shouldering his way into his coat, David turned back to Rachel and gave her a quick smile, then hustled her out the door. He sensed Annie's eyes on his back until the door shut behind him.

11

Passages

She stood there a moment longer, then continued upstairs to David's room. As she set about straightening up, her mind was in turmoil. She didn't like what she'd seen at the doorway, didn't like it at all. But what could she do about it?

Nothin', she thought. *He's a grown man. And cain't nobody do his thinkin' for him. He's got t'follow his own mind.*

"But how could he . . . ?" she muttered. "After all that's happened, how could he start up with that chile again?"

She saw his suitcase lying side down on a chair and went to it with the thought of setting it in his closet. Without thinking, she flipped it open.

Hm-humph! Didn't even take his clothes out. He sure don't mean t'stay long.

She saw one shirt, some underwear, and two pairs of socks.

Didn't bring much, neither. And his clothes—they look taken care of, but . . . well, he sure don't dress like he used to.

She started to unpack the suitcase herself—

Lay ev'rythin' in his dresser nice an' neat for him—

then thought better of it.

I sure don't wanna try to force him. Don't wanna upset him.

She lowered the suitcase lid and turned to the rest of the room. She'd remade his bed and was about to wipe down his desk when she saw that he'd found his old Bible. He'd left it lying open on his desk. She was surprised and pleased. She smiled wistfully.

Why, I r'member the day I gave him that. It was back in the days of the Tenderloin. His first Holy Communion Day. He was one proud li'l boy. Only nine years old.

She'd scrimped for a year to be able to buy him that small Bible . . . *even paid extra t'get his name written in gold on the cover.*

"You're a man, now," she'd told him. "A man in the sight of God."

The two of them had sat together, two or three evenings a week, and read it page for page. He had asked questions—

Good, smart questions—

And she'd done her best to give him good answers. And he'd believed— believed with his entire heart—in a loving God, a forgiving God.

He had such devotion, even more than Miss Lilian. Where'd it go?

When she mentioned that Miss Lilian had been buried in unconsecrated ground, his silence had said more than words.

What happened t'him? Whatever it was, it just 'bout ruint him. And kept him away. Kept him in exile.

He thought she believed he'd been working for the Movement all this time. But she knew better. Knew it in her heart. Something had gone wrong in his life.

"Terrible wrong," she said out loud.

Her gaze dwelled on the Bible.

At least, he took it out. Could be he's trying t'find his way back, God help him.

The Bible was open to the New Testament. A passage had been marked. Bending for a closer look, she squinted at the fine print.

"Matthew 26:57–75," she whispered and began to read aloud. "Those who had arrested Jesus took him t'Caiaphas, the high priest . . . Peter followed him at a distance, right up t'the courtyard of the high priest . . . A servant girl came t'him. 'You also were with Jesus of Galilee,' she said. But he denied it b'fore them all. Another girl saw him and said, 'This fellow was with Jesus of Nazareth.' He denied it again. Those standing there went up t'Peter and said, 'Surely, you are one of them, for your accent gives you 'way,' Then he b'gan t'call down curses on hisself and he swore to 'em, 'I don't know the man!' Immediately, a rooster crowed. Then Peter r'membered the words Jesus had spoken: 'Before the rooster crows, you will disown me three times.' And he went outside and wept bitterly."

She eased herself down into the wooden desk chair and touched the pages, wondering.

Peter's denial of Jesus: What's that got t'do with my David?

"'And he went outside and wept,'" she read again. "'Wept bitterly.'"

The page was well-fingered.

He been sittin' here and readin'—readin' and readin' 'bout how Peter denied his Lord. Why? Has he done somethin'? . . . Or has somebody done somethin' t'him?

o   o   o

She was peering into the display window of the Righteous Lady Dress Shop. From a distance, she looked pretty in a clean, simple way. Her coat was practical, but not stylish. And her little hat was modest. Her arms were full of groceries and at her side stood a small boy of about three dressed in knicker-bockers. He was playing with a bright green ball. As David's gaze moved from the woman to her child, his lips bowed in a faint smile. Once, he'd hoped to have a family.

The boy bounced his ball and it rebounded high. He tried to catch it, but it escaped from between his plump little hands and rolled toward the curb. He scrambled to catch it, but every time he reached for it, it slipped away. It wobbled until it hit the curb, then bounced off and rolled into the street. He followed. His mother, her attention on the display, didn't notice.

A milk wagon swung around the corner with a screech of tires. David glanced at it and his lungs contracted. The wagon had taken the corner way too wide and way too fast and was careening down the street. The boy didn't hear or see it; he was intent on his ball. It had settled dead in the middle of the street. Now it was just beyond his fingertips. He took another step and reached for it.

David's heart lurched. Then he was running. Running hard. Giving it all he had. He had a sensation of terrible slowness, of trying to run through mud. Somewhere, as though from far away, a woman screamed. Her sound of terror was muffled, as though he heard it through a glass wall. Now he was closing in on the child, surging forward with arms outstretched, conscious of the wagon bearing down on them. He got a brief glimpse of the boy's startled brown eyes; then he'd snatched him up and was diving forward, crashing against the pavement. His head hit the ground hard. He felt an explosion of pain and fractals of color went skidding before his vision. The wagon barreled by in a puff of smelly exhaust. David lay with the boy in a heap, the child resting on his chest. He closed his eyes for a moment, stunned. When he reopened them, he found himself looking up into a pair of wide, innocent eyes. A cute little face with round cheeks and a set of miniature teeth grinned back at him.

"Ooh, that was fun!" the boy giggled. "Can we do that again?"

What a little charmer, thought David. Then the boy's smile disappeared into a look of surprise as he was yanked away. David heard a woman sobbing and scolding—the child's mother, he assumed—in a mixture of love, anger, and relief. Then there were other hands, strangers' hands, helping him to his feet, brushing him off, clapping him on the shoulder.

"You okay, mister?"

"I'm fine." David nodded. He was still dazed, though, and his head was throbbing.

"Damn them wagons," someone muttered.

"Lady, you one lucky woman," another said. "I ain't never seen nobody move that fast."

David dusted himself off. The young woman stood nearby, holding her son in her arms. Up close, he could see the dark circles under her eyes. She was young, maybe in her late twenties, and she looked wrung out.

"Oh, baby, don't you know you coulda been killed?" she was saying, stroking her son's scratched and dirt-smudged cheeks.

Unshed tears sparkled in her eyes. The little boy looked at her with stupefied concern. He reached out with his small hands and touched her face. "Don't cry, Mommy. Please, don't cry!"

"You my precious angel. You all I got. If I lose you, I'll go outta my mind."

She bit down on her lip, trying to keep herself under control. An expression of horrified dismay crawled over her boy's small face. Then the corners of his lips turned down and his lower lip began to quiver. His face screwed up, his mouth dropped open, and he began to wail.

"But I wah-wah-wanted my ball!"

She tried to smile, but her lips trembled. "Honey, I've told you: If a ball goes out into the street, don't go after it. Let Mama do it." She wiped her eyes with the back of her hand. "Please, please baby. Let Mama do it. You promise? Don't never run out in the road like that again."

Fat tears slipped from his eyes, rolled down his cheeks, and fell in thick drops from his chin. "Unh-uh, I won't," he said. "I promise." He hugged his mother tight, nestling his head in the crook of her neck.

She looked up from him to David, extended a hand, and brushed David's sleeve with her fingertips.

"God bless you," she whispered.

"It was nothing." He reached out and tweaked the little boy's ear. "You're a fast one, chum."

The child managed a weak smile through his tears.

"Too fast," his mother said. "He ain't got no sense yet."

"He'll learn."

"He'd better." Now she did give her son a little jiggle to show her annoyance, but she was betrayed by the loving expression in her eyes. He looked up at her and the faint smile he'd given David grew into a mischievous grin for his mother. She grinned back, then looked at David and her eyes were humble.

"God was with us today, but I shoulda been payin' attention," she said. "I just bought him the ball. He was so excited and he wanted t'carry it. I told him not t'play with it 'til we got home, but I shoulda known better. He's just a baby. How could I expect him t'understand? Then I just stopped for a minute t'look at that shop window. They had a sign last week, sayin' they needed help. I shoulda been payin' attention," she repeated. She glanced down at her son, hugged him closer, and looked back at David. "Oh, Lord," she whispered. "If you hadna been here, I . . ." Her voice broke and the tears she'd been fighting to contain slipped from her eyes.

"Don't be so hard on yourself," said David. He reached over and stroked the small head. "He's fine. And he's learned a lesson. He won't be running out into the street again. Will you, little man?"

The boy nodded his head without lifting it from his mother's shoulder. The crowd had drifted away. David put a supporting hand under her elbow and escorted her back to the sidewalk. Her groceries lay spilled on the ground.

"I'll pack your bags for you," he said.

"You don't need to do that."

Their eyes met.

"Yes, I do," he said warmly.

She smiled and briefly averted her large chocolate eyes. He realized that she was quite pretty, despite the dark half-moons under her eyes. Her face was well scrubbed and her complexion smooth. She had high cheekbones and a kind mouth.

"This is awful kind of you," she said as he gathered the errant goods—a Hormel canned ham, a box of Wheaties, some Sanka decaffeinated coffee, a box of Quaker Quick oats, and two Snickers candy bars. He returned them to their bags and started to hand them back to her, but she was still holding her son.

"I can help you carry these."

Doubt flickered in her eyes. He understood. He had just saved her son's life, but he was still a stranger. In New York City, a wise woman did not let a strange man, even an apparently helpful one (in some cases, *especially* an apparently helpful one), walk her home.

"It's okay. I'll just take you to your corner, if you want me to."

She smiled, but shook her head. Putting her son down, she picked up her grocery bags.

"My ball," the boy protested.

David spied it lying in the gutter. He fetched it, pulled a worn silk handkerchief from his pocket and wiped the ball clean. Then he sank down on his haunches and offered it to the child. "Here you go."

The boy reached out and hesitated. He looked up at his mother. She nodded that it was okay to take the ball and he did so. Suddenly shy, he hid behind his mother's coat.

"Toby, say thank you," she said.

Toby peeked out from behind her coat and said, "Dankyu."

David laughed and straightened up.

"I'll be going now," she said.

Thanking David once again, she left him. Her tiny son firmly grasped her coat with one pudgy fist, his ball tucked under his other arm. David watched them go. She must've felt his eyes on her because at the corner she turned and gave a little wave. David waved back. Then she and her son disappeared from view. David dropped his arm, aware of an odd surge of sadness. The feeling bewildered him. A woman and her boy going about their lives—people he'd never seen before and would never see again: Why did the sight of their walking away make him feel so alone?

Shoving his hands deep into his pockets, he headed back toward Strivers' Row. As he walked, he had an image of the house, waiting for him with all of its empty rooms. And he recalled what he'd asked his father when he bought it.

"Why'd you buy such a big place, Daddy? What do we need all them rooms for?"

Augustus had laughed. "For grandchildren, son. Babies. The babies that you and the girls will bring home when you get married someday."

"We're a family," Lila had said. "And families need a place where they can be together."

David paused at a street corner, waiting for the light to change. Well, since his father's death, Gem had gone to Europe and he'd headed off down south. Only Lilian had remained in that big house, alone. Where were the grandchildren his parents had dreamed of? What had become of their vision of a large family, of generations gathered around the dining room table? Gem had never taken part in that dream, but he and Lilian had. Now Lilian was gone and he was the only one left. There was little chance of his marrying and having children. Not with the lie he was living.

Annie wanted him to fight for the house and he would do so, because he loved his parents, he loved Annie, and deep down, a part of him did love the house. He would fight and he would win, but in the end to what purpose?

The light changed; he was free to cross. But he remained standing there, rocked by a sense of loss. His family, he realized, was dying out.

Adrian Snyder leaned back in his chair and examined his fingernails. They were buffed to a nice soft gleam. He used a letter opener to dig a nearly imperceptible bit of dirt out from under the fingernail of his left index finger, then held his hand up to admire it. He heard a hiccup from his guest and looked up.

His "guest" sat in a chair in the middle of the room. Shotgun and Slate, two of Snyder's biggest, baddest men, flanked him. The guest fidgeted. He was bony and sharp-featured.

Something about him always did remind me of a ferret, thought Snyder. He hated ferrets.

The Ferret kept picking at the cloth at his knees, which he jogged up and down nervously.

"Nice pants," said Snyder in a conversational tone.

The Ferret tried to smile and failed.

"Did you buy them with my money?" Snyder asked.

The Ferret licked his lips. "Look, boss, I, uh—"

"Don't lie to me, Sully. Don't lie to me," said Snyder, still in a quiet tone. He never raised his voice. "There's only one thing worse than pickpockets and thieves and that's liars."

Sully flinched. He'd broken out into a cold sweat and his face was the color of wet putty. "Boss, I—I don't know what got into me. I swear, it'll never happen again."

"I'm sure it won't." Snyder examined a bit of loose skin on one cuticle. "So where's the rest of it? Or did you spend all twenty Gs?"

Sully's eyes shifted. "I—uh—I got it at home. In a box. Under the bed."

Snyder threw his head back and laughed. He had beautiful teeth. They caught the light and gleamed like pearls.

"C'mon, Sully. You can do better than that." He became serious again. "For your sake, you'd better do better than that."

He sent an eye signal to Shotgun, who dropped a brick-like hand on Sully's shoulder. Sully jumped and gave a little shriek.

"Okay—okay," he said, trembling. "It—it's in a box. Tied to a rope."

"Um-hmm," said Snyder. "And what's the rope tied to?"

"One of the pilings leading into the East River."

"I see." Snyder studied Sully, tapping the letter opener against one hand.

"I guess you didn't believe me when I said I can't stand liars." He paused. "I don't even tell lies myself." He drew a fingertip over the point of the opener. "You see, my boys already found the money. Wrapped in an oilskin and sunk in your toilet tank. Stupid move, Sully. It was one of the first places we looked." He gave a sigh of disappointment. "Now, I gave you two chances, two chances to tell the truth. And you fucked up. Actually, you fucked up three times, Sully. *Three* times. First when you stole from me. Second, when you lied to me. Third, when you lied to me again."

Sully was trembling. A wet stain blossomed at his crotch. Snyder saw it and shook his head with disgust. He glanced at Slate.

"Show him a slow twist."

Sully jerked forward in his seat, his face contorted in panic.

"Oh, God, no! Oh, please! It was Sheila, boss. She said she'd leave me if I didn't—"

The thin metal wire that was whipped around his neck cut him off in midsentence. His eyes bugged out. He turned and twisted, his skinny legs kicking at air.

Snyder watched without expression. "She said she'd leave you, did she? Well, I'm afraid you'll be leaving her."

Sully clawed at the wire as it cut into his neck. Droplets of blood oozed out along the line of the garrote. He pleaded with bulging eyes. Just before it looked like he was going to lose consciousness, Snyder signaled again and the wire was removed. Sully fell forward, clutching his neck.

"Oh, God, thank you. Thank you," he gasped.

Snyder got up and walked around his desk to where Sully sat. He towered over him.

"Look at me," he said.

Sully raised his bloodshot eyes. Snyder bent and brought his face close to the little man's. Snyder wrinkled his nose. The guy stunk of booze, piss, and fear. Sully reached out to him with bloody hands.

"Please . . . please, forgive me," he rasped.

"'Course I do."

Snyder's smile was affable. He gave Sully a little pat on the cheek. A tear ran down Sully's face. His eyes shone with relief.

"You forgive me, boss?"

"It's forgotten. Look," said Snyder. "I got somethin' for you."

He put a chummy hand on Sully's shoulder and hugged him. Sully stared into Snyder's eyes with gratitude. Snyder smiled, brought his right hand up, and plunged the letter opener deep into the base of Sully's throat. Sully's whole body jerked. He gagged and tore at the thing protruding from his throat. His eyes fixed on Snyder's. Then he pitched forward. Snyder stepped aside and Sully fell to the floor with a thump. He twitched for a few seconds, then lay still. Snyder looked down at the dead man with contempt.

"You dumb fuck. I told you to never listen to my sister."

He signaled to Shotgun and Slate. "Get rid of him. He's bleeding on the rug. Then come back here. I have another job for you. His name is McKay, David McKay."

David's head ached from having been smashed against the pavement. His eyes hurt even from the pale light of the overhung sky. And his thoughts churned restlessly inside his head.

A lot's done happened . . . A lot's done happened . . . A lot's done happened since you been gone . . .

Well, there was nothing he could do to change the past, but—

"Hey, mister, you wanna shine?"

David blinked and looked down. A grizzled old man with milky blue irises stood looking up at him. A battered hat sat jauntily on his round head. His lower lip hung a bit, revealing missing teeth and tobacco-stained stumps. His eyes gleamed with benevolence.

"Here, you wanna sit down?"

The old man gestured to a shoeshine stand built alongside a grocery store on the street. David saw then that the old man's hands were stained with boot black. His wooden shoeshine box stood nearby.

"No, thank you. I'm fine."

"You don't look it."

David had to smile at the old man's candor. Truth to tell, he didn't feel well. He yielded when the old man took him by the arm.

"Here, you sit down. Let me give you a nice shine."

"No, really, I—"

But the old man insisted. Finally, to be polite, David climbed up onto the mounted chair and placed his feet on the supports.

"I'm Roy," the old man said. "Roy, Roy, the Shoeshine Boy. See, it rhymes. Kinda catchy. Cust'mers like it. You new in town?"

"Not really, no."

Roy poured some drops of liquid shoe cleanser on David's shoes, spread it around with a soft little brush, then snapped open a strip of stained gray cloth and started to rub David's leather shoes with vigor.

"Set out to see Seventh Avenue, have you? That's what all the folk new to Harlem do. Well, it's pretty quiet today, but in the summertime, it's somethin' t'see. The gals strut they stuff and the crowds is deeper than deep. We gets all kindsa parades up and down the street. It sure is somethin' t'see."

Roy whipped out another rag from his back pocket, twisted open a tin of black polish, used the rag to apply the polish, and began to shine the shoes: from side to side, across the toe, around the back. He was quick and strong and while he worked he talked.

"Yeah, we's had lotsa parades." His voice trailed off. "But the one I best r'members, the one that meant the most, was back in 1919, when our boys come home from that there war over in Europe." He was silent a moment. "My son went t'France and didn't come back. My missus say he died for nothin', but I can't say that, don't want t'say that. The hurt done nearly killed her. That and believin' he died for nothin'." He looked up at David with cataract eyes. "You weren't here for that parade, son. Too young t'know what I mean."

"I was there," said David. "I was in it."

"You was over there? For real?"

"Yeah," David nodded. "For real."

The old man's eyes grew shrewd. "When d'you ship out?"

"Summer of '18."

"You was an officer, right?"

"A lieutenant."

Roy studied him. "You look way too young for them kind of mem'ries. But they're in your eyes . . . You got old eyes. My missus would say you got an old soul, son. A very old soul."

David said nothing, but he was touched.

"I bet you got a medal," Roy said. "You look the type."

"Do I now?" David smiled. "Well, yes, I did . . . I did, at that."

"It was hell over there, wasn't it?"

"Yeah . . . in many ways it was." *But the war over there,* he wanted to add, *was nothing—nothing compared to one over here.*

The knife of regret stabbed him.

Forgive me, Jonah. Forgive me. At least, you've found your peace. Maybe, just maybe, one day I'll find mine.

12

A Voice Stilled

"Excuse me, Mr. David, but I have somethin' for you."

Annie's voice brought him out of his reverie. He hadn't heard her as she entered the parlor, her skirts rustling softly. She reached into one of her deep apron pockets, withdrew a slender rose cloth-covered book, and handed it to him.

"It was Miss Lilian's."

Taking the book, he opened it. The book's delicate pages were covered with Lilian's fine script. His face registered surprise. He looked up at Annie.

"Did she leave other papers?"

Annie shook her head. "Mr. Sweet burned everythin' else. Even her last manuscript—"

"He burned her *book?*"

"Did it right after the funeral. But he missed this. I'd taken it. Hidden it."

He thanked her. She gave a slight bow and moved away. His suspicion and resentment of Sweet hardened. How could the man have destroyed her work? It was beyond callous; it was cruel. Or did the manuscript contain something Sweet wanted no one to see? That manuscript represented Lilian's last creative effort. It contained her last written thoughts.

But did it?

His gaze dropped to the diary. The book was new. He turned the pages one by one. She had written it as though it were a novel, recording the events like scenes from a book. Perhaps she'd intended to use it later as material. She'd begun it in October, the day Gem arrived. The last entry was dated last March. She must have stopped writing in it at about the same time Gem returned to Europe. Strange. He turned back to the first page.

> *Friday, October 31, 1924*
>
> Gem is back. How apt that she reappear on Halloween, the day on which ghosts return to bedevil the living. God help me. I

don't want her here. Not now, when everything is finally turning out well. I must get her out of the house swiftly, but she must leave voluntarily. I can't just turn her out. People will talk.

I sat on Gem's bed this evening, watching her unpack. She has tawdry taste. There was a slinky number in glittering crimson with a deep cut in the back ... *Vulgar* ... And the gold outfit that followed ... *Obscene*. And the shoes she had! Pair after pair after pair ... I had to ask her if this is how she's been spending Daddy's money, on trashy outfits.

Gem turned her nose up. "Darling, my clothes come from the best collections. There's absolutely nothing trashy about them. And I'll have you know, I didn't pay for a single stitch—at least not with cash."

She chuckled shamelessly. Then she proceeded to tell me what she's been up to. Living it up, as she called it. "Having a helluva time! In London, Amsterdam, Munich, Berlin! Fantastic city, Berlin. German lovers have incredible energy. No style, but lots of energy. And stamina."

She ground her hips into the air and thrust them forward roughly. Her manner was crude. Disgusting. She laughed at my expression and twirled exuberantly. She told me about her life in Paris. Montmartre, she said, is a playground.

"There's no other word for it. A playground. You need to go there. It's home-away-from-home for us colored folk."

She had a singing gig at Le Grand Duc, she said. I've heard of the club. Only the best people go there: Nancy Llewellyn, Raymond McMasters, Geoffrey Aragon, the Bendal sisters, Maria Noone, the Baltimore Tates. All of them fought to get tables to hear her, Gem said. And between sets, they begged her to sit with them and drink champagne.

"After hours, the Grand Duc was like a Harlem cabaret. Niggers from the other clubs would come over and we'd get down. Even Langston was there! He was working at the Duc, washing dishes. After hours, he'd come out of the kitchen and join in."

Gem's eyes sparkled; her cheeks were flushed and her skin glowed as though lit from within. I closed my eyes against the sight of her. She made me feel pale and drab, stiff and regimented, claustrophobic within my own skin.

My life has been dominated by obligation. It was never my

own. What did Gem do to merit such freedom? What did she ever do? Nothing. She took it as her right. Perhaps I should have done that, too. Simply taken my freedom, instead of having felt compelled to earn it.

When I consider all those years of teaching school . . . *Pure drudgery.* Daddy's voice would boom in my conscience every time I thought about quitting. *Duty, duty, first and foremost.* I would think of Gem and dream about what she was up to. I wanted to go out and experience life too, but I stayed put—because I thought I had to. I endured loneliness—because I thought I had to. This evening, listening to Gem, it seemed that my sacrifices weren't only useless, but foolish. An acute nausea crept up from the pit of my belly. Not once in five years had I felt this insecure—not once since Gem left. Only a few hours in the house and already she was affecting me.

I was suddenly angry, not just at her, but at myself. How could I let this empty-headed woman cause me to doubt myself? She's always had only one goal in life—to have fun—and she's never felt guilty about it. Such a goal would never have satisfied me and apparently it hasn't done much for her either. Gem has squandered her freedom. Otherwise, she wouldn't have come back. I let her prattle on about how marvelous her life in Paris was until I couldn't stand it anymore.

"If it was so wonderful there, then why are you here?"

Gem didn't miss a beat. "Because I missed you, sister dear. Missed you terribly."

"Are you sure you didn't miss my money more?"

Something flickered in her eyes. I told her about the letter I got from Aunt Clara the other day. About how well Auntie's doing. Settled in Chicago. On her third husband. He's even richer than the last, I said, related to the Johnsons. I told her that Auntie had asked about her.

"You were always her favorite. I'm sure she'd love to see you."

Gem caught my meaning. Her expression toughened and her left hand went to her hip. With her right index finger, she jabbed the air to emphasize every word.

"This is where I want to be. Here, in Daddy's house."

"*Daddy's house* no longer belongs to you. Remember? You sold your share to David and me."

"Well, I like it here. I'm going to stay—as long as I want to—and there's nothing you can do about it." She thrust her face up close to mine. "You don't have the guts to throw me out."

"Don't underestimate me. I've changed. I won't support you."

"Oh, but you will. You'll give me anything I want because you're afraid of people talking. And you know I know how to make people talk."

I stood to leave. "I won't let you destroy what I have. I've worked too hard to let you take it away. I'll see you out on the streets first."

She snickered. "Don't be stupid and don't try to scare me. I've run with the big boys. They play for keeps. And so do I."

David paused, remembering. Lilian and Gem had fought viciously in high school. Gem had been the one with the glittering looks and witty personality; the studious Lilian couldn't compete. The more people had urged her "to be like Gem," the harder she had fought to be different. She'd deliberately chosen to downplay her beauty and gain respect for her brains. They'd carried the conflict into adulthood. On Gem's first night home, they hadn't wasted time on niceties, but gone straight to the heart of the matter. They virtually declared war on one another. How in the world had they reached the point where they would go shopping together?

He found his place and read on.

Friday, November 7, 1924
Is something going on between Gem and my husband?

So, Lilian had begun to doubt Sweet's fidelity, after all . . .

Wednesday, November 12, 1924
Gem and I had lunch today. Her invitation was a surprise. Expecting the unpleasant, I planned to tread lightly and listen carefully. However, the conversation took an unexpected turn. I've decided to try to reconstruct it as accurately as I can because I sense that Gem's words contain a secret that I've yet to pierce.

Gem picked the Civic Club, because of its high social visibility, of course. When I arrived, she was seated at a center table, dressed in a buff-colored wool suit with a cream chinchilla stole. A bit much for so early in the day.

"You need to relax. Have more fun," she told me and chuckled. "I know you think I have too much fun. But you should try it. You might like it. Once I had a Buddhist lover. He'd pound me into the mattress for hours. Then he'd have the nerve to meditate for ten minutes and lecture me on moderation for twenty!" Gem gave a husky laugh.

Her voice was loud and I was sure her shameful words had carried. I glanced around, expecting to see ovals of shocked faces staring at us, openmouthed. Thank God, there were none. But I was still mortified. I looked back at her, at her overdone makeup, her supercilious air. She was the same old Gem: crude despite all her culture.

"You never will change, will you?" I said in a low, tense voice.

"Why should I?"

"That you have to even ask—"

"Listen, if I have too much fun, you have too little. Look at you. You're aging before your time."

This was an old argument between us. I wasn't in the mood for it.

"All right, all right," I said, waving her words away and hoping she would quiet down. The waiter was approaching with our tea.

As soon as he was gone, Gem produced a silver flask and before I could say anything, she had poured a dollop of whisky into my cup.

"Here. Eat, drink, and learn to be merry," she said.

I was tense and tired. My paper wasn't as well received at the Chicago conference as I'd hoped it would be. And I've been having nightmares. So I thought Gem might be right. I should relax. I took a sip. I didn't like it. I've never liked alcohol. But then I felt warmth spread through me and decided to take another sip after all.

Gem nodded approvingly. She waved her jeweled hand at the waiter and he promptly took our orders. Gem and I chatted. The conversation was going well and under the influence of several cups of tea, I began to relax. Indeed, I think now that I relaxed too much. The trouble began when Gem started criticizing me.

"You should do more for yourself. Take off those old-fashioned clothes. Doll yourself up a little."

"I'm as 'dolled up' as I need to be."

"Don't be a sap. Your face, your clothes—they're what people see first and remember last. Sometimes, I think you work to make yourself look like a zombie."

"I work to be respected. I don't want to be a bit of fluff on a man's arm."

"Like me, you mean?" She smiled saucily. "Why are you so stubbornly naive, dear? It was forgivable when you were younger, but it's tiresome now."

"Oh, please! My profession doesn't involve seducing men. Yours apparently does."

"Watch yourself, dear—"

"Getting a man was never as important to me as it is to you. I saw what Daddy did to Mama and I said I'd never let that happen to me. I knew that I could do without a man. Didn't want one. Didn't need one."

"Then why the hell did you marry one?"

"Men do have their uses. I wanted children—"

"You wanted sex—"

"No—you've had enough of that for both of us."

I stopped, appalled at what I'd said. But Gem smiled, unperturbed. She scooped up her flask and sloshed more whisky into my cup.

"Drink up, sweetheart. It seems to be doing you good."

I nudged my cup away. I'd had more alcohol than I intended to and now it was tricking me. Arguing with Gem was the last thing I wanted to do. The conference was exhausting. And this feeling, ever since I've been back, that something isn't right with Jameson . . .

My head ached. It felt as though an evil dwarf with a pickax had gotten inside my skull and was hitting an anvil with malicious regularity. I can't quite explain it, but something gave way inside me. I just didn't have the energy to pretend.

"The simple truth is that I was tired of being alone. I was in my late twenties and still single. I knew what everyone was thinking: 'How sad. What an old maid.' So when I met Jameson, I decided to marry him."

"Just like that?" Gem snapped her fingers.

"Just like that."

"Then why don't you do the work required to keep him?"

"What do you mean?"

"I mean: Be pretty, Lil. Give him something to look at."

"Jameson loves me the way I am."

"You believe that, do you?"

"Yes. I do. I'm plain. I'm old-fashioned. That's me, and I'm not ashamed of it."

"But why? You can look as good as I do!"

"Don't you understand? I don't want to look like you!"

"Well, be plain then! It's annoying to look at you. If you lose your precious Jameson, you'll be the one to blame, not me."

I didn't like what I saw in her eyes. "Why should I lose him?"

She didn't answer, but her lips curled maliciously. I suddenly felt cold.

"You want him, don't you? That's what this is all about."

"Yes, I want him, dear. But more to the point: He wants me."

The little man in my head struck his anvil a reverberating blow. I gambled when I married Jameson. For the first time in my life, I flew in the face of general opinion. And I did it quickly, afraid to give myself time to reconsider. But I've never been able to silence a nagging doubt . . .

Gem was studying me with the sharp, observant eyes of a hunter, eyes that missed nothing. And I wondered once more, why does she have to be a part of my life?

I closed my eyes, shutting out the outer world. I could hear the sounds of people drawing their chairs up to their tables, of napkins being snapped open; the obsequious murmur of waiters taking orders, the clink and clatter of silverware. I felt the suffo-cating quality of air in a closed room, and smelled the riotous mix of spices and oils in the sumptuous dishes laid out on surrounding tables. But I heard and felt and smelled everything from a dis-tance, as though I sat on the other side of a dampening curtain, isolated, alone with this throbbing pain, this exhaustion and this rapidly spreading dread. The only sensation that was up close and immediate was the penetrating impression of Gem's scrutiny crawling over me, probing, tasting, analyzing. Opening my eyes, I met her gaze head-on.

"I won't make it easy for you."

She laughed, but I didn't let that dismay me. I went on.

"You've always taken what you wanted—but not this time. I

have Jameson; I'm going to keep him. He'll never leave. He'll stay where the money is. And that's not with you. Perhaps you'll get him to cheat. Maybe you can teach him new tricks. But he'll bring them right back to me, to me and my bed. He will always come back."

Gem's face became as glacial as carved ice, her eyes as hot as molten lava. They virtually glowed with spite.

"Don't be a fool. You may be well off, but you're not rich. Not rich, little sister. I know rich. You are simply financially healthy. And you're not beautiful. You've got the material, but you don't want to use it. There are many other women who are either incredibly ugly but breathtakingly rich—or incredibly lovely but breathtakingly poor. Jameson would leave you for either one."

Her fangs had drawn blood and from my expression she knew it. My mind scrambled for a suitable reply. My thoughts ran hither and thither—I admit it—like a trapped mouse.

The waiter brought our orders. He swung our plates down on the table with a proud flourish. Gem picked up her fork and attacked her plate with gusto, but I'd lost my appetite. I tried to isolate Gem's venomous words with a mental tourniquet, but her poison had hit my veins. Self-doubt and apprehension burned through me. The dread of losing Jameson cut my breath to a painful wheeze. I couldn't lose him; I couldn't. I couldn't bear the shame.

Gem picked up a piece of celery and snapped it in two. "Wake up, dear. In this world, you've got to fight with everything you've got."

"He'll never leave me," I whispered.

"Baby, you don't even know what's cooking under your own roof. You need me to pull your pretentious little butt out of the fire. Well, I'm going to do you a favor. I'll save your marriage for you." Gem savored my stunned silence for a long delicious minute. "That's right. I'm going to help you."

"Help me? How?"

"I'll take you shopping. Get you acquainted with the seductive side of life."

The thought disgusted me. "I don't need your help."

"You're an idiot."

I felt sick. That little man with the pickax was swinging to a steady, bitter, battering rhythm in my head. "Since when would you be willing to help me?"

She didn't answer at once. Her expression softened and saddened. Gem, the tough woman of the world, suddenly appeared vulnerable. It was an amazing transformation.

"You asked before why I came back. You didn't believe me when I said I missed you. But it was true. Europe was magnificent, but it was also very, very lonely. Can you imagine what it's like to wander past the expensive shops of the Champs Elysées or struggle through the hordes clogging Berlin's Kurfürstendamm . . . year after year . . . and never once see a familiar face from back home?"

"But that's what you wanted."

"At first." Gem's gaze was distant. "Those first couple of years passed in a frantic haze. I was so busy, I could barely keep up. But then time seemed to slow, to stretch out. The days became longer; the nights lonelier. I missed Harlem. And I missed you." Gem's eyes refocused on me with a strange intensity. "Whatever happens, please believe that. I missed you."

Something in her tone gave me the chills. I tried to shrug it off. "All right, you missed me. That doesn't explain why you would be willing to 'save my marriage,' as you put it. If you want Jameson, then why would you help me keep him?"

"There are many men in the world, but I have only one sister. Does that satisfy you?"

"No."

She eyed me. She seemed to be measuring me, perhaps assessing just how much she could get away with.

"I want the truth, Gem."

"The absolute truth? All right, then."

She shrugged and snapped another celery stalk. It sounded like the breaking of bones.

"The fact is, I'm not interested in helping you keep Jameson, or any other man. I don't want to help you, period."

"That's more like it."

She laughed. "Truth is, I just like shopping. That's all. Especially when it's at someone else's expense. There, are you satisfied now?"

I eyed her.

"Come now," she coaxed. "What difference does it make why I help you? Just as long as I do?"

She was making me feel unreasonable. She had put me in an unforeseeable and disagreeable quandary. I'd always been free to blame Gem for our estrangement, but by offering to reconcile, she'd turned the tables. The onus was on me. I felt trapped. Manipulated. Outmaneuvered. And irritably, annoyingly, against all reason, vaguely guilty—I suppose for being so suspicious and unyielding, as though Gem has never given me good reason to distrust her, as if her demonstrated gift for deceit and deception is as insignificant as the dead leaves of autumns past, to be swept aside and discarded, without a second's qualm.

Was I being unreasonable? Perhaps Gem had indeed been homesick. Perhaps she had realized that those friends of hers in Paris were nothing more than opportunists who lost interest in her the moment her pockets were empty. Perhaps.

I would've liked to believe in Gem's avowed sisterly love, but . . .

Well, no matter what my doubts might be, one aspect was perfectly clear: As long as there was no proof of "an ulterior motive," I couldn't reject Gem's conciliatory offer in good conscience. And I didn't want to admit it, but I do need help with this marriage. So I relented.

Gem was delighted. That made me wonder anew. I still can't figure it out. And somehow, I can't free myself of the image of Gem signaling the waiter, then turning back to me with a grand smile, and saying brightly:

"Your bill."

Those two words made me shudder. Just what will I have to pay for? And what will be the price?

David closed the small book and leaned back, rubbing his eyes. He'd had no idea that Lilian was so lonely. Now he understood why she'd married so quickly. No wonder she hadn't informed him of her decision: She herself had never been at ease with it.

Like Lilian and Rachel, he wondered about Gem's sudden willingness to help. *Life does change people,* he thought. He knew that only too well himself. But had it changed Gem? Had the loneliness of her years abroad actually taught her to value her family or had it simply, as Annie put it, left her lean and hungry? And if Gem had indeed learned to care so much for Lilian, then where was she now? Why was she silent in the face of Lilian's death? Why the blatant indifference? Perhaps the reconciliation was short-lived. Did the diary hold the answer? Sitting up, he flipped it open and found where he'd left off.

> *Friday, December 5, 1924*
> Wonder of wonders . . . Dr. Steve agrees that I'm going to have a child.

David read the one line twice. She was *pregnant?* He sat there, stunned. But where was the baby? And why hadn't Annie said something? He'd seen no evidence of a baby in the house. Nothing, anywhere. And why had Lilian never written to him about it? He wasn't keeping a list of her emerging secrets, but maybe he should start.

He looked down at the slender book. What else would he find in there? For a split second, he was afraid to continue reading it. Would he learn something he didn't want to know?

> *Monday, December 8, 1924*
> I haven't told Jameson yet—I don't want to. This secret, this wonderful secret, is something I want to cherish alone. At least for a while, I want to enjoy it alone.

> *Sunday, January 18, 1925*
> There was a time when everything was going so well. I was writing regularly and my work was well received. Now when I put my fingers to the keys, they tremble so badly I can't type. This diary is now the only writing I do.

> *Tuesday, January 20, 1925*
> Gem has made friends with some rich whites, the Hardings. She brought them by yesterday. Horrible people. Always gushing about how "marvelous" Negroes are. But I suppose they were as sincere as ofays can be. It amazes me how white people observe so little and presume to know so much. Whites have hated and hunted us for years. Now they're fascinated with us. Their ignorance is deafening, their arrogance dazzling. Any colored man could fill an encyclopedia with what he knows about them, but it's

a rare ofay who could fill a pamphlet with a little truth about us. I believe they know more about their dogs. Certainly, I don't recognize myself or anyone else I know in the black characters produced by white writers. As for white patrons: They're only out to back what they think is "pure Negro art." As if they know us better than we know ourselves. I thank the Lord every day that I don't need the white man's money. I wouldn't trust a single one of them.

Tuesday, January 27, 1925

Jameson leaves me alone a great deal. He says he must, because of his work. That's true, but only to a certain extent. The truth is, he spends as little time with me as possible. He either locks himself in Daddy's old office or makes arrangements to meet friends, and he always meets them elsewhere, never inviting them to the house, carefully avoiding any overlap between his friendships and our marriage. I once asked him why.

Don't you want me to know your friends, darling?

He only smiled. Enigmatic. Charming. Unattainable.

But darling . . .

He never answered. His habit of evading my questions infuriates me. Like a cloud, he seems solid but is as insubstantial as mist when I reach for him. He's always gently kind, astutely considerate and sweetly polite when we pass in the hallway or sit down to dinner, but his manner is detached, as though I'm a neighborly acquaintance instead of his wife. He's gentlemanly and affectionate in public, holding my hand, supporting me by the elbow, making sure I'm properly seated in restaurants and at dinner parties. To all outer appearances, he's the perfect husband, but he leaves my side the moment our front door closes behind us.

We still share the same bedroom, but during the day he never enters the room when I'm in it, and on most nights, he eases into our bed only when he believes I'm asleep. Once a month, he exercises his husbandly privileges, but he's mechanical, distracted. I wonder why he bothers. Ours is a shell of a relationship, a lovely, beautiful shell . . .

Friday, January 30, 1925

He has never loved me. I knew it from the beginning. I hoped I could change him, but the more I do for him, the less he cares.

He's only interested in my money and his career. I'm scared to tell him about the baby. He doesn't want children. But I'm determined to have this child, come what may.

Sometimes I think of the years Mama endured Daddy's cruelty. I always sympathized with her; now I can empathize with her, too. But Mama had it better than I do. Deep down, Daddy did love her. And she sensed it. She felt that he needed her all along, even though he didn't know it himself. And that gave her strength. I wish I could feel that way about Jameson. But I can't. My only sources of comfort are my church and this child. All my hope I put into this one small human being. And all my love.

Wednesday, February 4, 1925

Jameson loves someone else. I'm sure of it. I've discovered that I can be intensely jealous. I've searched his jacket and coat pockets for bits of paper, checked his shirts for lipstick smears, read his mail. In short, I've done everything I could think of to find evidence that he's been somewhere he shouldn't have been, with someone he shouldn't have been. But I've found nothing. I should feel relieved. Instead, I feel worse. It sounds crazy, but the very lack of evidence seems proof that Jameson is being careful to hide something—or the existence of someone—from me.

Saturday, February 7, 1925

It's hard to remember the way it was when we first got married. I was so deeply in love with him, so grateful to have him, that it didn't matter that his ardor was weak. I wanted to believe that he was cool by nature, but loyal and committed. I was proud to have such a brilliant lawyer as my husband. But with the pregnancy, I can no longer ignore his lack of affection. I must find the strength to tell him about the baby.

Tuesday, February 10, 1925

Jameson continues to be solicitous and overwhelmingly kind, but today I realized that I hate him. I've heard of pregnant women coming to loathe their husbands, but my feelings don't stem from my condition. My feelings toward him have been changing for some time. I just didn't want to admit it. I wouldn't have believed that I could detest anyone so intensely.

Why did I marry such a lower-class social climber? What was I thinking of? Jameson should be grateful I even looked his way. Most women of my class wouldn't have given him the time of day, and here I went and married the man. Daddy would've never stood for it. I can't believe I made such a mistake.

I'm compelled to spend the rest of my life with him. That realization horrifies me. But the thought of losing him to someone else is worse. The shame, the scandal, would be unthinkable. Yet, I don't know how I can go on with him. The very sight of him makes me shake with rage.

Friday, February 13, 1925

If only I could get him away from me. But he's ever present, always there with his potions and medicines. I have to force myself to submit to his ministrations. I'm sure he can feel my loathing for him, but he ignores it. He's outwardly concerned, attentive and responsive to my every murmured wish. He pretends that the only problem is my "nerves," as he calls it.

I wish I had someone to talk to. If only Mama were here, but she's long gone. There's Annie, but as much as I love her, she's still just a servant and I can't see myself stooping so low as to confide in the help. I think of David. Often. But he has problems of his own. And to be truthful, I'd rather not have to admit to him that I've made a mess of my life. Then there's Gem.

The reversal in my feelings toward Jameson, dramatic as it is, still amazes me less than the change in my attitude toward Gem. After so many years, the two of us have come to share a closeness that I'd only heard other sisters speak of. She and I are at ease with our differences now. And we've discovered similarities that surprise us. Our rivalry will always be there, but it has lost its bitter edge. We can laugh and joke with one another.

Wednesday, February 18, 1925

I wonder whether Gem has noticed my changed feelings toward Jameson. She's very cool toward him. Sometimes I watch the two of them together. She's clearly not thrilled to see him when she runs into him. She's extremely cordial, but she seems blatantly relieved when he goes off on one of his business trips. I haven't told Gem about the baby either. I've tried several times, but I just can't bring the words out. I don't know why. Instead, I've confided in Rachel. That choice confuses me. I went outside the family. Why? It seemed right at the time.

For a moment, David stopped breathing. *Rachel? She told Rachel?* He closed the diary, too angry to read further. *If Rachel knew then surely Annie knew, too, and neither one of them said a damn thing.* He glanced at his pocket watch, left lying on his night table. It was nearly ten. Annie was in bed—it was too late to see her now . . . although he was sorely tempted to wake her—and Rachel was probably busy at the hospital. He sat for a moment, trying to get his emotions under control. *There are too many secrets in this house, too many.* His gaze dropped back down to the diary; he flipped it open. Only two more pages left.

Tuesday, February 24, 1925

I took a walk down by the Hudson River to see the sunset this evening. It was such a pleasure to get out of the house, away from the smell of medicines. The air was cold but crisp and clean. And the colors were magnificent. As though a mad painter had taken his brush and, in florid strokes, slashed the horizon with streaks of red, orange, violet, and gold. For one intense fleeting moment, I wished that I were as free as Gem, to simply pick up and go and never look back. But that will never be. I have responsibilities, status, property. I'm a wife and soon will be a mother. I'm rooted to my place, as firmly shackled to it as a prisoner wearing handcuffs.

Saturday, February 28, 1925

Our lives are falling apart. Snyder has broken with Gem. He did it in the most degrading way, right out in public, and now the town is buzzing about it. She has fled to the Hardings' estate in the Hamptons. I feel for her and I envy her ability to escape.

Monday, March 2, 1925

Gem has sent me a message. She's still at the Hamptons, feeling alone and humiliated. It isn't just the breakup with Adrian—she says there's no place for her here, with Jameson and me. I'm trying to convince her otherwise, but she doesn't believe me. It's ironic that this miserable marriage to Jameson has brought me closer to Gem. I'm almost ashamed to recall my earlier fears that she would try to take him. True to her word, she has become a loyal friend and ally. The thought of what has happened to her saddens me.

Thursday, March 5, 1925

My health seems to be worsening. Something must be very wrong with me. I'm so tired. I'm ready to collapse. My head throbs continually. The pain is almost unbearable. I seem to have lost my sense of balance and I stumble a lot. I'm afraid of falling and hurting the baby. I'm worried about my bouts of forgetfulness, too. These memory lapses are humiliating. And the dreams. Miserable, shifting images that invade my sleep. Maybe I'm losing my mind. I lay awake at night, the blood pounding in my temples, unable to raise my head from the pillow or even turn it sideways without stabbing pain. The doctors poke and prod but find nothing. Jameson wants me to see a psychologist. I don't want to. I'm not crazy. I know I'm not. I can't be.

That was the final entry, the last words of a voice now stilled. He would have to speak to the living to learn the rest of Lilian's story.

He closed the diary and weighed the little book in his hand. It was so small to contain such misery. He thought of Lilian's letters. What effort it must have cost her to sound cheerful. He recalled how her last letter had asked him to return and how he hadn't answered it. And he gave a long, deep sigh. He'd been so obsessed with his own dilemma that he had never considered, had refused to consider, that she might need him. And this . . . this was the consequence.

13

The Picnic

"Why did you tell me he was a good husband?"

"Because he was."

"Lilian's diary tells a different story."

"Her diary? You found her diary?"

It was late Monday morning and they were sitting in Rachel's living room. Her thin shoulders were hunched and tense under her cheap white cotton shirt. She folded her arms across her chest. He felt a spark of pity for her and quashed it.

"And why didn't you tell me that Lilian was pregnant?"

"Because I ..." Her voice was barely above a whisper. "Well, I wasn't sure. I mean I ... I knew she claimed to be—"

"*Claimed* to be?"

She licked her lips. "Remember, I told you there was a time when Lilian and I didn't see each other?"

He nodded. She took a deep breath.

"Well, there were two times when we did see each other ... two times that ..." She swallowed and looked at him. "David, this is so hard to tell you."

"Just spit it out. Nothing can be worse than what I'm thinking right now."

Something glimmered in her eyes, something hurt. "A year ago, in January, Lilian stopped by. She hadn't spoken to me in ages, but there she was. Pale as a ghost. Said she had to talk. But once she came in, she got quiet. Wouldn't say nothing. I let her be. And I made some coffee. Then the clock struck three. The kids started leaving the school across the street. We could see them through the window, all loud and laughing. Lilian started crying. And then she said she was pregnant."

"Why didn't you tell me before? Neither you nor Annie said anything about Lilian having had a child."

"Well . . . I guess that's because she didn't."

"You mean she *lost* the baby?" A horrible possibility dawned on him. "Did she kill herself because she lost the child?"

An indecipherable glimmer came into Rachel's eyes. Did it reveal sadness, perhaps agony, even a flash of anger? She swallowed and dropped her gaze.

"It would've made sense, wouldn't it? Losing a baby is . . . why, it's unbearable." She gave a little shake of her head. "But no, that's not what happened."

"Then what *did* happen?"

"I don't know," she said thickly.

"How far along was she?"

"She claimed she was in her fourth month, but there still wasn't nothing to see. She said she hadn't been sleeping. She talked a little bit about it being a boy or a girl. And then she said she was scared, that maybe it wouldn't turn out right. I told her a lot of women worry about stuff like that. But the baby almost always turns out fine. She smiled at me, sort of in a sad way. Then she got up to go. She stopped at the door and gave me a hug. She told me that she loved me, but she didn't come by no more."

"But that wasn't the last time you saw her?"

"No." She shook her head. "But it was a while that went by. She'd stopped coming to church, too, you see. For years, she'd come. Every Sunday, rain or shine. But after Gem, everything changed.

"The time came for our church's Fourth of July picnic. Even the blue bloods over in Brooklyn come over for it. Lilian was one of our best organizers. Folks at church were hoping she'd show up just to say hello."

"And did she?"

"Oh . . . she was there all right. Holding a big plate of food when I saw her. She wasn't eating it, though. Just picking at it. Like she needed something to do. She didn't look good. She'd fallen off. Her color was bad. And her belly was as flat as a pancake."

"What?"

"She tried to act like she didn't see me. So I went up to her and asked her about the baby. She turned white—whiter than a bleached sheet. Said she didn't know—didn't *want to* know—what I was talking about. I asked her if she remembered coming by my house that January. And her face changed. It just sort of . . . crumpled. She looked so sad. I asked her if I could do anything for her. And then she gave me this look." Rachel frowned. "This look, David, it was hard to describe. There was hurt . . . and anger . . . and, well . . . disgust—like she thought I was her worst enemy. Then she turned and ran.

She hightailed it out of there so fast you'd have thought the tax man was behind her."

"So she did lose the baby."

"David, don't you get it? When I asked her about visiting me, she really didn't know what I was talking about."

"How is that possible?"

"It's obvious, isn't it?"

"Not to me."

Rachel took a deep breath. Her gaze went out the window, to the school across the street. "Your sister wanted a baby. Wanted it bad. Don't you know what that kind of wanting can do to a woman?"

"Are you saying she *imagined* being pregnant?"

Rachel looked at him. "David, I don't think she killed herself because she lost a baby . . . but because she couldn't have one."

That possibility had never occurred to him. *Could she be right? Was that it?* He sighed. *Was that what brought Lilian down?*

"Now that you know, David, would you please, please leave this alone?"

He licked his lips and took a deep breath. "No."

"David, please—"

"I cannot . . . I will not."

She sagged down onto the sofa and put a hand to her forehead. He sat down next to her. His voice was quiet but penetrating.

"You might be right about the baby and her wanting one so badly. But there was another hand in this. Another reason."

"She got sick. That's all. She was sick and—"

"Yeah. Slit her wrists. I don't buy it."

"What're you saying?"

"I'm saying that all this talk of a mysterious illness makes no sense."

For a moment, she studied him and then her expression changed. She looked as though she were seeing him clearly for the first time. "I almost don't recognize you and that frightens me. All of a sudden, you're not just the grieving brother—you're an avenging angel."

He didn't deny it. "Look, there's something wrong here. I felt it before, but I know it now. And that something has to do with Sweet."

"I told you—Lilian wanted a baby and when it came to Sweet, she wasn't confident—"

"The diary, Rachel. The diary. Lack of confidence wasn't the problem. And I'm betting you know it."

She swallowed.

"Don't worry," he said. "I'm not angry. Not yet."

"What do you want me to say? I know how you feel—"

"You don't know a damn thing about how I feel. I'm riding a roller-coaster through hell. I want to know why it happened."

"You just want to blame somebody."

"Yes, I want to blame somebody."

"But there is no one to blame! Not you, not me. Not Annie, not Sweet. You've got to accept that Lilian did what she did because she had to do it. Something in her *drove* her to it. None of us could've stopped her. Why can't you see that? My God, it'd be better if you'd just stop thinking about it."

"Don't think about it? Hell, I can't think about anything else!"

He jumped up. She grabbed his forearm. He tried to wrench himself away, but she held firm. She stood up, put her arms around him, and laid her face against his chest. He was rigid.

"Please, let this go," she whispered. "Let Lilian rest in peace. Please, please, let her go."

"I wish I could. But I can't, not yet. Not until I prove—"

She looked up at him. "Prove what?"

"That he killed her."

Her eyes widened. "*What?*"

"That Sweet killed her. I know he did and I'm going to prove it."

She looked stunned, bewildered. "No," she breathed, "You can't mean that."

"Oh, but I do."

Her small face paled. She grabbed him and her hands were cold on his wrists. "But why would you think that?"

"They weren't happy—"

"So what! That's no reason to say he killed her."

"He didn't love her, Rachel. I know he didn't. He loved someone else."

She pulled back. "You can't believe that—"

"Gem wanted him. And he must've wanted her. Of course, he denies it, but that's to be expected."

Her sweet face was miserable. "But the police didn't find nothing wrong. Do you think you know more than they do?"

"The police didn't care enough to dig. I do."

They argued. She accused him of being suspicious due to his own sense of guilt. He denied it. She asked him whether he was just being a snob, suspecting Sweet because Sweet was born poor. He denied that, too. Finally, she accused him of being willing to do anything to fully reclaim the house.

"Yes, I want the house back! But that hasn't got a damn thing to do with it!"

"Think about this. Please! Sweet's not just anybody. He's got important friends. Byron Canfield treats him like a son. I'm afraid for you."

"You needn't be."

"But do you have any proof? Any evidence—"

"No—"

"Then why—"

"I have my instincts. And they rarely lie."

Her expression became grave. "My God, David, has your sense of guilt driven you this far? Is the idea of murder actually easier for you to live with than suicide? Murder's ugly enough, but suicide is even uglier, isn't it? Suicide makes you feel guilty. Murder means you can blame someone else." She stroked his cheek. "Oh, I ache with you. But why won't you understand that no one is responsible for Lilian's death? No one."

"*Someone is* responsible. And no, the idea of murder isn't easier than suicide. It amounts to the same thing. My sister's dead when she should be alive. And I refused to come back when she needed me."

Rachel dropped her hand. She stared at him and her eyes were beyond sad. "You're determined to go ahead with this?"

He nodded stubbornly and his eyes narrowed. "Now if you know something, then you'd better tell me."

She turned away, fidgeting with a button on her blouse.

"Turn around, Rachel. Turn around and talk to me."

Slowly, she turned to face him, her expression fearful.

He softened his tone: "Please tell me what you know. Tell me now."

A moment went by. She dropped her eyes. "All right," she whispered. "All right." She wrung her hands. "I knew Sweet was trouble to begin with. He was never no good."

"You *knew* it?" he repeated. "Why the hell didn't you say something to her, warn her?"

"I tried to, but Lilian wouldn't listen. She was lost the minute she met him."

He struggled to keep his mounting anger in check. "So, Lilian's diary told the truth. He never loved her."

"No." In the face of his furious stare, she squared her fragile shoulders. Folding her arms across her chest, she hugged herself. "Look David, Lilian was a grown woman. She made her own decisions—and her own mistakes. Eventually, like all of us, she came to regret some of them."

He looked at her, stunned, and his anger exploded. "How dare you! Who're we talking about here? You or Lilian? Let me tell you something, baby, you're not the first woman who's been left and you won't be the last. Now, I'm sorry I hurt you, but that doesn't mean I'll take you lying to me."

She looked as though she'd been slapped. "Get out," she said. "Get out!" She took a step toward him, her hands balled into fists, and screamed. *"Get outta my house! Get outta my life! GET OUT!"*

"Gladly," he said and left.

14

As Thick as Thieves

He'd never intended to have a fight with Rachel, but she'd gone too far—lying to him like that. She'd known Sweet was trouble—had known it all along and lied to him. What the hell had she been thinking?

He forced himself to take a deep breath. He needed to think clearly. Anger would only muddy the waters. He forced his thoughts in another direction. Back to the diary. What else had he learned from it? He'd learned that for Gem, the return to Harlem had been a misadventure.

He'd never spent much thought on Gem or considered the possibility that she could be in emotional pain. She'd been arrogant and overconfident, and then she'd been brought low. He found it ironic that Gem, who had felt so lonely abroad, had come to feel even more so at home. But her alienation from home was a foreseeable consequence of her years abroad. The trust that she had developed with Lilian still surprised him, although after reading the diary, he found it more tenable. A sense of failed dreams ran like a common thread between the twin sisters. Perhaps it was this shared disappointment in the world that had provided a basis for mutual understanding and helped them to reconcile. But if their reconciliation had been real, and they had learned to value one another, then again: Why Gem's silence?

"The story of Miss Lilian is the story of Miss Gem . . ."

Isn't that what Annie had said?

It occurred to him that he needed to know more about Gem, about what she'd been up to while she was in New York. He thought of Nella. She had offered to speak to him, not about Lilian, whom she claimed to have hardly known, but about Gem. Nella was a gossip, but an observant one. Despite her propensity for mixing dull fact with spicy fiction, much of what she could tell him would probably be true.

Yes . . . Nella was the next one to see.

•   •   ◦

Nella's Fifth Avenue living room was a lively combination of purple, rasp-berry, and turquoise fabrics used generously for weighty curtains and uphol-stered fat chairs. A Venetian glass chandelier hung from the ceiling, vases of calla lilies decked tables, and Oriental rugs covered the floors. Her desk near the window was a controlled chaos of glass paperweights, silver dolphins, and porcelain tigers. She greeted David's unexpected visit warmly.

"I thought you were leaving."

"I've decided to stay a while."

"Why?"

"I have my reasons."

She chuckled at his evasiveness and promptly had her maid make him a highball, to get him in "the right mood," she said. He decided not to ask her what she meant. He did, however, choose to sit in a narrow armchair a safe distance away from her, rather than join her on her couch. He sunk into the armchair, feeling claustrophobic and cramped, while she stretched out on her sofa, obviously hung over. She sipped her drink, laid her head back on a lace-covered pillow, and closed her eyes.

"I do love liquor," she sighed. "There are few things finer in the world than a good drink." After a moment, she opened her eyes and stripped him with a lustful gaze. Then she noticed that his highball was untouched. "Don't you drink?"

"I prefer wine."

She raised an eyebrow. "How very, very cultured of you."

He chose to ignore both the mockery in her tone and the desire in her eyes. "Did you know Gem in Europe?"

She needed a moment to shift mental gears. "No," she said finally. "I met her here. She came to see me." She paused, remembering. "I found her utterly marvelous. Full of primitive spirit. She was perfect for my villa gath-erings. She has that rare gift, you know: the ability to do nothing—and to do it with style. She's a woman of unbelievable conceit, but you forgive her for it because she's so full of life. I actually think I miss her."

She sat up and reached for a gold cigarette case on the marble coffee table before her. Pearls and emeralds had been worked together to give the case an intricate, eye-catching pattern.

"An original by Cartier," she informed him.

He waited while she fitted a twelve-inch gold-tipped filter to her cigarette, then held a light for her. She was smoking Chesterfields, he noted. Strong stuff.

"Does my smoking offend you?" she asked. "Do you think it improper for a lady to smoke?"

He smiled neutrally. "I don't mind."

"How very liberal of you." Her smile was saucy and her eyes impish. "Smoking is relaxing, David. Would you like to try it? Would you like to *smoke* with me?"

His eyes met hers. "No, thank you. Some habits I prefer not to develop."

He hoped she wouldn't press him. She didn't. Her eyes teased him, but she said nothing. She merely shrugged, sighed with theatrical regret, and took a drag on her cigarette.

"I was curious about Gem, wanted to know all about her. She'd been in Europe, she said. Seeing this person, visiting that one. She laughed, saying she didn't have a memory for details. I told her I had a feeling that her memory was excellent, simply highly selective. She didn't like that."

"Did she say why she'd come back?"

"I found out for myself. Like any lovely girl, she'd had several European sponsors. Her first was a Scandinavian cultural attaché in London. Her last was a Portuguese count—or claimed to be. He actually married her."

This bit of news was unexpected. The twinge of pride he felt was even more so. His sister, a girl from Harlem, had married a Portuguese nobleman.

"You sound surprised that someone would marry her," he said.

"I'm surprised that *he* did. Gem is a beautiful woman. But beautiful women are a dime a dozen in Europe. And usually these old fogies have nothing more in mind than fun."

"I suppose he loved her."

"Apparently, he did. He bought her a villa near Lisbon, and then conveniently died. His will was generous. Gem's life would've been set. But the children from his first marriage contested the will."

"And Gem ended up with nothing."

Nella smiled at him languidly. She sucked on her Chesterfield. Lazy puffs of smoke encircled her words. "Do you know why I like Gem?"

"Because she plays the exotic."

"Because she insists upon being herself. And she isn't a complainer. Despite setbacks, and she's had several, Gem still believes that the world is a nice place to live in. How many Negro woman see it that way?"

"Very few. But then, not many have always found someone else to pay their way."

Nella was amused. "You don't like Gem, do you? She said you didn't."

"Did she? Well, but you like her. That's what's important. You two spent time together."

"Yes, we did." Nella arranged herself more comfortably. "In the short time Gem was here, she set a new standard for beauty. She had a permanent table at Barron's. Only the best people go there. You and I should try it."

"I won't have time."

She tilted her head and regarded him. "You're like Lilian, aren't you? A bit prim?"

"I thought you said you didn't know her."

"Touché." She smiled. "I'm trying hard to provoke you. Why won't you let me?"

"Because I'm here to discuss my sisters, not me."

"But I think you're fascinating, David. You remind me of Gem."

David raised an eyebrow.

"I never knew what would happen with her," Nella explained. "Like you, she came and went as she pleased. And she never let anyone get to her. One night, we all decided to go to some downtown restaurant—Gem, Adrian, Nikki, and I. My chauffeur had the night off and the men didn't want to drive, so we all piled into a taxi. The cabby took one look at Gem and said he couldn't take Negroes. Gem said she didn't blame him. *She* couldn't take them either. Then she told him to put his foot to the pedal and drive. *Please.*"

David cracked a smile. Nella laughed merrily. She described how she and Gem had gone around together, dragging Nikki and Snyder in tow. The women loved to visit dance halls like the Renaissance Ballroom or the Rockland Palace, but they rarely danced. She and Gem stayed at their table, observing the others. The Charleston and the Black Bottom were all the rage then. The dancers could be wild, providing spectators with great entertainment.

"We went to Small's one night with Winston Charles, the playwright, you know. The music was copacetic. And those waiters! They're a show in themselves. Twirling their trays on their fingertips! Marvelous! Winston was so taken with the place that he tried to dance on our table. Smashed several glasses. Nearly broke his neck."

Nella and Gem shared several characteristics, thought David, *including a desire to watch and witness human foible, all the while remaining utterly blind to their own.* He could imagine Nella and Gem as thick as thieves, but it was nearly impossible to see Lilian in this same scenario. Now he thought he understood why Nella said she'd known Gem better. But why had Lilian pretended that it was she who was friends with the Hardings—when even in her diary she had confessed that she disliked them?

"Tell me more about when Gem first arrived."

"Well . . . she was short on funds. She was too proud to ask me for help and, naturally, she wouldn't approach Lilian. So I introduced her to Adrian, that marvelous man—"

"You're the one who introduced her to Snyder? How could you—"

"He's the perfect sugar daddy."

"He's dangerous."

"He treated her like an empress—"

"He dumped her."

"But he loved her dearly. It's just that Adrian's not the marrying type."

"Why didn't you tell her?"

"I assumed she knew. Everyone else did." Nella was darkly amused. "Come, come. Admit it, you're relieved. You wouldn't want your sister married to a West Indian."

"I wouldn't want her married to a racketeer."

"Well, then."

"Was he was the reason she left town?"

"It wasn't quite right, the way he did it. Still, I was surprised that Gem took it so hard. She wasn't heartbroken, you know. Just humiliated. They'd become quite the couple around town. Everyone knew them. She tried to say she'd left him, but no one believed her." Nella ground out her Chesterfield. She exhaled one last stream of smoke. "I don't think she loved him at all."

"That's not the point."

"The point, my dear, is that she used him as much as he used her. And I don't think he was the only reason she left New York. He was a front."

"For what?"

"It was more for *whom*."

"She loved someone else?"

"I never did find out who. She laughed when I asked her about it."

"Could it have been Lilian's husband?"

Nella laughed. "Jameson Sweet?"

"Did she love him?"

"No, she loathed him, absolutely hated Jameson Sweet. Apparently, he tried to seduce her in the parlor one day, but she'd have none of it. She said he was mad for her. She couldn't be in the same room with him. His eyes were always on her."

So this was Gem's version of events. David repressed a grim smile. It did not surprise him that Gem would have reversed the roles; it did surprise him that Nella, who seemed so astute, would have believed her. But then, why not? Gem was an attractive woman. It was easy to believe that all men would find her appealing. He himself was having a hard time believing that Sweet had continued to resist Gem's charms. It occurred to him to ask Nella about Sweet and she told him what she knew. This turned out to be quite a bit.

"Jameson Sweet is an impressive character. Extremely arrogant, but he's earned the right to be. His given name is Jimmy. He elevated himself to Jameson later on. An only child, his family was dirt-poor. They're from Virginia. His parents never finished school. Had no education to speak of. His father worked on the railroad, was away all the time. The mother took in wash. They were very proud people, clean, stable. They scrimped and saved to send him to school. Sweet himself has worked like a dog since he was a child. He's a dedicated civil rights attorney, determined to make a difference. By all accounts he has a brilliant future. He's sharp, cutthroat, and tough as nails."

"Sounds good."

Nella raised an eyebrow . . . and smiled. "Don't worry. He isn't perfect, dear. He doesn't hold a candle to you—not where it counts." She frisked him with her eyes again and sighed a sigh that came from her very core. David ignored it.

"What's his Achilles heel?"

"Come now, what do you think?"

"Money."

She nodded to compliment him. "Sweet's drawn to the lush life, but he's acutely aware of the handicap of his color. He knew he could never have earned it on his own. Privately, when it comes to women, Sweet has an appetite for dark chocolate. But he never let that stop him. He went through a succession of wealthy female friends, sometimes discreetly crossing the color line . . . before he found Lilian."

She watched him as she said this, but he knew his face expressed nothing. Lawyers learn fast to conceal their reactions. Inwardly, of course, his emotions were chaotic. She was confirming what he'd supposed. That relieved him; it also worried him. Having his suspicions about Sweet's character only increased his sense of urgency. He had to find proof of Sweet's guilt and find it quickly.

Then, there was the matter of Nella herself. Her ability to ferret out information both impressed and appalled him. After grinding out her last cigarette, she had immediately taken out another. He held her lighter for her.

"So what happened after Gem's breakup with Snyder?"

She leaned back and stretched out. "Gem came to me, desperate for a place to hunker down until the uproar over the breakup blew over. She felt that everyone was talking about her. I assured her it really wasn't quite that bad, but Gem is certain the world revolves around her. She wanted to use our house in the Hamptons. It's quiet there, very peaceful and beautiful. The perfect setting for a lovely woman who wants to withdraw from the world."

She exhaled and streams of smoke flowed out of her narrow nostrils. Then she rounded her lips and blew. A smoke ring emerged and floated upward. "That was the last time I saw her. I'm not even sure she stayed at the house a full two weeks. After about eight days, I received a note, saying she'd decided to catch a boat back to Europe. By the time the note arrived, she was gone. Left without even dropping by to see me." Nella actually sounded injured.

"Who gave her the money to leave?"

"I haven't a clue. Maybe she sold some of that marvelous jewelry Adrian gave her."

Nella sat up and ground the smoking cigarette into an ashtray. Standing up, she walked over to her window. David joined her. She had a captivating view of Central Park and lower Manhattan. Together, they looked down on Fifth Avenue. A mixture of cars and carriages snaked down the avenue. It was an impressive vista, but he didn't really see it. His thoughts were of Gem and Paris. The City of Light seemed unreal and unimaginably distant. What was she doing over there, so far away?

"Perhaps it was neither Jameson nor Adrian that caused her to leave," said Nella. "Gem was born with wings on her feet. Not even she knows what she's searching for. But she *is* determined to have a good time finding it."

Yes, that sounded like Gem. She had never had time to stop in any one place for too long. She'd been running, running, for years. But then, David caught himself, he was a runner, too.

"I haven't heard much from Gem since she went away," Nella said. "I used to get the occasional postcard, but they stopped a while ago. They always said essentially the same thing: that she's going to hell in a basket, and loving every minute of it."

She turned to him and her eyes searched his. "You come here and dredge up memories . . . Why, you've almost managed to make me sad."

She moved closer to him. Her perfume, a rich heavy musk, filled his nostrils. Then her fingertips were on his crotch, stroking the bulge in his pants. She massaged him and he felt the warmth of her hand even through the material. He looked down at her working hand; then back up at her. There was no mistaking the question in her eyes. And no mistaking the answer in his.

"What's the matter, Nella? Nikki been away too long?"

"We made a deal. Remember?"

He took her hand by the wrist and moved it away. She yielded with good humor, but raised a warning finger. "I'll let you slide—this time. But the next time you want answers, be prepared to pay on delivery. And the bill's still open for what I've told you so far." She raised an eyebrow. "With interest."

Upon leaving, he crossed Fifth Avenue and started walking uptown. It was frosty that day, yet many people were out: black nurses wheeling along their young white charges, chauffeurs walking pampered poodles. David intended to go home and get something to eat. Every now and then he had the odd sensation that something had cracked inside him. He could feel pain in his bones. In his fingertips. He wondered how Rachel could accept Lilian's suicide so easily and be so ready to move on. She did not seem concerned with the why of it. Perhaps it was because she was a nurse: She had learned to deal with death on a daily basis. He wished bitterly that he could be like her.

His thoughts returned to Gem.

She had lived the busy, madcap life in Paris. She had tried to settle down with the unlikely figure of a Portuguese nobleman, but fate had been against her. Stripped of her status and wealth, Gem had returned to New York. She had hoped to squeeze money out of Lilian, but had run into the obstacle of a husband. She had tried to seduce him, but that had failed, too. Then she had shifted in an unexpected direction. After having tried to destroy Lilian's marriage, Gem had ostensibly tried to shore it up: She had helped Lilian improve her appearance and found herself another man. Why?

Nella confirmed that Gem was penniless when she arrived, but she was unsure where Gem had gotten the money to leave. Nella also verified that Gem left after her liaison with Adrian Snyder collapsed. Yet she believed that Gem's departure was unrelated to her failed affair. She was convinced that Gem loved someone else, a Mr. X. But who could he have been? If Gem wasn't in love with Snyder, then it must have been Sweet.

Nella was adamant that Gem hated Sweet. She believed Gem's version of what had happened in the parlor that day. But David knew better. Gem had reversed the roles. Nella had been astute enough to sense that Gem loved someone, but not enough to see through Gem's ability to rewrite history.

David's forehead creased with thought.

Sweet was undeniably the type of man Gem was drawn to. And he had rejected her. That would have only served to boost her desire for him.

The creases deepened.

Hell hath no fury like a woman scorned: a particularly apt saying when applied to Gem. Yet she had apparently swallowed Sweet's rejection. She had done nothing more than publicly humiliate Lilian and rewrite the tale to favor herself. Given Gem's ruthless nature, David would have expected her to mount an all-out campaign to bring Sweet either to her bed or to his knees—or both. That she had done so much less—in fact, done nothing—puzzled him.

Gem had been accepting when he would have expected her to fight. She had swallowed rejection by two men, then simply fled town. Unthinkable.

And Lilian, dear Lilian, had acted totally out of character, too. She had rejected the intellectuals and artists whose respect she had worked so hard to attain, then befriended a woman she would have normally disdained. She had gone out smoking and drinking, then tried to fire Annie, a servant she loved. She had told Rachel she was pregnant, but instead of being happy, she had cried. Then she had repressed the memory—or pretended to—when she saw Rachel at the church picnic. But whether she had truly forgotten her claim or pretended to, she was not pregnant last July. So she had either lost the baby or, despite her claim of the doctor's confirmation, never been pregnant to begin with.

Annie, Rachel, and Nella: Speaking to them had produced more questions than answers. David ran his fingers through his hair distractedly. He was so deep in thought that he barely noticed when a black Lincoln pulled up alongside him. He was oblivious to the hidden hands that drew aside a dark curtain inside the car window and slightly rolled down the window itself. When he finally did look down, it was into the muzzle of a gun.

15

An Outsider Among Outsiders

"Get in."

David felt a rush of fear that sent his pulse racing. He sensed the blood drain from his brain and with it, his ability to think. His first impulse was to run, but his legs were as immobile as lead. His eyes darted over the street in an automatic search for help. There were plenty of people, but—

"If you make a move, I'll blow you away."

The window had been rolled down enough for him to see the speaker, or at least to see his eyes. That wasn't much, but it was enough to convince him that the man meant business.

He got in.

They blindfolded him and took him on a long, swerving drive. If the purpose of the whole exercise was to disorient him, it succeeded. Blind instinct told him that in forty minutes of driving, they hadn't traveled forty minutes' worth of distance, but he couldn't be sure. In fact, he decided he didn't want to know. If his safety depended on a certain degree of ignorance, he was willing to play along.

Once at his destination, he was led to a room that smelled of sandalwood. Perfumed hands removed the blindfold. The hands belonged to a lovely woman who smiled at him, then vanished. His eyes went to his host, who sat behind a large, handsome desk, sipping bootlegged brandy and smoking a cigar.

"There was no need to kidnap me," said David.

"Sorry," said Snyder. "Sometimes the boys get a little eager."

"Why did you want to see me?"

Snyder shrugged eloquently. "Curiosity, partly. Gem would never say much about her family. Naturally, that kindled my interest." He gestured toward an armchair. "Sit down."

"I would rather stand."

"As you will. A drink?"

"No, thank you."

David took in the room's spare Danish furnishings, the eclectic mixture of thirteenth-century Flemish and modern West Indian art on its walls. Two walls were lined with shelves of books. There were bound volumes of United States history, Virgin Island history, Danish history, German philosophy, and Western economic thought. His gaze went back to his host. This was a man who could effortlessly order another man's death, but he saw no immediate aggression in Snyder's black eyes: they were cold, yes, and watchful, but thoughtful, too. His rimless spectacles made him look more like a banker than a numbers king. He exuded the assurance of the self-made man and the charisma of one who knows how to build a following. He was a mobster, but intelligent, educated, and cultured. That, David would grant him.

Snyder rose from behind his desk and went to the leather conference chairs arranged in one corner. He gestured toward one of the matching chairs.

"We have to talk. Please, sit down."

David acquiesced. Snyder pressed a button. Another attractive young woman appeared with a tray of two fresh brandy glasses. Snyder urged one on David.

"By the way, you shouldn't be angry at Nella for having introduced me to Gem."

David was surprised at Adrian's bluntness, but he appreciated it. "She meant well, I'm sure, but—"

"There's always that 'but' with you dicties, isn't there?"

"I don't care about your being West Indian. I do care about your . . . business connections."

"That would concern someone like you."

David blinked. *Someone like you.* The phrase struck him as familiar but he was unable to place it. After a moment, he shoved the matter to the edge of his mind, where it hovered briefly before fading away.

"I enjoyed Gem's company very much," Snyder was saying. "I never intended for it to end that way."

"Then why did you break up with her?"

Snyder hesitated.

"Why did you *humiliate* her?" David pressed.

Snyder's dark eyebrows hovered like storm clouds over his face. "Because . . . she asked me to."

David's eyes narrowed.

"We were a scandal to respectable Harlem," Snyder said. "She always said she didn't care. But when I asked her to marry me, she said no."

"Because you're West Indian?"

"She said that had nothing to do with it. And I believed her."

"Why?"

"Because she said she wanted people to think that *I* had dropped *her*. She wanted a breakup and she wanted it big."

"But she couldn't have wanted you to publicly humiliate her."

"She *did*. She said she wanted to give the folks something to remember her by."

David gave Snyder a long, keen look. "Was there someone else?"

Snyder paused, the merest fraction of a second. "I would've known."

"Why else would she break up with you?"

"I don't know." A hurt look flitted across his face. "She laughed. She kissed me, and asked me to leave her. I thought it was a joke. But about a week later—we were at Barron's—she pitched a fit. The world was there. Everybody who was *any*body at the jump that night knew what was going on. She cried. She screamed. I had to play along."

"She left town after that?"

"Didn't even say good-bye."

"So you didn't give her the money to go?"

Snyder looked surprised at the question, and thoughtful. "No, actually not. Of course, I used to give her change, but she always spent it—"

"Then how could she afford passage? Nella told me that Gem was broke. You say you didn't give her the money. Well, someone had to."

Snyder took a swallow of his brandy. "You think she was two-timing me?"

"I think there are a lot of questions that need answering."

"I hope you believe I've told you the truth."

"Yes," David nodded. "I do. Gem's the kind of woman who does the leaving, not the type who's left. I'm not wondering whether you've told me the truth—but *why* you've told me. Not many men want it known that a woman left *them*."

"I'm not telling the world. I'm telling you."

"Again, why?"

"I thought you'd be glad to know."

"I am. But why should you care? You don't know me from Adam. So why would you want to do me favors? Why would you give a rat's ass what I think?"

Snyder didn't answer.

David studied him. He believed him, but he didn't trust him. "Did you ever meet Lilian?"

"A couple of times, when I was out at the house."

"And?"

"She was one of the most sensible women I've ever met. Not my type. Not that it matters." He paused. "What does matter, if I may say so, is that she wasn't the type her husband would go for either."

David's eyes met Snyder's. "Was Gem?"

"Yes," said Snyder reluctantly. "She was."

"And did Gem like Sweet?"

"She had absolutely no interest in him."

"Are you sure?"

"Very. Gem knew I wouldn't have tolerated two-timing."

David raised an eyebrow. Why should Gem care what Snyder would tolerate when she planned to break up with him? Surely, he saw that.

"Okay, let's be frank. You brought me here for a reason. And you told me the truth about your breakup—for a reason. You want me to find out what went wrong between you and Gem. Isn't that what this is all about?"

"I want to know what happened. It sounds crazy, but I can't get her out of my mind." Snyder leaned forward. "Tell me, have you heard from her? Why isn't she here?"

"Because she doesn't want to be."

"Did she write and say that?"

"She didn't have to."

Snyder's well-clad shoulders sagged. He picked up his glass of brandy and swirled the amber liquid, gazing into it. When he looked up, his eyes held a strange light.

"What's your story, McKay?"

"Does it matter?"

"You tell me. You've been gone for years. Now, you're suddenly back. You claim you've been working for the Movement, but nobody there can place you. No one knows who you are anymore."

"It's better that way."

"Everyone's talking."

"Let them."

Snyder smiled. "You don't plan on staying long, do you?"

"No."

David downed his brandy, set his glass on the table, and stood up. Snyder accompanied him to the door. He signaled to his man.

"Make sure he gets home." Snyder turned back to David. "I can understand why Gem doesn't like you. But *I* like you. Let's just say that I know what it's like to be an outsider among outsiders. If you should decide to stay, or ever need help, my door is always open to you."

Adrian Snyder, a murderer and crime boss, a man with whom respectable Harlem refused to associate, offered David his hand in brotherhood. And David, thinking of the odd code of honor that sometimes *does* exist among thieves, accepted it.

Snyder's men again blindfolded David and this time drove him home. Along the way, he reflected on what Snyder had said. Snyder's claim that it was Gem who left him was surprising, but the more David thought about it, the more it made sense. At least, it fit her personality. So much of what people had been telling him didn't. Gem was quick to leave a man—as soon as she found another.

So she must have had another sugar daddy waiting in the wings. Who else, if not Sweet? Some Mr. X with no face and no name? Possibly, but unlikely. If Gem had snagged a bigger fish than Snyder, then she wouldn't have hidden it. She sure wouldn't have gone to the trouble of making herself look bad.

So why had she done it?

He couldn't figure it. Leaving a man was one thing. But pretending to the world that he'd left her—that was another. Snyder saying that Gem had done that was like claiming he'd seen an elephant fly.

The problem was, David believed him. At least, he thought he did. He didn't know what to believe anymore. The more questions he asked, the more half-truths he heard. And the less he knew what to believe. It seemed as though everybody was either lying to him or holding back: Lilian never saying a word about getting married or Gem returning; Annie, who must've known, keeping mum about Lilian's pregnancy, real or unreal; and Rachel canonizing a devil like Sweet. He hated to think that the only people who had told him the truth—the full truth, as they knew it—were Nella and Snyder, a white woman and an island man. By everything he'd been taught, they were the kind of people you disbelieved on principle.

No, it didn't make sense that Gem would leave a man like Snyder for nothing and nobody. There was another player in that scene.

And it had to be Sweet; it had to be.

David could never accept that Gem had given up so quickly. She'd just hooked up with Snyder and strung him along until she landed Sweet.

But that didn't explain why she wanted a public breakup.

Gem said she wanted to give the folks something "to remember" her by.

That sounded like a good-bye—not just to Snyder, but to everybody. Like she was already planning on leaving town . . .

But why would she, when she planned on staying with Sweet? Or were they supposed to leave town together? Did something go wrong there?

No, that didn't make sense either. Why would Sweet give up his career and a nice setup like Strivers' Row?

Of course, men were known to give up even more for a woman, but . . .

Maybe he backed out at the last minute. Maybe he gave her the money to leave.

Or maybe it really wasn't Sweet after all—

But then, damn, who could it have been?

16

Clarifications

Early Tuesday, David went to see the family physician. Dr. Steve Johnson had delivered David and his sisters. Known to them as "Dr. Steve," he was short, chubby, and dapper. He had a habit of looking at patients over the top of his glasses. When David was a child, Dr. Steve's dark, merry eyes had reminded him of Santa Claus.

"I heard you were back," said Dr. Steve. He shook David's hand and offered him a seat. "It's good to see you. I'm so sorry about Lilian."

"It was a shock."

"I can imagine."

"I want to know what caused it. Did you see her during that last illness?"

"No," Dr. Steve shook his head. "No, I didn't. The last time I saw her was more than a year ago. She was pregnant and fairly healthy."

"Pregnant?" David felt his stomach tighten. "How far along was she?"

"In her third month."

"Was it a normal pregnancy?"

"Up to that point, it certainly was. But I never heard from her again, so I don't know how the rest of it went. It broke my heart to read about her dying like that. Odd, how the papers didn't mention a surviving child. What did she have? A boy or a girl?"

David paused. "There was no child."

Dr. Steve looked at him with disbelief. "But that's impossible. Was there a miscarriage?"

"Not that I know of."

Dr. Steve cleared his throat uncomfortably. Abortion was unmentionable.

"Well, then I don't understand."

"Neither do I," said David. "Neither do I."

David returned home. So Lilian *had* been pregnant . . . but there was no baby. Only a couple of explanations were possible. She wouldn't have had an abortion, because she wanted the child. Not unless she told Sweet and he forced her to it. David felt sick with anger at the thought of her in some filthy room with a back-alley cutter. But in all fairness, he couldn't accuse Sweet of that. Not yet.

According to Lilian's diary, she'd never even told Sweet about the pregnancy. Perhaps she'd had a miscarriage. But if so, then surely she couldn't have kept it a secret. Sweet would've learned about it. But if he *had* known, then he would've mentioned it—wouldn't he? He would've had no reason not to. On the other hand, Annie had said nothing. And she must've known. She must've.

But had she?

It occurred to him that he'd assumed that Annie knew. He went looking for her and found her in the kitchen. She was wiping down the top of the stove, humming to herself. She stopped when she looked up and saw his expression.

"What's the matter?"

"Did you know that Lilian was pregnant?"

Annie moaned. At the sound, David felt his temper rise. He fought to keep his voice steady.

"So you did know. And you said nothing to me?"

Annie looked away. "How'd you find out?"

"Her diary. And Dr. Steve just confirmed it. Why didn't you tell me?"

"I didn't know what t'say. Truth is, she never said nothin' t'me. I caught her being sick in the bathroom. And she was tired all the time. I guessed what was goin' on. And I tried t'help her, but there wasn't much I could do."

"But the baby . . . She didn't have it, did she?"

"No, she didn't. And I don't know why . . . I don't know what happened. One week she was sick ev'ry day. The next, she was fine. Just like that. Months went by. There was no baby. No nothin'. She never mentioned it no more."

"And you didn't ask her?"

She gave him a strange look. "I had a feelin' it'd be better not to. I had a feelin' . . . it was too late."

He felt a terrible disquiet. "What does that mean?"

"I don't know, Mr. David. I just had the feelin' that whatever was gonna happen had happened, that it was, well . . . over and done with."

It was a strange answer, one more intuitive than rational, one that chilled him. He started to ask her more but then stopped. She'd said exactly what she meant. She didn't know how to say more.

So he asked another question, on another subject, and framed it carefully.

"After that scene in the parlor, are you sure you didn't notice any particular . . . closeness . . . between Miss Gem and Mr. Jameson?"

"No," she shook her head. "Definitely not. There weren't no closeness b'tween them two. Miss Gem certainly had an affection for Mr. Jameson. She sure did. But that man didn't care nothin' for her. He was polite, but cool."

He felt he could trust Annie's observations in most instances, but this time he was unsure. Sweet would have taken great pains to hide his feelings for Gem, especially from Annie.

"He says he was in Newark that weekend . . ."

"That's right. Mr. Jameson said he had a conference. He *said* he'd be gone 'til Mond'y. He left Thursd'y. When he come back, Miss Lilian was already gone." She gave him a shrewd look. "Now, there ain't no way anybody *reason'ble* would say Mr. Jameson had anythin t'do with it. But . . ."

"Annie, you've never liked Mr. Jameson, have you?"

She hesitated. "Mr. David, you know I'm not one t'judge people. But I distrusted that man the moment he walked in the door. It was how he looked at the house. He stared so hard. At the furniture, the silverware, even the paintin's on the walls. I couldn't understand why Miss Rachel put that man in Miss Lilian's path. There was greed in his face. Greed. Just like the moneychangers Our Lord Jesus threw outta the Temple."

"Do you remember . . . the name of the hotel Mr. Jameson stayed at that weekend?"

She squinted, trying to recall. "The Newfield, I think." She nodded. "Yes, it was, the Newfield."

"And where's Mr. Jameson now?"

"He done left for work already. But he'll be back later."

He needed to talk to Sweet. But maybe he could use the fact that Sweet wasn't home to his advantage. Leaving Annie, David went to his father's office door, put his hand on the knob, and turned. Naturally, it resisted, but this time, he expected it to. With a little effort, he could pick the lock. And a little while later, he did.

"What'd you say the name of that hotel was?" the driver asked.

"The Newfield," said David.

The cabbie nodded. "Okay."

It was twenty minutes later. The break into Sweet's office had yielded results, but not the results David expected. Now he was out looking to check Sweet's alibi.

The hotel was a modest but attractive establishment. The woman behind the counter was polite but uncooperative. She refused to confirm or deny that Jameson Sweet had had a reservation at the hotel on the night David mentioned.

"We respect our guests' confidentiality."

"Listen, his wife died that night and I'm her brother. I just want to make sure he was where he said he was."

The woman's eyes became knowing. She looked to be in her mid-fifties, plump and gossipy. "You mean, you think he was stepping out on her?"

"I don't know what to think. That's the problem. All we know is that she's gone and there's a question . . ."

The woman nodded. "My baby girl had a cheating husband. It was terrible." She looked at David. "Look, I've got to go in the back for a second to check on something. People think I've got eyes in the back of my head, but I'll tell you a secret: I don't. So I won't have no idea of what you're up to while I'm gone. Just make sure you've cleared out before I get back. You hear?"

"Thank you."

With a wink, she turned her broad back to him and bustled into the back office. David spun the register book around and flipped the pages back for several weeks. He found Sweet's signature for the weekend that Lilian died. David scanned the room numbers and saw that Sweet had shared a room with another Movement official, Charlie Epps. David quickly copied Epps's name and address.

He took the hired car back to Manhattan and found Epps's building on 145th Street. It was midday. There was a small chance that Epps had come home for lunch. David rang the doorbell and waited. No reply. He rang again, long and loud, and waited. Still, no reply.

Disappointed, he turned away and went down the two steps leading to the street, then headed home.

17

Speaking of Secrets

Annie met him at the front door. "Mr. Jameson's back. He's sitting in the parlor."

"Good," said David. "I want to talk to him."

Sweet sat on Augustus's throne, reading a best-seller, *The Man Nobody Knows* by Bruce Barton. He glanced up when David entered and gave him a slight nod. David leaned against the fireplace mantel. "So, Sweet," he said casually, "did you know that Lilian believed she was pregnant last year?"

Sweet looked up. He appeared to be stunned. *"What?"*

"Lilian told Rachel she was expecting a child."

"That's impossible. Lilian never said anything to me about it."

"Maybe she was afraid to."

"Why? I would've been thrilled." He stared at David and then shook his head. "No, there was no pregnancy. There couldn't have been." He spoke more to himself than to David and his tone held the urgency of a man who was trying to convince himself more than another. "A pregnancy," he muttered. "That can't be true."

"How can you be so sure?"

He looked at David with resentment. "She would've told me. I was her husband."

"Yes, you were . . . weren't you?"

"What do you mean by that?"

"Just how well did you get to know Gem?"

Sweet's dark eyes took on a hard glint. "Not so well."

"How well?"

"Not as well as you seem to want to imply."

"Gem is a stunning woman—"

"But obvious. It was easy to see what she was after."

"And did you give her . . . what she was after?"

Sweet snickered. "Your train is running on the wrong track."

Annie came in with a coffee tray. David asked about Gem's absence.

"Strange that she hasn't responded to word of Lilian's death. I heard that they became close."

Sweet was quiet for a moment, then he laid his book aside.

"As far as I know, they *did* become close. Lilian told me she was receiving regular news from Gem."

"Letters?"

"Postcards."

"I'd like to see them, if you don't mind."

Sweet hesitated. *Did he burn them, too?* David wondered.

"Of course you may see them," said Sweet with glacial politeness. "But I'm not sure where they are. I'm not even sure she kept them."

Annie spoke up. "I b'lieve she did. Miss Lilian used to always read 'em at the desk in the library. She had a special drawer she liked t'put 'em in. I can fetch 'em if you like."

Sweet smiled thinly. "That's all right. I'm sure I can find them."

David accompanied Sweet to the library. Sweet went to the desk, pulled out one shallow side drawer. "Ah, here they are." He removed a small stack of postcards held together by a pink ribbon, handed them to David, then walked a little distance away. David sorted through the cards, then slapped the little packet against his palm. He ran a speculative eye over Sweet.

"Gem didn't write these cards. She has a lovely script. She's very vain about it. Whoever wrote these cards is barely literate."

"Lilian said these cards came from Gem. If Gem didn't write them, I don't know who did."

David looked down at the packet of cards. "When did they start coming?"

"About a month after Gem left. Look, McKay, Lilian had many secrets. Now she's gone and she took them with her. And I, for one, am glad to let them be."

"Are you?"

"I said I am."

"Well, I'm not."

A tic leapt near Sweet's right eye.

"Speaking of secrets," said David, "I've come across Lilian's diary."

"Her diary?" Sweet repeated tonelessly.

"It adds a whole new perspective to things."

"How interesting. Perhaps you'll let me look at it."

"Put it like this: When the time is right, I'll be sure to tell you what I've gotten from it."

David went upstairs to his room and gathered several handkerchiefs. Then he went to Lilian's room and headed for her private bathroom. There were shelves and a small medicine chest. The shelves carried only bath soaps and beauty ointments. He turned to the wooden medicine chest and opened it. Nothing. It was bare.

He's cleaned it out, thought David. *There was something in there he didn't want anyone to see.*

A hand touched his shoulder and he jumped. Then he saw that it was just Annie.

"Good grief," he said. "What're you doing here?"

"'Scuse me, Mr. David. Didn't mean to scare you." She nodded toward the medicine chest. "He emptied ev'rythin' outta there soon as the police left, the day she died."

David sighed. She put a hand on his wrist. He looked up and she crooked a finger, as if to say, Follow me.

Fifteen minutes later, he had thrown on his coat and set out for Seventh Avenue. His long muscular legs covered the distance quickly. Soon, he was standing before the Renaissance Pharmacy on the corner of 138th and Seventh. He shoved open the swinging glass doors and headed for the prescription counter. He had to wait until the pharmacist finished with a couple of elderly customers. Then he told the druggist what he wanted. The pharmacist did not comment. He simply extended his hand. David turned over a small bottle. He was told to come back on Thursday. The information he had requested would be waiting for him. David headed home, thinking about the other discovery he'd made that day, the one in his father's office.

18

Lyrics of a Blackbird

Lilian had started writing when she was ten. She'd kept a diary even then. The contents of her journal she'd kept secret, of course. But her poetry and short stories she'd shared. Sometimes with Rachel; mostly with David. While Gem and Rachel and Trudy Maxwell from up the street and Sally Mabel Stevens from down the street were all outside playing hopscotch, Lilian was indoors, busy with her "scribbling," as Augustus called it. He wasn't too thrilled about Lilian's fascination with the written word, but he tolerated it. Lila defended it. She was very proud of her daughter and encouraged her, but Lilian didn't particularly like to show her mother her writings. It was David she sought out. It was his opinion that made a difference.

"What d'you think?" she'd ask.

"You've got talent," he told her one day when he was twenty and she fifteen. He'd just finished reading a story she'd given him entitled, "The Man with One Green Eye." It was about a colored man who had one brown eye and one green one. He couldn't see out of both eyes at the same time, so he had to walk around with a patch on one eye all the time. He'd switch back and forth between eyes every day, "to give each eye an equal chance to see the world its way."

David could see the pride in her eyes, but she kept her expression serious. "That's very nice of you to say I have talent. But I *know* that. I need constructive criticism, David." She held up a warning finger. *"Constructive."*

And so he tried, as best he could, to give her some. "But I'm not like a teacher. I don't know the rules."

"You're better than a teacher. You're my brother."

He laughed and said, "Okay, your brother says this story's good enough for you to try to get it published."

Her eyes did shine then and her mouth sagged open. "You mean it?"

"Wouldn't have said it if I didn't."

"But, David, what magazine's gonna publish something from a colored girl?"

"Don't have to be a magazine. We'll try a newspaper. How about the *New York Age?*"

"They print short stories?"

He shrugged. "I don't know. If they don't, they'll change their mind when they see yours." He smiled. "There's always a first time."

She threw her arms around his neck and hugged him. "I've got the best brother in the whole wide world."

The newspaper did indeed publish "The Man with One Green Eye" and over the years it printed a couple of Lilian's poems, too, each of them after they'd undergone David's constructive criticism. And so David took personal pride in Lilian's literary accomplishments.

He now eased down in the chair before his desk. He pulled open the bottom drawer on the right and took out a package. He had found it in Sweet's office—Augustus's office. The package, wrapped in plain brown paper, was addressed to Lilian McKay. When he'd hefted it in his hand, he'd sensed the consistency and weight of a manuscript. *Lilian's last manuscript.*

The return address was Knopf Publishers. Her manuscript, sent back either because it was rejected or accepted but needed corrections, had arrived the day before.

How had Sweet managed to get his hands on it? Usually Annie was on hand to accept all the mail, but the package could've arrived while she was out shopping. It didn't matter. What mattered was that he, David, had now gotten *his* hands on it. Sweet probably would've burned it. He'd make sure Sweet never would.

David laid the manuscript on his desk. His heart beat a resounding staccato. *Her last words—last creative endeavor.* Quickly, he cut the twine holding the package together and ripped open the paper. Sheaves of typed pages were revealed. The title page read: "Lyrics of a Blackbird, by Lilian McKay Sweet."

Lilian had written him that *Lyrics* concerned secrecy and betrayal in a family on Strivers' Row. Beyond that, he knew nothing. Would it tell him more about Lilian's frame of mind before her death?

He began to read and once he started, he couldn't stop. On the surface, the plot was simple, but it held an underlying complexity that reverberated to his core.

It was the story of Georgia and Frank Johnson; their daughter, Helen; their sons, Mark and Joel; and their housekeeper, Alice. Alice and Georgia had started out as best friends, sharing a room in the Tenderloin with five others. Alice worked hard, but she could never keep two cents together. Georgia wasn't rich, but she had a little inheritance from her father, a white man who had never publicly acknowledged her. Despite her white blood, Georgia was as blue-black as the midnight sky. And Alice, who had no white ancestors she knew of, was as yellow as a sunbeam. It was Alice who met Frank Johnson, but it was Georgia who married him. An ambitious, self-righteous man with a touch for making money, Frank knew a good deal when he saw one. He may have loved Alice, but he needed Georgia's cash. Her little dowry gave a nice boost to his first real estate investment. But all did not flow smoothly.

Soon after Frank married Georgia, Alice learned that she was pregnant. Georgia offered to take the baby, a little girl with pale skin and silken curls, and raise her as her own. Alice could stay near the child—if she was willing to work as the servant. Under no conditions was she ever to tell Helen that she was her mother. Five years later, Georgia gave birth to twin sons. They too were cream-colored. But unlike Helen, they weren't so light as to pass for white.

As the years went by, Georgia realized that her husband's love, such as he was capable of, had stayed with Alice. And she suspected, though she could not prove, that their affair had never ended. She hated Alice—and she knew that Alice hated her. She saw that Alice was desperate to claim Frank and Helen as her own, but she didn't realize just how desperate Alice was. Not until it was too late.

Alice poisoned Georgia in the hopes that Frank would finally marry her. But Frank refused. He would never marry her now, he said. What would people say? A man of his stature, marrying the maid? Furthermore, he'd loved Georgia. Didn't she know that he'd grown to love Georgia?

The afternoon light slanting through David's bedroom window grew gray, then faded. He paused once to adjust his lamp, but otherwise he read the manuscript straight through. After turning the last page, he went and stretched out on his bed. He closed his eyes, feeling drained.

Things ain't always the way they seem, Annie liked to say. *She should know,* he thought, *she should most certainly know . . .*

19

The Lies of Kindness

There was a knock on David's door—"Yes?"—and Annie stuck her head in. "Miss Rachel's here to see you."

David got up and followed her downstairs, wondering what Rachel wanted. She was standing in the parlor, before the fireplace, nervously staring up at Augustus McKay's portrait and wringing her hands. She started and turned at the sound of David's entrance. Her face broke into a bright, edgy smile.

"I'm glad I caught you. I won't stay long. I just had to come by and say something after I . . ." She paused and looked away. "I wanted to apologize. I didn't mean to do anything wrong. I—"

He raised a hand to still her. "It's okay. I guess we both said things . . . things we didn't mean." He gestured for her to sit down on the sofa and sat down beside her. "I still don't understand, though. Why didn't you tell me the truth about Sweet when I first asked you? Did you just want to get back at me?"

She lowered her gaze. "Maybe I did. But mostly . . ." She raised her eyes to meet his. "Mostly it was because I didn't want to cause you pain."

"Cause me pain?"

"We can't bring Lilian back. It doesn't help to run around with extra heartache. I thought it'd be better for you to believe that Lilian was happy in her marriage." She was apologetic. "I'm sorry. I just wanted to help."

He heard her weariness and his anger toward her faded. He tried to follow her logic. Yes, it would've been nice to think that Lilian had a good husband. It would've been nice to believe that she'd received support from at least one of the people she loved, trusted, and depended upon. It would've been nice to believe that not everyone who mattered—her husband, her brother, and her sister—had failed her. "It would've been nice," he mused, "but it wouldn't have been true." He looked at her. "Just help me find the truth, Rachel. It'll be better that way."

"Okay, I'll do whatever I can. I loved Lilian. She was the closest I'll ever have to a sister. And I hate to think that I didn't do everything I could to help her." She laid a hand over his. "And now to help you."

"Thank you."

"What're you gonna do now?"

"Keep on digging. You know about my having been to Dr. Steve. After I saw him, I went out to New Jersey—"

"Jersey? What's out there?"

"The hotel Sweet said he was staying at the night Lilian died. I wanted to see if they remembered him being there, or if not, find out the name of the man he shared his room with."

"And did you?"

"They wouldn't say, but I got the roommate's name. Unfortunately, he wasn't in when I tried to see him. I'll have to go by later."

"And suppose he says that Sweet *was* there all that night?"

"We'll cross that bridge when we come to it." He smiled. "Anyway, I have an ace up my sleeve."

"What's that?"

"I went to Lilian's room looking for the medicine Sweet gave her. Naturally, he'd cleared everything away. But Annie"—he grinned—"had set some aside."

"You mean Annie suspects something, too?"

"You could say that."

"But what did you want the medicine for?"

"To have it tested."

She looked at him with concern. "Oh, David, you're working so hard at this."

"I have to. The least I can do for Lilian, now that she's gone, is to clear up any questions about her death."

She went into his arms and the pain swelling his chest eased. For one intense moment, he wanted nothing more than to pretend that the last four years had never happened. He crushed her to him with a slow, deep sigh.

"Come home with me tonight," she whispered.

"I can't," he said. "I—"

"Please, don't make me beg."

"I'll only hurt you and I don't want to. Not ever again."

"Please. I'll take what you can give. I know I can't keep you." She caressed his cheek. "Let me be with you while you're still here. Let me at least have that."

Her eyes smoked and her lips found his. Her fingertips caressed the base of his throat and with nimble fingers she freed the top buttons of his shirt. Then she drew a fingertip over his lips and kissed him. With a husky groan, he gripped her shoulders and kissed her back, savoring her taste, her smell, her softness. Vaguely, he heard the doorbell ring. Moments later came Annie's voice.

"Mr. David?"

Rachel started; David dropped his hands. He felt a surge of adolescent guilt. Clearing his throat, he said, "Yes, Annie? What is it?"

"There's a messenger from Miss Nella Harding," she said and moved to one side.

A uniformed chauffeur stepped smartly forward. He whipped out a white envelope and presented it to David.

David took the note, read it—"Have urgent information you might consider invaluable. Come now."—then refolded it.

"I have instructions to drive you, sir, if you so require."

David nodded, and then turned to Rachel. "I'm sorry. I have to go."

She jumped up and smoothed her skirt with short embarrassed hand strokes. "That's all right, I—"

"It's late and dark. I'll take you home."

It was a short distance to Rachel's house. During the two-minute drive, she stroked the leather seat covers and every now and then gave David a shy smile. When the car pulled up in front of her building, she started to open the door on her side, then stopped at the restraining hand David put on her wrist. She looked at him, not understanding. He nodded toward the chauffeur. "Wait."

The chauffeur was getting out. He walked around the car and opened the door for her. She glanced at David, smiled, and got out. Then she turned around, leaned back into the car, and kissed him.

"Promise me one thing," she said.

"What?"

"Let me help—really help. If you want me to go anywhere or talk to people and ask questions, you'll ask me. Okay?"

He cupped her face and kissed her again. "Okay."

She drew back and the chauffeur closed the door. She stood on the curb, waving good-bye, a lonely figure in an oversized coat. David returned her wave until the car turned the corner and she was gone from view.

20

Playing with Fire

"Here, I've come up with something special for you. Something I think you'll like." Nella pressed a tall, chilled glass into David's hand. "Drink up."

He eyed the glass suspiciously. Its contents were a murky white. "You wouldn't be insulted if I were to ask you what this is?"

"I would be, so don't." She took her own drink and stirred it. "Some things," she said with a wicked grin, "are better left unsaid."

"Some things, perhaps, but this isn't one of them."

"Why don't you trust me? You really should."

"I should?"

"Yes."

"Why?"

"Why not?"

He didn't bother to answer. He lifted the glass to his lips and took a cautious sip. It *was* good. He commented with raised eyebrows. She raised her drink to him in a silent toast, then drank half of it straightaway.

"Prohibition is such a bore, don't you think? I do hope they get rid of it soon. Nikki thinks it's marvelous, though. He says liquor is so much more fun when it's forbidden."

"Aren't you worried about drinking around a sworn upholder of the law?"

"Darling, I never worry—about anything. It's against my principles. Just last week, Nikki and I were visiting a judge friend of ours. He treated us to some of the most delicious highballs we've had in ages. If I'm not worried about drinking with a judge, why would I worry about drinking with you?" She sipped and smiled. "You're a perfectly marvelous man, David. You do know that, don't you? I just can't understand why some lovely little Negress hasn't snapped you up."

"Nella, I'd like to sit and chat, but I can't. It's late and I'm tired. Now, you summoned me here. You said you have information—"

"It can wait—"

"It can't."

"It'll have to."

She crossed the room, her dress rustling, and went around behind the sofa where he was sitting. He felt one of her hands ease onto his shoulders. She began to massage the side of his neck. His hand snapped up, grabbed hers, and held it away.

"It's time to pay up," she whispered. Bending down, she nuzzled his earlobe. "I've got a taste for chocolate, that special McKay brand of cream. A connoisseur's special. A gourmet's delight. Be with me, David. Here. Tonight."

"I can't do that."

"Can't? Or won't?"

"Does it matter?"

With a hiss, she tore away and slinked across the room. "I told you from the beginning: I don't give information for free. We had a deal and you're going to stick to it. One way or another, you're going to pay." She had left her Cartier case lying carelessly on a divan near one window. Scooping it up, she yanked out a Chesterfield and lit it from a candle burning in a tall golden holder. She took short, angry puffs and stood staring into the flame.

What was she thinking? he wondered. *What was she up to?*

"I do love fire," she said suddenly. "It's beautiful, mysterious, and very, very lethal."

He felt an increasing unease.

"Take this tiny flame," she said. "Think how quickly it can grow when fed. How quickly it can consume a man and bring death."

She turned and spoke those last words directly at him. He rose to his feet. He was pale.

"That's the problem with you light-skinned Negroes," she said. "Everything shows on your face. You don't know how to hide anything. I dare say, in some ways, the really inky spades are much better off."

"What do you want?"

"I've told you."

"This is not the way to get it."

She came up to him. "Don't try to act virtuous, darling. I know you like vanilla."

"Why would you think that?"

"Your life in Philly. You have a weakness for white women, don't you?"

He stared at her in bitter disbelief, then almost laughed out loud. "Is that what you think it's all about?"

"Obviously. Everyone knows that colored men—"

"What *everyone knows* doesn't amount to a hill of beans." His dark eyes flashed. "I have never licked vanilla—and I never intend to."

She shrunk back. Her delicate nostrils flared. "I see."

"Do you?"

"More than you realize." She turned away. "Don't think I'm interested in you personally, darling. I'm interested in your *type*. I write. People aren't real to me. They're *characters*. Gem will definitely make a star appearance in my next book. And so will you. I knew you had a story the moment I saw you. Your modesty, your asceticism: What lay behind it?"

"I'm no one special."

"Of course you are—you're the star of my next book. Shall I tell you its title? *Duplicity*. It deals with denial and deception. It's about double lives and double meanings. Do you think the title gives away too much? Maybe I'll pare it down."

"I'm not the man to try this with."

"Believe me, I'm not your enemy. I could destroy you with a phone call and you know it. The right word in the wrong ear . . ." She snapped her fingers. "And that would be that. But why should I harm you? I like you."

"You have a strange way of showing it."

"I'm not a hypocrite. Neither are you. That's one reason I like you. But I have to show you who has the upper hand here."

"May I remind you that slavery went out more than sixty years ago? You can have your dogs sniff out my trail, but you cannot haul me in. You don't *own* me."

"Are you sure?"

His expression hardened. She went on.

"As cliché as it might sound, it's fair to say that your fate is at the mercy of my pen. If you're nice to me, I'll make sure no one knows who I'm writing about. Think it over."

"There's nothing to think about. A little notoriety never hurt anyone."

"It would destroy you."

"I would survive."

"Not without help." She sighed, exasperated. "My God, why do I like you so much? Think, David. *Think*. Someday, they're going to find out, whether I write about it or not. Someday, you're going to need my help. The moment you came back to town and confirmed where you'd been—the moment you stepped foot on that train in Philadelphia—you put yourself in danger. You can't stay in Harlem—not for long—not without a protector. I can be that person. I can be your advocate."

"And what would Nikki say? Or do you have a *deal* with him too?"

"Don't be cynical. It doesn't fit you."

"Nella, I am not for sale—not at any price. I'll get what I need from someone else, some other way."

"There is no one else. There *is* no other way. And payback is always a bitch."

"Your bill is paid, lady. I got information on my sister and you got information on me. We are *even*."

He grabbed his hat and went to the door.

"You make it hard to be your friend," she said.

Something in her tone stopped him. He paused in the doorway and turned around. He saw her standing there in the middle of her vast, over-blown room and it was as though a veil had lifted. He saw her for what she was: Not just a spoiled dilettante craving illicit attention, but a lonely figure surrounded by the cold baubles of wealth. He understood her frantic partying, drinking, and socializing with blacks: Like him, like Gem, she was trying to escape her demons by taking flight into an alternate reality. He also knew the answer to his earlier question: Nikki had indeed been away too long, and if he guessed right, that was often the case.

David walked back across the room. They stood for a moment, facing one another. Then he took her by her shoulders and a little light of hope came into her eyes. He drew her to him, and kissed her, very gently, on her forehead.

"Good night," he said. "And sweet dreams."

She leaned against him and moaned. But when he pulled away, she didn't try to stop him. At the door, he turned around once more and gave her a little smile. He tipped his hat and said:

"When Nikki comes back, would you tell him something for me?"

She looked at him, a little sad, a little surprised. "Yeah. What's that?"

"Tell him I said that you're a hell of a woman . . . and that he's a fool." He thought of Rachel. "He can take it from me: It takes one to know one."

21

The Lost Weekend

On Wednesday morning, Annie knocked on Sweet's office door. "Mr. Jameson, this here letter just come for you."

He nodded, giving her permission to approach. He still hadn't made up his mind what to do about her. She moved about the house with the familiarity of a family member. Her presence was pervasive. He'd realized early on that if not handled properly, she could be a threat. He'd hoped to make her closeness to Lilian work to his advantage. He'd even rehired the old woman after she had been fired. Now, Annie would be loyal to him too, he'd thought. She'd seen how sick her mistress was. She could testify to Lilian's mental state as having deteriorated to a dangerous level. Should the need arise, she could also testify to his husbandly devotion. Who'd be a better character witness than the woman whose dedication to Lilian was long-proven?

Of course, he'd only need such a witness if questions were raised. But why should anyone doubt that Lilian had committed suicide? Lilian's own behavior made her suicide likely. Lilian was a witness against herself.

He'd been shocked when Annie found McKay's address and he'd never anticipated McKay's tenacity. Worst of all—and he could've kicked himself for this—he'd never foreseen McKay's attachment to the house.

In hindsight, it seemed obvious. Once Annie found that address, the battle for the house was inevitable.

Sweet told himself that he really wouldn't have any trouble if the matter went to court. His legal claim was straight and clear. But he would—*Naturally*—prefer to avoid court if he could.

Sweet took the letter, thinking that this could be the answer. He dismissed Annie with a curt nod, watched her leave, then ripped the envelope open. It was a response from the operative in Philadelphia. He leaned forward into the light and read the opening lines.

They were good. He smiled. Very good.

•   •   •

Charlie Epps seemed to be out of town. He was certainly never home. It was Thursday. David had been by Epps's house three times now—morning, noon, and night—and never gotten an answer.

He'd been back to the Renaissance Pharmacy, too, but the drug analysis still wasn't ready. In the meantime, he'd had another couple of nasty run-ins with Sweet and he'd received the distinct impression that Sweet was up to something. He was tempted to simply have someone come, pack Sweet's things, and move them to a hotel room. But as inviting as the idea might be, it would be only a temporary solution. He needed something permanent. That led his thoughts back to Lilian . . . and Gem. He telephoned Nella. She agreed to see him late that evening.

"Let's make a new deal," he said at her apartment. "You think you've found a story in me—but your story doesn't have a context and it doesn't have an ending. I'll give you both. I'll talk to you, if you talk to me."

"So you *are* willing to sell yourself."

"To sell my history, yes. But *not* my name."

She reflected. "All right, but there's one thing you should learn about me. I have ears everywhere. So don't try to hold out on me."

He stiffened inwardly. She watched him for reaction.

"I heard about your meeting with Adrian and I know what was said. I also know that you went to Newark to check Sweet's whereabouts the night Lilian died, and that you're having a druggist test the medicine Sweet gave her. One plus one equals two, my boy: You've got it in for Jameson Sweet."

He refused to give her the pleasure of showing either surprise or dismay. Instead, he asked: "Did you suspect what Snyder told me?"

Her eyes narrowed. "It surprised the hell out of me. The little bitch lied to me—and I believed her."

"You still know Gem better than anyone else—even better than Snyder. Can you figure why she left him? Snyder loved her. He's attractive, urbane, witty. He has money and position—"

"But he would've never gained acceptance among Harlem's elite—"

"All the more reason. Gem is a rebel and she loves mavericks. Why did she reject him? And why did she insist that the breakup be so public?"

"I really couldn't say—but even if I could, I wouldn't tell you, not until you tell me what's going on inside that handsome head of yours. What have you got against Sweet and how did you get it?"

"Sweet killed Lilian. His motives: greed for Lilian's money and love for

Gem; his method: an as-yet-unidentified poison; and his opportunity: one lonely weekend when everyone, including his victim, thought he was away at a Movement conference."

"Your proof?"

He glanced away. "I don't have any. Not yet."

"So you have nothing but bitter suspicions."

He looked back. "Suspicion, supposition: Without them, no investigation would ever begin."

"Listen to me. Lilian is dead. You can't bring her back. You want to prove she was murdered and you want to blame Sweet. That's all very well, but if you're honest, you'll admit that there's more evidence—hard evidence—for suicide than for murder. Let's just say for the sake of argument that Lilian *was* murdered. Do you really want to dredge up the whole thing? It would mean a lot of unpleasant publicity. How do you think the Movement would feel about having one of its most talented attorneys accused of such a miserable crime? Given your history, do you think Harlem would stand by you or stand by him? Then take Sweet. He's a dirty player. If I could find out about you, so could he. Is that what you want? What would it do to that proud family name of yours? Lilian's death would be forgotten in the scandal over your crime."

"I have to get at the truth."

"The truth? Don't disappoint me by turning into a hypocrite. People who live in glass houses should never throw stones."

"Are you really telling me that I should let him get away with it?"

"I told you: I'm your friend. I only want to make sure you know what you might be getting into."

"I do know."

"I don't think so."

There seemed to be no point in staying longer. She wasn't going to tell him anything. He took up his hat and coat and thanked her for her time. He was almost out the door when she asked: "Do you like bedtime stories? I'm good at them."

He turned around; she chuckled wickedly at his expression.

"Don't worry. I've lost interest in you. You're no good to a live woman, anyway. You're too busy with the dead. Sit down. Over there." She waved imperiously toward the divan across the room. "If you won't let me tuck you in, at least let me give you something to dream about."

David glanced at the divan, then at Nella. Slowly, he crossed the room and sat down.

o   o   o

"Listen carefully. What I'm about to tell you could save you a lot of trouble."

She lit herself a fresh Chesterfield and played with her lighter.

"After Gem left, I became curious about Lilian and her husband. I invited them to dinner. Gem had told me that she and Lilian were identical twins, so I should have been prepared. I wasn't. I was shocked and intrigued. I'm afraid my manners weren't very good. I stared at Lilian the whole evening. At first, it was as though Gem were there, but of course, she wasn't. She was thousands of miles away, across the sea. It didn't take long to see the differences. As Gem said, it was mainly a matter of personality. Lilian was shy and diffident. She let her husband speak first and never contradicted him. A couple of times, she opened her mouth to comment and he silenced her. It took no more than a glance and she would simmer down. It was terrible. I could have hated him myself—almost. But I have a weakness for good-looking men. And when they can be disarmingly charming, well then . . ."

Nella flicked a bit of ash from her dress.

"Anyway, Nikki invited Sweet to sit by the fire and enjoy a coffee. Lilian and I retired to another room. I hoped that she would open up when we were alone. But she was even more reticent, if that's possible. She answered my questions with monosyllables and wouldn't look me straight in the eye. I decided there must be something seriously wrong. I told her that if there was anything I could ever do for her, she should call me right away. She nodded but said nothing. I left it at that.

"I was surprised to hear from her about two months later. It was in May, I believe. Remembering my promise, I asked her if anything was wrong. No, she said, there wasn't. She sounded quite gay, actually. She asked if she could come out and visit. I was thrilled and very curious. I told her I was giving a party in the Hamptons that evening. She was welcome, of course. Given what Gem had told me about Lilian—and what I'd seen myself that evening—I didn't think she'd come. You can't imagine my surprise when she appeared at my door that night. She was dressed beautifully. Her style was entirely different from Gem's, but it was every bit as effective. She had a touching innocence that made one want to protect her. In her own way, Lilian could be as devastatingly manipulative as Gem. It was a wonderful discovery.

"It took a while for her to warm up to me, but eventually she did. I liked her very much. Lilian was a lovely woman. But she never toughened up. She was very gay during the times I saw her. Sometimes, she even reminded me of Gem. We used to talk about Gem and wonder what she was up to in Paris. Lilian had a natural gift for mimicry. She used to do marvelous imperson- ations of Gem for me. It was almost like having Gem here with me. Lilian could sense how much I missed her sister. It didn't seem to bother her. She was never jealous of my affection for Gem. I admired her for that. It was another difference between the two sisters, a difference that put a plus next to Lilian's name. Gem would've never stood for being in second place. But Lilian was simply happy to have a place at all. I've often wondered why the two turned out so differently. Objectively speaking, Lilian was every bit as pretty as Gem. But she lacked something. Perhaps it was the self-love, that extra drop of poisonous narcissism that makes Gem so pitiless and yet so attractive to men and women alike.

"Lilian and I saw one another off and on for several months. I always invited her to my soirées. If Jameson was out of town, she would come. I told her the invitation included them both, but she merely laughed and said my parties were meant for her alone. Then the time between her visits length- ened.

"Nikki and I went to Europe last July. I tried to contact Gem during a long stopover in Paris, but I wasn't successful. When we got back in Septem- ber, I sent a note to Lilian but she didn't respond. I was a bit concerned, but with one thing and another, I got busy and didn't get around to trying again. Months went by. I started hearing from Lilian again in December. She came out to the house once, in January. She'd missed both my Christmas and New Year's Eve parties. I couldn't believe she'd done that, but she said Jameson had made other plans. Looking back, I remember thinking she didn't look well. It was nothing specific, just a general sense that something was off. After that visit in January, she promised to come again. That was how things stood until a month ago.

"Late that Friday morning, Lilian called sounding confused and depressed. Jameson had left that day on a business trip and she was alone at home. She was incoherent. She claimed the place was haunted. She begged me to let her come out to Harding House. Of course, she could, I said. She asked if Nikki or I could go and get her. We couldn't. Nikki was out with the car. She was quiet, and then she said she was sure she could get there on her own. She did arrive—hours later. I was horrified when I saw her. She was exhausted when she stepped out of her car. She looked like death warmed over. I know it's a terrible choice of words, but you get my meaning. Her face was bloated and gray. Her clothes hung off her carelessly. She looked nothing like the exquisite Lilian I knew.

"I wasn't quick enough to hide my shock. She didn't say a word. Just grabbed her suitcase, ran into the house, and shut herself in our biggest guest room. I went upstairs to her. I was afraid she wouldn't let me in, but she did. She was lying on the bed. I urged her to spend the weekend with us. I'll never forget her answer.

"'Whether I stay or not, I'm going to die, Nella. I'm going to die. But we've all got to die sometime, don't we? Some of us just have a better notion of when.'"

Nella shivered.

"She was talking like a madwoman. Yet her tone of voice was absolutely sane, even sensible. Lilian seemed convinced that a ghost was haunting her house and would kill her.

"I offered to help her unpack. When she didn't answer, I took it upon myself to start. But when I opened her suitcase, I found that she'd packed just one outfit, a cocktail dress, a bright red one with a glittery top. I couldn't understand why. My husband and I hadn't spoken of any party. We hadn't planned on having one. The dress was totally inappropriate. And it was the only bit of clothing she'd brought. Otherwise, she had only what she needed for her hair and face."

Nella pulled a Chesterfield out of a jeweled box on the table. She let David light it for her, and then stretched out. She stared at a large painting of Cape Cod on the wall opposite her.

"Lilian came down for dinner that evening. We served steak. She ate like someone starved. Said she was thrilled to have some real food, finally. Nikki and I exchanged glances. She consumed enormous amounts. I lost my appetite watching her.

"After dinner, she told us she had to go take her sleeping powder—I didn't know she'd been taking any. She said she was going to bed, but then she asked me to sit and talk with her until the medicine took effect. I was quite willing. I hoped she'd tell me what had happened to change her so quickly. So, I went upstairs with her. I couldn't believe how much sleeping powder she took. It was incredible. Suddenly, her mood changed. She said she wanted to be alone and sent me from the room.

"I went back downstairs. My husband and I talked for a while. Then we both went up at around ten. Her door was closed and there was no light shining from under it. We went to sleep thinking—hoping—all would be well. Then began a night I will never forget.

"I heard her screaming at around three that morning. She was shrieking out her own name. I ran down the hall and wrenched open her door. She was sitting stiffly upright in bed. Her eyes were wide and staring. Fixed on the window opposite the bed. Her hands were pressed over her ears. She was shaking her head from side to side. And she was babbling, imploring someone she thought was in the room. It wasn't me; she wasn't seeing me. I couldn't make out her words. They were utter nonsense. But she was afraid. Scared out of her wits. She kept saying her own name. But it had turned into a terrified whimper. I ran to her and shook her. She fought me and God forgive me, I slapped her. That seemed to bring her out of it. She collapsed in my arms, weeping. And begged me to stay with her until daybreak. I sat with her for two hours. She refused to speak. She lay with her eyes wide open, staring at the ceiling. I tried to talk to her, but she acted as though she hadn't heard me. At one point, she closed her eyes. I thought she'd fallen asleep, but the moment I tried to leave her, she reached out a hand and grabbed me. She was as thin as a rail, but she had the strength of two men. At around half-past five, she finally fell asleep.

"I crept back to my own bed, exhausted. I slept late, but Nikki was up early. When I woke, he told me that Lilian had come downstairs, eaten a hearty breakfast, and then gone back to bed.

"Lilian spent most of Saturday in bed reading or in the bathroom soaking in the tub. That evening, she came downstairs with her bag packed and announced that she had a very important appointment. She didn't say what it was. I can still see her. She went to the door, suddenly turned around and said: 'I love you, Nella. You're the only other one who lets me be me.' I was so stunned, I didn't know what to say. Before I could answer, she went out.

"Nikki and I didn't know if she intended to come back or not, but she reappeared that evening, after about three hours. I heard a car drive up at around ten-thirty and went to my bedroom window. It was Lilian, getting out of a taxi."

"A taxi?"

"There was no sign of her Packard. I ran downstairs to let her in. She was smiling and cheerful. She was all dressed up in her red dress and she seemed very energetic and decisive. She didn't give me time to put questions, just kissed me lightly on the cheek and dashed up the stairs to her room. And then the night before was repeated. It was ghastly: the whole thing, at three A.M., the crying out of her own name. That night, she asked me to bring her water for more sleeping powder. I was afraid she'd kill herself if I did, but Nikki told me to go ahead and do it. She took another big dose, slept again.

"Nikki and I like to have a good Sunday brunch. Lilian ate well and with enthusiasm. She seemed to be her old self again. Afterward, she said she was tired. She went upstairs and when I checked on her later, I found her sound asleep. She slept around three hours. When she woke up, she said she felt better, so much better in fact that she wanted to go home. Jameson wasn't back yet; I was afraid for her to be at home alone. I tried to talk her out of it, but she wouldn't listen. She had firmly decided to go home. She said that a Dr. Hawthorne—I take it he was her therapist. Clearly, she must've been under treatment. Anyway, this Dr. Hawthorne had found a nurse for her and the woman would be at the house Monday morning. She also said she had a lot to do before Jameson got home. I agreed . . . reluctantly. Nikki said he would drive her. They left at around six that evening.

"When Nikki got back hours later, he was very upset. Lilian had cried the whole way home. She'd talked about going back with him. Several times, he'd wondered whether he should turn the car around and bring her back. But when they drove up to the house, she'd suddenly become calm. She took out her keys and got out. She asked Nikki to go through the house with her, to make sure that no one was there. He did. The house was empty. But she didn't believe him. She said that her sister was there, that she could smell her. She asked Nikki to check again. But again, he found no one. He left her standing by the parlor window, gazing out into the empty street. And that, dear David, was the last time either of us ever saw her."

David closed his eyes and leaned forward, resting his head in his right hand. He suddenly wanted a cigarette badly. Never mind that he didn't smoke. And he would have been happy to down one of Nella's bizarre cocktails. He could almost believe that Lilian had killed herself, had seized a butcher knife from the kitchen cutting block, gone back to her bedroom, and systematically sliced down deep into her own flesh. He could almost envision it.

Almost.

Nella gave him a piercing look.

"You still don't want to accept that Lilian killed herself. But you must. Forget about Sweet. Forget him. I'll tell you something more: I was curious about where Lilian went that evening, so I contacted the taxi companies working the area near my house. Sure enough, a driver did remember bringing a young colored woman to Harding House. He had picked her up at a cheap hotel. The cabby gave me the name of the place. Only one word to describe it: squalid, absolutely irredeemably squalid. I don't want to imagine what Lilian was doing there. I spotted her Packard in the parking lot. The keys were still in the ignition. Unbelievable. Anyone could've driven off with it. I think the proprietor had been using it himself. He was very reluctant to part with it. The car is in my driveway in the Hamptons. You can pick it up the next time you come out. The hotel owner also showed me the room in which Lilian spent three hours that evening. I found a letter. It isn't addressed to anyone and it isn't very coherent, but I can show it to you."

Nella went to a small side table and slid out a narrow, shallow drawer. She withdrew a piece of folded blue paper and handed it to David. Other than the hotel's moniker, the page was nondescript. It was covered in a small nervous scrawl. The handwriting was barely legible. It was difficult to recognize as Lilian's.

> It's her fault. It's her fault,
> My sister, that sister of mine,
> She's trying to kill me, to slay me,
> With her dead, blind eyes.
> She chokes me with sadness.
> Her plainness, her grayness,
> Are a suffocating shroud.
> But I am a bird that will survive.
> I will fly, far away, high up on high
> She will see. I will destroy her.
> I will survive.

David shuddered. Nelly nodded grimly.

"Finally," she said. "You understand."

A little ways uptown, Sweet was handing Canfield a letter. They were sitting in Canfield's study. Canfield read the missive, his expression deepening from curiosity to displeasure to fury. Finally, he looked up.

"Good God, is McKay out of his mind?"

Sweet took back the letter. "He would seem to be."

Canfield stared pensively at the letter in Sweet's hands. "The Movement will have to make a formal statement, cutting him off."

Sweet looked pleased. "Were it up to me, I'd have him disbarred."

Canfield looked up at him. "Just what *are* you going to do with this information?"

"I don't want to destroy the McKay name, or damage the family. When it comes down to it, I *am* part of that family now. And I respect Augustus McKay's memory, even if his own son doesn't. So I wouldn't want to harm it. But David McKay can't be allowed to go on like this. And I won't let him drive me out of the house." Sweet tapped the letter against his palm. "For the moment, I'll hold on to this for a little insurance. When the time's right, McKay and I will have a talk. Right now, I have to go to Chicago to take more depositions. I can't put the trip off and I'll be gone about ten days."

"Yes . . . the Richards case. We can't afford to let anything distract us from it. Try to talk to the dead man's widow."

"That'll be almost impossible."

"The key word is 'almost.' Find a way." Canfield drew himself up. "And don't wait too long on the McKay matter. Now that I know what he *is,* what he's been doing, I can't afford to have him associated with the Movement." He gestured toward the letter. "Your operative will bring the evidence when he comes?"

"Oh, yes," said Sweet. "He'll bring evidence. He'll bring plenty."

22

To Be with Rachel

Upon leaving Nella's, David decided to walk home. It was nearly ten o'clock at night. Fifth Avenue was cold and damp and for the most part empty. The street lamps glowed with a ghostly light through the fog that had descended over the avenue.

It was a good stretch from Nella's apartment to Strivers' Row and not all of it was through hospitable territory. Negroes still took their hands in their lives when walking through parts of Manhattan. Even so, he decided to walk that night; he hoped it would clear his head.

He had to admit that the picture Nella had drawn of Lilian strengthened the contention that Lilian killed herself, but he was not free of his suspicions of Sweet. Not by a long shot. He was being stubborn and he knew he looked like a man on a personal vendetta, but he was not prepared to give up. Not yet.

He kept up a good pace and in a relatively short time he'd reached lower Harlem. Soon after that, he was passing 130th Street. He immediately thought of Rachel. He recalled that last lonely image of her standing at the curbside, waving. Without thinking about it, he turned down her block.

She answered the door still wearing her hospital uniform. She was obviously tired but she pushed aside her fatigue when she saw him. Her soft eyes filled with concern. "Have you eaten?"

He shook his head.

She started banging about in her small kitchen and soon the air was fragrant with sizzling bacon. She dug out some potatoes and onions and fried them. David told her to stop. "I don't want to cause you work." She smiled and kept on cooking. David ended up helping her. They ate and afterward, as they were washing the dishes, he told her what Nella had said about Lilian's lost weekend.

"It was horrible, listening to her. And the thing is, I'm sure she's telling the truth."

"Would she lie?"

"No," he said with a sigh. "I don't think she would." He rubbed his eyes. They were still irritated from the onions. "It doesn't really mean anything, what she said, you know. Even if Lilian was a bit . . ."—he searched for the word—"a bit confused that weekend . . . it doesn't mean that she killed herself."

"Have you talked to the man who stayed with Sweet at the hotel?"

"No, but I will. And I'm still waiting on the man at the drugstore to tell me what was in that stuff Sweet was giving her."

"You're sure the news is gonna be bad—I mean good, good in the sense that it *was* poison?"

He paused, then said: "I think it very likely, yes."

She looked away. "But suppose he . . . doesn't find what you're looking for? Does that mean you'll be ready to stop looking? To move on? Does that mean you'll be leaving?"

He cupped her chin and turned her face to him. Her eyes twinkled like emeralds. He recognized unshed tears. On impulse, he put down the dishtowel and took her in his arms, wishing that he could reassure her, but how could he, without lying? He felt her soften against him and felt himself respond. He remembered how soft and supple she'd been. They had moved instinctively to the same inner song, so closely intertwined they could have shared one skin. Her body fitted perfectly to his.

Too perfectly, he thought, and released her. "I'd better go."

"Stay." She gripped his hand. "Just a little while longer. Please."

"Rachel . . ." He gazed at her and felt his desire harden, but he shook his head. "I can't."

She kissed him, muffling his refusals. His resistance weakened. Before he knew it, he was returning her kisses, his hands pressing into the small of her back. After a while, she interlaced her fingers with his. "C'mon," she said and drew him down the hallway.

She had a small bedroom. The bed itself wasn't much more than a glorified cot, but like the rest of her place, it was very feminine, very inviting. To a man coming out of the desert, it looked like paradise.

He tried to turn off his thoughts, tried not to think about how he'd feel later, and for a time, he succeeded. But when it came down to it, he couldn't go ahead. Poised over her, he stopped. He gazed down at her, tightened his jaw against the throbbing in his groin—and made himself think. He closed his eyes and deep-breathed. He became aware of the thudding of his heartbeat and concentrated on every inhale-exhale.

Rachel moaned beneath him. "David?"

When he thought he was calm, he opened his eyes.

"David?" she said again, this time a little worried.

He kissed her, then rolled away and sat up on the edge of the bed.

"What's the matter?" she asked, pushing herself up on one elbow. "What's wrong?"

His hands began to shake. Soon, his whole body was shaking.

"David?" She put a hand out and touched his elbow, more than a little worried now.

"I'm all right," he said. He inhaled deeply, trying to get his trembling under control. "But I can't—I can't do this. It wouldn't be right. I gotta go." He patted her hand. "Rest, now. Sleep, if you can."

"The hell I will." She half-raised up.

He stood and started getting dressed.

"You can't leave me like this," she cried.

His response was to finish getting dressed and walk to the door. There he paused, with one hand on the knob. With a low groan, he dropped his hand, went back to the bed, planted his fists on it, and leaned over her.

"Don't you understand?" he said. "The problem isn't that I don't want you. It's that I want you too damn much. I can't be messing around and still concentrate on what I got to do."

He grabbed her face and kissed her hard. Then before she could say anything more, he was gone. The sound of her weeping followed him as he took his hat and coat down from the wall hook by her door. He ran down the stairs, cursing himself. Crossing the street, he headed toward Lenox Avenue and forced his thoughts back to the business at hand.

Annie hesitated, then she said, "Just r'member what the Good Book says, Mr. David. What ye sow, so shall ye reap. R'member them words." She sighed and rubbed her wrists. "I think I'll lay down now. These old bones just ain't what they used t'be."

David was nearly out the door when the telephone rang. He had a sense of impending disaster the moment he realized who was on the line.

"What's this all about, Doctor?"

Dr. Steve cleared his throat. "After our last conversation, I went over my notes on Lilian. It seems there *was* some question about whether she was indeed pregnant—"

David was stunned. "What?"

"Your sister was displaying all the signs of early pregnancy when she came to see me. But pregnancy wasn't the only explanation for her symptoms. I agreed with her that she probably *was* pregnant, but I cautioned her that I could not be sure. Not at that time. And I told her to come back."

"Why didn't you tell me this before?"

"Because I did believe that Lilian was pregnant. Looking back, it was partly because she was so sure herself—many times a woman knows these things. However, I did caution her. You yourself told me there was no child. We both know she was not the kind of woman to have had an abor—a termination. And surely, someone would've known if she miscarried. I'm sorry. But given what I later heard about Lilian's state of mind, there is the chance it was a hysterical pregnancy that simply went away by itself."

"Thank you, Doctor."

David hung up. He stared at the phone for a long time.

When Charlie Epps answered his doorbell, David thought that maybe his luck was changing. Epps turned out to be squat, round, and partially balding. He had beady brown eyes and full cheeks. He was nibbling on a ham sandwich with buckteeth when he opened the door. He acted friendly enough until David explained the reason for his visit and started asking questions about Sweet.

"Who'd you say you are?" Epps asked.

"I'm a lawyer. And I'm inquiring into a family matter."

"Is Sweet in some kind of trouble?"

"Not that I know of. Why would you ask?"

"No reason." Epps shrugged indifferently, but his eyes shifted uneasily. He put the sandwich down on a plate left lying on the living room coffee table. "What exactly did you want to know?"

"Whether Sweet was in his hotel room the entire night of Sunday, February twenty-first. Was he?"

Epps folded his arms across his chest. "This sounds like something serious. I don't know if I should be talking to you. Does Sweet know you're here?"

"Is there a reason why you wouldn't talk to me? Do you have something to hide?"

"Of course not."

"Does Sweet?"

"Look, man, I don't want to get involved in—"

"Just answer my question, that one question, and I'll leave."

Epps coughed and rubbed his throat.

"Well, what's your answer?"

Epps averted his eyes. "Sweet never left his hotel room that night. He went to bed at nine with a stack of briefs. I couldn't sleep because his lamp was on half the night." He looked back at David. "Now please go."

"Are you absolutely certain that Sweet was in the room all night?"

"Mister, I don't know who you are or what you want, but you've gotten all you're going to get out of me."

David left. Epps's statement had disappointed him, but when he thought about it, he couldn't say that it surprised him. Sweet was clever. He would have made sure that he had a sound alibi in the unlikely case that anyone raised questions. So he had either gotten Epps to lie or convinced Epps that he was still in the room for the hours he presumably left it.

I've got one more chance at bat, David thought. Epps's statement counted as a strike. And Dr. Steve's call certainly chalked up as another one.

Two strikes. Three and I'm out.

Of course, if Nella's description of Lilian's lost weekend was counted . . . well, then he'd already struck out.

But I don't count it, he thought. *There was too much room for Nella's opinion.*

The druggist's report, however, would be empirical evidence.

It would prove him right.

It had to.

The druggist greeted David with a smile. "There wasn't nothin' wrong with that medicine you brought in. Harmless stuff. Bet you're glad to hear that, huh?" The old man peered down at him from his raised counter. "Just what'd you think you'd find?"

What indeed?

David hid his disappointment, paid for the analysis, and turned away.

He'd run up against a wall. Hit it full speed running. His intelligent face was grave. He had proven neither method, nor motive, nor opportunity. He was angry and frustrated—and scared.

Am I wrong? he asked himself. *Am I wrong to suspect Sweet?*

Did he really think Sweet was guilty? Or did he just want him to be? Without a doubt, Sweet had been a lousy husband, but was he a murderer?

Back in his room at home, he forced himself to reflect. True, he had no proof, but his suspicions had a solid basis, didn't they? What about the questions his talks with Annie, Rachel, Nella, and Snyder had raised? The contradictions?

What contradictions?

He wasn't even sure what they were anymore. The gravest of them all—Lilian's pregnancy—was apparently no contradiction at all. It was the question of her pregnancy that had formed the underpinning of his suspicions. Without a confirmation of the pregnancy, without the druggist's confirmation of poison, he had nothing. He was sinking into a quagmire of doubt. It was getting harder and harder to think.

Were his suspicions valid? Or were they simply the effort of a weary mind and even wearier heart to blame someone else for his failure to answer Lilian's call for help?

Has your sense of guilt really driven you this far? Rachel had asked. *Is the idea of murder actually easier to live with than suicide? Murder means you can blame someone else . . .*

He would have to tell her. He went downstairs to head out again and saw Annie.

"You haven't had lunch yet," she said.

"I'm not really hungry."

"I can fix you something real quick."

"That's all right. I'm going to see Rachel. Maybe we'll have a bite to eat together."

"Miss Rachel?" she repeated. "You goin' t'see Miss Rachel *again?*"

He looked at her. "What's on your mind, Annie?"

Her nostrils flared just a bit. "'Course it ain't my place to say . . . but I hope you ain't meanin' t'start up somethin' you can't finish."

Relieved that her concern wasn't over something more serious, he gave a wry smile. "I'm not."

"That young woman done been through a lot. Please don't go makin' no promises you know you can't keep."

"We're friends. That's all. Friends."

"Does that mean what I hope it mean?"

"It means that I won't hurt her."

Her stern expression softened, somewhat, but he could tell that she still wasn't satisfied.

"I know I hurt her when I went away," he added. "I know she hoped for more, but . . ."

"But what?"

"But sometimes," he hesitated, then looked at her. "Sometimes we can't have what we want."

She studied him. "In them four years you was gone, what happened t'you? What'd they do t'you *out there?*"

He shrugged and gave her a kiss on the cheek. "Nothing important," he said. "Nothing that a man can't learn to live with."

He felt a pang of guilt when Rachel opened her door. She looked exhausted. Evidently, she'd just returned home, hadn't even had time to remove her coat. The dark circles under her eyes were pronounced and her heart-shaped face was pale. After he'd left the night before, she'd been called back in to work part of the overnight and early morning shifts, she told him. Two of the other nurses had called in sick.

"I'm sorry," he said. "I should go."

"No." She stayed him with an outstretched hand. "Come in. Please. Seeing you is good for me."

She went to the kitchen. Rapidly, she put up water for coffee and took out chocolate cake. Finally, he got her to sit down. He spoke in low, intense tones of his failure to prove a case against Sweet.

"Sweet's hotel roommate claims that Sweet was in his room the whole night Lilian died. All of a sudden, Dr. Steve says he's *not* sure Lilian was pregnant. And now, the druggist says the medicine Sweet was giving Lilian was harmless."

"Oh, David . . . what you've been through."

"When I add all that to what Nella said, I . . . I have to say I . . ." His voice trailed off.

"Maybe it's for the best. You've done all you can. Now you'll have peace of mind. Now you know it *was* suicide. I mean—you do see that now, don't you?"

He was silent.

"David McKay, you're one of the most stubborn men I've ever known. You've got to accept what happened. You've got to let Lilian go. That's the only way to survive this. Your thoughts belong with the living, not the dead."

Nella had said something similar *Why can't I let go?* he asked himself. *Why can't I admit that I might be wrong?* The fact was, he *did* want Sweet to be guilty. He needed him to carry the blame.

"Promise me you'll forget about Sweet," she begged. "For your own sake, you've got to promise me that you'll move on."

"Rachel . . . I can't."

There was a long uncomfortable moment.

"What are you going to do now?" she asked.

"I don't know."

She studied him with bleary eyes. Then she rose from the table with the slow, stiff movements of a sleepwalker. "I'm very tired now. I'd like to sleep."

She was kicking him out. He stood up. He looked at her narrow shoulders hunched miserably under her thin coat, remembered what Annie had said, and felt ashamed.

"I'm sorry," he said.

She turned away from him. He laid a light hand on her shoulder. At his touch, she gave a dry sob. He put his arms around her. She turned, laid her face against his chest, and openly wept.

"It was so horrible," she sniffled. "All those months with Lilian and then her dying that way. And then I heard that you were coming back. And it sounds terrible, but I thought that maybe her death was meant to be . . . that it was worth it . . . if it could bring you back. But then you said you weren't going to stay. I don't want you to leave Harlem, but I can't make you stay. And I don't want you to stay, not if it's going to be this way. Not if all you can think about is getting Sweet."

She babbled on, like a heartbroken child. The kitchen clock ticked loudly. The sounds of laughter floated in from the street. *Happy people, normal people,* David thought, glancing out the kitchen window. *Do such people still exist?* Sometimes, it seemed to him that he was mired in sadness, that everyone he knew was struggling with tragedy. Perhaps it was his work in Philadelphia; perhaps it was only his own skewed view of the world.

Gradually, Rachel calmed down. The remaining traces of her perfume, mixed with the hospital odors of sweat, disinfectant, and sickness, wafted up to him. He kissed the top of her head. She moaned and looked up. Her green eyes intrigued him. Sometimes, they were as clear as dewdrops; other times, as opaque as a forest at midnight. Right then, they were tired and reddened but they bore an expression that made him yearn for a sweetness he had no right to taste again. He felt himself swelling. He moaned. Even the agony of saying no was beginning to feel good. He was tempted, so tempted to cross the line. If he didn't get away soon, he'd burst—

"Stay with me," she whispered.

Somehow, she'd managed to slip off her coat. His was coming off, too.

With nimble fingers she unbuttoned his shirt and rolled it back over his shoulders. Spreading her fingertips over his chest, she covered it with hot, moist kisses. She began to lick him, the tip of her tongue fluttering lightly over his nipples. Her lips traced a line of fire, downward, while her fingers undid his belt, burrowed inside his pants and touched him there . . . there . . . and *there*. His eyes slid closed; his breathing grew ragged. What was the point? Why couldn't he—for once—just let go?

He sensed her slide to her knees. When he realized that she was parting his fly, he clasped her by her shoulders and drew her up. She looked at him, wondering. Had she done something wrong? Was he going to leave?

No, he shook his head. "I want to be here, with you," he said and caressed her with his eyes. "It's just that . . . I didn't think we could ever have this again. I didn't really think . . ."

A wealth of relief and happiness flooded her face. He stroked her cheek.

"Let's take our time," he whispered. "Let's take it slow . . . and easy."

With his right hand, he cupped her cheek and kissed her lips. When he drew back, he saw that her eyes were closed, her lips slightly parted. He drew a fingertip over one of her eyebrows and she opened her eyes. They were like green flames now. Taking her face in both hands, he slowly ran his tongue along her upper lip, then made his way down her chin. Tilting her face upward, he gently sucked on her throat.

Moaning, she pressed herself against him. Her body quivered. Then, she pulled away. "Wait," she whispered and left the room. He heard the sound of running water. When she came back, she took his hand and led him to her bathroom. He saw that she'd filled the tub, a deep claw-footed one. She'd also set lighted candles on the tiled floor. Their small flames cast flickering shadows on the bathroom's yellowed ivory walls.

Slowly, they undressed one another. She had him lie back in the tub. Then she stepped in with him, kneeling between his legs, facing him. When he reached for her, she pressed his arms down.

"Relax, baby."

Tenderly, she lathered him with a sponge and a bar of soap scented with sandalwood. Gently, as though she were handling a child, she lifted his arms and soaped his armpits, then moved down over his chest. His erection arched over his stomach like a bird about to take flight. He reached to cup her breasts, but she swatted him away, and then she began to wash him with calm efficiency, a woman reclaiming her lost lover as her own.

For a time, he watched her slender hands at work. Then he closed his eyes, slid deeper into the warm water, and gave in to the sweet sensation of her hands moving over him. Now and then, she would kiss him and where her lips touched him, he ached.

He would never feel as captured by a woman as he was by Rachel. As she bathed him, he imagined a cleansing that went deeper than the skin, one that took him back to earlier times, before shame and exile.

He moaned as she cradled his balls and lathered them. He closed his eyes and let his head fall back, and then he felt her mouth envelop him. A sharp stab of pleasure shot through him. He looked down. With her tongue, she was caressing him from base to tip, tip to base. She looked up, saw his expression, and smiled her Mona Lisa smile, then gave him one last lick. Still on her knees, she took his right hand and placed it between her thighs.

He curled his fingers into her soft dark triangle. Her breath caught as his middle finger slipped inside her and she bit her lower lip. For a brief moment, she closed her eyes and shivered from head to toe. Then her eyes opened to dwell on him, as warm and inviting as the Caribbean. Silently, she leaned forward and kissed him long and hard on the mouth. All of her pain, her longing, went into that one kiss. He drew her to him, sliding her forward through the water, and kissed her eyes, her lips, her throat. Then he washed her, too.

They dried one another with short, rapid strokes of the towel, then went to her bedroom. Once there, they got close, loving hard, loving deep, sweating to make up for lost time. Once he woke her to lick honey from between her thighs. When the day had given way to early evening, she laid her face on his chest and asked:

"So, is your honey-stick sore?"

"It aches, all right."

She chuckled and played with him lazily. "You were a hungry man."

"Four years without a dip in the pot can do that."

"Four years?" she repeated with wonder, turning his exhausted member this way and that. "Why? Were you sick?" She looked up. "Or were you in jail?"

He saw the morbid interest in her eyes and felt only faint surprise. He'd always suspected that she had a dark side and yes, he was attracted to it. He chuckled.

"Yeah, I saw the inside of a couple. But not in the way you mean."

She twirled some of his chest hairs around her right index finger. "Does loving me cause you pain, David?" She pulled on the hairs a little, watching his skin lift, and whispered, "Do you feel ashamed?"

He shook his head.

She smiled sweetly at him, then gave his chest hairs a swift, sharp yank, ripping some out by the roots. He jerked up and grabbed her hand.

"What the fu—"

"Do you feel ashamed?"

Their gazes locked. She stared him down.

"Yeah," he said, finally. "I guess I do."

Her feline eyes appraised him. "But still, you love me." Her grip on his hairs loosened, and with a contented little smile, she lowered her head and nuzzled her cheek against his chest.

He let himself sink back against the pillow. One hand he threw across his forehead; with the other, he stroked the top of her head, drawing her hair back from her face. "Why d'you ask?"

Her voice, when it came, sounded as though it was floating from somewhere deep within him.

"Because . . . it's no good when the loving's easy. It's got to hurt . . . and hurt bad. That's the only way a body knows it's for real."

Years later, looking back, he would wonder at the power of pain, at how some people are more attracted to anguish than to ecstasy, how for some they are one and the same. But at the time, he only perceived that Rachel connected with him on a level that no other woman did. And that he was grateful to have someone with whom he could express, without explaining, the pain he otherwise had to hide.

He found that he'd forgotten his keys and had to ring the doorbell. Annie shook her head at the sight of him. Hers was the expression of a teacher who had seen his homework and was none too pleased. It was in the set of her mouth, the way her eyes moved over him. She hung up his coat, gave him another dark glance, then headed off down the hall. He pursued her and put a light restraining hand on her arm.

"Hey, Annie, what's the matter? Come on, look at me."

She turned around, her arms folded across her bosom, her lips pressed tight. "Yes?"

"What's the matter?"

She looked at him hard. This was more than disapproval. It was fury. "Mr. David . . . Her smell's all over you. You reek of her."

Normally, he was slow to anger, but her words threw his switch. "And what of it?"

"Looka here, I sees you runnin' over there all times of day, disappearin' early in the mornin' and comin' back at night. Now I don't know what you doin', but I can guess and it don't seem right, not after all that's happened."

He took a deep breath to try to calm down. "Annie, I love you and I respect you, but I won't let you mind my business. Now I know you're upset about Lilian—so am I—but that don't give you the right to—"

"This ain't got nothin' t'do with Miss Lilian. And you know it."

He stared at her, not comprehending. "I know *what?*"

She looked at him skeptically.

"Annie, tell me what-all I'm supposed to know!"

She studied him, still mistrustful, then told him to follow her into the kitchen. Once there, they sat down. She talked; he listened. Twenty minutes went by.

"Are you sure?"

"Go back 'n'see her. Talk t'her. But no matter what she says, please r'member this: There's some things a woman never forgives or forgets. Miss Rachel may not want t'carry her mem'ries round with her—I'm sure she don't—but she ain't got no choice. Them mem'ries is cut into her heart, burned into her soul. She'll never come free of 'em. Hear what I say, Mr. David, hear what I say. Them mem'ries will be a part of her 'til the day she die."

And so they would be. Rachel would never forget the day when the sun turned dark in her inner sky and bitterness settled like a permanent night over her heart. It was the twentieth of January 1923. David had been gone exactly three months. She'd visited Lilian. They were in the McKay family parlor. Rachel had sat nervously on the edge of the fireplace armchair. She was weak after days of vomiting. Her eyes were reddened from nights of crying. She saw that Lilian couldn't bear to look at her. They were old friends, but Lilian was ashamed and embarrassed. She obviously wanted her out of the house as quickly as possible.

Lilian took a step toward her, then faltered. Her expression was grim, but decided. "I'm sorry, Rachel. You're like a sister to me, but I can't help you. You're asking for something I cannot give."

Rachel's heart thumped painfully. "But why?" she pleaded. "Just tell me where he is."

"No."

Rachel's small hands balled into fists. She willed back the tears she feared were about to spring to her eyes.

Lilian's pale pink lips pressed together firmly. "Rachel, you're to blame for the trouble you're in. No decent woman would've let a man go as far as you did."

Rachel cringed inwardly but she forced herself to speak up. "It's not like I got this way by myself. David was there, too. I didn't force him to love me."

"My brother was only reacting like a healthy man. It's always the woman's place to keep matters within proper limits." Lilian's control snapped. "You should've known better."

"We were together only once."

"And this had to happen!"

"You think I did this on purpose to make him marry me?"

Lilian gritted her teeth. "I have nothing against my brother marrying you, but I won't let you use him. I don't believe he loves you. If he loved you, he would've come back."

Rachel wailed, "He'd come back if he knew—"

"I'm doing you a favor, Rachel. You don't believe it, but I am."

"It wouldn't be the way it was between your parents—"

"How dare you!"

Rachel saw that she'd said the wrong thing. What could she do? Finally, she begged. "If you won't tell me where he is, will you at least tell him about me, about . . . ?"

Lilian's eyes narrowed. A little smile appeared on her lips. "Yes," she said. "Of course I will."

"I knew she was lying before the words left her mouth." Rachel's eyes moved over David's face. "I mean, she did lie, didn't she? You never knew, did you?"

"No," he said. "I never knew."

His eyes burned in his head. He had left Rachel to face this alone. As for Lilian—he struggled to understand—how could she have done this?

"Didn't she do anything to help you?"

"She offered me money, in your name. To finance a new start, she said. *Elsewhere.*"

Of all Lilian's secrets, this was the worst. That she had known where he was, known that Rachel and his child needed him, but failed to tell him.

"She only wrote me that you'd left town."

"I didn't take Lilian's money. Mama bought me a bus ticket—a one-way ticket—to Chicago. She thought it'd be better for me if I went away. She was afraid the gossip would hurt me. But nothing could cut deeper than know-ing you were gone. After that, nothing mattered. But I couldn't stay. I had to think of Mama, too. She gave me all her savings. I went to the station by myself. But I didn't go to Chicago. I went to D.C. Somehow, I had a notion you were there. But you weren't. At least, I couldn't find you. I bought a cheap ring. Found a rooming house. And said I was a widow."

"And the baby?"

The expression in Rachel's eyes softened. "A little girl. I named her Isabella."

Pain blossomed inside David like a blood-red flower. "And did you put . . . Isabella . . . in a home?"

Rachel smiled dreamily. "She was so pretty. Sometimes I can still feel her soft little cheek against mine."

He had a sinking feeling. "Rachel, where's the baby?"

Rachel's smile abruptly faded. "Dead. Caught pneumonia. Died right before Christmas." Rachel's eyes became wet. She blinked and swallowed hard. "Maybe it's better that she's gone. She wouldn't have had much of a life. But I loved her. God, I ache for her. Mama said Isabella suffered for my sins, but I wonder what kind of God would punish an innocent baby. Sweet Jesus, she was five months old."

Rachel clenched her teeth and shut her eyes. Her small fists flexed and curled in her lap.

"I was afraid to . . . I didn't have the money to . . . bring her back here. I had to bury her there. To leave her down there with nobody to visit her. Sometimes I dream about getting the money together to go back. Just once. Just to put some flowers . . ." She bit her lip. "I left the same day as the funeral. Came back here. Mama fell ill three months later. She was gone within a week."

David took her in his arms. "My God, Rachel . . ."

She sagged against him, blinking rapidly to hold back her tears. "Lilian came to see me. My mama was dead. My baby was dead. And now, she wanted to know if there was anything she could do. I told her, no. No, thank you." Rachel forced a smile. "But you know something? I'm not bitter. I'm just glad that I had Isabella. So grateful that I had her at all."

He convinced Rachel to lend him her sole picture of Isabella. She relin-quished it only after he promised to return it. Later, ensconced in his arm-chair before the parlor fireplace, David fingered the small rectangle, studying it. His fingers trembled. His little girl had had his eyes, almond-shaped, dark and liquid. Her small lips were pert and soft like the leaves of cherry blossoms. She was a beautiful child who stared into the camera with a sense of expectation and curiosity about what life would bring. The magnitude of his loss hit him. He felt gutted. So much had happened while he was away. How could he have ever thought his disappearance wouldn't matter?

"You want another cup of coffee, Mr. David?"

Annie's gentle voice brought him back. She stood next to him, pointing at his still half-full cup on the nearby side table. "It's sat a long time. Probably done gotten cold. You want a fresh cup?"

Yes. He needed warmth, to drink it and hold it, to stave off the cold that was creeping around inside him.

"Thank you," he said, then asked: "Why didn't Lilian tell me that Rachel needed me?"

"The first of the Seven Sins," she said promptly.

Pride, he thought. *Puritan pride. They were friends. Like sisters, for years. But when it came down to it, Lilian didn't think Rachel was good enough. And it didn't matter that Rachel was carrying my child. She didn't just turn her back on her friend—but on her own flesh and blood . . . because of pride.*

He fingered the small photograph, still thinking of Lilian.

Just one more sign that I didn't really know her. No more than I know Gem.

His thoughts slowed.

Gem . . .

Who was he to judge her? After what he'd done? After what Lilian had done? Gem was his one remaining blood relative. They'd never made much effort to get along, but now—he wanted to. Suddenly, he was determined to.

But first, he had something else to do. A plan fully formed had presented itself to him. And to his tired mind, the plan made sense. He'd failed his father, his sister, and his child. What was done was done and they were gone. He hadn't done right by them, but he could still do right by Rachel, do what he should have done to begin with.

Marry her.

Yes . . . that's what he had to do. A sense of relief, as well as of inevitability, swept over him. He saw with startling clarity that he was not in love with Rachel. He felt at most a deep affection for her. She could certainly make him desire to touch her more than any other woman he had ever known, but lust had nothing to do with love. He saw that while part of his decision to marry her grew from a sense of guilt, another part stemmed from his awareness that she was a tie to his roots. They were bonded by a common history, one of shared pain as well as pleasure. After living for four years as a stranger in a strange land, he was desperately lonely and needed someone with whom he could be himself.

His plan required him to give up his life in Philadelphia, but he knew with sudden, brilliant clarity that he would not miss it. What he desired most was a new start. He could do that with Rachel. When he left town this time, he would take her with him.

The idea of marrying someone he was not in love with seemed familiar. Why? Then he thought of his mother and Lilian. Inaccessible husbands, neglected wives. One-sided marriages were the McKay way.

He'd long ago stopped trying to understand his parents' relationship. Or rather, he thought he *had* understood it and because that understanding brought him no comfort, he'd finally left the matter alone.

Lila had suffered under Augustus. She was lithe, pretty, and accomplished. But her skin likened to chocolate, not honey; her hair to wool, not silk—and those were the deciding factors. She adored her tall, light-skinned husband. There was no sign, however, that he loved her. Quite the contrary: His eyes filled with resentment when she entered the room. He dismissed her love but demanded her loyalty. Any respect he showed her was due to her station as his wife, not her worth as an individual. And any need on his part to love or be loved was satisfied in the arms of the high-toned mistresses he took on with a vengeance.

"Why do you have to humiliate me?" David had once overheard his mother cry. He'd been walking past his father's office door. It was shut, and normally, you couldn't hear a thing through it. But his parents must've been standing just on the other side. Augustus was trying to get Lila to leave. She'd broken into his inner sanctum and he wanted her out. She had no intention of going, not without saying her peace. David listened with a sense of shame.

"I can't take it much longer—"

"You'll take whatever I give you. You wanted me. You got me. Now, leave."

"Augustus, please—"

"Leave!"

David hurried away, ducking into the parlor just in time. He peeked out. His mother stepped outside his father's office. She turned to look at Augustus and he shut the door in her face. As David watched, she bent her head and wept. She muffled her cries with a handkerchief.

His blood pounded in his head. He was filled with hate and shame—hate for his father and shame that he couldn't protect his mother.

Why did Daddy marry her? If that's the way he's going to treat her?

She straightened up and held her small head erect.

That's right, Mama. Don't let him get you down.

Was there ever a time when it had been good between them? When his father had treated her with love and respect? David searched his memory for instances and found precious few.

His mother went toward the kitchen, then paused on the threshold and turned back. Her face had a peculiar look when she did that. He'd noticed that she never entered the kitchen when Annie was in there. She and Annie rarely spoke to one another, exchanging words only when it was necessary.

She started back toward the front of the house. David withdrew into the parlor and went behind the door. He didn't want her to see him standing there, *spying on her.* Through the crack between the door and its frame, he watched as she passed and went up the steps.

He'd once heard his father mutter that marriage to a "high yaller" would've helped him businesswise, would've brought him good social contacts. No doubt Augustus believed that and the wisdom of the times backed him, for it dictated that everyone in the race "marry up." But if that was the case, then one had to wonder, why *had* he married Lila?

David had heard rumors and he'd done simple arithmetic. It took a woman nine months after marriage to bear a child. Why had she needed only six with him?

So what if he married you because he had to, he wanted to say, as he watched her climb the stairs. *That doesn't give him the right to treat you this way.*

That was the message he wanted to give—and one day would. But he had to find the right words. The wrong words would hurt her, would make her feel cheap, and God knows that's not what he wanted to do. He wanted, if anything, to relieve her of the burden of keeping a secret. A secret he already knew. *Mama, it's okay. I understand,* he wanted to say. *Someday, Daddy's going to know what he had in you. Someday, he'll be sorry.*

He'd stood there with clenched fists, thinking that yes, in time he'd find the right words . . . the words and the courage. But time ran out before he found either one.

Lila died under the wheels of a trolley car on Thanksgiving Day in November 1920, eight months after they'd moved to Strivers' Row, one week after he'd overheard the scene in his father's office.

On the eve of her funeral, David watched as his father approached Lila's casket in the parlor. Augustus broke down. His tears ran freely. In his remaining months, he wandered through the house, a tired, insignificant-looking old man. Without Lila's love and adoration to inflate him, he seemed to shrink. He withdrew, disapproving of any "outsider" who stepped through the door, and filled the house with his mournful spirit. He held his children to him with a dark magnetism that silenced all thoughts of resistance. By June, he was gone, too.

David now resolved that his marriage would be different. He would give his wife attention and affection. He would do his best to be a good husband. Ironically, his past neglect of Rachel would guarantee that he would treat her well.

His mind made up, he decided that the marriage would take place as soon as possible, but his plan for a fresh beginning would have to wait a while. Even if he did manage to accept the idea of Lilian's death as a suicide, he still wanted Sweet out of the house. Once Sweet was gone, a decision would have to be made about the place. Glancing around the room, David knew he would never sell the house, but he couldn't live there either. He hadn't lived in it long before going south, but in that short time, it had accumulated too many memories. And goodness only knows how long he could stave off questions about his past if he remained in town. He would retire Annie—she would hate that, but he had no choice—rent the house (with Annie in it, if necessary), and he and Rachel would start anew.

Later that day, he went to Annie in the laundry room and told her: "I just thought you should know. I plan to ask Miss Rachel to marry me."

Annie was folding towels. She was quiet at first, getting used to the idea, he supposed. Then she looked at him. "Do you love her?"

He was quiet for a moment. "I care for her."

She took a deep breath and went back to folding "So, it's really 'cause of the baby?"

"Sort of." He folded his arms across his chest. "And because I need someone. I can't stay in Harlem—don't ask me why—and when I leave, I'm going to take her with me." He touched her elbow. "Don't you like her? I thought you'd be . . . well, happy, to hear that I'm going to do right by her."

"Two wrongs don't make a right," she said and went back to folding a bath towel, taking extra care to match the corners. "I'd like to see you marry somebody you love. I know that girl's been crazy 'bout you since she first laid eyes on you. She so fulla love for you, she cain't see straight. And right now, it prob'ly won't matter t'her much that your feelin's ain't the same. I mean—you ain't lied t'her or nothin', has you, sayin' somethin' you don't mean?"

"No, I've been honest."

"Well, I guess she don't know it yet—or she don't care—but she'll find out. It can be awful hard on a woman livin' with a man that don't love her. All them feelin's goin' out and nothin' comin' in . . . it's kinda like starvin'."

He thought again of Lila and Augustus, of Lilian and Sweet. "I'll take good care of her. It doesn't have to turn out badly. Maybe the love'll come later."

"Maybe . . . But maybe, it won't." She looked at him. "You really think it's gonna come with you?"

"I don't know."

"Well, you best be thinkin' long and patient 'bout it, Mr. David, 'cause when you say them words 'I do,' you cain't never take 'em back."

She picked up another towel and spread it out flat on the countertop. "And what you gonna do 'bout the house?"

He licked his lips. "I wanted to talk to you about that. Annie, like I said, I can't stay here—but I'm going to make sure Mr. Jameson's out of the house."

"He ain't going nowhere if he finds out you ain't gonna stay here."

"He'll leave. One way or another, he'll go. What I want to talk to you about is what happens after he's gone."

She looked at him with sudden understanding. "Don't tell me you gonna sell this place—"

"No . . . No, I'm not. But I am going to have to rent it out."

Panic flashed across her face. "Oh my God, you gonna put me out?"

"No, of course not."

Stunned and hurt, she put a hand to her mouth. A little sound escaped. She blinked and turned away. He put an arm around her shoulder.

"Don't worry, please. No matter what, you're going to be able to stay here."

She just shook her head, soundlessly.

"I am *not* going to put you out," he repeated. "And I'm not going to let anyone else do it either."

She put a trembling hand on the counter to steady herself. "Oh, Mr. David, you don't understand. You just don't understand." She turned her wrinkled face toward him. Tears shimmered in her eyes. "This house," she whispered. "This house—I done spent more'n halfa my life takin' care of you and your fam'ly. I don't wanna work for nobody else. I *won't* work for nobody else."

"Annie, calm down."

"You just don't understand."

"I do understand—"

"No, you don't. You don't understand nothin'—not nothin'."

She turned away. He let his hands drop and sighed.

The problem was, he did understand. He just didn't know what to do about it.

25

The Proposal

The sun hung low in the sky with a dull, metallic gleam, like a watch dangling from a banker's gray pocket. The air was cool and damp and looked like it would stay that way forever. It was that time of year when it's hard to believe there ever was or will be another summer.

David had begun his day with another visit to Lilian's grave. He stood there for a long, long time. A tidal wave of resignation and despair surged inside him. He tried to contain his pain, his hands clasped tightly before him, but as the emotional pressure in his chest swelled and expanded, he felt as though he might explode. Closing his eyes, he let the pain wash over him. He rolled with it, like a man tossed and tumbled by the sea. His chest constricted; he couldn't breathe. And like a man adrift, he wondered, *Will I ever reach shore again?* Finally, the pain subsided. Numbness set in. He sank down on his haunches by the grave.

"I'll never stop fighting for you, never," he whispered, "but I have other responsibilities, too. What we did to Rachel—it wasn't right. She deserved better. I wish we could change the past. But we can't. And now there's no turning back. You must understand. There is no turning back."

Rachel had the day off. David picked her up late that afternoon. They walked through the park path along Riverside Drive. Couples strolling along hugged one another against the cold. Others took turns pushing prams. A few children rode battered bicycles while their friends ran alongside. David thought of Isabella. She would have been three years old, able to run, climb, get into mischief, and keep up a constant chatter. He caught himself. He was yearning for a child he would never hold. Putting one hand on the small of Rachel's back, he guided her to the edge of the path. It was a quiet spot, from which they could clearly see across the Hudson River.

The water was a filthy blue-gray. And the skyline beyond it was less than significant. Yet the scene had its own melancholy beauty. David's gaze dwelled on the water. The Hudson had always fascinated him. Its swift current had stirred his young man's heart with thoughts of travel. It had beguiled him with hints of life beyond the horizon, of days filled with adventure, danger, and delight. There were fortunes to be made and worlds to be conquered if only one had the guts to step beyond the shore. The river, the river: It promised the freedom to wander, but never once mentioned the loneliness of exile.

"Rachel, you've told me it's time to look toward the future. You're right."

He felt her tense.

"You're leaving?" she asked.

"Yes . . . but—"

"Don't worry. I won't try to keep you."

He took her hands in his and brought them to his lips. Her fingers were cold. Exhaling puffs of warm air on them, he massaged them gently.

"I want to buy you some gloves. The warmest I can find."

"That's very kind, but you don't need to."

She withdrew her hands from his and put them into her pocket. Her sudden coolness dismayed him. He tried to remember all the sweet words he'd rehearsed, but could recall none of them. So he went straight to the heart of the matter. Reaching into his coat pocket, he brought out a small jeweler's box covered in blue velvet. He opened it to reveal a ring, a tear-shaped diamond on a slender gold band. Her eyes widened at the sight of it and she gasped as he slipped the ring onto the fourth finger of her left hand.

"I'm asking you to be my wife. I promise, here and now, to honor and respect you, as long as we both shall live." He took a deep breath and his voice broke. "Marry me, Rachel. Believe in me. Trust me, again. And the loving won't have to hurt for it to be real."

She swallowed hard. Tears welled in her eyes as she looked at the ring. "It's beautiful . . . but I can't accept it."

His heart thudded. "Why not?"

"You're only proposing out of guilt."

"I should've asked you long ago."

"You're only asking now because of Isabella."

"Isabella was simply the kick I needed."

Silent and skeptical, she turned her face away. He cupped her chin and made her look at him.

"Rachel, I know life's been hard on you, but it's been hard on me, too."

"Hard on *you?* You're a McKay. You have a name, money."

"But I don't have you. And that makes all the difference. Now how about it? You gonna make an honest man of me?"

For a moment, she didn't answer. Tears slid down her face. Then she smiled and nodded jerkily. It was all he needed. He grabbed her up and kissed her face, her eyes, her lips, and the tip of her nose. He picked her up and swung her around. His heart had never felt lighter, his soul freer. He had finally done something right. He would be able to leave all the madness of Harlem and Philadelphia behind him.

"We'll go somewhere, start fresh."

"You mean not live on Strivers' Row?"

"No. Once Sweet's out of the house, I'll rent it. We'll find a new place. Start over."

For the first time in years, he felt hope. He was so engaged with his vision of their future that it took him a while to notice that her smile had faltered.

"What's the matter?"

Rachel hesitated. Her gaze went out over the Hudson, to the world beyond the river's shore. "I was thinking about what leaving Harlem might mean. I don't know if I can do that."

His smile died. "You can't mean that."

"But I do."

"Don't you ever want to experience life outside of this place?"

She was quiet. "I did. Once. I never want to step foot outside Harlem again."

"It'll be different this time. You'll be with me."

"No, it's not what you're thinking. I don't know if I can explain it. I need this place, somehow. Seeing the people in the neighborhood going about their daily lives. I don't know—I feel strong here."

He had never expected her to refuse to leave Harlem. There were black communities elsewhere that had something to offer. Yes, he could understand that like thousands of Harlemites, she might be indifferent to white New York. She might admire items on display in its downtown shops, applaud shows at its theaters, browse through books in its libraries, and every now and then sip coffee at one of its restaurants. She might peruse its newspapers and cluck her tongue over "the doings of white folks," then promptly use the newsprint to wrap potato cuttings in. Never once would she consider herself a part of the silver metropolis. Hundreds of wealthy whites might stream toward black Harlem to visit its cabarets, but essentially white New York had nothing to do with her, or she with it, and she liked it that way. David could understand all that. But it surprised him that she had absolutely no curiosity about life outside New York. Did she actually intend to live her life within the strict confines of Central Park to the south, Fifth Avenue to the east, St. Nicholas Park to the west, and 145th Street to the north?

It was as though she'd heard his thoughts.

"This is my portion, David, and I'm satisfied with it." She faced him, her eyes darkly somber. "We have a home here, a place to build on. The house on Strivers' Row might have bad memories now, but we can fill it with love. Think, David. We have friends here, a community. And we're so lucky we do. We're living in the heart of the world's most exciting Negro community. No, I don't want to leave it. And you wouldn't either if you only thought about it."

He gazed at the horizon with profound longing. He should have anticipated her desire to live on Strivers' Row. She was a realist. The house was one reason why she was attracted to him; the house, the status and the stability that it stood for. That didn't bother him because he was sure she loved him. He had sensed her adoration since the first day she had seen him, when they were children, so many years ago, long before his family became rich. He wished intensely that she had been prepared to go away with him, but why should she? What could he offer her but vague promises and undefined dreams? His shoulders slumped but his smile was valiant.

"We'll stay here, Rachel. I promise you the house and all that goes with it. If that's what you want, that's what you'll have."

He felt like a prisoner who'd been given a glimpse of freedom, then yanked back into his cage. He then saw the delight and joy in her eyes and that comforted him.

"One more thing," she said. "I want you to accept that Lilian's gone. You can't bring her back. You'll get Sweet out of the house—I don't want him there either—but otherwise, you'll leave him alone. No more trying to say that he killed Lilian. Agreed?"

She squeezed his hand gently and looked up at him. He was quiet, his head bent, his jaw clenched. There was a long silence. This was not what he had intended. She kissed him.

"I don't want you to spend our married life chasing down Sweet," she said. "I don't want you wasting *our* time."

He looked at her.

"I have a right to ask that of you," she said. "God knows, I've waited for you long enough."

He smiled dryly, but he thought to himself, *She's right.* He had kept her waiting, too long. And how much of a life could they have with him always looking back? On the other hand, how could he let Sweet get away with . . . He sighed roughly. Rachel drew a fingertip across his chin. He gazed down at her. He did care for her. And he wanted to make her happy. Perhaps she was right. Perhaps it made no sense to continue to rake up the past. Perhaps . . . it was indeed time to let Lilian rest in peace. With an effort, he pushed his misgivings aside. He took Rachel in his arms.

"All right. It's agreed."

They headed back to her apartment. She invited him in, but he turned her down. He wanted to be alone. Noting the concern on her face, he hugged her again. Then he was gone.

26

In the Belly of the Whale

If she only knew what that promise might cost us.

Public shame and social ostracism: The McKay family name, which represented such genteel dignity and pride of race, would become muddied with cowardice and mired in moral disgrace. The doors to the elegant homes and elite salons she so desperately wanted to enter would be slammed in their faces. They would not be able to walk down the street without encountering stares of disdain.

She might even leave him. What irony. He would stay in Harlem to give her pleasure, but it was this very decision that would cause her pain. Nevertheless, he would try. He owed her that much. He had abandoned her when he left Harlem those four years ago, not that he had planned to leave her, to leave anyone, when he went away that October day. It was the seventeenth of the month, 1922. He had expected to return after a couple of weeks' work, but it hadn't happened that way.

His assignment had taken him to Charlottesville, in Boone County, Georgia. He could still hear the train wheels screeching as the locomotive ground to a halt, the confused babble of hurried, excited voices as people climbed off, met friends, and tried to find their way.

Charlottesville was a rich little town in the southernmost part of the state, near the Florida border. David's intent was to investigate the lynchings of five Negroes—four brothers and one of the men's sons, an eleven-year-old boy—two weeks before.

Passing himself off as a white reporter for the *New York Sentinel,* David found it easy to get the locals to talk. They didn't try to hide their part in the lynchings, but talked volubly, sometimes with pride. They described the torture, mutilation, burning, and hanging of the five victims with the same enthusiasm one would expect in a recounting of a day at the circus. Many took out their "souvenirs" from the lynchings: the burnt stump of a wooden stake, a bloodstained stretch of rope, charred bones, and pickled body parts removed while the victims were still alive. At the same time, however, none of the whites he spoke to would name names. If he pressed for the identities of the mob leaders, a funny look would flit across their faces, a sudden suspicion, and he'd find the conversation ended.

Certain facts were not in dispute: Over the course of three days, October 8 through 10, 1922, mobs executed Hosea Johnson, his brothers Solomon, Jeremiah, and Ezekiel, and Ezekiel's son Caleb. The men were accused of having murdered a white farmer, Ray Stokes, and of raping Stokes's wife, Missy.

There was no doubt that Stokes had been killed, but was it premeditated murder? Had his wife indeed been raped? And if so, what, if anything, did the Johnsons have to do with these events?

The Johnson brothers were family men. Stable. Hardworking. Even the whites conceded that. After the men were killed, their homes were burned to the ground. Their widows and the remaining children, a total of twelve, were whipped, then driven out of town with only the clothes on their backs.

Talks with the locals also quickly gave David a picture of Stokes. Big and burly, Stokes had owned a large plantation in Boone County. He was known for beating and cheating his Negro workers. After a while, no blacks would voluntarily agree to work for him, so Stokes found a way to force them to. He regularly visited the courthouse and checked the docket to see what black man had been convicted and couldn't pay his fine or was sentenced to work on the chain gang, Stokes would pay the fine, get the man released into his custody, and have him work off the debt on his plantation.

Hosea Johnson fell under Stokes's shadow in just this way. His thirty-dollar gaming fine had been beyond his means. Stokes put his money down and had himself a new man. Johnson labored on Stokes's property until the thirty dollars had been worked off. Perhaps the situation would've turned out differently if matters had ended there. But they didn't.

Johnson's wife was pregnant with their fifth child. Money was more than tight and work was hard to come by. So when Stokes offered to "let" Johnson work additional hours, Johnson agreed. Days went by and Johnson's labor added up to a considerable amount of service. After a week, Johnson asked Stokes for the money due him for the extra time; Stokes refused. Witnesses said the two men argued. That was on October 7. That evening, Stokes was found dead on his front porch, an ax embedded in his meaty chest.

The call went out and men swarmed to the Stokeses' plantation. Suspicion immediately targeted Hosea Johnson. Somebody mentioned how close the Johnson brothers were and pointed out that they'd all had trouble with Stokes. No doubt, the brothers had committed the crime together.

Men were deputized and went looking for the brothers, but word of Stokes's death and the ensuing manhunt had spread; the Johnson brothers and their families had disappeared into the woods.

On October 8, Solomon and Jeremiah Johnson were captured about five miles outside Charlottesville. They were lynched on the spot. Hung upside down, they were literally ripped apart by a furious fuselage of more than five hundred bullets.

Sheriff Parker Haynes caught Ezekiel that afternoon and placed him in the nearby Putnam city jail. That evening, Hayes and the county court clerk took Ezekiel out of jail, ostensibly to transport him to the county seat at Lovetree for safekeeping. Haynes told David that a mob had "ambushed" him near the fork of the Dicey and Lovetree roads, just two miles from their destination. Outarmed and outmanned, he said, "I had no choice but to stand by and watch."

Ezekiel was handcuffed and slowly strangled. First, the lynchers chopped off his fingers. They then strung him up three times, letting him down each time to give him "a chance to save his immortal soul by confessing." Finally, they just let him swing. He died maintaining his innocence.

Ezekiel was left on display for two days. Crowds in autos, buggies, and on foot strolled by to point and snigger.

Meanwhile, the hunt for Hosea continued in vain. After two days of searching, people assumed that he'd successfully fled the area. On the afternoon of October 10, a black man named Moses Whitney burst into Haynes's office and told him that Hosea was hiding out at his house. Hosea had come to him for food, Whitney said. He'd given Hosea food and promised him supplies, but when Hosea had fallen asleep, exhausted, Whitney had slipped out of the house.

The sheriff's men surrounded Whitney's house. There was an exchange of gunfire but Hosea was taken alive. He was attached by rope to the back of a car, dragged down Crabtree Boulevard, the busiest street in Charlottesville, then taken out to a place called the Old Indian Cemetery, on the edge of town. There, they hung him upside down, doused him with kerosene, and burned him alive. David visited the place. It was beautiful and still, and it was hard to believe it had been the site of such recent evil. The only testimony was the scorched remains of an isolated tree.

Now, according to the newspaper reports David had read, Hosea Johnson had confessed to the murder and the assault before he died. David tried to see

Mrs. Stokes, but was told that she was still suffering from shock. He was able to gather information from servants, however. It was Mrs. Stokes who had found the body. As soon as she saw her husband lying there, she'd run to her father-in-law's house, screaming that Hosea had "axed my Christian man."

She was hysterical but said nothing about Hosea having attacked *her*. The family physician, who happened to be a dining guest at the home of Stokes Sr., quickly sedated her. Despite the fact that Mrs. Stokes lay unconscious for nearly two days, City Superintendent Sharkey Summers claimed that he'd talked to her the morning after the murder. "She told me what the nigger done to her," he said in one newspaper article. He became one of the leading advocates for the burning of Hosea Johnson.

David read and reread the newspaper reports. The papers had fed the lynching mania. Not a single one had urged due legal process for the accused when captured. All had predicted with malevolent glee that Hosea Johnson would be hung and burned, virtually passing sentence and prescribing in detail the mode of execution.

Nor had any report attempted to explain the death of Ezekiel's son, Caleb. One wrote that "the nigger child's death was too insignificant to explore."

David talked not only to white locals, but also to black residents. At least, he tried to. Most had fled into the woods and were only slowly daring to return. They professed absolute ignorance of what had occurred while they were gone. Others admitted that they'd seen and heard enough to have something to say, but they refused to speak.

Over a three-day period, David canvassed about forty ramshackle homes on the black side of town. Most wouldn't even open their doors. Finally, he gave up. There was a late afternoon train. He'd be on it. Back at his hotel, he wrote his report, packed his bags, and headed for the railway station. It was there he happened upon a man who *would* talk. And the man's name was Jonah.

"Caleb was a bright youngster," said Jonah. "He was there when they dragged his poppa from the woods. Later, somebody heard him say that he'd write to the Movement, tell who it was done what. That night, they came back for him."

"God," murmured David.

At the railroad station, Jonah, a porter, had whispered instructions to meet him at Miss Mae's Rooming House, then gone back to work, hauling luggage. David had gone ahead to the house and Jonah had showed up ten minutes later.

"The next train ain't 'til tomorrow," Jonah had said. "But you can stay here tonight."

Miss Mae's was a little two-story construction, not much more than an oversized hut, and David had had his doubts when he saw it. Miss Mae eased his concern the minute he stepped inside the door.

"What a fine young man!"

She welcomed him, a stranger, with outstretched arms. She was so thin; it hurt David to look at her. He gratefully accepted the hug and the pat on the shoulder she gave him, and gently hugged her back.

"You just come on in and rest yourself," she said. At the sight of Jonah, her smile grew wider. "Jonah! You come on in here. I ain't seen you for way too long."

Before David could blink, Miss Mae had sat him and Jonah down at the table and laid out some thin peach pie and watery coffee for them. It was a meager spread, but it was all the woman had and David was touched by her generosity.

Miss Mae sat at the table with them. She refused to eat, but said: "Y'all take as much as you want." Her voice was as soft as a whisper. She looked at David and her eyes twinkled with curiosity. She wasn't fooled by the lightness of his skin. "You one of us, ain't you?"

David smiled and nodded.

"So, where you from?"

"He's from up north," said Jonah.

David sipped some coffee to wash down the hard, crusty pie. "I'm working for the Movement. Took the train down from New York. I'm here to find the truth about what really happened."

Miss Mae and Jonah exchanged glances. David sensed a palpable sadness enter the room. Jonah rubbed his chin. He was thoughtful.

"In a way, what happened here," he began, "weren't nothin' special. Nothin' we ain't seen b'fore. It was bad. Yeah, it was real bad. But bad happens to us colored all the time. It happened here, but it coulda happened in the next town over. Y'understand?" He looked at David, who nodded. "There's a lot of Charlottesvilles waitin' t'happen," said Jonah, his brown eyes mournful. "Us colored folk . . . we's born under the hangman's noose. We never know when he'll come a-knockin'. Could be, he never comes. Could be, he comes on the morrow, any time, any day. And we accept." He was silent, staring at his large hands, which he clenched and opened, clenched and opened. David looked at them too, thinking of their size . . . and their impotence in the face of the white man's rule. Jonah looked up at David. "We cain't do nothin' 'bout nothin' down here, so we accept. We just . . . accept." He dropped his hands to his lap, and there was something very close to despair in his eyes. "My name is Jonah and many times I wonder . . . will I end up in the belly of the whale? I just hope the Lord'll deliver me if I do."

"Hush your mouth," Miss Mae said. "Ain't no need t'be scarin' this young man. He a stranger—"

"That's right," said Jonah. "He a stranger and he don't know nothin' 'bout what's going on down here. But he need to."

"That's why I'm here," David said with confidence. "It's my job to take a look-see. Ask questions. Get answers."

After that, he and Jonah had moved to the front porch. Now Jonah was sitting in Miss Mae's creaky rocking chair, hunched forward. David was perched on the wooden railing, his arms folded across his chest, his face grim.

"The reports say Hosea admitted to killing Stokes and assaulting the man's wife. Is that true?"

"He ain't gone nowhere near Missy Stokes, but yeah, it's true he said he killed the white man."

"They tortured it out of him?"

"Didn't have to. He fessed up all right. Free 'n' clear. Told Whitney all 'bout it."

"Whitney? The one who turned him in?"

"That's right."

"You believe what Whitney said, considering the fact that he turned him in?"

"Yeah, I b'lieve it. Most times, you cain't b'lieve Whitney, but this time I b'lieves him. See, Hosea said he killed Mistah Stokes all right, but he said it was an accident. He went back t'see Mistah Stokes 'bout the money. Mistah Stokes tole him that if he chopped him some mo' wood, he'd maybe get his money. Hosea said he wasn't 'bout to do that. Mistah Stokes got angry. Took out his gun and aimed t'shoot. Hosea—he threw his ax at the man and run. He say he heard the man grunt, but he ain't look back, so he didn' know that the ax had killed him."

"And what about this business with Missy Stokes? Did he say anything about that?"

"He say he guessed that Missy Stokes was in the house, but he ain't never seen her. Said he just threw that ax, turned tail, and headed for the woods."

David looked at Jonah for a moment. Everything Jonah had said made sense. David sighed, dropped his hands to the railings, and shook his head, reflecting on what he'd heard. He looked at Jonah. "I'm glad you decided to talk."

"I hope it'll help."

"It will. And don't worry, I won't name your name in my report. Nobody'll learn from me that we had this conversation." He smiled and stuck his hand out.

Jonah shook David's hand with his callused one. They'd been talking for more than an hour. David had missed his train. He didn't want to spend another night in town, but it looked as though he'd have to. He cast his eyes to the western horizon. The winter sun was setting. Brilliant streaks of red, orange, and gold were layered behind the trees. His gaze took in the lush green foliage crowding the edge of Miss Mae's yard. In stark contrast to the decrepit rooming house, it was a rich display. As he looked, a branch swayed, leaves rustled, and a twig snapped. He frowned, his gaze hardening into a stare. Jonah, following David's look, said:

"Maybe we better go inside."

David glanced at him, then back at the bushes. They were still and silent. "Yeah ... maybe we'd better."

Night fell. Jonah had wished David good luck and gone home. After updating his report, David had retired to the upstairs room Miss Mae had given him. His sleep was troubled. He was standing in a narrow street, caged in by rickety buildings on either side. He could hear a low rumbling, a churning sound, like an approaching river. It was getting nearer. He looked up—just in time to see the rising wave of water rushing toward him. He had to get out of the way before he was crushed. He started to run—

And jerked himself awake. He lay there for a moment, stunned. Gradually, he realized that the rumbling he'd heard in his dream was still there. He sat up in bed, his ears straining to understand the sound. He was aware of his heart beating heavily, of cold sweat trickling down from his armpits. Creeping to the room's sole window, he peeked out. By the ghostly light of a full moon, he saw dusty clusters of white men swarming up the town's main street. It was the muffled sound of their running feet that he'd heard, and the blurred murmurs of their agitated voices. They carried homemade torches. All bore arms: everything from shotguns and pistols to iron clubs and bullwhips.

David dressed quickly in the dark. Miss Mae was standing on the landing when he left his room. Her sad, wrinkled face was drawn. She held a candle; it threw flickering orange shadows over her shrunken face. Her bony shoulders shivered under her thin shawl.

"Don't go out there," she whispered. "Please!"

"Don't worry. I'll be all right."

He gave her a hug, and then raced down the steps and out into the street. He'd never felt such fear, not even under fire in Europe. Yet a desperate need to know drove him on. He followed the growing mob. The crowd, which included women and children, had stopped at a clearing at the farthest end of the Old Indian Cemetery, where the grass grew thin, not far from the tree where Hosea had died.

David looked around. The area had a few other trees, but they were young—nothing sturdy enough to support a man's weight. That gave him hope—a hope that withered when he looked at the faces in the crowd. He saw grim, maniacal expressions, pale eyes that glittered with homicidal determination. The air crackled with pent-up anticipation and repressed exhilaration. Few words were exchanged. The ground began to vibrate. Then came the rumble of galloping horses and the cries of men raised in exultant triumph.

David turned.

The crowd had parted. A single white rider appeared, galloping at full speed, kicking up a billowing cloud of reddish-brown dust. Out of the cloud emerged the form of a ragged bundle, dragged by a rope attached to the rider's saddle horn. Soon, other riders appeared. And men on foot who waved their arms. The horsemen thundered through. David's recognized the victim. His heart thumped.

It was Jonah, bloody and battered.

Four men lugged in two short wooden stakes. They pounded them into the ground—not too deep, because they were in a hurry, but deep enough to make them hold. Stretching Jonah out on the ground, they yanked his hands over his head. His wrists they bound to one stake; his ankles to the other. Meanwhile, people in cars were arriving. They parked and left their headlights on, illuminating Jonah in a glaring, ghostly white light. From the cars erupted men with cameras and tripods. Within minutes, the atmosphere had gone from grim to festive. A party was about to take place and a torture-murder was going to be the main attraction.

In a spasm of terror, Jonah twisted and yanked at his bonds. Onlookers jeered, enjoying his struggles. He bucked and pulled, but the stakes held.

Finally, he let his head drop back and closed his eyes. He lay there, his chest heaving. Then he raised his head again and looked around. His gaze jumped backed and forth across the crowd and then . . . they found David.

David felt something inside him spasm and a pain shot through him that reached his fingertips. Just a few hours earlier, he and this man had been sitting at Miss Mae's together. *Will I end up in the belly of the whale?* Jonah had asked. Now, Jonah's eyes, full of wrenching despair, held the answer.

One of the whites followed Jonah's stare. "Hey, I know him!" he yelled, pointing to David. "He's the one been hangin' around, askin' questions."

"He the one I seen at Miss Mae's," another cried. "He was sittin' and jivin' with the niggers just like he was a one of 'em."

"Maybe he *is!*" the first said. "A Yankee nigger!"

Angry murmurs rumbled through the crowd. The mob seemed to contract, then it surged toward David like a murderous claw. He couldn't move. His instincts said run, but his legs wouldn't carry him. He could never outrun that crowd. His eyes went to Jonah. Their gazes locked. It couldn't have been more than a split second, but David would never forget the agony, the dignity and fellowship in Jonah's eyes. *Save yourself,* Jonah seemed to say, *and live to tell my story.* David heard Jonah's message in his heart. He did not remember opening his mouth, but he heard his own voice, anguished, broken and husky.

"I'm not a nigger," he whispered. "I'm not . . . one of *them.*"

"You spoke t'him at the railroad station. And then you was at that ole nigger woman's house. I saw ya!"

David's chest heaved. "He said she wasn't feeling well. I went to help. But I don't know him . . . don't know him at all."

"You's a lying uppity yella nigger!"

"Come down here to spy on us!"

"Let's burn the bastard!"

"Yeah!"

David tried to swallow, but his throat had gone dry. With a leaden finger, he slowly tapped the collar of his well-cut jacket. His voice was heavy with shame. "Would a colored man be dressed so fine? Speak so well? Would a colored man stand here and watch while another colored man dies? Wouldn't I be running . . . if I was a colored man, too?"

Hoots and snickers went up.

"Hey, we's wasting time," a voice cried out. "We already got a nigger to burn!"

"Yeah!"

"Let's get to it!"

The mob lost interest in David. The people began to turn their backs on him. He took a tentative step forward and asked: "But what has this man done?"

One of the white men slowly turned. He was tall, nearly skeletal and had a fanatic's gleam in his eyes. He held a coiled bullwhip. "What d'ya mean, what's the nigger done?" he hissed, looking David up and down. His gray eyes glinted with renewed suspicion. Gesturing toward Jonah with the bullwhip, he said: "Niggers don't need t'do nothin' to die, but this one's done a-plenty. He's been spreadin' lies about them nigger deaths."

"Take him to the sheriff," said David. "Whatever you think he's done, he deserves a fair trial."

More laughter, but bitter this time and laced with poison.

"Damn! Where you come from anyway?" the lanky man asked. "A fair trial? It's the American way, right? Well, hell, down here, son, *lynching* is the American way. Y'see the niggers down here—*our* niggers—they gets a hot tongue—a very hot tongue—when they forgets their place."

The lyncher turned back to the crowd. Laughing amiably, he slowly uncoiled his bullwhip. Then he spun around and brought the lash down across David's left shoulder. David reeled backward with a cry. The material of his jacket tore and his shoulder reddened with blood. The lyncher pulled the whip back with a resounding crack, and then flicked it forward. It wrapped around David's ankles like a thick snake. The lyncher yanked and David's feet went from under him. He lay in the dust, sprawled on his back. The lyncher stood over him.

"Now I don't b'lieve in whippin' no white man. But I will if I have to. If you know what's good for you, you'll just settle down, enjoy the show. This here's gonna be a good one."

A babble of malicious chuckles and comments went up. The mob surged back to their victim. Children were sent to scavenge for twigs, urged on by their parents' pointing fingers. It was a game to see who could gather the most. Some of the children were no older than three. Jonah watched mutely as they ran hither and thither, laughing and giggling. The oldest staggered back quickly, their thin arms laden down with twigs, their small faces suffused with pride. Kneeling down next to Jonah, they arranged the branches snugly at his side.

Can they bring themselves to look in his eyes? David wondered. *They're old enough to realize that he's a human being . . . old enough to know better. Don't they know what they're doing?*

What they were doing was their parents' bidding, as the cheering yells of the adults testified.

The hedge of kindling grew higher.

One of the men raced forward with a small knife. Another darted forward. He too, held a blade. David, confused, thought they were going to stab Jonah. But no, the men knelt down on either side of him. They yanked on his ears, pulled them away from the side of his head, and sliced them off. Jonah arched at the pain and bit back a scream. The first man stood and gave a great yell, waving Jonah's right ear in his hand. The other man soon did the same with the left ear. Others scurried forward, their knives held ready. They stripped the skin from his face and hacked away at his fingers. Through it all, Jonah never once gave them the satisfaction of a cry or an appeal for mercy. Only once, as the dull knives were being used to doggedly—and slowly—cut off his fingers, did David hear Jonah speak, and then it was to moan, "Oh, Jesus."

"Clear away!" came the sudden yell. "We're gonna set to it!"

The souvenir hunters ended their bloody work. Other men came forward. One laid down his shotgun, grabbed hold of Jonah's jaw, and forced open his mouth; another poured in kerosene. As Jonah lay there choking and gagging, a third dropped in a lit twig.

The flames bubbled in Jonah's mouth for a moment, then shot up with a whoosh. The crowd cheered. Jonah's exhalations were literally on fire. And every time he inhaled, he sucked the flames deeper into his body.

God, no! David inwardly cried. *They're burning him! My God, they're burning him! For having talked to me! They're killing him!*

Flashbulbs popped, blitzing the area with white light, as photographers took pictures for later sale as postcards. From the west came the soft rumble of faraway thunder. Meanwhile, dull cherry-red flames licked and kissed Jonah. He writhed in their embrace. His major blood vessels burst and the blood boiled in the heat. His agonized face was contorted in silent screams. The crowd fell silent. A few pointed and snickered but most stared dumbly. One or two even turned away, sickened by the sight. Others shielded their eyes with their hands, but peeked through their fingers.

David watched, impotent and overwhelmed, and as he watched he prayed, prayed harder than when he was in the woods of Belleau and the Germans were racing toward him.

God help him. Help him help him, please.

Now, there was nothing but the sound of the crackling flames. The air was nearly unbreathable, heavy with the stench of burning flesh.

Jesus, please!

Finally, Jonah's struggles stilled. A bolt of lightning tore the sky, illuminating the faces of the people in the mob. In that flash of cold, blue light, they all appeared dead.

We're all walking corpses, thought David. *We all look like we're out for a night on the town in Hell.*

The last of the carnival atmosphere was gone. A vague unease settled over the mob. The people glanced at one another, then looked away, suddenly unable to meet one another's eyes. They shuffled in place. For one split second, something very like terror rippled through the crowd. David could feel it. He could see it. People began to sidle away. One by one, they left. Men pulling away wives, mothers dragging away children; in some cases, shielding their children's eyes from the very sight they'd brought them to see.

David stayed. He kept witness until the bitter end.

Jonah's torso arched and his legs drew up as his muscles contracted in the heat. After about forty eternal minutes, his roasted body had been reduced to an unrecognizable smoking mass. The flames sputtered and popped, briefly flared up again, then went down.

David turned away. He was alone. The others were long gone. Stumbling a short distance, he collapsed on a boulder and vomited. The war in Europe, despite its vast horrors, had not prepared him for what he'd just seen: the specter of God-fearing, churchgoing, patriotic Americans burning a fellow man to death.

For talking to me. For telling the truth. His breath came in hitches. *I was a fool. All us colored who fought for this country—we were fools.*

He felt worse than a fool. He was ashamed to be black. *We're a race of victims. Always at the mercy of some white man's whim. That's what we are. Always at the mercy of some white man's whim.*

Then he heard another voice, a voice that would come to haunt him.

You did nothing. Nothing. But stand by and watch.

Self-hatred surged through him and he spilled hot tears. If he were honest . . . if he faced the truth, he would have to admit that he was less ashamed of what he was, than of what he had done.

You betrayed the Movement. Betrayed it and everything you swore to uphold.

There was nothing I could do!

Nothing? Nothing but stand by and watch?

He couldn't have saved Jonah. What could he have done against a mob? Saving himself was the least—and the most—he could have done. But an implacable voice, a voice that sounded so much like his father's, condemned him as guilty of unforgivable cowardice.

David wept like a child raped of its innocence. That single atrocity had done what a year of war failed to do: savage his hope for humanity, his belief in his country, his faith in God—and his respect for himself.

He was still sitting there when the rains came, hard and heavy, drenching him to the skin. Casting his eyes to the sky, he held out his hands, palms upward. He felt the slanting rain splatter against his face and laughed harshly. *So, now you send the rain. Too late, my friend, too late.*

He clenched his fists, closed his eyes, and whispered a bitter prayer. *You're guilty too. You know that, don't you? You and I, we both did nothing. Nothing but stand by and watch.*

He dragged himself to his feet and staggered back through the muddy streets to the rooming house. Early the next morning, he went to see Sheriff Payne and told them what he had seen.

"Leave town," was Payne's polite advice. Saying it was for David's safety, Payne had him escorted to the station and put on the next train that came through. Five men were waiting at the next stop; Payne among them. They dragged David off the train, down into the dust.

"You one lucky white bastard," Payne said. "We hates Yankee nigger-lovers down here, almos' as much as we hates niggers themselves."

He delivered a ferocious kick to David's side. One of the men standing alongside slammed the toe of his boot into David's lower back. The others moved to join in, but Payne held up his hand. Bending down, he grinned in David's face with brown, tobacco-stained teeth.

"Don't worry. I ain't gonna let 'em kill you. I wouldn't do that t'one of my own. But you gots t'learn how we do business down here. You gots t'learn not t'stick your nose where it don't belong." Straightening up, he nodded at the others. "All right. Get to it, boys. I ain't got all day. Just don't kill the sonuvabitch."

David awoke days later in a hospital in Lovetree. Railroad workers had found him lying by the side of the tracks. The doctors and nurses had assumed he was white and treated him better accordingly. Broken spiritually, mentally, and physically, he did not correct them.

After leaving the hospital, he drifted. One morning, he woke up in a filthy flophouse in a city he did not know. He did not remember where he had come from or when he had arrived. His reflection in the small mirror over the washbasin indicated that it had been weeks since he had shaved. His new beard was hard and matted. His hair was newly touched with gray. He cleaned himself as best he could, then left the flophouse and began walking.

He learned that he was in Philadelphia. He walked for hours. Finally tired, he decided to rest on a park bench. A black woman sat there, neither old nor young, but visibly bent under the weight of sorrow. Her sobs were silent but her shoulders heaved. He half-turned, intending to walk on. But something told him not to. Something in that woebegone figure drew him back. In her hunched figure was the personification of his own desolation.

She looked up. Alarm flickered across her face at the sight of him. His face was clean but unshaven and his clothes were dirty and disheveled. He realized that he appeared disreputable, so he spoke quickly.

"I don't want to bother you, lady. I just want to ask if I can help."

She drew back and shook her head, but she seemed reassured. Her thoughts apparently went back to her troubles. Her gaze drifted away and her head bowed again. He took a step toward her.

"Maybe it would help to talk. I'm good at listening."

She ignored him. He hesitated, then slid onto the bench next to her, not too close, but not too far away either. He waited patiently. Minutes passed.

"My boy," she said in a sudden whisper. "They've got my boy."

He waited, but she said nothing more. "Who's got him?"

"My boy," she whimpered. "He ain't but fourteen. The police. They gonna put him away."

"What do they say he's done?"

"Robbed a store. Killed the owner."

He took this in. A Negro teenager in a situation like that barely stood a chance. "You got a lawyer?"

"No money for one." She hugged herself and rocked back and forth. "No money. And no way to get none."

He was quiet. A squirrel scampered down the trunk of a nearby oak tree and found a tidbit in some last-minute pre-winter scavenging. The little animal grabbed it up and scampered away with a switch of bushy tail.

"I'm a lawyer," David heard himself say. "I could defend your son."

She looked at him, surprised, doubtful, and a bit alarmed. "You's a crazy man, ain't you?"

"I admit I don't look like a lawyer." He smiled apologetically. "But I am one. And if you want me to, I'll talk to your son. My talking to your boy wouldn't hurt him, now would it?"

"No . . . I suppose it wouldn't." She scrutinized him. "And you say you's a lawyer? You sure?"

"Yes, very sure." His soft eyes twinkled.

They talked a little more about the details of the case and she seemed to feel better. She gave him her name, her son's name, and where she could be reached. He scribbled it all down with a pencil stub on a piece of paper he'd found in his pocket. As he stood to go, he clutched the bit of paper like a man adrift who has found a life raft. He was flush with a new sense of purpose. She looked up at him, her face a mix of worry and hope.

"Why," she asked, "would you want to help my boy?"

He was the one who looked away then. How could he explain that she was doing him a favor? He gave a little half-smile. "Because . . ." He shrugged. " . . . because I can."

"Well, maybe you can." She was thoughtful. "Being a white man makes a difference in this city. Maybe you can make 'em listen."

His smile froze. It had never occurred to him that she might take him for white. He started to correct her, then stopped. She thought he was white and that gave her hope. Why disappoint her? He was an experienced pretender. The Movement had given him the moral mandate to pass as white in order to investigate lynchings; he'd abused that trust when he disavowed Jonah. Now, he might once again put his lies to good use. He suppressed a bitter laugh. Passing was becoming a curse.

"I can't promise you anything."

"You promise to do the best you can?"

He nodded.

"That's enough. That's all anybody can do."

He won that case. It became the first of many. They came to him because he was dedicated, inexpensive, and apparently white: an unbeatable combination.

The switching of identities required no effort. He simply let people take him for what he appeared to be. Many times, he wished he hadn't had the freedom of choice, for it was a temptation and a responsibility. His father had always been adamant about "standing tall as a colored man," about identifying himself, but what would his father have said under the present circumstances? What purpose would he serve in destroying his credibility and with it, his ability to help the people who needed him?

Most of his clients were small-time offenders. He was their main hope and the main one they lied to. He became used to them evading, denying, obfuscating—telling anything but the truth. By and large, they were gauche, uneducated, unemployed men—either too reckless to realize that they would end up in jail or too desperate to care. Most had never had a chance to be anything other than what they were.

When David had an odd moment to reflect, he would compare their lives to his sheltered upbringing. After what he had done with his life, he was in no position to criticize them. Streetwalkers, alcoholics, and thieves: It was an education to serve them. His previous life took on the blurred appearance of a dream. He changed his name and severed contact with everyone from his past, everyone but Lilian. He felt alive, challenged, and productive. This was his path to redemption—even though it meant living in exile, living a lie.

Now Lilian's death had summoned him back to Harlem, back to Rachel. He would never find the strength to leave Rachel again. And given what he now knew, he wouldn't be able to live with himself if he did.

He thought about his furnished room in a Philadelphia boardinghouse. The house sat back from lovely, inviting, well-manicured lawns, but the room itself was desolate and plain. It contained nothing for him to return to: a thin bed, a table, and a dresser; a sink attached to one wall; a closet with two extra suits, some simple ties, and his one luxury—a second pair of shoes. The room was a monk's cell, a place to sleep. Alone. Night after night, alone.

He was concerned, however, about his clients, about the cases he had dropped. There were depositions to be taken, briefs to be written, court dates to be kept. He could not abandon his clients. He would write letters to them and to the courts, offering some explanation. And he would write his colleagues, asking them to take over his cases.

He turned his thoughts away from Philadelphia. It too now belonged to his past. His future in Harlem worried him. He hoped that his marriage would be strong enough to overcome the difficulties it would no doubt face.

27

Toby's Mother

He found himself on the corner of 137th and Lenox, in front of a slightly battered-looking establishment called the Mayfair Diner. On impulse, he stepped up to the door and went inside. He simply wanted somewhere to sit down. The place was half-empty with the late lunch crowd; there was one waitress, wiping a table at the farther end. She seemed familiar. He recognized her when she turned around. It was the woman whose son he had saved, Toby's mother. She came toward him. Her tired expression softened at the sight of him and his heart felt oddly lighter.

"Well, if that don't beat all," she said. "Take a seat."

He slid onto a stool at the counter. "How's your boy doing?"

"Fine. He asks about you."

"Nah."

"Sure he does. You his hero."

David smiled. "Thanks."

"What for?"

"For making me smile."

She cocked her head to one side as she poured his coffee. "Had one of them days, huh?"

"You could say that."

"Well, don't worry. Whatever it is, it too will pass. That's what my pappy used to say."

"Did he now?"

"Yes, he did. And he was a wise old coot."

David chuckled. "Where're you from?"

"Virginia. My folks was sharecroppers."

"Big family?"

"There was nine of us kids. We was poor but we had a good time t'gether. I guess you could say, we didn't know no better."

"Been here long?"

Her smile faded. "I come up here with my sister a few months ago—but she went back. Sister couldn't take the city. She wanted to take Toby back with her, but he's mine and I'm keepin' him. His daddy don't want him. He up and took off. I can't have him thinkin' that his mama don't want him, neither."

Was this the way Rachel would've spoken about him if Isabella had lived? He would've wanted Isabella, though. If he'd had the chance, he would've protected her, given her everything he had.

"You really are havin' a bad day," she said, looking at his face. "How 'bout somethin' to eat?"

He shook his head, glancing at the stitching on the pocket of her shirt. He hoped to see her name but it was simply the name of the diner. "Just a cup of coffee."

For the next twenty minutes, he watched her move up and down the counter, exchanging lighthearted banter with the other customers: truck drivers, busboys on break, drunks, and drifters. He saw the way she managed to bring a crooked smile to even the saddest face. Finally, she paused in front of him.

"Anythin' more I can get for you?"

"Just more coffee, please."

His gaze fell on her hands as she poured. In her rough skin and broken fingernails, he saw a lifetime of sewing and scrubbing, cutting and chopping. He watched her move away and again wondered what her name was. He could imagine her hands kneading dough for fluffy biscuits, patting a baby's bottom, massaging her man's back. She would give comfort and strength. She looked like a woman a man could trust, someone he could bare his heart to.

He blinked, faintly disturbed at the course of his thoughts. Standing, he signaled her. She caught his gesture out of the corner of her eye and moved down the counter toward him. Taking out his wallet, he drew out an extra ten bits and laid them in front of her. She took the money, went away, then returned with his change. He waved it aside.

"Keep it."

She touched the money and looked up at him. "This is way too much."

"It's way too little for the price of a smile."

She studied him with light amusement, as though she didn't know what to make of him. He liked what he saw in her eyes and he liked the way it made him feel—like a man standing in sunshine after spending years in the rain.

"Good luck," she said. "I got a feeling you need it. Maybe even more than I do."

She tucked the money into her apron pocket. He watched her move away, then turned to go.

"Hey," he heard her call to him. He turned around. "I get a break in five minutes," she said. "You wanna take a walk?"

He paused. "Yeah, okay."

She looked suddenly shy, perhaps realizing how "forward" she'd been. "Okay."

He slid into a booth to wait and looked out the window. Some members of Marcus Garvey's Universal Negro Improvement Association were parading down the street. The men were dressed in military-like uniforms with generous applications of gold braid. Many of the women wore long pale dresses with wide cloths tied about their heads like missionary sisters. These people were trying to keep up the spirit of Garvey's Back-to-Africa Movement, but the UNIA was in tatters, and their leader, the Black Moses—a short, charismatic Jamaican who had galvanized thousands of Harlem's poor with talk of returning to their ancestral homeland—was himself locked in the Atlanta federal penitentiary, serving a five-year sentence for mail fraud.

"I'm ready," David heard a soft voice say and turned around. She was bundled up in her coat and had stuck her little hat on her head. She looked adorable.

"All right," he said. "Let's go."

As always, the Avenue was crowded. It was even more so that day because of the parade. Though small, it was enough to attract attention. They joined the onlookers for a minute, admiring the UNIA's smart color guard, then turned away and headed downtown. On the left, they passed the Renaissance Casino & Ballroom.

"You ever go to a dance there?" she asked.

"A long time ago."

"It's real nice, ain't it? I heard they got receptions and basketball games and everything."

Directly across from them, on the corner of 135th, was Small's Paradise, the place where Nella's playwright friend had danced on the tables. Not a block away was Saint Philip's. The last time David had been there, it had been for his father's funeral. They reached the corner of 135th and paused for a stoplight.

"NAACP secretary James Weldon Johnson used to live around here," he said. "I met him once."

"What's he like?"

"Got a good sense of humor." The light changed and they started across the street. "Fats Waller and Florence Mills live only a couple of blocks down the way."

They walked in comfortable silence, pausing at the corner of 133rd. To the left and right stretched "Jungle Alley," the main drag of expensive Harlem cabarets. David's memories came to life. The Nest Club, Kaiser's, Barron's: Once he'd been a regular at them all. Farther down Seventh was the Lafayette Theater. There was no better place to see tap-dancing greats Bill "Bojangles" Robinson, Honi Coles, Bunny Briggs, Chuck Green, and Baby Laurence.

Then there was the Band Box Club, just off the Avenue on 131st. A man could go there and hear the purest jazz he could hope for. And what about the Tree of Hope? Folks said it had magic. Entertainers hoping for a break would rub it. On a good night, a man could see any number of stars under it: jazz singer Ethel Waters, Fletcher Henderson, and Eubie Blake. Across the street was Connie's Inn. Bill "Bojangles" Robinson and Earl "Snakehips" Tucker entertained hundreds of guests on Connie's raised dance floor nightly. Below Connie's was the Barbecue, the best rib joint in Harlem.

David took a deep breath. There was talk everywhere about Harlem enjoying a heyday, and if he could believe his eyes, that was certainly the case. But what no one wanted to talk about was the poverty lurking behind the glitz.

"I'm glad to be here," she said suddenly, "but Harlem ain't an easy place to live. Ever since I been up here, I been hearin' talk about the 'New Negro,' but what does it mean? I feel the same and I don't see where nothin's changed. There's a lot of white folks steppin' up here t'go clubbin'. But what d'we get out of it? A few jobs and nothin' more. The places they go, we cain't go. There's a lucky few—some colored writers and painters and singers I hear tell about. But there's always a lucky few that breaks through, whose star gets t'shine a li'l brighter. But what about the rest of us—the reg'lar folk? When'll it be our turn?"

He smiled at her. "What would you do if you had the chance?"

"I'd paint," she said. "Every now and then, I'd paint." She laughed. "But them's all dreams. My pappy, he said dreams is like water: Too li'l of 'em and you dry up. Too much of 'em and you drown." She shook her head and looked up at him. "Don't get me dreamin'. I can't afford t'do that." She looked down at her work-worn hands and sighed. "No, I can't afford t'do that."

28

For Richer, For Poorer . . .

David married Rachel the following Tuesday in a City Hall ceremony, then took her to the Bamboo Inn for a small celebratory dinner. When he brought her home, there was no party, great or small. Rachel would have preferred one, but she acceded to his wishes for privacy and quiet.

"I want to be with you alone," he said.

"Perhaps we can have a party later. Introduce me to society?" she asked.

He hesitated, then agreed. He carried her across the threshold of the front door. She slid to her feet as agile as a kitten. She stood for a moment, just looking around, then piled her coat and purse on Annie's waiting arms. Slowly, as David watched, Rachel walked through the house, touching things here and there.

"So beautiful," she whispered. "These are all ours . . . For as long as we both shall live."

Turning to him with an adoring smile, she threw her arms around his neck and gave him a deep, lingering kiss. He groaned. Loving Rachel was addictive. Bending, he grabbed her up and carried her up the stairs to his room. Once in bed, she opened his shirt and covered his bare chest with hard kisses. She ran her fingertips lightly over his body, playing it as though it were a familiar instrument, as though she had loved him every night in her dreams.

"It's hard to believe that I'm finally here . . . with you," she whispered afterward.

He kissed her naked shoulder and gathered her in his arms.

"Are you happy?" she asked.

"Quite."

"You're so quiet."

He smiled. "That's because I'm sated with love."

She slapped him playfully on the cheek. "You and your fancy talk. Don't make fun of me."

He shook his head. "Never," and hugged her.

She sighed happily and gazed around the room. "It's a bit dark in here. Lilian's room's brighter. And bigger." She inclined her head. "Y'ever think about moving in there?"

"No. And if I ever *had* thought about it . . . well, I wouldn't want to do it now."

She nodded. "I know. I can understand that." She was quiet for a minute and then: "But the room . . . it's just too nice to go to waste."

He half-raised up. "Rachel, I'm not moving in there. That's where my sister died. Eventually we'll do something with the room—it will not 'go to waste'—but we are not, I repeat *not,* moving into it."

"Shhh. I didn't mean to upset you. I was just asking, that's all."

He eased back down. "It's just difficult, you know? Just difficult."

She leaned down and kissed him. "Know what I'm thinking about?"

"I have no idea, but I'm sure you're going to tell me."

"I was remembering these boys at school when I was eight."

"Not even one day married and you're already thinking about other men?"

"Hush. These boys—I wish they could see me now. They told me I was dog dirt. Got me in a corner one day and tried to do nasty things to me. Then they yanked my hair and made fun of my clothes. And there was this rhyme they kept singing over and over.

> *Cat on the scene, cat on the scene.*
> *Yella sits pretty in a black limousine.*
> *Brown sits humble in a Model-A Ford.*
> *They goin' somewhere. Oh yes, my Lord.*
> *Monkey on my back, monkey on my back.*
> *Black gals climb on a donkey's back.*
> *They never getting nowhere, eatin' out a sack.*
> *They never getting nowhere, just ugly and fat.*

"It was the first time I realized that my own people can cut deeper than any ofay." She paused. "I never expected nothing from whites no-how. I trusted my own people. But they was the very ones who tried to knock me down.

"I remember looking for a room to rent. So many times a Negro landlady took one look at me and slammed the door in my face. And then, when I was trying to find a nurse's job, one supervisor said to me: 'Children is afraid of dark skin. We can't afford that.' Can you imagine?"

He stroked her back. "Rachel, a lot's been done to our people to make us hate ourselves. Sometimes we colored folk . . . we're our own worst enemy."

She snuggled up closer to him. "Well, I'm protected from all them evil people now. I got you."

He sighed, thinking of the danger his past represented. It was time he told her. He opened his mouth to speak, but she hushed him with her fingertips.

"I don't want to talk no more. Not right now. I don't want no more looking back."

They snuggled deeply under the blankets together. She began to dream aloud of the parties she'd give. She named the names, like the Nails up the street, of the people she intended to invite.

"We'll have luncheons, bridge parties, and formal, white-tie dances. And we need a new car. And a boat. And didn't Augustus buy a summer house in Martha's Vineyard?"

He listened with half an ear. His thoughts were elsewhere. "Sweet's due back in about a week."

She looked up at him, realizing that he hadn't been paying attention. She wasn't annoyed, though. Getting Sweet out of the house was a real concern. "I'm sure he'll want to move out. Now that you've decided to stay, Sweet won't feel comfortable."

"Perhaps. Perhaps not."

"I'm sure you can handle it." She gave him a kiss on his chin. Then, apparently unconcerned and full of confidence in her beloved husband, she closed her eyes and went to sleep.

But he lay awake, worrying.

I should've told her. And I should've done it before we got married. When she could've made a choice, when she was still free to—

C'mon, an inner voice said, *she would've married you no matter what and you know it.*

Yeah, but—

And she still wouldn't have wanted to run away. She's a fighter. Be glad you've got her in your corner. No, my friend. She's not your problem. You're the problem.

David rubbed his eyes. He'd arranged by telephone with his secretary in Philadelphia to shut down his office there. He'd also give her a list of colleagues who would be willing to take over his cases. His life in the City of Brotherly Love was over. Now he had to deal with the question of just what kind of work could he do *here?*

The same kind you did in Philadelphia. Defend the indigent. Just under your own name, as yourself.

Then to have it all destroyed by, how did Nella put it? The right word in the wrong ears? How much time would he have to build up anything *anyway?* He would've liked to rejoin the Movement, but how could he? With his past hanging over him and with Sweet in the Movement?

Speaking of . . .

Was he really going to let Sweet get away with his part in Lilian's death?

He sighed. *Be patient,* that inner voice said. *Sometimes it takes years to gather proof and evidence and put them together in a way that means a conviction.*

And what about Rachel? he wondered. He'd promised to drop the inquiry.

That little voice laughed mirthlessly. *Are you kidding?*

29

The Lizard Lounge

Over breakfast Wednesday morning, he watched Annie and Rachel avoid one another, circling one another like cats in an arena. It was subtle, but it was there. Rachel, for example, would tell him what she wanted, and it was up to him to tell Annie. And Annie had an odd way of acting as though Rachel didn't exist.

He took a deep breath. Annie wasn't happy about his decision—*stated* decision—to drop his inquiry into Lilian's death, and though he hadn't mentioned Rachel's part in it, Annie seemed to sense the connection.

He watched her move about. She was indeed much slower than she used to be.

She looks exhausted, he thought. *But after more than half a century of cooking and cleaning for others, she has every right to be.*

Since reading Lilian's manuscript, he'd watched Annie and listened to the words behind her words. He knew little of her life before she'd joined his family—to him it seemed that she'd always been there—but he did remember a story she'd once told him about her childhood. He was twelve and angry that Augustus had made him stay home to do extra homework. Annie had brought milk and cookies to his room. There, she'd sat down with him.

"Want to hear 'bout my tenth birthday?" she said. "I'll never forget it. I was so excited. I'd been dreamin' of this doll I'd seen in a store window. She had this long blond curly hair and a pretty dress. I'd never seen nothin' like her. I didn't know how much she cost, but I do r'member thinkin': Mama's gonna get me that doll. I just know she will. Well, the day of my birthd'y come and I bounced outta bed real early. And there was Mama, and Uncle Clement. And sure 'nough, they had a big box, wrapped up all pretty. Jumbo size. I couldn't believe it. And then I opened it." Annie sighed. "You won't believe this—I didn't at first. It was a bucket. A bright, shiny, spankin' new washerwoman's bucket. And while I was tryin' t'get over *that,* Mama went and fetched my second birthd'y present. Guess what it was. A mop. That's right. A mop.

"I was ten years old and my Mama was givin' me a mop and a bucket for birthd'y presents. That hurt. That cut deep. Up 'til then I'd always gotten a toy, even if it was just a rag doll. And I woulda been happy with another rag doll. Mama knew she didn't have to gimme that 'spensive doll, but why'd she have to go and gimme a mop and a bucket? Well, I took one look at her face and I knew. It was the end of my chilehood. Mama said I'd been playin' long 'nough. I cried. Told her she was bein' mean. Said she wasn't being *kind* t'me. I'll never forget her answer. Not as long as I live.

"'I am bein' kind, honey,' she said. 'I's bein' as kind as a mama can be. I'm givin' you the most important thing I got t'give: a way to survive. I'm gonna teach you how t'fend for yourself. Gonna make sure you learn. And I'm gonna start right now.'

"And you know what?" Annie smiled. "My mama was right. If she hadna taught me how to cook and clean, I wouldna found this here place with you and your sisters. Mama *was* bein' kind, as kind as she knew how. And I learned, from that day on, t'always 'preciate kindness—no matter what form it takes."

Kindness. Would she say that kindness was what Lilian's manuscript was all about?

He remembered the cautionary ending to Annie's tale: "Sometimes, you gotta be a little cruel t'be kind. And sometimes, what people claim for kindness ain't nothing but cruelty."

He looked at Rachel across the table and recalled what Lilian said in denying her help: *I am doing you a favor.* And then he reflected on his own decision to marry Rachel although he wasn't in love her.

Was he guilty of a milder form of cruelty masquerading as kindness?

As Annie pottered about, stacking the used dishes on a tray, Rachel's eyes followed her. The moment Annie left, Rachel asked:

"You ever think about letting her rest?"

"You mean, retire her? Not really, why?" Of course, he had. Why was he lying about it? *You feel guilty. That's why,* his inner voice said.

She shrugged. "I just don't think it's right to make such an old lady work so hard, carrying groceries and wash baskets and such. She's done her share for your family."

"That she has. But she'd be miserable if she wasn't working." He took a sip from his coffee, then set the cup down. "You don't like Annie, do you?"

She looked surprised. "What gave you that idea?"

"I don't know. It's just a—" He shrugged. "A feeling."

"Well, it's all in your mind. Oh, I had my run-ins with her in the past, but that was then. I was young and silly. Annie's a member of the family. And she's a great help, but I do think you take advantage of her."

"All right then, I'll talk to her about it. See what she wants to do."

It was something to say. He knew full well what Annie wanted, but he wasn't about to tell Rachel. He didn't know much about women, but he knew a territorial cat-fight when he saw one. And if he got caught up in it, it would be *his* blood that was on the floor.

He looked at his new wife across the breakfast table and smiled. For her, the world could hardly be more perfect, but he still had certain steps to take in order to rebuild *his* life. Marrying Rachel had been one step; regaining control of the house would be another.

Reestablishing contact with Gem would be a third.

Rachel did not greet this news warmly. Her clear eyes darted over his face. "But why would you do that? Why contact Gem all of a sudden?"

"Because she's the only family I have."

"But you've never liked her."

"Well, it's time I learned. She's the only sister I've got left."

Rachel appeared stupefied. Her reaction to his decision to find Gem surprised him, but he thought he understood it. She had never liked Gem, and all brides tend to be on guard against in-laws. Well, once Rachel saw that Gem would not be a threat, she would calm down.

She would have to.

The idea to find Gem had seized him with incredible power. He *would* find her, even if it meant sailing to Paris. The time and money would be worth it. He would not try to convince her to return. Just seeing her would be reassuring.

Reassuring?

Why that? He felt a sharp ping of anxiety. It hit him that he was *worried* about Gem—indeed, had been for some time—but he'd been so fixed on Lilian he hadn't noticed. Why worried? What was the source of his unease? He reflected.

It began with those postcards.

Yes. They disturbed him. And Snyder's words and Nella's admission that she couldn't reach Gem in Paris troubled him, too.

Acknowledging his concern was like opening the trapdoor to a crowded attic. The old fearful questions tumbled out, one after another. Why did Gem demand that public breakup with Snyder? Who sent those postcards and why? Why didn't Gem respond to Nella's calls? Gem was flighty and free-spirited, but she'd always make time for a rich friend, especially one as generous as Nella. Why didn't Gem respond to word of Lilian's death? *What if something had happened to Gem, too?*

That afternoon, David paid a visit to Birdie's grocery store and went downstairs. "Jolene, you got an idea where I could find Shug Ryan?"

Jolene leaned across the bar. "Try the Lizard Lounge, up on 140th. Shug likes to shoot pool when he's in town."

Stella came up and caught what Jolene was saying. "The Lizard Lounge? Don't send him up there. Them some nasty jigs."

Jolene shrugged. "It's his life, Mama." To David, he said, "A broad named Bentley runs the place. Tell her I sent you. And tell her quick, b'fore one of them saps gets itchy."

It would've been generous to call the Lizard Lounge a "hole in the wall." David only found the place because he trudged up and down the east and west sides of 140th Street, from one side of Harlem to the next, checking out each door along the way. The place had no sign to mark it and that in itself told him what to expect inside.

The Lizard Lounge consisted of a long, narrow room with no windows and one door. Through the haze of smoke and the murky light, David could barely see, but he could feel several pairs of eyes on him. Why would a sax player be hanging out in a dive like this? Usually, musicians went to places that catered to entertainers. As his eyes adjusted to the light, he made out the six pool tables, with green baize lampshades dangling over them. He saw the patrons.

The Lizard Lounge was apparently a hangout for vicious hustlers, red-eyed gangsters, and men who were experts at giving pain. It was the kind of place where a man could literally get his throat cut for batting an eyelash at the wrong time. He figured he had better follow Jolene's advice and find Bentley.

He scanned the room for a woman. There was only one in sight. She was sitting at a fold-up wooden card table on the far side of the room. She was fat, about fifty, with black and gray finger waves and large cheap golden earrings. She was playing Solitaire, laying out the cards methodically, and just as methodically, watching him. He felt the eyes follow him as he walked over to her. Felt them like tips of daggers pressed against his skin.

"Evening," he said. "You Bentley?"

"Who's askin'?" She slid a hand under the table.

"Jolene told me to look you up."

Bentley's jaundiced eyes widened and a sound like a hiss left her mouth. Before he could blink, she'd whipped out a gun from under the table and trained it on his chest. He stepped back and slowly raised his hands in the air. Very slowly. Only the breadth of the card table lay between them. If she cut loose, there was no way she would miss.

"Yo, lady, chill," he breathed.

"Jolene ain't never sent me nothin' but trouble. The last time, trouble was packin' a switchblade. He tried to bury it in my ribs."

"I don't know nothin' but nothin' about that."

Her eyes narrowed. "Sure you don't."

He sensed two men behind him. He glanced back over his shoulder. One had pale green snake eyes; the other was fat and soft-looking but crusty, like dough that had been left sitting on the counter too long. Bentley smiled at David, revealing brown, rotting stumps for teeth.

"Baby, don't you know who you messin' with?"

"I guess I'm about to find out."

Her broad nostrils flared. She nodded to the two men. They took him through a back door he hadn't seen to the alleyway. The moment they were outside, Snake-eyes bashed him in the head from behind. Pain scissored through him as he dropped and twisted. Doughboy aimed a kick at David's ribs and David rolled on the ground, gasping. They pulled him to his feet. Snake-eyes gripped David from behind and held him, while Doughboy tore into him with his fists. Doughboy was fast and vicious despite his looks. He pulled back for a killing blow and David ducked. Doughboy's fist connected with Snake-eyes' nose. There was the thin crunch of broken bone and Snake-eyes yelled, stumbling backward. David whirled and slammed his fist into Doughboy's throat. The fat man sputtered and sagged to his knees. By then, Snake-eyes was back on his feet. He had a blade. David glanced around, saw a rusty lead pipe, and grabbed it. It took two good blows before Snake-eyes went down. David didn't know if Snake-eyes was alive or dead. He didn't have time to think about it. Doughboy was gone. That meant that reinforcements were on the way. David dropped the pipe. He had to clear out. Fast.

The moment Birdie saw David he raised his hands. "Hey, David, I'm sorry. If I'da known—"

"Let me go downstairs."

"Can't do that. He's my brother."

"Well, your brother's gonna have a rat's pack of trouble if he don't haul his sorry ass up here."

"I—"

"I don't wanna shut you down, Birdie. But he shouldn't have done that. Now get him up here."

Birdie nodded. "Okay. No hard feelin's b'tween us, I hope."

"Naturally not."

"So you stay up here and keep a lookout for me while I go get 'im, okay?"

David smiled. "Sure."

Birdie went downstairs. The moment he was out of sight, David left the grocery store and went around the back way. A set of parallel iron stairs ran alongside the building and down to the cellar doorway. A minute later, the cellar door flew open and Jolene came busting out. David snatched him by the collar and slammed him against the building's brick wall. Jolene sputtered and clenched at his throat, staring at David with one bulging eye.

"It was just a joke. I ain't mean no harm."

"You've got a strange sense of humor. It could get you killed one day."

Jolene fumbled at his pants pocket. David slammed him again. Jolene threw his hands back up.

"Easy, man. Easy. You wanna know where Shug is, right? A bird told me he'll be playin' a rent party tonight."

"A bird told you that, huh?"

Jolene nodded. Beads of sweat had popped out at his temples. "No lie this time."

"So where's the jump?"

"Card's in my pocket."

Jolene gestured downward with his right hand. David dipped into Jolene's pants pocket and drew out a cheaply printed square.

"It's a woman named Lulu Smits," Jolene said.

David nodded, "Lulu, huh?" and read the card.

> *Hey, papa, come on and shake that thing.*
> *Bring pretty mama and let it swing.*
> *We gonna hop and pop and rattle the room.*
> *We're gonna shimmy and shally and shatter the gloom.*

David tucked the little card into his breast pocket and looked at Jolene. He was tempted to deck him, but resisted the urge. Jolene cringed.

"Man, don't cut me," he begged. "Please don't hurt me."

David shoved Jolene back against the doorway, looked at him with disgust, and released him. He felt dirty from having touched him. David turned to go. He had taken two steps when some minuscule sound warned him to turn around. Jolene was coming at him with a switchblade. David sidestepped the lunging blade, then pivoted and swung around in a neat movement. He put his fists together and brought them down like a hammer between Jolene's shoulder blades. The ugly barkeep went down with a grunt. David stood over him. He deliberated for a moment. Then he gave Jolene a deeply satisfying kick in the ass for good measure.

30

Neighbor, Neighbor

It was still way too early to go to Lulu's, so David headed home. He wanted to get cleaned up before going to the party, anyway. He'd just turned the corner onto his street, when he ran smack into Byron Canfield.

"My God, can't you look where you're going?" Canfield brushed off his coat sleeve as though he'd collided with something dirty. Then he realized he was speaking to David. "Oh, it's you!" He looked David up and down, noting his slight dishevelment. "Yes, well . . . I did hear that you'd stayed."

The derision in Canfield's tone was unmistakable, as was the hint of unsavory knowledge and superiority. And the look in his eyes—that, too, was unpleasant.

David was tempted to curse his luck at this chance meeting but realized that it had been inevitable. As a young lawyer, just starting out and still hoping for a career within the Movement, he'd wondered what it would be like to try a case with the great Canfield, a man as known for his arrogance as for his intellect. David now realized that such a collaboration would've been unprofitable. He realized that the antipathy between them wasn't simply the product of the present situation, but stemmed from disparities that went much deeper. Remembering his manners, David donned a polite smile.

"Circumstances forced me to change my plans," he said.

"Did they, now? Well, fancy that. So you're staying?"

"For a while, yes."

Canfield nodded to himself, as if to confirm some private thought.

"Well then, there's no reason you can't come by for dinner," he said. "We'll do it immediately. Tonight. You're not busy, are you? Even if you are, you'll cancel."

David understood that he was not being invited but summoned. He briefly entertained the idea of firmly but politely saying no. He was tired, he felt ill: Any one of a hundred excuses would do. But Canfield would know them for what they were, a way of avoiding him. And Canfield's curiosity, already aroused, would grow stronger.

David found himself recalling one of his teachers at Howard: Professor John Milton. Milton was a gifted strategist and an enthusiastic instructor. He was full of good advice and pithy mottoes. David could hear him now, saying, "If you want to know your enemy, then go visit him: Just drop by, sit down, and enjoy a nice, long chat."

"Thank you for the invitation," David now said. "I'm looking forward to it."

They shook hands and Canfield turned to go. Then he hesitated and turned back, as though he'd remembered something.

"Oh and by the way," he said, "you needn't worry."

"Worry?"

"Yes. There won't be anyone there tonight—no one except you and my wife and I."

David's pleasant expression froze. He clamped down on the chill and fear that Canfield's words had given rise to and forced himself to use a normal tone of voice.

"A small gathering? How nice. I'll bring my wife."

"You're married?" Canfield seemed surprised. "But you were single the last time I met you, weren't you? My wife prides herself on knowing about everything that occurs on Strivers' Row. I don't see how she could've possibly missed hearing about your wedding."

"It happened rather quickly."

"Well, well . . . you're full of surprises."

"My critics have never accused me of being boring."

"I'm sure I would agree with them."

They parted, David having agreed to show up for dinner at eight. Rachel was delighted at the invitation. The Canfields were exactly the type of people she wanted to impress.

"Have you met Mrs. Canfield? Is she nice? Do you think they'll like me?"

"They'll adore you." David kissed her. "Just be yourself and you can't go wrong."

As he escorted her to the Canfields' that night, he watched her admire her new neighborhood.

"It's so beautiful here," she whispered. "So very, very beautiful. And quiet."

He only smiled in response. As always, he was caught between guilt and pride that his family lived there.

"Isn't it amazing that colored folk ever managed to get into such nice buildings?" she said.

"Yeah, I can remember Daddy's joy when he bought our house."

"I hope I can fit in here. I've been waiting for this all my life, but now . . ."

She looked up at him. She seemed so fragile. He hugged her and kissed her forehead.

"Don't worry. You'll do fine."

Dinner was pleasant enough, but David was glad to see it end. Afterward, Emma Canfield led him and Rachel into her parlor while her husband went off, looking for a favorite wine in his pantry.

The Canfields were the perfect example of a Strivers' Row couple. They were educated, traveled, refined. They saw themselves as influential, but benign and modest. They were also hopelessly out of touch with the concerns of Harlem's poor.

"I don't understand those people out there," said Emma, gesturing toward her windows. "It's as though they want us to become what they are. They've got this blind hatred of us. Just because we read and keep our property clean, they say we're snobs. We're not snobs. We just enjoy knowledge and we want to live well. It's as though they've accepted the popular idea that the only genuine Negro is an ignorant, dirty Negro."

David felt Rachel tense. He glanced at her. Her lips were bent in a forced smile, but her eyes regarded Emma with resentment. He could tell that she wanted to speak up. She was biting her lip to keep silent. He took hold of Rachel's hand and gave it a squeeze.

Like most of the doctors, lawyers, and educators who composed the bulk of Strivers' Row residents, the Canfields were committed to doing everything they could to make sure that their street would not be sucked into the slum beyond. They had convinced themselves that they could provide a shining example to other blacks of how a winsome neighborhood could be maintained. But the effort was failing dismally, and they were bewildered by the reaction they were getting. The more manicured Strivers' Row became, the more mockery it drew from Harlem's poor. The more elevated the Row became, the greater the cleft between it and the rest of the neighborhood.

David, perhaps because he'd lived for so long among Philadelphia's poor, understood what Emma could not.

"Mrs. Canfield, let's be honest," he said. "If the people who don't live on Strivers' Row resent the people who do, it's at least partly because the people on the Row deserve it. The people 'out there,' as you put it, simply resent the sight of Negroes who not only live well, but don't seem to care that others live poorly."

"We do care," Emma cried. "But there's no way we can help them if they won't help themselves. No one helped us. My husband and I—and all the rest of us here on the Row—why, we have what we have because we worked for it and worked hard. Nobody gave us anything. Nobody urged us on. And now that we have something, it's our own people who want to tear us down. I don't understand it."

David found it ironic to hear her echo Rachel's complaint.

Emma set her bone china teacup down on her glass coffee table with a rattle and fixed David with her jet-black eyes. She was a matronly woman of about fifty. She had a round, soft figure and a pretty face. One would have thought her the soul of tolerance and generosity from the sweetness of her expression, but the hardness of her eyes reminded David of granite. She was assiduously groomed and everything about her displayed an exacting perfectionism. She was, David thought, the perfect match for Byron Canfield, from the top of her perfectly coiffed head to the tip of her polished kid leather shoes.

"Strivers' Row is about more than black-tie dinners, bridge parties, and balls," she said. "It's proof that not only whites but blacks can make it. If we're smart enough, stubborn enough, tough enough. It proves that DuBois is right, that the best of us, the 'Talented Tenth,' will succeed if we commit ourselves to American ways and reject that Back-to-Africa nonsense. We try to be role models and an inspiration. I wish they'd think of us that way."

"But how can we be role models when we're increasingly cut off from them?" David asked. "Most of the people on the Row don't know a single soul who lives out there."

"And why should we? They're shiftless, lazy. If they worked, they could have what we have. Or nearly as nice. If their houses are dirty, it's because they dirtied them. And if they're living five and ten to a room, it's—"

"It's because they can't afford the rents, Mrs. Canfield. Open your eyes."

"Those people—"

"They're our people," said David. "And they need us. Harlem's not just the well-feathered beds of Strivers' Row. It's the hot beds of shift workers. It's battered tenements, cramped kitchenettes, and bleak rented bedrooms. It's the wheelers and dealers on Seventh; Mr. Jones's barber salon on 125th, and Mrs. Johnson's beauty salon on 122nd. Harlem is storefront churches and jackleg preachers. It's people finding faith wherever and however they can:

young folk visiting the conjure man on Friday and the jump joint on Saturday; it's old folk giving up their nickels and dimes to the preacher on Sunday,
singing and praying and singing some more at the First Baptists, Good Sav-
iors, and Little Bethels that dot nearly every Harlem street."

"You just don't understand. My husband says you've been away a long
time—"

"Yes, I have—but maybe that's why I see so clearly."

Emma's response was cut off by her husband's arrival. Canfield came in,
proudly displaying a red wine bottle.

"Found it," he said. "A lovely Beaujolais I brought back from France during the war."

"You should be honored," Emma told David. "My husband is very dis-
criminating about who he offers his wine to."

David smiled politely and buried the words that had sprung to his lips.

With Canfield's presence, the topic of conversation changed. Eventually,
it turned to the ideological dispute that was threatening to splinter the
Movement. Its leaders were divided as to whether the Movement should
fight for total integration or accept compromises along the line of "separate
but equal." In the February issue of the *Black Arrow*, Canfield had written an
editorial suggesting that it might be wise to accept limited racial segregation.
When Walker Gaines, the Movement secretary, saw it, he'd had a fit. He
wrote a scathing counterstatement that attacked segregation "in any form"
and committed the Movement in perpetuity to a war against it. Gaines had
expected his piece to be published in the March issue, but Canfield had
blocked it. Gaines accused Canfield of considering himself beyond reproach.
David, like many others, had been stunned by Canfield's essay, and he'd
watched in dismay as the ideological debate crystallized into a power struggle between the two men. Now he found himself listening to Canfield as he
set forth his position.

"Cultural nationalism," said Canfield, "is the most important goal our
people can aim for. It can be seen in the light of the Zionists' desire for political separation."

David felt Rachel shift next to him. She was intimidated and bored. Canfield warmed to his subject.

"Cultural nationalism relates to ethnic pride as well as political strength.
It's an important concept and rather radical, because it bespeaks a certain
amount of self-imposed 'segregation.'"

David felt a prickle of annoyance. "But segregation is what we're fighting
against—"

"We can't denounce segregation in theory without denouncing the Negro church, the Negro college, or any other purely Negro institution."

"It's one thing for us to choose ethnic privacy; quite another to be forced into—"

"Simple-minded people try to avoid the issue by distinguishing between voluntary and involuntary segregation. But to put it rather colloquially, we can't have our cake and eat it, too."

David's temper surged. "Sometimes 'simple-minded' people are the most perceptive. *They* have a mental clarity that many intellectuals seem to lose. *They* don't lose sight of priorities and they don't cloud the issues with irrelevancies. Desegregation is, and was, one of the Movement's primary goals as a means to an end."

"You're mistaken. Or misled. The Movement has never 'defined' its position on segregation, merely taken concrete steps to oppose it in its baser forms."

David looked at Canfield, wondering if he had heard correctly. Then he leaned forward, and took a deep breath.

"Mr. Canfield, I have to be blunt. If the Movement isn't openly opposed to segregation, then it's lost all meaning." His eyes met Canfield's. "And its leaders have lost all credibility."

Canfield stared at him. "How dare you—"

"Any first-year law student—no, any man in the street—knows that the black man's desire for ethnic privacy in his lodges and his churches does not exclude his right, his basic human right, to integration and equality in the public sphere."

"David, please," said Rachel.

She touched him on the elbow. He shrugged her off—he was beyond caution—and pressed on.

"For the time being, we've got to live with Jim Crow's rule, but it's an anathema. It must go. You wrote of accommodation, Mr. Canfield, of compromise. Well, you can forget compromise. The Devil doesn't make compromises. Neither can we. It doesn't matter whether you or I survive to see Jim Crow die. We have to fight it—to crush it—or we're all lost. Black and white, we're all done for."

Blistering silence. The two men gazed at one another with open enmity. Finally, Canfield cleared his throat.

"Thank you for that little lecture. It's good to know that you haven't lost your dedication, or your energy for debate. One wonders, you know, about a man who's been away for so long."

Clearly, it was time to leave. David stood and drew Rachel up alongside him. He thanked the Canfields for their hospitality and bade them a good night. Rachel spoke up the moment they left.

"What did you have to insult him like that for? He's a powerful man. He could've been our friend."

"With a friend like that, a man doesn't need enemies."

"So what if you don't like him. I don't particularly care for his wife, either. But she knows all the right people. She could make sure that we're invited everywhere. Now, I'll have to—"

David rounded on her. "Rachel, you're my wife and I want to make you happy. But I won't play the hypocrite, not even for you."

"But if you'd just—"

"Don't." He held up his hand. "Just don't."

31

Lulu's Home Jam

Lulu lived in the poorest section of Harlem. Shatter the gloom, her card had said. Well, he could understand that. In Harlem, if the rent was not paid by Sunday, the landlord put the furniture on the street by Monday. So people would do just about whatever necessary to raise the money. That included rent parties: opening their homes to strangers and charging admission, from a dime to a half-dollar.

Lulu's place was on 131st Street and Eighth Avenue. David got there at around one in the morning. The door downstairs was broken open. Broken glass, discarded bottles, cigarette butts, newspapers, and one curiously flattened dead cat littered the entryway. From the back of a dark, narrow hallway emerged the distant sounds of a party in full swing. David could make out a piano playing ragtime. He followed the sound to the stairs at the back of the hallway. Lulu's apartment was on the third floor. The apartment door was ajar. Inside, he found an incredibly fat woman sitting at an itsy-bitsy table behind the door.

"Come on in, brother," she said. "Make yourself comfortable. Corn liquor's in the kitchen. Fifty cents a pitcher. You alone, son? I'm sure we can find you some comp'ny."

The room was hot and funky. It stunk of smoke, sweat, and booze, collard greens, chitlins, hog maws, mulatto rice, and hopping John. Scores of folks had paid their nickels and dimes to get in. The place was jumping, packed with young studs looking for mischief and pretty young things out for fun. David recognized poets, novelists, even a civil rights official or two; there were painters, truckers, and policemen, and a fair assortment of queens in drag. David glanced back at his hostess. She was watching him with amusement.

"Don't be shy, sugar, we got somethin' for everybody."

"I'm looking for a sax player. Name of Shug Ryan. He playing here tonight?"

"Baby, I got a box-beater and that's that. If Shug was s'posed to come, I don't know nothin' about it." She held out a grubby hand. "So you stayin' or what?"

He paid his quarter and moved into the crowd. It turned out to be a five-room apartment. A poker and blackjack game was up and running in one bedroom; a "private party" was going on in the next. The parlor and dining room had been nearly cleared of furniture. The music had changed to a slow, bluesy number. A sole red lightbulb cast a lurid glow over dancing couples, who shuffled in place, grinding their hips together. From the shadows along the edge of the dance floor came pants and whispers, grunts and groans. The floorboards sagged and creaked as the dancers slow-dragged around the crowded floor.

The box-beater—or piano player, as he'd be known in more "polite" society—was a narrow, thin man with tired eyes. He swung into a mad folly of light notes tripping over one another. A fat light-skinned girl with dark eyes and long straight black hair climbed atop a chair. She twisted her top so it exposed her midriff and pushed down her long skirt until it sat on her fleshy hips. Raising her arms, she started to rhythmically jiggle her hips to the music. The piano player picked up speed. One loose key flipped off the keyboard. David couldn't help but think that if that old piano had been alive, it would've rocked on dancing feet. He smiled, shook his head, and tapped his feet. After a while, the music started to wind down. David went and bought two cups of liquor and had one waiting for the box-beater when he took a break. The piano player smiled readily when David asked about Shug.

"Yeah, he's here. Over there, in the corner. C'mon. I'll introduce you."

Shug Ryan was in his early forties, a short, bald man with a high forehead and flabby cheeks.

"Let's go in the kitchen," he said.

David bought Shug some corn liquor and asked a few questions about Paris, thinking he'd gradually lead the conversation back to Gem. Shug was eager to talk. He'd hated the Paris scene as much as he'd loved it.

"Don't get me wrong. It's hot, all right—just sometimes, a tad *too* hot. Us niggers would head into them nightspots in Montmartre. Pockets full when we got there, pockets empty when we left. Drinkin' that cheap champagne, makin' it with the white girls. Them chicks knew how to wheedle free drinks and food out of a man. They'd get hold of a fellah and have him jim-clean before the night was through. But we didn't care. We wanted fun. Wanted to be *out there*. We was like kids in a candy shop." He smiled. "We'd get all hopped up, smokin' that bamboo, tuckin' into some snow—whatever and whenever we wanted it." Then he shook his head and said to himself again, "Yeah, them streetcorner Sallies fleeced us clean."

"What made you decide to get out?"

Shug took a drink from his cup and set it down. "Well, it was like this. My friend Julian Campbell was playing with the group Jukebox '29. One night, he fell down dead while blowin' his horn. Had a stroke. Right in the middle of a set. The life did him in. He was young, but the life killed him. Well, that brought me up straight. It sure did. I caught the next boat back."

"How long you been back?"

"'Bout a month."

"How's your luck holding?"

Shug grinned. "Ain't got nothin' but holes in it, man. Nothin' but holes."

"So, did you see Gem McKay over there?"

"Nah, man. Ain't laid eyes on her in more'n a year."

"But I thought you were friends with her."

Shug hunched his shoulders and raised his hands in an I-don't-know gesture. "Hey, a woman like her don't have no friends. You know that. You say you her brother, so you got to know that."

"Well, if you didn't see her, did you at least hear about her? Where she was, how she's doing?"

"Far as I know, ain't nobody heard nothin'. And I mean nothin'."

David tucked ten bits in Shug's hand and turned away. The word "disappointed" did not cover how he felt. He'd been so sure that Shug would give him the information he needed. So sure th—

Wait.

Perhaps Shug *had* given him something . . . something important. It was odd—*No, downright strange* that Shug hadn't heard anything about Gem. He was part of her crowd. Of course, there was always the possibility that she'd left Paris, gone south to Marseilles or off to Madrid or Barcelona if she'd found a new friend.

But what if she didn't leave Paris?

He closed his eyes.

What if she never even got there?

32

On the Town

They'd been married for two days. Every minute that ticked by was borrowed time. Whether that time could be counted in months or weeks or even days, he didn't know. That was all the more reason to make the most of it. He decided to surprise Rachel with a night out and so reserved tables at a cabaret. When she returned home from work that day ("When are you going to quit?" he kept asking. "I can't right now," she'd say, "They still need me"), he told her to get fixed up.

"We're stepping out," he said. "But first, let's see if you like this."

He pulled out a slender blue box that was tied with a gold ribbon and set it on the bed. Her face lit up like a child's at Christmastime. He sat nearby and watched her. She tore the ribbons open and lifted off the cover. When she saw what lay within the box, her mouth formed an O of surprise.

"My God," she whispered, and covered her mouth.

A string of pearls gleamed on a bed of blue velvet. She reached out to touch them, then drew her hand back.

"Go on," he said. "They're yours. Try them on."

Apparently, she couldn't. She appeared stunned. With a smile, he got up, took the necklace from the box, draped it around her throat, and fastened it. He put his hands on her shoulders and steered her toward the mirror. She stared. She stroked the pearls and regarded her reflection with wonder. He laughed and hugged her.

"And now, my dear, you're supposed to say, 'Oh, David, you shouldn't have.'"

She looked at his reflection. "Am I supposed to say that?"

He nodded.

"All right," she said, warming to the game. "'Oh, David, you shouldn't have.'"

"And then I say, 'But aren't you glad I did?'"

"And then," she said, turning to face him. "And then . . . I get to show you just how glad I can be."

An hour and a half later, they were walking east across 139th Street toward Lenox Avenue.

"Where we're going," he said, "used to be one of my old stomping grounds, Jack Johnson's Club Deluxe. Of course, it's got new owners now, and a new name, but I'm sure it's just as fine."

They turned north. When they reached the corner of Lenox and 142nd Street, they saw a long queue of limousines pulled up in front of the club's marquee. People in ermine and top hats pressed around the entrance, waiting to get in. Rachel and David joined the crowd. He noticed that a few glances were thrown at Rachel, then at him, but he thought nothing of it. After all, Rachel was a pretty woman and the new clothes she'd bought did her justice. The crowd moved forward and soon they were just inside the entrance. He missed the hesitant look the doorman gave them.

An usher came up, wearing an unctuous smile. He was young, white, and skinny, and already starting to bald. He glanced at Rachel and his smile disappeared.

"May I help you?" he asked.

"Why, yes," said David, "we have reservations—"

The usher's eyes again went to Rachel. "I'm afraid that can't be."

Rachel tensed.

"What do you mean?" said David, perplexed and irritated. "You took my reservation yesterday."

"You must be mistaken. We've been booked out for weeks, months—"

"Years?" added David. "This is ridiculous. I—"

"Perhaps it would be better if you spoke with the manager." The usher bowed himself away, leaving David and Rachel standing there.

"David, let's leave," Rachel whispered.

He put an arm around her shoulder. She edged closer. The usher reappeared, this time with a large, fat, bullet-shaped man, who was also white. The usher gestured toward David and Rachel, then stepped back. The big guy surged forward with a definite I'm-in-charge attitude. He had Mob written all over him, from the loud checks of his sack suit to the scowl on his face. He jabbed a thick thumb in the direction of the cowering usher behind him.

"My man here tells me you folks got some kinda problem."

"No problem," said David. "We just want our table."

"You've made a mistake. All our tables are taken."

Rachel's grip on David's arm tightened. "Please, let's go."

"No." He turned to the fat man. "If there's been a mistake, then you've made it. I was here yesterday. I made reservations and your man said everything would be fine. Now we're going to sit at our table. If somebody else is sitting there, you'll just have to ask them to leave."

The fat man glared at David. "Buddy, you're the one who's leaving. You wanna hang out with a spade, that's fine with me. But you can't do it here." Two muscular men appeared at his elbow. "I suggest you don't ask for trouble."

"David—" Rachel tugged at David's arm. "It's not worth it. They'll have us thrown in jail—or worse." She threw them a terrified look. "Now please. I just want to be with you. It doesn't have to be here."

"Rachel—"

"*I don't want to stay here!*"

As they left the Cotton Club, they were silent. He could've kicked himself. He should've known better. He'd heard that some of Harlem's best clubs had gone white, but it hadn't really registered. He looked at Rachel. The worst part was that he didn't know what to say to her. He didn't know how to make it better.

I'm protected from all them evil people now . . . I got you.

He stopped, took her in his arms, and hugged her. "I'm sorry, Rachel. I should've checked. It was my fault."

"It's nothing, David. It don't matter. Don't matter at all."

But looking down deep into her eyes, he could see that it did. She laid her head against his chest and wept.

33

Augustus

Friday evening Rachel and David were sitting in the parlor, reading. He had a copy of J. W. Johnson's *Autobiography of an Ex-Colored Man*. She peeked at him over the top of her magazine. He'd asked her if she wanted to go out again that night and she'd said no. She could tell that he'd been relieved, but he felt guilty. He assumed that she was still upset over what had happened at the Cotton Club. She was, but that's not the reason she'd wanted to stay home. In fact, he was more upset about the evening before than she was. She simply wanted to stay home because she had this sudden desperate desire to keep him all to herself. She didn't want to share his attention, not with any-one, not even an admiring social circle. She knew this was unreasonable, but the impulse was so strong it didn't have to make sense.

He glanced up, caught her staring, and smiled, then went back to his book.

I can't believe he belongs to me . . . that I'm here with here with him . . . and that no one, but no one, can ever order me away again.

Her eyes rose to the painting over the mantelpiece. Augustus McKay's portrait looked down at her with stern disapproval. She felt a little chill crawl up her spine. For a moment, she actually thought the eyes in the portrait were alive. They seemed so full of displeasure at the sight of her.

I bet you're rolling over in your grave to see me here. Well I am here and you can't do nothing about it.

Her memories of Daddy McKay were vivid. He'd been one of those suc-cessful colored men who were not only proud of their achievements but acutely aware of their responsibility toward other "less fortunate" members of their race. As far as she was concerned, he'd been obsessed with "the race issue." He'd systematically subscribed to every protest magazine and reli-giously read every sensationalist newspaper printed by the Negro press. He was always ready to discuss, debate, and deliberate on the injuries and humil-iations done to his people.

"Rachel, I don't want you over there so often," her mother had told her one day. "Don't be hurt when I say this, honey, but I don't think Daddy McKay likes you."

At the time, Rachel was fifteen. She'd put down the book she was struggling to read, *Jane Eyre* it was, and scowled. "Well, I don't like him neither."

"Then what you goin' over there for?" Minnie asked, letting her knitting sink to her lap.

Rachel felt a surge of impatience. Her mother would never understand. "Leave me alone, Mama. I can't explain. Just let me be." She picked up her book and tried to find her place.

Minnie was hurt. "Lord, Lord, help my child," she whispered, just loud enough for Rachel to hear.

With an irritated sigh, Rachel laid *Jane Eyre* aside. She went over to her mother where she was sitting in the rocking chair, hugged her, and gave her sunken cheek a kiss. "I'm sorry, Mama. I didn't mean to be rude."

Minnie gave a wan smile and squeezed Rachel's hand. "That's okay, baby, but you be careful."

Rachel nodded, although she really wasn't sure what her mother was warning her against. Daddy McKay might not like her, but he'd never harm her. She was, after all, the family's pet "uplift" project. Her dark skin and her poverty made her perfect for that role, though absolutely unsuitable for any other.

She had nothing but contempt for the man.

What a hypocrite.

He preached against "social inequality" but he believed in social "distinction." He would have scornfully refused any invitation from a white, had he ever received one. Certainly, no white was ever made welcome in his home. He swore that every wretched black sharecropper deserved as much respect as any world leader. But he looked down his chiseled nose at his people's earthy spiritualism, their hearty meals, their love of bright colors and light-hearted tomfoolery. He viewed their everyday ways with detached contempt. He never permitted criticism of black art, music, or literature, but he had no personal affinity for his people's songs, their dances and softly cadenced speech. He despised and distrusted white people, but he admired their clothes and emulated their manners. Like other elitist "brown" men of his time, he lived in a world of "society" events and self-serving perceptions that insulated him from a harsh reality while rewarding him the status the white world denied.

"Don't worry, Mama," she said. "Daddy McKay ain't violent—just weird."

"That's not what I meant," Minnie said, but Rachel wasn't listening.

"He likes to have these meetin's," she said.

"Meetin's? What kinda meetin's?" Minnie was quick to be suspicious.

Rachel smiled and for a moment, she looked much older than her years. "Oh, they ain't got nothin' to do with sex or religion, if that's what you're thinkin'."

Minnie gasped. "Why, Rachel Hamilton, you—"

"They's got to do with somethin' much worse—politics."

"Politics!"

"Yes, ma'am. He gets David and the twins together once a week—and if I'm there I get pulled in, too. We get to sit in his office and. . . ." She let her voice trail off and gave a shrug that said, *What goes on in Daddy McKay's office ain't worth the effort of describing.* But now that she'd mentioned the meetings, Minnie wanted to know about them. In detail.

"Sit, and yes—then what?"

Rachel sighed. "Don't be such a worrywart. We listen. That's all. We just get to listen. For at least an hour, while Daddy McKay rants and raves about the sins of white folks and the responsibilities of black ones. His children have a mission to advance the race, he says. He's given them money and education—"

"Well, that's true."

"And he expects somethin' for it."

"'Spects *what?*" With a raised eyebrow.

Rachel smiled, bemused. "Why, he don't expect nothin' much—just that his children become big, important Negro leaders, members of the Talented Tenth."

"The Talented *what?*"

Rachel looked at her. "Oh, you heard of that, Mama. Why, that's a theory of Mr. W. E. B. DuBois. He says that there shall arise a Talented Tenth of the Negro people and they shall lead us to the Promised Land."

Minnie failed to catch the cynicism in Rachel's voice. "Is he some kinda false prophet, this Mr. DuBois?"

Rachel shrugged. "I don't know. To me, he's just like one of them white folks that think the better-offs should get more and the rest of us should keep struggling."

"He ain't black, is he?"

"Sure 'nough is, Mama. One of them light-skinned educated race men, done studied in Europe."

"Humph," said Minnie. "Well, that explains it." She picked up her knitting.

Rachel suppressed a chuckle. "You know somethin', Mama? I think you got more wisdom in your pinkie than Mr. DuBois's got in his whole head. But a lot of people respect him. They think he's done good things for our people."

"Has he, now? Well, I ain't never heard of him. And from what you tell me, I can't b'lieve he's interested in doin' anythin' for poor folk like me." Minnie paused to catch a dropped stitch. "What d'you do when Daddy McKay's carryin' on like that? What d'you say?"

"Nothin'," Rachel answered. "He'd never ask our opinion about nothin'. He just wants to hear himself talk. So, yup." She sighed. "That's all I do . . . is listen."

And that's hard enough.

Even if he did ever ask her opinion about anything, she'd be crazy to actually try to talk to the man. To tell the truth, he not only irritated her, he amused her. Who'd have ever thought to find so much racial ardor in a family that was by and large insulated against the ravages of racial prejudice? Of course, sometimes she *did* tire of his speeches on the ignorance, arrogance, and malevolence of white people. Sometimes, she wanted to stand up and cry out: *What do you know about it,* really?

Instead, she always sat quietly, appearing to listen dutifully, while her thoughts and eyes wandered elsewhere—elsewhere inevitably meaning David.

And now, finally, unbelievably, she was his wife.

Her eyes went back to him and she thought of Isabella. *She looked so much like him.*

He looked up again, to find her eyes on him. Concern crossed his face. He closed his book, putting a finger between the pages to hold his place, and leaned forward.

"You all right?"

For a moment, she looked as though she were about to cry. "I'm fine."

He laid his book on the side table and went to sit next to her. She snuggled into his arms and raised her face.

"You do love me?" she whispered.

"Hm, hmm . . . Of course I do." He kissed her on the top of her head.

"Then tell me. Say the words."

His forehead creased. "What's wrong, Rachel?"

Her eyes searched his. She saw what she suspected and something painful pinged inside her. She dropped her gaze and looked away.

"What's the matter, baby?"

"Nothing. I was just being silly, that's all."

34

Nella Comes Clean

"You weren't quite truthful with me before—"

"I don't tell lies—"

"But you don't always tell the whole truth either."

It was Sunday. David was seated in Nella's immense living room with a glass of suspicious contents pressed into his hand. She put a platter of sweets on the coffee table. Choosing what appeared to be a chocolate-covered cherry, she popped it into her mouth whole.

"Just what is it you want to know?"

"How to find Gem."

"I told you—"

"You told me that while you were in Paris, you tried to contact her."

"I told you that I was unsuccessful."

"But you didn't tell me that you didn't give up."

She stared at him, stunned. "How did you know?"

"You're a stubborn woman. The kind who doesn't change her mind once it's made up."

An admiring smile slowly spread over Nella's face. She did not answer directly, but ate another cherry and chewed thoughtfully.

"Remember our deal. Information for information."

"Yes, yes, I remember," he said mildly. "Now please, do what you do best. Talk."

"David, you have a way with you—a way that . . ."

She clenched her jaw and pressed her lips together. Words failed her. She lit herself a cigarette and jabbed the air with it. "If anyone else ever spoke to me that way, I'd have him thrown out on his ear. Not even Nikki—"

"Nella, you don't have to throw me out. Just answer my question and I'll leave."

Her eyes narrowed. "I'll let that last little quip slide," she said, "but don't—"

"Nella, please—"

She held up a hand. "All right, all right." She took a deep breath. "You're right. I didn't give up. After several attempts to contact Gem, I decided to go see her, to drop in on her unannounced. I knew it would be in bad taste. But I felt entitled. After all, she hadn't taken the time to even answer my notes. The boy I'd sent told me there was a girl who accepted the messages. Clearly, the girl wasn't Gem, but he said she seemed capable enough. He didn't doubt that she was passing my notes on. It was Gem's fault that she was about to get an unexpected visitor.

"I took a taxi to the address on the postcards Gem had sent me. I was very surprised when the driver pulled up in front of the place. It wasn't at all what I might've imagined for someone like Gem. It was dirty; slummy in fact. The driver assured me that this was the address I'd given him. He was getting anxious about his money, so I paid him and got out. Then, on second thought, I turned back, gave him a little something extra, and asked him to wait.

"A young woman answered the door. I assume she was the one who'd taken my messages. She was rather tall, but stooped and starved-looking. Her clothes were fashionable, but they didn't fit her well. They looked like the cast-offs of some wealthy, chic girlfriend. The young woman herself wasn't chic at all. Her makeup was poorly done. Her jewelry, a long pearl necklace à la Chanel, was a cheap imitation that clanked when she moved. Her fingernails were broken and dirty; her fingernail polish, a bright garish red, was chipped and peeling.

"My opinion of her must've shown in my face. She immediately drew herself up and tried to play *la grande dame,* but she was too young and much too uneducated for the part. She told me in guttural French that Gem wasn't there. She wasn't exactly impolite, just brusque. Something about her made me curious. Her eyes kept flicking from side to side, glancing up and down the street. Obviously, she wanted me away from her door as quickly as possible. I think she wanted to shut the door in my face, but she was afraid I'd make a scene. I practically forced her to let me in.

"I followed her down a short hallway that opened into a small parlor. The room had a very low ceiling and one tiny window. It was like being in a dark hole. The place stunk—a repellent mixture of garlic, cheap perfume, and stale cigarettes. The room had dirty white walls with cracked and peeling paint. There was a lumpy red sofa, a couple of tables and a lamp, and not much else. She probably worked as a cheap fortune-teller. I noticed some battered Tarot cards laid out on a table.

"She and I seemed to be alone. She rolled herself a cigarette. I was sure that she was hiding something. Slyly, she admitted that she was. She wanted money. Naturally she asked for too much. We haggled. She was greedy, but I'm very, very stingy. Most rich people are.

"Finally, she came out with it. Gem had never been there, she said. She'd been collecting Gem's mail and messages for months. I showed her a post-card I'd received. She admitted she'd written it herself. She said Gem had been paying her to regularly make up messages and send postcards to certain people in the States, had given her a list in fact. She showed me the letter from Gem that told her what to do. I made her give it to me. If you want, I can show it to you. I brought it back."

Nella jumped up and walked briskly out of the room. David waited impatiently. When Nella returned, she handed him a sheet of once-white, once-very-expensive stationery. There were only three sets of names and addresses written on it: Lilian's, Nella's, and Snyder's. The page itself had been handled a great deal. Fingerprints smudged it and one part of it buckled under an old brown coffee stain. Nella caught David's look and shrugged.

"That's the condition it was in when the girl gave it to me."

"Why didn't you tell me all this before?"

Nella sighed. "I didn't see what relevance it might have to Lilian's death. But then it occurred to me that Gem's silence might be causing you pain. I don't want that. If you hadn't come today, I would've sent for you. I realize that many people don't think well of Gem. But I like her. Gem isn't that callous. She hasn't said a word because she doesn't know about Lilian. I'm sure she would be here now if she did."

Interesting how two people can interpret the same thing differently, thought David. Nella was dismayed by Gem's silence. Nothing more. She didn't find it alarming—at worst, inconvenient. David wished he could feel that way, too, but in his state of mind, anything out of the ordinary seemed sinister.

"Well then, where is she?"

Nella shrugged. "I haven't the faintest idea. But I'm sure she's fine. It's obvious, don't you see? Gem doesn't want to be found. She's played a little trick on us. It's just her way. She'll pop up sometime. We must be patient. We have no other choice."

But we do, thought David. *We do.*

35

The Bitter Truth About Sweet

His worry about Gem had reawakened his doubts about Lilian's death, doubts he had never been able to fully put aside. He rubbed his temples. *I'm tired,* he thought, *so damn tired of trying to believe in explanations that make no sense.* He thought of Lilian's disappearing pregnancy and of Gem's faked postcards; of Lilian's hatred of Sweet and of Gem's breakup with Snyder; of Lilian's friendship with Nella and of Gem's refusal to answer Nella's calls.

Things ain't always the way they seem. His inner voice, echoing Annie's words, spoke to him now more loudly than ever. But the words were indistinct, muffled by conflicting thoughts and distracting opinions.

Back home in his room, David reviewed all the questions he had raised and the few answers he had found. Visualizing the details of what he had learned as puzzle pieces, he mentally shifted them around, trying to interlock them, breaking them apart. Gradually, he discerned a pattern. One by one, the pieces of the puzzle fell into place.

Why had it taken him so long to see the obvious? He knew—undeniably and completely—that Lilian had indeed been murdered. He knew who had killed her. He understood why Gem had given up her attempts to seduce Sweet; why she had offered to help Lilian; and why she had staged that raucous breakup with Snyder.

He thought about Sadie Mansfield, a former client. She had cut her wrists after her husband left her. He would never forget her body. Her wrists were covered with the small incisions she had made as she worked up her courage to die.

With rapid fluidity, his thoughts flew to a book he had once read in his father's library. French sociologist Émile Durkheim had written that suicide victims always give their act a personal stamp, one that reflects their temperament and the special characteristics of their circumstances.

David found a sheet of paper and a pen. He wrote first the name "Pierre

Lorraine" and underlined it heavily. After a moment or two, he wrote the word "conceit." Then after a space, the question: "Why not take the easy way?"

He sat quite still for about three minutes. In his mind, he could hear Rachel asking him, "But why would Sweet kill her?" and his answer, "Because he not only didn't love her—*he loved someone else.*"

He thought of Nella and vanilla. And his heart gave a hard little thump. Something heavy and cold landed in the pit of his stomach. He had been close to the truth before, very close—but two false assumptions had kept him from it. He saw it all now. He had the solution, he had it—but how he wished he hadn't.

There was a knock on his door. Annie stepped in. "Mr. Jameson's back. I just thought you might like to know."

"Thank you."

She turned to go, then hesitated.

"Yes?" he asked.

"Mr. Jameson—he don't know 'bout you and Miss Rachel. Maybe you better tell him—b'fore she comes home from work."

"Yes," he said slowly. "I'll be sure to talk to him—about that and many other things."

Going downstairs, he found Sweet relaxing with a newspaper in Augustus's throne. Sweet was humming the popular song "I'm Sitting on Top of the World."

David stood in the doorway, watching him. Sweet shivered. Perhaps he felt a cold wind at his back. He swung around, took one look at David, and rose to his feet. The two men stared at one another.

"You don't miss my sister at all, do you?" said David.

Sweet looked at David as though he were mad. Sweet opened his mouth to reply, but David raised a hand. "Please. The last thing I need is to hear more lies."

David entered the room. Sweet watched him warily. David remembered how impressed he'd been with Durkheim's insights. He'd never foreseen that he would have to recall Durkheim's words twenty years later to solve his sister's murder. He spoke thoughtfully, explaining in a methodical tone.

"I returned because I was told that Lilian had committed suicide. That she'd become mentally unstable and taken her life. I was told that Gem had suddenly reappeared after five years' absence and . . . just as suddenly left again. So I was told, and so I was supposed to believe. But none of it made sense. None of it reflected the people I knew my sisters to be. So, I asked questions. Annie, Rachel, Nella Harding, you. On the surface, you each told the same tale, but when I looked closer, listened harder, I found too many contradictions to ignore. The Lilian I knew was not the Lilian people described."

Sweet's expression was faintly contemptuous. "I told you—her illness changed her."

"No illness could explain these changes."

"Which changes?"

"Lilian's pregnancy, for one."

"It was imagined—"

"Her doctor, at least initially, confirmed it."

Sweet looked genuinely stunned. "He couldn't have. She would've told me—"

"She wouldn't have told you and she didn't tell you—for reasons we're both aware of."

Sweet's lizard-like eyes narrowed. "I refuse to believe there was a pregnancy. But go on. You spoke of several—what was the word?" He paused. "Oh, yes. Contradictions."

"Suffice it to say there were enough to make me wonder. When I first started asking questions, Annie warned me that things aren't always the way they seem. The more people I talked to, the more applicable that warning seemed to be."

Sweet smirked. "Let's be blunt. You think I killed her, don't you? You feel guilty about her suicide, so now you want to say *I* did it."

"No. Not at all."

Sweet's surprise was obvious. David gave a cryptic little smile.

"Naturally, there was someone else who could've killed her—someone who like you would've benefited, or hoped to benefit, from her death."

Sweet tensed. David kept his voice calm and restrained.

"I know Gem was interested in you and that you rejected her when she approached you openly. Gem found herself another lover, Adrian Snyder. She showed how much she disliked you when Lilian was around and offered Lilian the benefit of her sisterly advice. Finally, she ran weeping to the Hamptons after her breakup with Snyder. But nothing was as it seemed: Gem neither despised you nor loved Snyder. He didn't break up with her— she broke up with him. And she wasn't ashamed of the public breakup. She wanted people to know about it. They had to believe she had good reason to suddenly leave town.

"While the gossips were still atwitter, Gem packed her bags. She fled the cold grayness of New York for the stillness of Harding House. It's a lovely place. Relatively isolated, set on an outcropping of private beach, with a small private dock and a boat for short excursions. Nella's house fitted Gem's needs perfectly. The water was too cold to swim in, so Gem probably sat on the beach the first couple of days, letting the hours slip by peacefully, watching the sun sink lower over the horizon. I can see her hugging herself, as the air grew chill with the setting sun. She prepared simple suppers and ate them alone. She probably read for a while, before going to bed. She spent several days like this, in self-imposed isolation. Then one night, lying in the dark, let's say she watched a cloud pass over the moon. And she knew it was time to do what she planned next.

"She telephoned Lilian, invited her to visit. When Lilian arrived, Gem went on to the next step of her plan—a plan that was exquisitely simple and brutally direct. She killed Lilian—shot her, stabbed her, I don't know—and hid her body on Nella's property. Then Gem dressed herself in Lilian's clothes, drove back to Manhattan, *and took Lilian's place.*"

Sweet said nothing, but he looked dismayed. David went on.

"This would explain why the last entry in Lilian's diary was dated just after the breakup. It would explain why no one had a chance to see Gem before she left. Why Lilian was suddenly no longer pregnant. Why she lost interest in her friends and sought out Nella. It would explain a great deal. And it would explain it with sense."

"But that couldn't be! It couldn't! Don't you think I'd know if Gem had been pretending to be my wife?"

"A good question," said David. "Very good."

Stillness.

Sweet cleared his throat. "This is ridiculous. I know it was Lilian. If it had been Gem, she would've been healthy. But the woman who came back from Harding House was as sick as ever."

"You said she was well for some time after Gem supposedly left."

"Just for a short time—"

"Enough time for Gem to develop Lilian's symptoms."

"Preposterous! Impossible!"

"Think about it—about the mental strain Gem was under. She'd gotten Lilian to confide in her, so she felt sure of her familiarity with Lilian's life, but there must've been many perks to Lilian's personality, areas about Lilian's life, that Gem didn't know about, and they must've tripped her up. What was worse was conforming herself to the ways and habits she did know about. It was an ironic twist: Gem the free spirit had trapped herself in a situation where she had to adopt the mannerisms of the sister she'd scorned, the woman she'd killed. As time went by, Gem must've felt imprisoned by glass walls. And she felt guilt. Intense, unbearable guilt. Yes, she'd been cold enough to kill her own sister. But she wasn't cold enough to live with it.

"Gem was haunted by Lilian's dying gaze. That would explain a letter Nella Harding found, a letter that reads like a poem. 'It's her fault. It's her fault. My sister, that sister of mine. She's trying to kill me, to slay me, with her dead blind eyes . . .' Gem was the family poet. She's the only one who could've written those words. I think she dreamed constantly about what she'd done. She was tortured by nightmares. That's why, on a visit to Nella's house, it seemed as though she was screaming out her own name.

"When you urged Gem to see a psychiatrist, she panicked. She couldn't afford to let a stranger probe her mind, but she couldn't hold out. She probably told the good doctor what she thought he wanted to hear. She knew exactly what to say to make him cluck or sigh or tsk or simply nod his head in empathy, sympathy, or feigned understanding. *What a dear old fool,* she thought at first. And that was fine, because she found it entertaining to manipulate him, but then he became a 'tiring old fool' when she began to suspect that he was seeing through her, was indeed learning more about her through her lies than any of the few truths she volunteered. She broke off her therapy. She turned to liquor and drugs."

"Gem would've never committed suicide. She's the most self-loving woman I've ever met."

"And one of the most self-destructive. Liquor, drugs, and guilt can bring anyone down." David paused. "Still, I agree with you. Gem did not kill herself. She didn't die by her own hand any more than Lilian did."

Sweet's dark eyes were bleak and grim. Several uneasy minutes passed by.

"You might've gotten away with it, Sweet. But you're a sloppy killer."

Sweet started, and then caught himself. "Lilian wasn't the only one with mental problems, I see."

"Yes, well . . . All of us McKays are cursed with a rather creative intelligence," David said mildly. "Unfortunately for you, you aren't. You didn't do your homework. You didn't study your victim enough."

Sweet said nothing, but he swallowed once.

"Is your throat dry?" David asked. "Nervousness—fear—will do that to people. Make yourself a drink."

Sweet licked his lips, but he didn't move.

"I once read that every suicide chooses his death, marks his death," said David, "in a way that reflects his special temperament. Seen in that light, it was a bad idea for you to have shown that suicide note to me. Neither one of my sisters would've written something like that.

"You quoted Lorraine. I'm sure you thought you were being brilliant. But Lilian hated Lorraine. You didn't take enough interest in her to learn that. Why would Lilian quote a writer she disliked? When I realized that it wasn't Lilian, but Gem who had been found upstairs, the note seemed even odder. Gem would've never written such a thing. At most, she might've grabbed a page of stationery and in her pretty script, written 'See you in Hell.' She would've never typed it. She couldn't type. But that's irrelevant. Neither Gem nor Lilian would've thought to write anything so personal on a machine."

Sweet's eyes were riveted to David's face. He listened, unwillingly captivated, as David continued.

"Gem's thinking patterns never interested me before. I never found her scintillatingly unpredictable. She was one of the most boringly predictable people I've ever known. Why? Because she was unerringly selfish and vain. She always chose the easiest way out. And she always wanted to look her best. So why would she choose such an ugly, not to mention painful, way to die? Why didn't she use the drugs that were right there? Why would she instead take a knife and butcher her own flesh? It didn't make sense." There was a momentary pause, then David added, almost as an afterthought: "There was also the matter of the slashes."

"The what?" Sweet stirred. "The slashes?"

"On her wrists. Suicide victims usually make one or two shallow cuts while working up their courage. But Annie described two clean wounds."

"But the shallow cuts were there. Annie just didn't see them."

"But you did?"

"Yes—I did. You can't trust that old woman's memory. The shock of finding Lilian's body probably drove everything else out of her mind."

"I see. So you want me to believe that the discovery shocked Annie, but it didn't shock you? Well, I'm quite willing to believe that. I'm willing to believe that you knew exactly what Annie would find when she returned that day."

"Don't twist my words."

"I don't have to. They speak for themselves. Every inconsistency reflects a certain truth."

That nervous tic leapt near Sweet's right eye.

"I've thought a lot about that weekend when my sister supposedly killed herself," said David. "She told Nella Harding that you'd be gone the entire time. You certainly went to a lot of trouble to make it look that way, setting up an alibi, including a witness. The man who shared your hotel room claims you were there all Sunday night. But we both know he's lying. It's easy to buy false testimony. But given time and determination, it's also easy to break it. I'm sure Epps will think twice when he learns he's part of a murder investigation.

"You hid while Nikki Harding searched the house. And came out after he left. Gem suspected that you were here and she wasn't happy about it. She'd come to fear you. She wasn't sure why. In her confused state, the best she could do was talk about ghosts.

"You waited until she'd gone to sleep. Then in the night, you crept up on her. As she slept, you took her hand. You uncurled her fingers and—" David raised his hand and, with a swift slicing motion, mimed the flash of a blade over flesh. "The pain woke her. Her eyes snapped open. She saw her blood squirting from her wrist. Perhaps she clapped her other hand over it, but the blood would've just bubbled up between her fingers.

"Maybe you went so far as to tell my sister that it was time for her to die. You held the knife away from you so it wouldn't soil those nice new clothes her money had paid for. Maybe you tilted the knife, turned it this way and that. No doubt some of the blood trickled down onto your hands. Maybe you looked down at them, admired them. For their strength. For their ability to destroy a woman."

The twitch at the corner of Sweet's eye was pronounced. He strode to the writing table and poured himself a drink. He gulped half of it down, turned, and eyed David with intense distaste.

"Tell me more. I'm sure there is more."

"You're the kind of killer who takes pleasure in explaining how clever he is, so you explained to her what you would tell the police. You would say you found her dead. That she'd been depressed but had refused help. That she'd apparently taken matters into her own hands. That's all you'd have to say. They would call it suicide for you.

"You went on to tell her how everyone would believe you. That no one would suspect. After all, you're the man who loved her, the good husband who'd stayed at her side. They'd believe anything you said. And my sister listened, mute from the pain, the terror of finding herself trapped with a madman. Maybe she found her voice and asked you, 'Why?' You had the money, the house. Why weren't you satisfied?

"I can imagine your answer. You thought you were talking to Lilian. She was a wonderful woman. But for a man like you, she was too quiet, too thoughtful. You would love another kind of woman—someone who plays the game of life as you do: a fighter, a dirty player. You wanted Gem. And you were prepared to kill in order to be with her. The great irony is, *you killed the very woman you loved.*

"I'm sure my sister pleaded for her life. I know she fought. For all she was worth. Blood everywhere, Annie said. On the sheets, the canopy, the walls. Drugged or not, Gem would never have died easily. You must've had to drag her down, pin her down like an animal, to do what you did."

Sweet's eyes were dull and cold.

"Yet you two deserved one another," David said. "Both ruthless, both greedy, disdainful of humanity and unable to love anyone other than yourselves. Gem, unwilling to risk another rejection, determined to have you at all costs. You, driven by a sick love for the woman you couldn't have and contempt for the one you did."

A hostile silence followed. Finally, Sweet tossed back the last of his gin and set his glass down on the writing table with a thump. Slowly, he raised his big hands in the air and began to applaud loudly, mockingly.

"An excellent performance. Too bad you didn't sell tickets."

David's smile was frosty. "Would you like that? A public display? That's what I want, too. You, charged with first-degree murder in a very public courtroom."

"What proof do you have? None. If you did, you'd be talking to the police right now." Sweet's expression grew venomous. "Where do you get the nerve to accuse me? Where were you when Lilian needed you? I was the one who carried her, who soothed her nightmares and cradled her when she slept. I was the one! Not you!"

Sweet drew himself up. "You have no right to play judge or jury. I know about you. Don't think I don't. I contacted an operative down in Philly, a good, no-nonsense kind of guy. Fast, efficient, accurate. I thought he'd have to look far and dig deep, but he said you were easy. It seems you're a local hero. Marvelous press clippings."

David's expression became stone-like.

Sweet laughed. He was enjoying himself. "That's right. Your secret is a secret no longer, my friend. Soon, everyone who is anyone will know your game. You and your accusations. What a hypocrite!"

"I don't care what you say about me, as long as I live to see you behind bars. It might take time, but you'll pay for what you did." David turned to leave, then paused. "Oh, and one last thing. While you were gone, Rachel Hamilton and I got married. You know her, I believe?"

Sweet blinked as though he'd been hit. His face drained of expression. "You and Rachel?"

"She's at work. I want you gone before she gets back. Pack your bags and get out."

Sweet's face congested with blood. He balled his hands into fists. "McKay, I warn you. I will not let you send me to prison. I'd rather die first. I've always been a man to choose my own destiny. Neither you nor anyone else will dictate my end."

Sweet stormed past. David watched him go with a grim, set expression. A long fight lay ahead. No doubt, Sweet would make good on his threats, but David found that he was relieved. He was tired of running and ready for a fight. If public humiliation was the price to pay to see Sweet in jail, then he was willing to pay it.

His first concern was to protect Rachel. The uproar over his past would hurt her—more than it would hurt him. He cared nothing for the stifling *café au lait* society that would bar them, but Rachel would hunger for entry. He'd had years to prepare for a day of reckoning, but Rachel would be caught like a deer in headlights.

He had to send her somewhere safe, where the vicious tongues would be still. Aunt Clara's in Chicago. His father's younger sister was practical, tough-minded, and independent. And she loved a good fight.

Aunt Clara always said that the best defense is a good offense. He had to find proof that Sweet killed Gem. Of course, Sweet would battle any attempt to have Gem's remains exhumed, but David felt that he could box it through. He rubbed his jaw. An exhumation would demonstrate the switch in identities, but would it yield proof that Sweet wielded the knife?

First things first. He had to prepare Rachel. She would soon be at the epi-center of a storm. He had a sudden silly—*very silly* impulse to buy her flowers.

Of all the times to be thinking about that . . .

But what better time than now? After so much misery, and with so much more ahead, why not try to enjoy the moment?

His mind clicking, David left. It took him about forty minutes of running around in the cold to find the bouquet he wanted. The flowers were lovely, yet the instant he held them in his hand, his heart sank.

Rachel will know that something's wrong the moment I give them to her. She'll know that I have something difficult to say.

He headed home, trying to organize his thoughts so that he could tell her *in a cohesive way* about Jonah and Philadelphia—*a way that she'll understand.*

He glanced at his watch. Rachel should be home now. There would be no purpose in putting it off. He'd have to tell her immediately. He climbed the front steps to his house, his heart heavy. As he entered the house, he heard heated voices coming from the parlor. Then a shot rang out.

36

Heavy Bracelets

Dropping the flowers, David rushed to the parlor doors and ripped them open.

Jameson Sweet lay dead on the floor, his face a crimson mass. A gun was in his right hand and Rachel was kneeling beside him. Her face and throat and the bodice of her white nurse's uniform were splattered with blood. She picked up the gun and looked at it, dazed. David ran to her, kneeled, and gathered her in his arms.

"My God, what happened? Are you hurt?"

"He—he killed himself. Shot himself. I—I co—couldn't stop him. I tried but I—I couldn't." An anguished sob broke from her throat. She dropped the gun and buried her face in David's chest, whimpering. He looked over her shoulder. A ragged wound had gutted the left side of Sweet's face. When it exited, the bullet had taken part of his skull with it, causing an explosion of blood and brain matter.

No one deserves to die like that, he thought. "We have to call the police."

"We can't. I—I fought with him. I tried to get the gun away. They'll think I killed him."

"Calm down."

Rachel gulped. "What—what'll I say?"

"Tell the truth."

David hugged her. The coming police interview would be difficult, but once it was done, they would be free of the nightmare. His secret would be safe; he and Rachel would be able to live out their lives in peace.

He stood by Rachel, his hand on her shoulder while she gave her statement. A homicide detective, a man named Peters, listened with the ill-concealed cynicism of a man who was used to being lied to. Peters was gray and tough-looking, like a faded bulldog, of medium height with a balding head and bloodshot blue eyes. Peters also questioned David but there was little he could add since he hadn't seen the actual shooting.

"Are you aware of any personal problems that might've led Mr. Sweet to take his life?"

David paused. What was he to answer? To say yes would open a Pandora's box. Everything about his sisters might come out. To say no would undermine Rachel's credibility.

"I didn't know my brother-in-law well. But I believe he'd been in a critical frame of mind since my sister's recent death."

Peters turned back to Rachel. "Did Mr. Sweet say what was bothering him?"

"He talked about his wife. He couldn't come to terms with having lost her."

"She committed suicide, too—"

"After a long illness."

"They were close?"

"Yes."

"And you say you tried to stop him from killing himself?"

"I talked to him. And then I tried to get the gun away."

"Were your hands on the gun when it went off?"

Rachel felt for David's hand. He gave her shoulder a reassuring squeeze.

"What's behind your question, Detective?" he asked.

Peters smiled blandly and snapped his notepad shut. "Just looking for the truth. We'll have to test your wife's hands for gunpowder residue."

Rachel started. She turned to David. "But I—"

"It's normal in situations like this," said Peters.

David comforted her. "It *is* procedure. Don't worry. You have nothing to fear."

"No," she murmured. "Of course not."

David caught the fear in her voice. It echoed his own. How could he have thought that Sweet's death would mean an end to their troubles? It now appeared that Sweet would pose an even greater threat in death than he had in life.

Peters returned the next day and asked for Rachel. Annie told him Rachel was resting, so he asked to speak with David. She left the two men in the library. David rose from his armchair to shake hands with the detective and asked him to sit down. Peters spoke without preamble.

"Your wife tested positive for gunpowder residue."

"Of course she did. She said she tried to get the gun away."

"But she *didn't* say she was holding it when it fired."

"Are you accusing my wife of murder? I saw Sweet's body. The wound that killed him was consistent with suicide: close contact, to the head."

"Yes . . . it was fired at close range," Peters said. "But there's a problem. The muzzle must've been pressed against his cheek. Most people shoot themselves in the temple. Let's say Sweet was sitting down—or he was standing." He waved his hands to stave off argument. "It doesn't matter. Either way, it would've been simple for her to come up behind him. He would've been dead before he knew what hit him."

"A big man like that? You're saying a big man like Jameson Sweet would just let someone creep up on him, put a gun in his face, and fire?"

"If he trusted her enough not to look behind him."

The two men studied one another.

"Don't try to arrest her."

"I have a warrant."

"You don't have a case. You don't even have a motive."

"We have Byron Canfield."

David's eyes flashed. "What does he have to do with this?"

"He says Sweet had hold of a secret that could've destroyed you. We've checked it out and his story is solid. Your wife offed Sweet to protect you. To protect your name. Your money. And her status."

David stood. "You—"

"David?"

Both men turned around. Rachel was standing in the doorway. Framed by the archway and an aureole of soft late afternoon light, she seemed ethereal and delicate. David went to her. Peters rose to his feet.

"Mrs. McKay, I have to ask you to come with me."

"No!" she cried.

David stepped between them. "If you take her, then you'll have to take me, too."

Peters looked at David. "I could charge you with obstruction—"

"You can charge me with murder if you want to. Just don't take her."

Rachel looked frantically at David.

"Are you serious?" Peters asked.

"Very."

Peters was silent. He looked at David with a calculating hunger.

"Think about it," said David. "This is the best offer you'll have all day."

"I can't just forget about the gun residue test."

"We both know they're notoriously fallible. Look, man, I'm offering to go with you. We both know I make the better suspect. After all, I was the target of the scandal."

The detective's eyes narrowed. "May I take that as a confession of guilt?"

"No, you may not."

The metal handcuffs were cold and heavy and cut into his skin. Annie watched silently from the kitchen doorway, her eyes full of pain. Rachel's wails followed him out the house. Then Peters slammed the door behind them, cutting off the sound of her cries.

Two police officers were waiting by a squad car. They came up to him, one on either side, gripped him by his elbows, and led him from the house to the waiting car. It was late afternoon, bright enough for the world to see his disgrace. He was painfully aware of the parting of delicate French curtains up and down the street, of brown noses pressed against windowpanes and wide eyes staring. Humiliation overwhelmed him. Although he had volunteered to be arrested for a crime he had not committed, he was sick with shame. That they should see him this way. That his life should have come to this. Yes, he was innocent of *this* crime, but he was guilty of another—and soon everyone would know it. As Sweet said: *Everyone who is anyone will know your game.*

He was roughly grabbed by the back of his collar, forced to bend down, and shoved into the backseat. The car reeked of stale cigarettes, cold sweat, and dried semen. An odious mixture. An officer climbed in next to him. David looked at him, at his resentful, muddy brown eyes and blotchy complexion.

"It stinks in here."

The young officer grinned at him. "You'll get used to it."

David turned his face away. He tried not to think of the stench and peered out the grimy window of the police car instead. The world whisked by. He caught glimpses of a young woman in a wheelchair with a small girl on her lap, a teenage boy pedaling a rusted cart, an old man in tattered clothes shuffling along with the help of a cane. For a moment, he forgot about himself. What about those people? Look at the burdens they had to bear. What would be their end? An awareness of the brevity of life pressed itself upon him. The words of a psalm Lila had loved rose within him.

Lord, make me to know my end. And what is the measure of my days, that I may know how frail I am. . . . Do not be silent at my tears, for I am a stranger with you, a sojourner as all my fathers were. Look away from me that I may be radiant, before I go away and am no more.

Years had passed since he'd thought of those words, but now they returned unbidden. Why? He thought for a moment and he knew. Death, in its psychic form, awaited him. He stood on the edge of a mental precipice. His arrest, his incarceration, the trial and the public excoriation that would undoubtedly follow would push him over the edge. Life as he knew it would end. But would that be so terrible? He had been blessed in many ways. Life had been generous to him. It had granted him more advantages than it did most people, black or white. But to what benefit had he used them? That woman in the wheelchair, the teenage boy, and the old man: Their struggles—disability, poverty, and age—had been forced upon them. His problems were of his own making. He'd made too many wrong decisions. He had failed at every determining moment. Why hadn't he fought for Jonah—even if it meant dying at the hands of that lynch mob? Wouldn't it have been better to die with honor than to live in shame? Wouldn't it have been better if when he'd seen that woman in Philadelphia, upon offering to help her, he'd had the guts to tell her who and what he was? And why, dear God, why hadn't he answered Lilian's last letter?

If he had made the right decision at the right time, he would have been able to return. He would have been there to support Rachel and save Isabella. He could possibly have dissuaded Lilian from marrying Sweet. He could have protected his women. He could have made a difference. He felt the heavy handcuffs cutting into his wrists, pressing into his back, and his shame left him. An odd calm washed over him. Life, he told himself, had once more been generous with him. It had granted him a chance to make amends.

They took him down to the City Prison at 101 Centre Street, also known as the Tombs. Once there, he was led to an office and seated in a chair before a long, battered wooden table. The room was dark, except for one glaring light, which was angled so that it shone directly in his eyes. He winced, blinded. Several officers stood over him with their shirtsleeves rolled up. They asked him his name and told him to tell them what had happened. He told them everything—beginning with the day he returned, ending with Sweet's last words that he would not allow himself to be jailed. They urged him to confess to murder. They demanded. They cajoled. They threatened. He refused. Then the beatings began. Still, he refused.

The "interrogating" and fingerprinting lasted well past midnight. They threw him into a small, narrow cell that reeked of urine and vomit. He was grateful, however, to have a cell alone. When the guard extinguished the light, it was pitch-dark. David couldn't see his hand before his face. Feeling his way in the dark, he stumbled into the cot shoved up against one wall. The mattress was thin and hard and it stank of mildew. He lay down, his body a mass of bruised and aching parts, his right eye swollen shut. Staring into the gloom, he waited for panic to set in, but he felt eerily calm. A warm liquid numbness that began in his fingertips spread slowly to the rest of his body. He closed his eyes, sure that he would be unable to sleep. But he did, uneasily.

Early Monday morning, he was chained to two other men and hustled to court for a hearing. He looked and felt horrible. His hair was dusty. He had a nasty taste in his mouth and his clothes stunk of rot after a night of sleeping on the cell's filthy mattress. The skin over his swollen eye was purplish and tender.

He was charged with first-degree murder in the death of Jameson Sweet. Bail was out of the question. As he stood before the judge, he glanced around the courtroom, looking for Rachel. She was nowhere to be seen. Yes, he had told her to stay away and he was glad she had listened. But he was saddened. He missed her. Annie was there, however. And so was Byron Canfield.

37

The Confessional

Later that day, David sat on his thin mattress, reading. A pile of newspapers lay scattered on the floor at his feet.

"RACIAL TREASON: MCKAY LIVED AS A WHITE IN PHILLY!" screamed the headline of one paper. "POLICE: MOVEMENT LAWYER SLAIN BY NEGRO PASSING FOR WHITE!" proclaimed another. "MCKAY'S DOUBLE LIFE: DID HE KILL TO PROTECT HIS DIRTY SECRET?" said a third.

The Negro press was full of his arrest; more accurately, they were full of Canfield.

"Young Sweet was like a son to me," Canfield was quoted as saying. "I showed him the ropes, brought him along. We had just returned from Chicago, filled with joy over our landmark victory in the Boston Richards case. Then this happened. Sweet's work on the Richards case was impeccable. His death is a loss to every colored man, woman, and child.

"David McKay, on the other hand, is a source of shame for us all, most especially for those here at Movement headquarters. We placed our faith, our trust, our hopes in him. He fell lower than any of us could've imagined. He murdered a man to keep his dirty lies a secret. He killed in order to steal the money and the house, to which Jameson Sweet had a legitimate right. We are cooperating with the prosecution in every way to purge our community of such a cowardly monster."

The man makes good copy, I have to admit. David smiled grimly. He shuffled through the other papers. Apparently, Canfield talked to anyone who would quote him, and most of the Negro newspapers did.

A guard appeared at his cell. "Get up. Someone's here to see you."

Surprised, David laid the newspapers aside. Was it Rachel? He'd love to see her. But what would she think when she saw him? They'd given him a basin of cold water, and he'd done his best to wash and shave, but he still felt grubby. To make matters worse, he now wore a jailhouse uniform. He hoped his appearance wouldn't shock her.

He touched his bruised eye. *Does it hurt to love me?* she'd asked. Well yes, he sighed. It did.

Heart thumping, he tucked his shirttail tightly into his pants, ran his fingers rapidly through his hair, and went through the opened gate.

The guard escorted him to a tiny visiting room. David stepped inside and stopped. A muscle in his chest twisted painfully. She sat on the other side of the wall of iron bars that divided the room. She was as lovely as always, but looked wrung out. She paled at the sight of him. He smiled to reassure her. Crossing the room, he slid onto the seat opposite her. The guard warned him to keep his hands in his lap, and then stepped back. David leaned toward her.

"How are you?"

She gave a wan smile. "The reporters have been annoying and the neighbors are gossiping up a storm, but I'm okay."

"You look wonderful. But you shouldn't have come."

"I had to." Her eyes glowed with loyalty. "The stories in the papers about Philadelphia. Why didn't you tell me?"

He sighed. "I wanted to. I intended to—but everything happened so quickly."

"It don't matter, you know," she said. "None of it matters to me."

"I'm so sorry."

"Don't be. You did what you had to do to survive. I'd rather have you this way than not at all."

"I've been a fool. All those years wasted. I wanted to come back, but I couldn't."

"Shush—"

"I have one hope. One chance. I've got to face up to what I've done. If I survive that, I'll be free, really free, to live my life with you. To stay here, at home, where our roots are." He looked around at the dingy institutional walls encompassing him. "A man has a lot of time to think when he's here. I've thought a lot about what you said that day, Rachel. The fact is, you were right. The world out there will deceive a man. It can bring him down. What I've been looking for, I had right here." He gaze went back to her. He tried to smile, but failed miserably. "What a husband, huh?"

"Oh, David," she moaned. "But they have no proof against you!"

"This is 1926, baby. They don't need proof to try a colored man. To execute him, either." If only he could hold her, at least touch her hands. He had to get her through this situation as smoothly as possible, to protect her from the scandal as best he could. "Rachel, promise me that you'll stay away when the trial starts."

"But I want to be with you—"

"You will be. In here." He touched his chest.

Tears shimmered in her eyes. She reached out to him. The guard stepped forward and gave a warning signal. She let her hand drop. "I'm going to be there, in that courtroom every day," she whispered.

"No."

Tears spilled down her cheeks. "Yes."

Annie visited him. "I can't stay long. They won't let me." Her wise face crinkled with a sad smile. He assumed that she had heard the gossip from the neighbors and read the newspaper reports. She must be so disappointed in him. She answered him as though reading his thoughts.

"You oughta know I'm not here to judge. I want to listen and listen well. Tell me if what I've heard is true."

David looked up at the room's sole window. How to explain? The light inside the small visitors' room darkened as clouds moved over the sun. It rained. Heavy, pelting drops that beat furiously against the windowpane. Finally, he began. He spoke at length and Annie listened without interrupting. If she was shocked at what he told her, she kept it to herself. Every now and then, lightning would snap overhead and thunder would roll; a storm cloud would burst and needles of rain would come slanting down to punch against the windowpane. It seemed as though it would rain forever. David talked until he could say no more. It all came out: the years of running, pretending, his effort to make amends.

"It wasn't just the evil of those supposedly God-fearing people that got me. It was what I saw in myself. God, I'll never forget the moment when I realized what I'd done."

The visitor's room had taken on the air of a confessional. A contemplative silence had settled over it. The rainfall quieted. Even the rumble of thunder seemed to come from far away. Annie looked at David's wretched face.

"Son, what do you think life is? Don't you know that in many ways, it ain't nothing but a battle with yourself?"

"But I saw something in myself that horrified me."

"You think you the first one that's happened to? What 'bout all 'em people out there drinkin' and cussin' and carryin' on? Who d'you think they runnin' from? People start out with all kinds of high-falutin' ideas. And then things happen, bad things, t'test a man's grit. And don't nobody know how they gonna react 'til their time comes."

"I was so sure of myself when I set out, so sure of what I was capable of—"

"When you left here, you didn't have the faintest idea where you was goin'. Or what you'd do when you got there."

David remembered how he'd responded with confidence when Jonah and Miss Mae expressed their fear. They must've thought him a fool. He gave a rueful smile. "Maybe you're right. Being knocked down can clear a man's head of a lot of nonsense."

"You had a choice: t'lay down and die or get back on your feet. And you chose t'get up. Some folks might not agree with how you did it, but you did it and *I'm* proud that you did."

His eyes shone. He blinked rapidly. "I love you, Annie."

"And I love you." Her eyes dwelled on him for a bit, then she said, "I got a present here for you." Reaching into her purse, she pulled out his worn childhood Bible. "Take it and read it. The Lord'll stand by you if you stand by Him."

He looked at it, knowing that his faith was long gone. "Thank you. You'll have to give it to the guard. He'll pass it to me."

Annie leaned toward him. "I know you feel alone, but trust in the Lord. You got friends, son. Not just me. Powerful people. Some of 'em in the strangest places."

David thought about Snyder and what he'd said. *I know what it's like to be an outsider among outsiders.* And what about Nella? Despite her manipulative ambition, she had sincerely tried to help him. And he sensed that he could always count on her for eccentric but oddly dependable support. A West Indian rackets king and a wealthy white socialite: The prejudices of his time rigidly classified them as his enemies, but they had shown themselves to be his allies. He, of all people, had been forced to learn once more that in life so little is as it seems.

"You done traveled a long hard way, and you got a ways t'go. But I b'lieve you'll be all right. I do b'lieve you'll be just fine. Just remember: *Ev'rybody* gets tested. And sooner or later ev'rybody fails. Discovers somethin' 'bout themselves they don't wanna know. Ev'rybody's got secrets, young man. *Ev'rybody.*"

His eyes dwelled on her and his expression saddened. He had a heavy feeling in his chest. For once, it had nothing to do with his own guilt. "Even you, Annie?"

There was a long silence and then the edges of her smile began to tremble. "How long you been knowin'?"

"I found a copy of Lilian's manuscript. It was all there." He paused. "Why didn't you tell me? After Daddy died, you could've said something."

She didn't answer for a long, long time. "I wanted to. All these years, I wanted to. But I made a promise—"

"You made a pact with the Devil."

"I knew he'd give his son the best."

"But to make you a servant—"

"Hush. It was the only way. He'd married my best friend. It was over. It was done. You was on the way. And you was all I had. I didn't wanna give you up . . . And I didn't wanna have t'raise you alone. When Lila found out, she had the idea. And I agreed."

It's a hard thing for a man to realize that the people he has most loved and trusted have lied to him all his life. It takes strength to resist the temptation to be bitter. He thought of all the times he'd seen her and his father together.

"And did you still love him? Did you two keep on loving each other through all those years?"

"No." She shook her head. "When he married my friend, that was the end of anythin' that coulda been between us. All I cared 'bout was you gettin' his name."

Was this how Rachel felt when she was carrying Isabella? He thought of the parallels between Augustus and Annie, and himself and Rachel. Were sons always destined to repeat the sins of their fathers?

"How did Lilian find out?"

"I don't know. She never said nothin'. But there were days I caught her lookin' at me—and I knew. It was the same way you started lookin' at me after you went into Mr. Jameson's office. I didn't know what you'd found, but I was pretty certain what you'd learned from it."

David drew a deep breath. "It's time for the lying and pretending to stop, don't you think? It's time for a little honesty . . . from all of us."

There were tears in her eyes as she whispered, "Yes . . . yes, it is."

"Remember me?" the old man said when David was shown into the visitors' room.

"'Course I do. You're Roy—"

"That's right! Roy, Roy, the Shoeshine Boy. How ya doin', soldier boy?"

"Fine," said David, then thought about it. He gave a sheepish grin and gestured toward his surroundings. "Well, not so fine, actually."

Roy shook his head. "Ain't this a mess? When I saw your face in the paper . . . read what happened, I just had t'come. How can they treat a fine soldier boy this way?"

David slid his seat closer. "Listen, I'm glad you're here. I couldn't sleep last night and I got to thinking about what you said, about the war . . . and your son and all."

Roy's sunny expression dimmed. "Sorry 'bout that. I was just flappin' my lip. Went and put my foot in it."

"No, I'm glad you said what you said, about your wife thinking your son died for nothing and what that does to you. As you know from the papers, my sister recently died and the hardest part of it all is the notion that she died before her time. But that's not what I wanted to talk to you about. Not directly. You see, I had a time too when I was bitter about having fought in that war, about having risked my life for Mister Charlie."

"But you're a hero. You got a medal."

"I was in the wrong place at the right time—if you can imagine."

"And you ain't bitter no more?"

"No. I realized last night that I'm not." David paused, trying to find words to explain. "I was twenty-seven when I signed up, too old for any romantic notions about the battlefield. Our civil rights leaders were telling us that colored patriotism in the trenches of Europe would mean social equality for us at home. I didn't believe it. We colored folk fought in the War for Independence and every war since then. Our courage had never been acknowledged or rewarded. I didn't understand what made DuBois and the others so sure it would work this time. How could they ensure that we wouldn't just come back to broken promises? And there was nothing going on to make a man feel better.

"There was that mess over in East St. Louis. All those colored folk killed—hundreds dead and thousands more torched out of their homes. That was in July. In August, a riot tore through Houston. The colored soldiers stationed outside the city got tired of putting up with the white boys' nonsense. Seventeen white folk died. To avenge them seventeen, Mister Charlie hung thirteen blacks, court-martialed sixty, and jailed scores for life. But you know all this. Kill 'em or lock 'em up: That was the way to keep colored men in line. Understanding why the riot happened was the last thing on the white man's mind. So, things couldn't have been much worse."

"But you and my boy, y'all signed up anyway."

"I believed we couldn't let a chance go by without at least trying. The army had set up this training camp for colored officers at Des Moines. DuBois was urging educated colored men to go there. But once I was there, it didn't take long to see that those white folk were giving the higher commissions to the fellows with little or no education. They viewed educated colored men with suspicion and treated us with contempt.

"That fixed it for me. My dying over there wouldn't mean a damn thing over here. I'd be just one less nigger to deal with. As for civil rights, white mobs would go on lynching, killing, burning with impunity; the ballot box would remain off-limits; southern university doors would remain closed, and good jobs would be a luxury for a lucky few. Me and the other fellows at the camp, we used to ask ourselves why we should go overseas and risk our lives for a democracy we were denied at home. We never found a good answer. But we went anyway.

"Army life confirmed my worst fears. They confined us colored men to camp. Made us go through hourly checks. We were a threat to white women, they said. We were lazy, stupid brutes, they said. But we were strong and they worked us like dogs. Sometimes fourteen hours a day. We were poorly fed, physically abused, mocked, and humiliated. They forbid us to consort with French civilians and they told the French to have nothing to do with us. We were sexually depraved, they said, cowardly, incompetent. And the French, they didn't know any better, so they listened.

"I remember that first French village my company entered. The village folk were scared to death. But we won them over. We worked hard at it, doing all we could to help. And it worked. We won their trust. We won their friendship. Best of all, we won their respect. They invited us into their homes. They shared their food, their stories, their losses, and their luck with us. And they appreciated what we did for them. It was so different from here in the U.S., where the white man says nothing we do is good enough.

"France was an eye-opener. I'd never dreamed that black and white could coexist like that. Some of those French folk were even willing to fight Mister Charlie to defend being friends with us. I remember one time when a riot broke out in a club. A white American officer had insulted a colored Frenchman for talking to a white girl. The girl's brother understood some English and caught what was said. Those French people took off after those soldiers. Nearly tore up the place. Don't get me wrong. I knew that France wasn't perfect. They gave the Senegalese something to complain about. But there was no sign of the endemic, systematic, and deadly contempt that the white folk here got for us.

"When it was over, the white boys left us all the clean-up work. My last memories were of the military cemetery at Romagne, near Verdun. It was the eve of General Pershing's visit. Those white boys refused to help bury their own men, the guys who'd died in the battle at Meuse-Argonne. We colored had to do it. We'd rise at dawn and go back to the battlefield, collecting the dead. We bent our backs from dawn 'til dusk. From Romagne, we went on to Beaumont, Belleau Wood, Fay-en-Tardenois, and Soissons. God, those names I'll never forget. Twenty-two thousand white crosses we planted. The white boys got to go home. We were left to do what they refused to do. We were the last to go.

"Of course, by then, lots of the fellows didn't even want to come back. They'd had enough of this country. They were going to stay in France. Study. Open clubs. They wanted me to stay with them, but I had other ideas. I had a promise to my father to keep. But it wasn't just that. I really thought I could make a difference. I'd seen the way it was in France. I knew it wouldn't be easy to make changes here in the States, but I thought it was worth a try. I was naive. I know that now. But what I wanted to tell you, Roy—what I want you to tell your missus—is this: Before he died, those French villagers gave your son, gave all of us Negro soldiers, a gift. And it was this: a vision, a taste, of what it's like to be viewed with respect and treated like a man. Something most of us would've never had if we'd stayed here. Now, I don't know *how* your son died . . . but I know he didn't die for nothing."

There was a silence. Roy's lips began to tremble. He pressed them together, then put his hand over his mouth. He closed his eyes and his chest heaved. Tears leaked out from under his eyelids. He produced a torn but clean handkerchief and swiped his damp face with it. He looked at David with grateful eyes. "I came here to comfort you. Now you's the one comfortin' me. Thank you." He smiled through his tears.

Roy left soon after that and David was returned to his cell. His memory stirred, he was swamped with images from the summer he'd returned, the "Red Summer" they called it, referring to the streams of Negro blood sent flowing down American streets. By the year's end, bloody race riots had erupted in two dozen cities or counties, scores of blacks had been lynched and burned, and the Ku Klux Klan had resurged in popularity. David had read the reports, sickened. Still invigorated by his memories of France, he had planned to attend Howard, and then join the Movement. But as he contemplated a newspaper photograph of a black man's scorched remains hanging from a tree, he knew there wasn't a snowball's chance in hell of re-creating the openness he had seen in France in the United States, at least not in his lifetime. But he promised himself that he would do what he could. He vowed to work until he dropped to at least make it safe for black men, women, and children to walk the streets of American towns. As for what happened to that vow, that was the most painful thought of all.

David's next visitor couldn't have been more of a surprise: Toby's mother. She drew her chair close to the grate separating them. Her gentle eyes were actually amused. She couldn't believe he had killed Sweet, she said, but she didn't know what to think about the rest. Had he really led a double life? He explained and when he was done, she simply nodded.

"Well, I suppose a man's got to do what a man's got to do. And sometimes that means wearing a mask to survive."

He smiled at her pragmatic way of seeing the situation, but his conscience rejected it. It seemed that while part of him yearned for redemption, another part strove for condemnation, and the more his friends forgave him, the more he demanded punishment.

"What happens," he asked, "when that mask becomes your second skin? You forget how to live without it. You forget what your own face looks like. What's worse, you're not sure you want to know. And when a chance comes to take it off, to tell the world, 'This is me. This is who I am,' you pass it up. Life behind the mask has become too safe, too comfortable. That was me."

"You know, you think too much. It's always bad t'think too much. I got a sister who's passin'. She ain't found nothin' comfortable about it. She the loneliest person I know. At least you did it t'help people. She ain't int'rested in helping nobody but herself. Ev'rybody in the fam'ly know what she's doin' and why she's doin' it. And we still love her. We just don't never see the need t'talk about it." Her eyes went over him. "You got to stop lookin' back. You done your best. The Lord don't ask for more."

For an instant, she reminded him of Annie. "I don't know what the Lord asks for. I used to think I did, but that was . . ." He grimaced. "I was a child."

"My pappy used to say we got to love with the heart of a child and think with the mind of a man."

"Your pappy wasn't talking about abandoning his friends. Lying about his identity."

"No, he was just talkin' 'bout survivin'." She looked at his woebegone face and shook her head. "I done known a lot of people in a lot of trouble, but you take the cake. I got t'admit, though, you'd look good in stripes."

He could feel a smile coming on. "Could be I'll be wearing them for some time."

"Don't think so."

"No?"

"A man like you got a plan."

"Have I now?"

"Um-hm. Men like you always got a plan. So, what you gonna do?"

He thought about it. It was getting harder to hold back that smile. He gave a wry grin. "Well, like you said, a man's got to do what a man's got to do. And a man can't live his life looking backward, now can he?"

"Not if he don't want to get an awful crick in his neck."

He couldn't hold it in anymore. He laughed out loud, grateful for her mischievous humor. He asked her to tell him about Toby, something she was happy to do. He liked the way her eyes lit up when she spoke of her little boy. The minutes allotted them passed quickly and soon it was time for her to leave. She would attend the trial, she said, whenever she could, and nothing he could say would dissuade her. He needed friends and she meant to be among them. He watched her go with an odd warmth in his heart. It was only then he realized that he'd again forgotten to ask her name.

Nella stopped by. She was bold and to the point. "So tell me the truth, dear boy. Did you shoot him?"

"Would you blame me if I had?"

"Not a bit. But you didn't, did you?" She sighed. "How unfortunate."

"Why?"

"It would make my book oh so much juicier if you had."

Snyder puffed on his cigar and fixed David with a paternal eye.

"You didn't have to kill Sweet, you know. I can understand why you did it, but I wish you'd left him for me."

"I didn't kill him."

"Too bad," he said, but it was with an amused expression. "It always amazes me that I like you. But I do. And now I know why. When I first looked at you, I sensed an old wound—a deep wound—and I sensed the strength that went into hiding it. You're a strong man."

"Am I?"

"I don't trust men who don't feel pain. Men who don't risk pain are cowards, and those who can't carry it are weak."

"Well, if that's the case, then my muscles should be busting through my shirt."

38

Lies and Whispers

The leaders of the Movement demanded that the accused murderer of Jameson Sweet suffer the full brunt of the law. David McKay had not only destroyed one of the Movement's best legal minds, but sullied the reputation of the Movement itself. Calling upon their white allies, the Movement's officials put the heat on police and legal authorities.

On Monday, April 5, one week after David's arrest, a grand jury needed just twelve minutes to indict him. The trial was scheduled to begin two weeks later, on April 20. In the interim, both the prosecution and the defense scrambled to prepare.

Byron Canfield became the prosecution's mainstay. In a major deposition, he recapped how David had disappeared years earlier, then "conveniently reappeared" following Lilian's death. He described David's evasive answers at Nella Harding's party and repeated Sweet's complaint that David wanted to eject him from the house. Finally, he related the results of Sweet's private investigation into David's life and Sweet's plans to expose David's duplicity.

Detective Peters subjected Annie to hours of grueling interrogation. She was uncooperative, sometimes flatly refusing to answer. He threatened to jail her until she reconsidered. Annie was sent away with a proud mien and her lips sealed, but twenty-four hours in a cold, damp cell weakened her. With tears in her eyes, she "admitted" to having urged David to fight for the house and said, yes, she'd overheard him argue with Sweet on the day Sweet died. But she was sure she "heard Mr. David leave a long time before Mr. Jameson got shot. Miss Rachel was in the house when that happened. Mr. David wasn't." That last statement was given short shrift. She went home sure that she'd put a noose around her own son's neck.

David didn't learn of Annie's ordeal until it was over, but Rachel was there when Peters took Annie away and she saw the old woman's sorry state when she came back. For the first time since the nightmare began, Rachel stepped forward to speak to reporters. With taunting, angry words, she denounced the way Annie had been treated and proclaimed David's innocence. When reporters asked Peters for a response, he dismissed Rachel's statement with a shrug. "A woman," he said, "is expected to stand by her man."

The scandal raged, and it spread beyond Harlem. White-owned publications with national circulation picked up the story; even the *New York Times* and one of the Washington papers expressed interest. As Mason Rugby, an influential white editor, put it:

"This is not just an everyday murder, in some filthy Harlem back alley. Here we have a top attorney in the national civil rights movement slain— not by white men, but by one of his own: another civil rights attorney, the rich scion of a Harlem success story. Jameson Sweet wasn't just any victim; David McKay isn't just any accused killer. They represent the *crème de la crème* of *café au lait* society—the hopes of the Negro people, the best that the black man can produce. And all they could do was try to kill each other. What does that say about the Movement? What does it tell white America about the so-called New Negro? I'll tell you what it says: It shows that them niggers can't blame us whites for all their problems, can they?"

The scandal divided not only Harlem, but the conservative black societies of Atlanta, Philadelphia, Chicago, and Washington, D.C. They were riveted and horrified. Everyone, it seemed, had an opinion. Not one fancy parlor— or funky pool hall for that matter—was free from debate.

Passionate syndicated columns for and against David ran side-by-side with confused reports that presented rumors as facts. The newspapers continued to quote Canfield heavily, and he was merciless. He had David tried and convicted before his first court date. For his part, David neither hid nor scurried. He let reporters see him. He gave quiet, lucid, concise statements. By the time he was to appear in the packed courtroom, he had attracted much sympathy, especially among women, but few believed him—male or female—when he maintained his innocence. As the time approached for jury selection, the very newspapers that had inflamed the public now expressed concern as to whether a panel free of prejudice could be found.

Nevin Caruthers, a superbly educated and privileged black man, offered to act as David's attorney. In his mid-fifties, Nevin was of short physical stature but immense presence. His salt-and-pepper hair was closely cropped and his mustache was copious but carefully groomed. His walk was robust and energetic. Behind his eyeglasses, his dark brown eyes reflected a gentle heart and perceptive intelligence.

"I was a friend of Lilian. I admired her work. Lord knows, she could be temperamental, but she was a talented woman. I won't see her brother go down without a fight."

District Attorney Jack Baker, a ruthless cross-examiner, formed the prosecution. He was hungry for a high-profile conviction that would bring him closer to his goal: the New York State governorship.

Nevin warned David that Baker would crucify him.

"This is not about whether you killed Jameson Sweet. This is about Philly. You've done what most every colored man at one time or another wishes he could do but would never admit to. You committed the unforgivable. And you got caught doing it."

"When the time comes, let me testify," David said. "Let me tell them why."

"Nobody gives a damn about why. They only care that you did. *You* are every white man's nightmare. Someone who looks like them, sounds like them, but isn't one of them. Someone who can pretend to be the Man Next Door. Character. It's all about character. The prosecution is going to do its best to paint you as a devil and Sweet as a saint."

"Canfield and the papers have already done a good job at that."

"We have to reverse those images. We'll remind them that you're a war hero. We'll bring in witnesses who'll testify to the compassionate work you've been doing in Philly. Friends, people you work with—"

"No, not that. I won't let you."

"But why not?"

"I won't have them involved. It's bad enough that they'll be mocked because I tricked them—"

"If they're your friends, they'll want to help."

"I can't ask them to."

"Maybe you can't, but I can."

"Don't do it."

Nevin leveled a steady gaze at his client. He saw despair and regret and something else, too. "David, are you afraid that none of the people you helped, that none of the friends you made, would stand by you if given the chance?"

David didn't answer. His eyes dropped away and his jaw worked. "I don't know if they would. I just know I won't ask them to."

Nevin shook his head, frustrated. "All right. We'll leave it alone for now. But we do need character witnesses. It's crucial. So you think about it."

He looked down at his notes, scribbled a comment, and sighed. "While we're on this difficult topic, we might as well broach another. Your best witness, you know, would be Rachel."

"No."

"I figured you'd say that."

"No one will believe her. She's my wife."

"She was present when you struggled with Sweet. She can speak to his suicidal intent. People will wonder why she doesn't testify on your behalf. Even if they're set against believing her, they'll want to hear her. Her appearance in court is crucial."

"I won't have her exposed like that."

Nevin rubbed his forehead and sighed. "David, I—"

"My answer's no. Now let's move on. I take it the second part of our strategy has to do with dressing down Sweet?"

Nevin looked at David and shook his head. He paused to rearrange his thoughts, then went on. "If you don't want Rachel to testify, we have to find another way to convince the jury that Sweet chose to die. That means, we've got to provide a motive for suicide. A good, strong motive that'll compensate for the lack of physical evidence, like a note. To show motive, we've got to shore up your contention that Sweet killed Gem. Make them believe that he preferred to die rather than face a humiliating trial. The fact that the prosecution will put Sweet on a pedestal could then work in our favor. Sweet was a man with a lot to lose. Many proud men in his position have taken the same way out."

Gray skies heavy with rain clouds darkened lower Manhattan on the opening day of the trial. A loud, angry crowd assembled before the courthouse. Authorities decided to bring David into the building through a side entrance. They posted twenty policemen in front of the courthouse and sent another ten inside to guard the courtroom.

With a blow of his gavel, Judge Sylvan Richter called the session to order, and District Attorney Baker took center stage. A skeletal man with parchment-colored skin and raven-black hair, Baker had small, marble-like eyes that seemed curiously dead behind round, rimless spectacles. He launched his case by calling Dr. Hubert Thatcher to the witness stand. Thatcher was broad and squat, with bulbous eyes and pencil-thin lips. His nose was so flat that it barely rose from his face and his nostrils were merely horizontal slits. With his pale, waxy skin, oddly tinged green, he resembled a large toad struggling for dignity in a tight black suit.

Thatcher began by testifying as to the time of death. His first statement was not a matter for contention; his next one was.

"I can say without doubt that the blood and human tissue found on David McKay's right hand and coat collar belonged to the victim, Jameson Sweet."

"Did you conduct a laboratory analysis?" asked Nevin in cross-examination.

"I didn't need to," said Thatcher. "Everybody can tell a Negro's blood just by looking at it."

Nevin checked a smile of satisfaction and glanced at Baker. A look of irritation flashed across the D.A.'s face. His first expert witness had just revealed himself to be both a racist and a sloppy technician, the second quality being by far the worst.

Nevin turned back to Thatcher.

"Could David McKay have picked up the blood and tissue through contact with another person at the death scene?"

David's breath caught. How could Nevin do this, when he'd pleaded with him not to involve Rachel?

Thatcher's eyes shot over to Baker hoping for a hint as to how to answer. Finding none, he looked back at Nevin. A thin layer of sweat enhanced the waxy sheen of his forehead. "I suppose it's possible. But I, uh . . . I find it highly unlikely."

"But it *is* possible?"

Thatcher hesitated. "Yes . . . it's possible."

Thatcher was dismissed. Baker then sought to demonstrate that David was the last person to see Sweet alive. He called a reluctant Annie to the stand. Since she was a hostile witness, he was given leeway in questioning her. She answered with brief sentences and her eyes never left David. An expression of relief crossed her face when Baker sat down and Nevin rose to cross-examine her. He gave her a chance to emphasize that she was sure, "Mr. David was outta the house when it happened." But on re-direct, Baker asked her whether she'd actually seen David leave and she had to admit that she hadn't.

Next came Byron Canfield. He told his story with devastating simplicity. David was forced to listen to an amalgam of circumstantial evidence that maligned and misrepresented him.

To back up Canfield's testimony, Baker summoned Frank Nyman, the white private detective Sweet had hired. David took one look at Nyman and sensed danger. Nyman was the kind of witness who could do damage. He was small, wiry, and scruffy. He was poor and made no attempt to hide it. He had chosen to wear a shapeless black suit and dusty shoes. His tie was crooked and his shirt none too clean. His hair was unkempt and a shock of it, black mixed with gray, fell over his narrow, lined face. His heavy-lidded eyes were as black as pitch. His lower lip was full and fleshy, and his upper lip, thin and cruel and bitter. He was indisputably ugly and more than slightly seedy, but David saw at once that none of that mattered. None of it made a damn bit of difference because Nyman was also utterly charming. In fact, his ugliness made his charm all the more disturbing. It allowed him to sneak up on you, to take you unawares. Humor flashed in his eyes, wisdom rested in the corners of his lips, and an easygoing lassitude rode his shoulders every time he shrugged. Despite his rough, uncouth manner, or perhaps because of it, he was entirely credible. He knew exactly what was expected of him and he delivered. He seduced the members of the jury and they never knew what hit them.

As David listened to Nyman testify, his heart sunk. Nyman's comments, though succinct, were colorful. With a few vague words and several fairly explicit gestures, he implied much while saying little. *An out-and-out con man's trick,* David thought, *but the judge and jury bought it.*

At one point, Nyman hinted that there was much he could tell about David's "relations with white females," but he would prefer not to "out of respect for the ladies present."

Nevin objected. This testimony had nothing to do with the murder charge, he said. Baker countered that the testimony was directly relevant since it elaborated on the personality of the accused. Richter found for the prosecution. He not only approved further testimony along the same lines but ordered Nyman to "give details." First, however, he said, the courtroom would have to be cleared of women and children. There was a flurry of movement; the courtroom doors opened and closed behind little feet and straight skirts. Then Richter told Nyman to continue. The private detective obliged with a graphic description of how David had "preyed on innocent white women who had no idea they were being seduced by a Negro."

There was a hush in the courtroom, then a murmur, then an angry hum. David thought of bees when they discover an intruder who's trying to steal some of their honey.

Richter banged for silence. Again, Nevin moved to have Nyman's lascivious descriptions stricken from the record, and again Baker objected. Richter denied Nevin's motion to suppress, and whites in the all-male courtroom erupted in vigorous applause.

"My God, Nyman's destroying me," David whispered to Nevin.

He patted David's hand. "Don't worry. The prosecutor's entitled to a few good moments."

David shot Nevin a troubled look. "Let's just make sure he doesn't have too many of them, shall we?"

Nevin gave David a reassuring smile. "I got some good news this morning that'll give this case a whole new complexion." He chuckled at David's expression and patted his hand.

Despite his outer calm, Nevin knew that David's concern was justified. Nyman had been convincing. It was time for damage control. For more than an hour, he cross-examined the private detective, trying to get him to admit that much of his report was regurgitated hearsay. He did get Nyman to concede that some of it was based on secondhand gossip, but Nyman wouldn't budge about the core of his report: David McKay's pretense of being white was a well-documented fact.

"There's no end to the proof," Nyman said.

He'd collected Philadelphia newspaper reports on David's cases and statements from white friends and colleagues who were shocked at the mere suggestion that the man they knew might be black.

Nevin thought it wiser to stipulate that David had indeed lived as a white man in Philadelphia—arguing against a given fact would simply decrease David's credibility—but he asked the jury to remember: "This does not constitute proof that he killed Jameson Sweet."

David's guilt seemed to be a given, however, for the city at large. Front-page speculation, innuendo, and rumor continued to characterize news coverage of the trial. Someone in the D.A.'s office leaked a copy of Nyman's provocative report to the press. Many newspapers thought Nyman's direct testimony too offensive to quote extensively, but they reprinted his written report in full. Once again, as the trial went into its second day, officers posted outside had to stand off a mob.

Baker called Peters to testify about the crime scene itself, to tell what he saw when he entered the McKay parlor that day. Peters delivered his statement in a dry tone that contrasted vividly with the gruesome details he conveyed. Baker asked Peters how he had come to arrest David McKay. Peters looked David straight in the face and said: "The defendant admitted to knowing that Sweet had the goods on him, but he only gave himself up when he knew his wife would have to take the fall."

Not only the whites but also the black viewers in the courtroom shook their heads.

Baker had Peters describe Sweet's fatal wound, but he noticeably failed to ask about any gunpowder residue on the hands of the accused or fingerprints that might've been found on the murder weapon. Nevin asked, though, in cross-examination, "Whose fingerprints were lifted from the gun?"

Peters licked his lips and joggled one knee. This was a question he would've preferred not to answer.

"Detective?" prompted Nevin.

Peters cleared his throat. "There were two sets of prints. One belonging to the victim; one belonging to the defendant's wife."

"Are you telling me that the defendant's prints weren't found on the gun at all?"

"No, they weren't."

"A little louder, please. It's only fair if those people in the back rows can also hear you."

"No," said Peters a bit louder, in a faintly squeaky tone. "David McKay's fingerprints were not found on the gun."

There was an instant of heated murmuring before Richter clipped it with a bang of his gavel. Baker began his redirect.

"If McKay's prints weren't on the gun," he asked Peters, "then why did you arrest him?"

"Because he was on the scene; he had the best motive and, of course, the best opportunity."

"Once more, Detective: Was this the typical wound of a suicide?"

"No," said Peters with renewed confidence. "I've never known a suicide to shoot himself in the cheek. It's usually the temple. Almost always, the temple."

Late that afternoon, Nevin began to present his case. Nella had offered to testify as a character witness in David's defense.

"I'm going to let her," said Nevin. "She's a prominent person."

David had his doubts. "Nella's not just prominent. She's white and she's a woman. What all-white male jury will heed a white woman defending a colored man? Do you think they'll listen, especially after what Nyman said about me? She means well, but her testimony could do more harm than good."

Nevin conceded the danger, but said: "We need her. She's not just the best witness we've got. She's nearly the only one."

Nella took the witness stand and surprised David and his attorney with a blithe lie. "David McKay generously offered me his biography some time ago to use in my next book. He wouldn't have killed Sweet to conceal his life story—he'd planned to have it published anyway."

"Did you know she was going to say that?" David whispered to Nevin.

"No."

As Nella stepped down, Nevin whispered miserably to David, "She tried."

David smiled gratefully, fleetingly at Nella as she switched past him. She bent to give him an encouraging tap on the elbow. He did not agree with her having lied, but he was touched by her effort to help him.

"You didn't have to."

"Of course I did. I owe you. Thanks to you, my book's going to be a best-seller."

Annie stayed home on the third day of the trial. The arthritis in her knees was sometimes so painful, she had to bite her lip to keep from crying out. It was especially bad when she first eased out of bed in the morning. On rainy days, she could barely walk. David knew nothing of her condition. She had never told him and never intended to, partly because she feared that he would retire her, but mostly because she felt he had enough troubles to deal with. Relaxing on the window seat in the parlor, she thought once more of that passage she had seen marked in his Bible.

He's tried so hard to make good, Lord. Won't you help him?

She wanted to help him, too, but she didn't know how.

Show me . . . please.

The doorbell rang. Annie jumped at the sudden sound. The bell rang again. Parting the curtain, she peeked out the window with a suspicious eye. Since David's arrest, strange people had been stopping by the house, some threatening to put a curse on the family—*what was left of it,* thought Annie grimly—others offering to help with spells, voodoo, witchcraft, and such. *I don't hold with none of that stuff.*

A boy of about fourteen stood in front of the house. He wore a brown cap and blue jacket and was holding a piece of paper in one hand. He looked harmless enough. As the bell rang again, she stood uneasily and went to the vestibule. She hesitated, looking at the door, still undecided. Finally, she answered it, her mind set to give the stranger a good tongue-lashing. Before she could say anything, the boy politely whipped off his hat and spoke. He had a message from the Renaissance Pharmacy. He thrust the sheet of paper into her hand, then stood nervously fingering his cap, obviously hoping for a tip. She found a nickel in her apron pocket and gave it to him.

After he left, she stood in the vestibule, studying the page he'd given her. She couldn't read all that fast and many of the words were unfamiliar, but she could make out enough for her to understand the gist of it. Her face light-ened with interest, then darkened with puzzlement. When she was done, she stood quite still for a minute. *Thank you, Lord,* she whispered, then hurried to her room and fetched her coat.

In court that afternoon, Nevin called Adrian Snyder to the stand. David looked at Nevin, surprised.

"You're calling *him* as a character witness?"

Nevin patted David on the shoulder. "Have faith."

David held his head high but inwardly battled despair. His star character witnesses were living scandals: a suspected crime figure and a white woman known for socializing with blacks. Leaning into his hand, David rubbed his forehead wearily. He sensed waves of hostility and contempt flowing from Canfield. The aristocratic old lawyer had pointedly placed himself in the first seat directly behind the prosecutor. David resolved to ignore Canfield. His ears picked up the melody of a Negro spiritual, sung softly in the courtroom behind him. He glanced over his shoulder. Annie sat four rows behind him. She must have just arrived. She hadn't been there earlier. And sitting next to her—his eyes widened—was Toby's mother. She gave him the thumbs-up sign. His heart lifted. He looked back at Annie. She gave him a smile. It was sweet, sudden, and oddly dazzling. It warmed him. He glanced at Rachel. She sat in the first row, slightly to one side of him, so she could see his face easily. She smiled at him, too, but he saw fear in the tightness around her eyes. He returned her smile, and then gave his attention back to the theatrics of his trial.

Nevin took Snyder through a brief description of his courtship with Gem, and Gem's decision to end their relationship. Baker objected.

"This testimony is irrelevant."

"Your Honor, the relevance will become clear," said Nevin. "I'm trying to lay the foundation for causal evidence."

Richter looked from Nevin's mahogany-brown face to Baker's alabaster-white one. Then he brought down his gavel, sustained Baker's motion, and brusquely ordered Nevin to move on. A frustrated Nevin was forced to dismiss Snyder. He called his next witness.

"Homicide Detective Bill Rogers."

A short, portly white man in his late forties waddled to the stand, identified himself, and took the oath. He worked in the Hamptons, he said.

"Now is it true that you were summoned to Harding House last night?" asked Nevin.

Rogers nodded.

"Please tell us what you found."

"Mr. Snyder there and some of his men said they'd gone fishing on the Hardings' estate. They reported finding a skeleton, and sure enough, they had—mired in the waters off the Hardings' private dock."

A wave of gasps and whispers rolled across the courtroom. Richter banged his gavel. He beckoned to Nevin and Baker. Richter, a broad-faced man with rolls of fat under his chin, scowled down angrily at both men.

"Just what the hell is going on here?" He looked at Baker. "Did you know about this?"

"No, Your Honor."

"Baker, the report is on your desk," said Nevin hurriedly. "We couldn't get it to you sooner. We only learned about it ourselves this morning."

Richter glared at Nevin, then asked, "What does this have to do with the case at hand?"

"Everything," said Nevin. "Jameson Sweet's death was simply the culmination of a series of murderous events that began with the victim found yesterday."

Richter looked down at Baker. "You going to object?"

Baker looked worried, but shook his head. "No, Your Honor, but I reserve my right to do so."

"All right. Get on with it."

Nevin turned back to Rogers. "Can you describe the remains?"

"The skeleton had been in the water for some time, probably a year. It was a woman, not too old, not too young."

A wave of murmurs stirred the courtroom.

"Colored or white?"

"Can't say."

"How'd she end up in the water?"

"Put there."

"Didn't fall in?"

"She was bound and weighted down. Probably dead before she hit the water. Looks like the bullet we pulled from her sternum's gonna match the bullet we took out of Jameson Sweet—"

Baker jumped to his feet. "Objection, Your Honor. Testimony is irrelevant. I move to have it stricken from the record."

Nevin went to Richter, his arms raised. "Please, Your Honor. This man's testimony substantiates my client's claim. It will show that Gem McKay murdered her sister, Lilian, then took her place—only to be killed by Jameson Sweet, who committed suicide when faced with his crime."

Richter turned to Rogers. "Is there any way to identify this woman?"

"Not definitely."

"Any way to prove that she was Lilian McKay Sweet?"

"Not likely."

Richter banged his gavel. "Objection sustained."

"But Your Honor—" cried Nevin.

"Objection sustained!"

Nevin gritted his teeth. *That was our trump card,* thought David. *That was it.* Behind him, Annie sang softly. David closed his eyes wearily. He had never been so tired in his life. Nevin dismissed Rogers.

"We're not finished yet," he whispered to David.

"Let me testify."

"No."

"Please—"

Nevin ignored him. He straightened up and in a ringing voice, said: "Inasmuch as neither my learned opponent, the prosecutor, nor anyone else can prove what happened in the McKay parlor that day, I move for a dismissal of the charges against David McKay, based on lack of evidence."

Richter raised his bushy eyebrows in disbelief. With a great sweeping motion, he raised his gavel high, as though it were the hammer of Thor, and brought it down swiftly with a thunderous blow. "Motion denied!"

Nevin threw his hands up in the air.

The court took a ten-minute break. Rachel hurried to get to David's side, but he was swept out of the courtroom before she could reach him. A phalanx of guards surrounded him to keep the reporters at bay. She tried to press her way through the jostling crowd, but was pushed back.

Annie was waiting for David in the crowded hallway. She waved frantically from the edge of the crowd, trying to catch his eye. He was almost past when one of those odd momentary partings in the crowd allowed him to catch sight of her. He sent a guard to bring her to him.

"I gotta talk to you," she whispered.

Out of breath from the effort to get through the crowd, she stumbled and nearly fell. David grabbed her under one elbow. Nevin showed them to a private room with guards posted outside. Rachel staggered out of the courtroom just as Nevin was leaving the room. She caught a glimpse of Annie and David, their heads bent together, before Nevin closed the door behind him.

The moment they were alone, Annie told David about her visit to the druggist. She laid the druggist's report in his hands. "They said they made a mistake. They got your medicine mixed up with somebody's else's. But this here"—she tapped the paper—"this here's the report they shoulda given you."

David looked at her with anxious eyes, then at the paper she'd pressed into his hand. "*A homemade mixture expertly made,*" it said. "*Can be used to treat bad nerves, but overuse will cause tremors, blurred vision, fatigue, headaches, and loss of balance. Hallucinations, anxiety, a pounding heartbeat, stroke and death.*"

His hands began to tremble. He fumbled for the chair behind him and slowly sank down into it. The report neither shocked nor surprised him, but he was horrified by what it implied. He'd had his suspicions, of course. He'd felt that something was wrong all along. But he had hoped and prayed that those suspicions were wrong. For once in his life, he would have been grateful and relieved to be wrong. Dead wrong—

There was a knock on the door. Nevin came in.

"It's time to go back in."

David nodded. He pushed himself up and stood unsteadily. His olive complexion was ashen and his hands shook. He folded the sheet of paper clumsily and shoved it into his inner breast pocket. A look of concern came over Nevin's benign, round face.

"C'mon," he said and rushed them back to the courtroom.

Nevin called a forensics expert to counter the state's testimony about the wound that killed Sweet. The witness, Harold Schmuck, a sallow, dry little stick of a man, was obviously proud of his expertise. He took great pains to answer each question in excruciating detail. He multiplied words impressively but ineffectively. He was a bore and painful to listen to. David saw that the jury had not only lost interest but was becoming hostile. Why was Nevin keeping the man on the witness stand? It was obvious to those few people who were listening that Schmuck refused to take sides. Given the nature of Sweet's injury, he said, it was open to fair interpretation whether the wound was self-inflicted or not. Schmuck's argument weighed like a well-balanced scale that tipped sometimes this way, sometimes that. *Unfortunately,* thought David, *the decisive weight tipped the scales most certainly against him.* As Nevin had told him privately, "The problem for us is that Sweet left no physical sign, no proof, not even a hint that he intended to do away with himself. He neither said anything to anyone nor left a note to clearly demonstrate premeditated suicide. And accidental suicide would be equally hard to prove. What we need," concluded Nevin, "is paper evidence."

David closed his eyes. The pathologist droned on, his statements punctuated by Nevin's brief, precise questions. David only half-listened. His head ached. He thought of the druggist report in his pocket. *Here's your paper evidence, Nevin—but I can't give it to you.* He felt nauseated.

Annie and Nella had given him the answer. Right at the beginning, they had told him what to look for. Annie had described how Sweet told Gem that he could never love "someone like her." And Nella had told him that Sweet liked dark women. That should've told him immediately that Sweet's words to Gem meant that he could never love someone light-skinned. And when he met Sweet himself, he had sensed immediately that Sweet would want a woman with street smarts, a fighter.

David shook his head at his own stupidity. There had been many signs, but he had refused to heed them. The direction in which they were leading him was too painful for him to follow. He had chosen to look away. And that first erroneous druggist report had helped him do it. It had reassured him. But this one—there was no mistaking the meaning of this one. *A homemade mixture—so well made it must have been done by an expert.*

A fighter. An expert. A nurse.

His thoughts went back to the vestibule that day. He had heard voices coming from the parlor, heated voices. *If only he'd returned a few minutes earlier, he would have heard everything.*

Sitting behind him, Rachel was thinking the same thing and she was wondering about what she'd seen out in the hallway, that glimpse of David and Annie with their heads bent together. What did it mean? Did it mean *anything?* He'd barely glanced at her since returning to the courtroom. Something was wrong. Was her luck running out? No . . . it couldn't be. Not when it had held out this long.

She thought of Sweet, of that last wretched conversation with him, and again saw him dead on the floor. She hadn't wanted it to end that way. She could say with all honesty that she'd tried every trick in the book to dissuade him from his plan. Nothing had worked.

He'd been upset. Had wanted to clear out, and had wanted her to go with him. Naturally, she'd refused.

"Don't be silly. It's worked out perfectly well. We both got what we wanted."

"Got what *we* wanted? I didn't get what I wanted—I wanted you! Who do you think I did it for? For you, woman! You, not me! It was you who wanted the big house, the fancy clothes. And not just any house. It had to be the McKay house, the McKay money."

"You love money as much as I do. And you hate the McKays as much as I do. You've always hated dicties."

"But my hate didn't drive me out of my mind. My love for you did that. Damn it! I risked everything for you. I killed for you." He shook his big fists at her. "How could you choose that yellow nigger over me? How could you? And after what he did to you?"

Her sweet face screwed up with contempt and though she was the shorter one, she managed to give the impression of looking down on him.

"Don't you understand?" she hissed. "David is the one I want, the one I have *always* wanted. How could you have ever thought I loved you?"

Sweet's face twisted bitterly. "Woman, don't do this to me."

"You disgust me, 'cause you're no better than me! But you don't know it. Darkies like you and me—the world is never gonna let us amount to anything. We can't do nothing for each other but bring each other down. We need to marry up to survive. You with your obstinate pride, your talk of Negro dignity—you're a fool. A stubborn, stupid fool. I could never let myself love a man like you. Now go away. Build yourself another life while you have the chance."

"What chance? He knows. Don't you understand? He *knows.*"

"He doesn't know. He suspects. And he only suspects you—not me."

"Rachel." Sweet's chest heaved. "We go together or not at all. Either you come with me or I tell everything."

"You would do that to me?"

"I'd have to."

"I see." She turned away. She could hear him breathing heavily behind her, waiting for her decision. Her shoulders sagged and she seemed to deflate. All the fight appeared to leave her, like hot air seeping from a balloon.

"All right," she said in a listless tone. "When do you want to go?"

"Right now."

She was standing at the writing table. Her large purse lay on top of it. She went into it and took out her compact. While she dabbed her nose, she watched him in the mirror and noted how far away he stood.

"Won't I have time to pack?"

"No."

She went back into her bag, dropped the compact, and found the other item she wanted. It had taken her an hour that morning to find where Gem had hidden it in Lilian's bedroom. She had started looking the moment David left to see Nella. *Time well spent.* She felt Sweet come up behind her and left her hand hidden within her purse. He gripped her shoulders.

"It's better this way," he whispered. "You wouldn't have been happy here. With him."

"No, perhaps not." She turned to face him, her right hand dropping deftly behind her back.

"We belong together," he said. "We're two of a kind, you see."

He took her in his arms and she raised her face for him to kiss. He closed his eyes and she at the last moment pulled away, put the gun to his cheek, and fired. For a split second, he looked surprised, then all expression was gone. She sagged to her knees at his side. She'd just curled his fingers around the handle of the gun when David appeared.

Lies and whispers. Whispers and lies. Where would we be without them? Was that a line from a song she'd heard? If it wasn't, it should be.

Sitting in court, she stared at David's profile. How many more days would she have to drag herself to this damn courtroom? She was sick of the reporters, the neighbors; sick of having to play the loyal wife; of having to visit her "beloved" in that stinking jail. When would this stupid trial end?

Her eyes went to the jury members, two rows of pale strangers: They had the power to convict David, to put the period at the end of his sentence. She smiled grimly. Only once the jury spoke, could her life—the life she dreamed of—go on.

The trial went into its third day. Nevin took stock of the situation. There seemed to be no way to prove that Sweet had killed himself. He had tried to introduce evidence that Sweet's death was the brutal end to a chain of homicidal events, but the strategy had backfired. Baker had objected to the introduction of the allegation, and Richter had bent over backward to oblige. The judge had ruled out any testimony that extended beyond the immediate murder of Jameson Sweet, yet in effect had given Baker leeway to use the allegation to bolster his own case. David's belief that Sweet killed Gem, Baker said, provided David with an additional motive to commit murder.

David, too, had done his share in tying Nevin's hands, with his adamant refusal to let Rachel testify or seek help from his friends in Philadelphia. As a result, Sweet's reputation remained pristine; David's was ruined. The hundreds of backbreaking hours he had logged in Philadelphia were dismissed; the lives he had salvaged forgotten.

Nevin now turned to David and said in a fierce whisper, "All right. We play it your way. You get to testify. But remember: If you say one wrong word—just one—you're dead. Those good citizens on that jury will lynch you. And they'll do it legally. They'll fry your ass in the electric chair at Sing Sing. A flick of the switch and you'll be as dead as a nigger hanging from a southern tree."

David rose slowly. He straightened his tie and walked forward. Climbing the steps into the witness stand, he placed one hand on the Bible offered him and swore to tell the truth, the whole truth, and nothing but the truth.

Nevin led David through a formal restatement of his innocence and a description of his confrontation with Sweet, and then paused dramatically.

"Your Honor, members of the jury, and honored guests, because the claims against my client hinge on his alleged motivation, I think it would be appropriate to hear my client himself speak to this matter." Nevin turned to the prosecutor.

"Does my learned colleague concur?"

Baker nodded. "No objections."

Nevin turned back to David. "You're up to bat now," he whispered. "Don't strike out."

David looked out over the courtroom. He was intensely aware of Rachel. And of Canfield. The influential lawyer resembled an eagle waiting to pounce. David decided to look beyond them to Annie and Toby's mother. To Nella and Snyder. And Roy, crowded into a seat in the back. David took in all the faces of those present, the faces of poor people, people educated not by books but by hard licks. It was these people, as much as the white jury, who would decide his future. Even if he convinced the jury, but failed to sway the folk, he was doomed. For himself, he was unconcerned. But his parents deserved better. They had worked hard to make something of themselves and the family name. His friends and all those who had written to him in jail or otherwise extended their support—they too deserved better. Holding his head high, he began.

"When I left Harlem four years ago, I never intended to be gone long. I thought the job would take a week, two at most. But my life was about to change . . . I just didn't know it."

Every soul in the courtroom hushed. They had been waiting for this. Most of the black onlookers were southern. David's words evoked pictures they had hoped to forget. As he touched the crucible of his tale, they listened uneasily.

"I drifted for weeks after leaving that hospital. I don't even remember arriving in Philadelphia. One day, I met a woman. Her son was in jail. I offered to defend him. She took me for white. I started to correct her, then thought better of it. Her mistaken belief seemed to increase her hope. Why take that away? I won that case and more came to see me. That's how it all began. I did not decide to pass for white. I did decide to let people see what they wanted to see."

David turned to the jury. Some of the men looked away; others frankly met his gaze—with varying degrees of interest, sympathy, belligerence, and accusation.

"I lived as Daniel Kincaid. No one but Lilian knew where I was. I explained the name change as a discretion that was necessary for my work. I think that as time went by, she began to suspect what was happening. But she never once criticized or denounced me.

"I started a law practice, representing poor colored who couldn't afford good lawyers, who thought they were getting a sympathetic 'white' attorney. I thought about revealing the truth. I came close once or twice, but hesitated: What purpose would this particular truth serve? It would destroy my effectiveness as an attorney—and thereby allow others to question the moral and legal validity of every court decision I had won. It would not only endanger my former clients, but end my ability to help future ones. And so I kept mum.

"I helped a lot of my people. I know I did. But the gratitude in their eyes was a dagger in my soul. I had confirmed their belief in the white man's power over them, for better or for worse. If they had won their cases or gotten good sentences with the help of an obviously colored attorney, their faith in a Negro's ability to determine his own fate would've been strengthened. I robbed them of that. I cheated them. It was subtle, but it was there. And it was wrong.

"Most of all I harmed myself. I thought my decision would set me free, but I just exchanged one burden for another. I wanted to walk without fear, but I was never more afraid in my life. I thought I could finally be myself, but that's exactly who I *couldn't* be. I wanted to be free, but I had to repress the best part of me. I wanted to be seen as an individual, not as a racial symbol. But when my clients looked at me, that's all they *did* see—a symbol of benevolent white domination.

"I'm not proud of what I did. But having said this, I must add that I don't fully regret it either. I don't regret having wrenched back some of the authority that's been bullwhipped from the Negro in this country. I certainly don't regret having used it to relieve my people's suffering. For once, the color prejudice of the legal system worked to the black man's advantage."

David extended his gaze to encompass the courtroom. There was shame, sympathy, anger, frustration, and bewilderment in the brown faces he saw. He thought he detected, hoped he detected, expressions of support, too. Perhaps not all of them agreed with what he had done; but every single one of them had to understand why he had done it.

"I'm accused of having killed Jameson Sweet because he threatened to unveil me, to shame me before the world. I admit he repelled me. This man tortured my sisters, plotted to murder one, and ended up murdering the other. That I couldn't forgive. But when he said he had discovered my secret, I felt grateful. He had freed me from a burden I was tired of carrying. I needed Jameson Sweet to live. So no, I didn't kill him. I have never knowingly been destructive toward anyone. No one but myself."

The courtroom was still and it was a silence no one dared break. In that profound silence, David hoped that his words had penetrated the hearts of his listeners. Eventually, someone coughed. The rough sound, though slight, broke the spell. The onlookers stirred; they began to murmur among themselves. Richter banged his gavel and recessed the trial until the next day. David returned to his single jail cell uncertain as to whether the truth had significantly helped his case, but deeply relieved at having told it. He looked forward to a restful sleep that night, but Rachel's spirit kept him awake.

He'd confronted her the evening before. He didn't know what reaction he'd expected, but it was not the one he received: She'd laughed and her pretty mouth had curled with spite.

"If you're waiting to hear me say I'm sorry, you'll be waiting a long, long time."

Her green eyes were as incandescent as gems and just as hard. Had he only imagined that less than one month ago, they had shone with love for him?

"Our wedding night. The love we shared. The vows we made. They meant nothing?"

She gave him a pitying look. "You should know better than to ask. Lies and whispers. Whispers and lies. Where would we be without them?"

Nevin turned to Baker: "Your witness."

The district attorney rose. He leaned forward, planted both fists on his desk, and nailed David with an unblinking stare.

"Thank you for yesterday's exciting narrative. We were all caught up in your tale of woe. Now let's clarify a few points."

The jury turned to David.

"Mr. Kincaid or Mr. McKay—which do you prefer?"

"It doesn't matter."

"Doesn't it? In this courtroom, we're inclined to take a serious view of aliases. However . . ." His attitude suggested that he would be generous and let the point slide. With a long finger, he checked his notes, then looked up. "Mr. McKay, it would appear that when those men in Georgia approached you, you lied about being a Negro?"

"They would've killed me if I'd—"

"You lied, did you not? A yes or no will do."

"Yes."

"Thank you. And when they asked if you knew their victim, a man who had befriended you, you lied then too?"

"Yes."

"And later, in setting up your Philadelphia law practice, when identifying yourself to the authorities, you also lied?"

David hesitated. "I didn't fully tell the truth."

Baker's tone hardened. "You knew that everyone believed you to be white and treated you as white. You permitted, if not outright encouraged, that belief?"

David took a deep breath, knowing that he was about to hand himself over to his enemies. "I did nothing to correct it. No."

That admission was all Baker needed. A master at verbal savagery, he scourged David with ridicule, contempt, and innuendo. He twisted David's words and interrupted his answers. He took obvious pride in putting him to the verbal lash. David took the flogging with dignity. He gritted his teeth and bore it, but that only incited Baker to more. Nevin tried several times to object, but David signaled him to sit down. He would not cringe or dodge or deny, but gradually, despite his determination, his strength left him. The merciless brutality of the questions—the inflexible manner in which he was allowed to answer—all wore him down. Like a bullwhip, the questions came faster, fell harder, cut deeper, and dealt a sharper sting. He was virtually being flayed alive. His admissions, like blood, began to pour from him.

"So in effect you lied to the courts?"

"Yes."

"Lied to your clients?"

"Yes."

"Lied to your colleagues and friends?"

"Yes! Yes!"

"And once back here, when asked what you've been doing, you said—"

"I said nothing—"

"You let people believe you've been working for the Movement, but this too was a lie?"

"Yes, a lie."

"And isn't it true that you would be back in Philadelphia if it weren't for your marriage? Wouldn't you still be deceiving? Concealing? Living your lies?"

"I would be living—another life. Yes."

Baker moved in for the kill. "The fact is, Mr. McKay, you've lied to your family and friends, to your clients and colleagues, day after day, month after month, year after year—*for four years*. Do you know what the truth *is* anymore? Do you even *care?*"

David gripped the railing of the witness stand. "I give you my word. I didn't kill—"

Baker slammed his fist down. "Why should we believe you? Why should we trust you? Why, when it seems that you do nothing but lie?" He looked at the judge. "No more questions, Your Honor. We are finished with this *witness.*"

Nevin stood. "Redirect, Your Honor?"

Richter nodded.

Nevin leaned on his desk—the onlookers leaned forward in their seats. With a sonorous voice, Nevin intoned: "This then is the truth: That you accused Jameson Sweet of having killed your sister; that he said to you: 'I will not let you send me to prison. I'd rather die first,' that you left him alive, and when you returned he was dead?"

"That's what happened. That's the truth."

"On your oath before God?"

"On my oath before God."

"Thank you."

Nevin sat down heavily. His kind face was grave. The cross-examination had been damaging. There was no doubt about it. The judge dismissed David with a curt nod. David stood stiffly. The stares of the jury seemed to burn into his back as he walked to his seat.

"You did well," Nevin told him. "You did fine."

o   o   o

Baker's summation was delivered with consummate skill. He reminded the jury that it was the defense that had introduced the possibility of a second powerful motive, "McKay's obsessive belief that Sweet killed his sister," and that it was a Negro civil rights official who had brought police attention to the racial aspects of the case. David McKay's own people saw him as a traitor to the Negro race and a shame to humanity, Baker said. In bringing in a verdict of guilty, members of the all-white jury need not fear accusations of racism. They need not be concerned with allegations that McKay lacked a fair trial. Nor would the fine city of New York suffer claims "against its reputation as a place of refuge for the honest and hardworking, no matter what their shade or hue." None of these matters need concern the jury. What the jury did need to consider was the calculated cruelty of the crime and the deceitful personality of the defendant.

"Through his words and deeds, David McKay has shown himself to be an opportunist, a chameleon who changes colors the way others change clothes. He lies and thinks nothing of it. He abandons his family and thinks nothing of it. He sees a good friend burned to death, stands by, and does nothing about it. Would such a man stop at murder? I think not.

"David McKay is a spoiled Negro. A spoiled Negro? Two terms some would say are mutually exclusive. But there it is. He had more than any decent Negro could hope for; yet he wasn't satisfied. Cowardice, greed—would a man with such qualities stop at murder? I think not.

"Jameson Sweet, on the other hand, was a hardworking man, a good example to Negroes everywhere. He overcame daunting disadvantages to become an attorney. He was a giving man, a brave man, dedicated to making life better for his people. He was a loving husband who patiently nursed his ailing wife . . . only to be cut down by her self-serving brother."

Baker leaned on the rail separating him from the jury. He looked each member of the panel in the eye, taking his time. His normally stern visage was softened by the hint of a sad smile.

"It's up to you," he said. "You have the power to make David McKay pay." He raised his fist and brought it down on the railing in an intense, silent blow. The touch of compassion in his expression was gone, replaced by one of hate. "Make him pay! *Make him pay! MAKE HIM PAY!*"

Nevin paced slowly, thoughtfully, back and forth before the jury box. An impressive figure and a gifted speaker, he had inherited his father's eloquence as a Baptist preacher. Nevin knew exactly what he wanted to say. His slow pacing was meant to give the jury members time to recover from the dark emotions stirred by Baker's speech. Every trial attorney knows that the fight for the jury's vote entails a battle for its heart as well as its mind, the first often superseding the other. When Nevin sensed that the jury members had settled down, had focused on him, he began.

He opened by thanking them for their time and patience, and he expressed confidence that they would reach a fair and well-considered verdict. As he moved to the core of the matter, his tone was conversational, reasonable, and quietly but intensely passionate.

"Evidence," he said. "*Evidence.* That is the *crux* of the matter. Remember: In this country, a man is innocent until proven guilty. Proven by *evidence.* Only two sets of fingerprints were found on the gun that killed Jameson Sweet. Did either of them belong to David McKay? No, they did not. Did one of them belong to Jameson Sweet? Yes, they did.

"I repeat: *Evidence.* Look to the evidence. But how can we? There is *no* evidence that David McKay shot Jameson Sweet. There is, however, evidence that Jameson Sweet shot himself."

Nevin's voice took on the rolling cadence of the pulpit preacher. His walk became more vigorous as he strode the span of the jury box. He was no ordinary attorney; he was a craftsman. His soaring, vital voice drove on. Steadily and precisely, he depicted the fallacies of the state's case.

"The charges against David McKay were based on his alleged motive: to keep his double life a secret. Since the trial began, a second alleged motive— to avenge his sister's death—has been brought to bear. These motives remain unproved. Yes, David McKay wanted to retain his privacy, but he had already agreed to give Nella Harding details of his life. Yes, he wanted his sister's killer punished, but it was a legal, a judicial punishment he planned to seek. Gentlemen of the jury, this case boils down to the word of the state against that of the accused.

"My learned colleague, Mr. Baker, sees no reason to believe David McKay. David McKay is a liar, says Mr. Baker: David McKay has lived a lie for four years. Has denied his own people for four years. This man, implies Mr. Baker, is a murderous coward. But I remind you: This man is a war hero. This man has faced what no member of this jury will ever face—the blood-lust of a lynch mob."

Nevin leaned on the jury box. "Who among you would have acted differently than David McKay? Who is ready to cast the first stone? David McKay did not turn from his people—he turned from injustice. Shall I repeat his words? He said, 'I did not decide to pass for white. I did decide *to let people see what they wanted to see.'*"

"I ask you: What kind of moral code requires a man to constantly identify himself as a target for racial hatred? Or to make himself a willing victim for the proponents of genocide? Tell me, men of the jury, which one of *you* would have stepped forward to endure the hangman's noose or the burning pyre?"

Nevin paused to let his words sink in. "David McKay's initial denial of his racial identity was born of terror. But his long-term decision to no longer brand himself as either black or white stemmed neither from fear nor cowardice, but from despair. Despair at the murderous stupidity of lynch mobs; despair at the haunting political impotence of the black race; at the rigidity of America's caste system and the knowledge that the democracy you fought for overseas will turn a blind eye when you're lynched at home.

"As you know, in this country, a man's worth is irrevocably determined by his racial identity. David McKay thought his decision to be *neither black nor white* would free him from America's whole mad obsession with race, and in his sense of racial responsibility, he worked privately, feverishly to help as many of his people as he could. How can you see a man who cares that much, who labors that hard, as a murderous coward?"

David thought of his clients in Philadelphia. Now he knew how they felt when they were on trial: the helplessness and frustration at the beginning; the despair and resignation toward the end. He had always tried to give them hope. He had asked them to have faith. He realized with a sinking heart that retaining faith was the most difficult of all things to do. He found himself praying as he hadn't prayed in years, for hope, for faith, for courage to endure what he was sure would befall him.

They took him to another room in the courthouse to await the jury's decision. He asked Nevin to leave him alone, then sat down on one of the hard wooden chairs furnishing the barren room and stared out of the barred window.

Inevitably, his thoughts returned to Rachel. She had offered to serve him choice bits of truth on each successive visit.

"What shall I tell you today?" she would ask. "What do you want to know?"

"Tell me," he'd said the evening before, "about Jameson Sweet."

"Jimmy? Now what's there to say about him?" She played at being surprised. But her mocking tone was softened by a bittersweet smile.

"He was your sheik, your sugar daddy?" he asked.

"And my friend." Her look was teasing. "Jealous?"

"No," he said mildly with a little shake of his head.

"Just curious, huh?" She was suddenly bitter. "You never loved me."

"No, but I cared. For a while, I cared very much."

"And now?"

"Does it matter?"

She eyed him. Her heart-shaped face was tight with anger. "No," she said coolly. "It don't matter. Don't matter at all."

"I didn't think so."

Her eyes narrowed. "You want to know about Jimmy? Well, he loved me. Adored me. Always had. From the time we ran the streets as kids."

"You never talked about him."

"Why should I? I knew the kind of people I wanted to be with—and he wasn't one of them."

For the first time since he'd known her, David saw the naked ambition in her eyes, the sense of ruthless calculation that drove her. He did not fault her for it; given her life, he even understood it. Nevertheless, it repelled him.

"I saw less of Jimmy as I grew older. Years went by. Then I ran into him two years ago, right after I moved back from D.C. Jimmy knew about the baby. Seems like everybody did. I was tired, broke. Jimmy tried to help. After Mama died, he offered me everything he had. He thought he could make me forget. But he was wrong."

Her soft voice was heavy with hate. "I wanted to make you people hurt the way you hurt me, and I wanted Jimmy to help me do it." Her voice trailed off, as she remembered. "He tried to talk me out of it. He promised to deliver the sun and the moon and the stars, if I'd just give up my idea. But I wouldn't. Finally, he gave in. He loved me too much to let me try it alone."

David had never expected to feel sympathy for Sweet, but for a moment he felt something quite close to it. He rearranged his normally expressive face into a mask, but he found it impossible to keep the rage from his eyes.

"What was your plan?" he asked in a dull voice.

"It was simple: Jimmy was to marry Lilian, fake her suicide, then wait a while and marry me."

"As simple as that?"

She arched an eyebrow. "Yeah, as simple as that." She smiled provocatively. "You're very handsome when you're mad."

"Is that what you told Sweet before you shot him?"

The smile disappeared. She was furious. "What d'you care what I said to him? What I *did* with him on the parlor sofa—before he died?"

He gave a slow, studied shrug. "You're right. I don't give a damn what you two did together. I just want to know about my sisters. You introduced him to Lilian, didn't you?"

"Well, what of it? She wanted to marry a dark-skinned man. To make herself look good. To prove her commitment to the race by marrying 'a real Negro.' My, my, she was something. A pathetic snob who knew nothing about men." Scorn distorted Rachel's pretty features.

"But Rachel, when you learned that she was going to have a child—"

"That changed nothing."

"You still planned to kill her?"

"Of course." She gave him a long, long stare and a strange light came into her eyes. "I wanted Lilian dead. You hear me? Dead. You think I should've had pity on her 'cause she was carrying a baby. But she didn't have pity on me. Lilian as much as killed my child—our child, David, our child. I didn't owe Lilian a damn thing. Isabella would've lived—if only she'd gotten good food, good medicine—if only she'd had you."

Something convulsed inside him. His blood pounded in his face. "Tell me the rest," he said thickly.

She gave him one last resentful look. Then her features composed themselves. Her passions, so dramatically evident one second, disappeared the next as though some mental door had swung shut behind them. Within a minute, her face was calm.

"Everything was going fine. Then Gem arrived. That worried us, but we decided to go ahead with our plan. We didn't know Gem had plans of her own. Not until later, when Gem told Jimmy what she'd done to Lilian at Nella Harding's house."

A look of injured self-righteousness swept over her face. "You think I'm cold-hearted. Well, what about Gem? She killed her own sister: shot her in the heart. Right on Nella's dock. Gem said she'd wondered how it would feel to kill. But it was no big deal. She said she'd had more fun shooting rabbits. So there."

David knew that she expected a response; he gave her none. He believed what she said about Gem, of course. He believed her one hundred percent. It was more or less what he had figured out. But that made the confirming details no less painful to hear. And Rachel knew it. Telling him how Gem had murdered Lilian was part of her revenge. She wanted to wound him and she was doing a good job of it. He felt as though she were raking his heart with claws, but he was determined not to let her know it, so he met her vicious tongue with silence. He knew that she would be unable to hold out and he was right. Her own need to tell him everything drove her on. She began speaking in a low, vehement tone. And he listened—he had to. He was truly a captive listener. He had sought the truth and now he had it, delivered in its most brutal form. She told him how Gem had stripped Lilian's body on the spot.

"That's when she saw Lilian's belly. It was a little too round. She touched it and nearly rocked on her heels. A baby. Gem thought back on how Jimmy had acted—how he and Lilian had acted together—and it hit her like a thunderclap that maybe Lilian hadn't told Jimmy about the baby. It was a slight chance. Slighter than the crack in an ant's behind. But still there. And if Lilian *had* told him . . . Well, Gem figured she'd have to have herself a little accident. Maybe a fall down the stairs.

"Anyway, she didn't waste time worrying. She dragged the body to the edge of the dock, tied it up with some rope and rocks, and rolled it off the pier. The next morning, she put on Lilian's clothes and drove back in Lilian's car.

"Jimmy didn't suspect—at first. But Gem was a lousy actress. Too conceited. Didn't like having to pretend to be somebody else—especially when that somebody was Lilian. Finally, Jimmy said something. She admitted everything. Even bragged about it.

"Jimmy said he'd turn her in. But she said she'd say he helped her. It would've been his word against hers. Then she told him he'd be smarter to just play along and let her 'keep Lilian alive.' No one would be the wiser. You were the only one who could tell the difference, David. But you'd been gone for years. Gem was sure you'd died in some southern cornfield. No one else could guess. Not even Annie. Gem didn't know about me. So, Jimmy and me let her think she was getting her way. We decided we'd just wait a while, then kill her, too."

David was past being shocked. Still, he stared at her, wondering. Her face was familiar—her eyes, her nose, her delicate throat—but he felt as though a stranger sat before him. Where was the desirable woman he had married? Had she ever existed? Usually, he had good instincts for people. Why had he never perceived the bitterness, the ruthlessness that simmered within her? There *had* been times when he had sensed something . . . something not quite right. That was the best choice of words he could come up with. But his remorse had blinded him. His sense of guilt and regret had disabled him. *Now I'm free of such constraints,* he thought bitterly. His mind was once more free to follow a logical train of thought, no matter where it led him.

"Was it was your idea to drive Gem out of her mind using drugs?"

Rachel's smile was smug. "We'd done it to Lilian. I stole the drugs from the hospital. Jimmy mixed them with Gem's food, put them in her drinks. Then he brought me into the house. To help 'take care of her.' We waited a year. A whole damn year. Long enough for everyone to know she was sick. I got tired of it, so I said: 'Jimmy, go do it.' He picked the weekend he was supposed to be in Newark."

"And what about his alibi? The roommate who said Sweet was there all night—did Sweet buy him?"

"He didn't have to. Charlie Epps. Good ol' Charlie. He don't know if Jimmy was there all night 'cause he wasn't there himself. He spent the night having fun with a lady friend. Naturally, he didn't want the missus to find out."

"So Sweet was supposed to be *his* alibi?"

She laughed. "He didn't know he was going to be Jimmy's alibi, too."

"Clever," was all David said.

Her smiled faded. "I'll tell you who was clever—*I* was." She leaned forward, her small hands curled into fists. "Jimmy came back here, did what he had to do, and drove back to Jersey. It went down fine. Then Annie found your address. As soon as I knew you were coming back, I decided to go to work on you. Jimmy didn't like it. But somebody had to keep an eye on you." Her tone became syrupy sweet. "I knew you'd trust me."

His temples throbbed painfully. How many times had she misled him? In how many ways had she masked her lies? She had been so fearful when he shared his suspicions against Sweet and so relieved when he found no evidence to support them. In his mind, he heard her voice denying the importance of her history with Sweet; praising Sweet as a husband; dismissing Lilian's pregnancy as imagined; and trying to dissuade him from seeking Gem . . . because she herself had ordered Gem's death.

He listened, outwardly calm, as she told him that at the beginning, she had simply wanted to keep him in line—and get him to leave Harlem as soon as possible. She had pressed him to accept Lilian's death as suicide. But then she had seen that he was determined to dig deeper, and that had frightened her. Horrified at his discovery of Lilian's diary, she'd tried every argument to dissuade him from taking on Sweet. And when that didn't work, she'd had to do some quick thinking.

"I decided to tell you what you wanted to hear."

"And when you offered me your loving—"

"It was a little insurance. I had to get you to trust me again. And yes, I wanted you." She leaned toward him. "I'm not as terrible as I sound. Part of me, the part that was scared of being found out, couldn't wait for you to leave Harlem. The other part, the part that still loved you, ached at the thought of it. Every time you came by, I thought it might be the last time I'd ever see you.

"When you showed up, asking about Isabella, I was shocked. And then when you proposed . . ." She shook her head. "I just couldn't believe it. It looked like the Lord was finally gonna answer my prayers. Everything I ever wanted was right there for the taking. I could have it all. Not just the house, but the McKay name. I was so happy . . . And then, I remembered Sweet."

She felt, she said, as though she was walking a tightrope. On the one hand, she hoped desperately that he would never uncover what Sweet had done, for that would mean her own unmasking; on the other, she hoped that he would get rid of Sweet for her, so she could fulfill her dream of living with him on Strivers' Row. She only killed Sweet, she said, because Sweet forced her to.

"Letting me go to you was Jimmy's biggest mistake. He never guessed that I'd fall in love with you again."

"Rachel . . . I don't think you have the faintest idea what love means."

Was that pain in her eyes? She looked stung. "Don't judge me. Your family put me through hell. I know what you think of me. I can see it in your eyes. You think I'd use anyone and anything to get my way. You see something wrong with that and maybe you're right. But your family ain't no better. That pile of money you sitting on, your daddy didn't earn by doing good deeds. Anybody and everybody'll tell you that. Maybe that's why he was so fixed on making you into some kind of social hero."

"My father never plotted to kill—"

"He put people out on the street. In the middle of winter, in ice and snow. Whole families, children and old people. When they couldn't pay the rent, he'd take the best of their furniture, sell it and trash the rest. Now don't act like you don't know about that."

Yes, he did know about his father's cruelty. Thank God, he also knew about Lila's kindness. She'd made it her business to quietly find new homes for every single family Augustus evicted. Everyone in the neighborhood knew about it; everyone but Augustus.

"Perhaps you have a point," he said firmly, "but we were talking about you."

"Fine. I did what I had to do to survive. But I didn't use you, David. I gave you what you wanted. A way to ease your conscience. You felt guilty about Isabella. But it wasn't me making you feel guilty. That was you. It wasn't even me who told you about Isabella in the first place. That was Annie—"

"You knew she'd eventually tell me—"

"It wasn't her place. Me, I wouldna never said nothing. I got too much pride for that. When you asked me to marry you, I even turned you down. I gave you a chance to back out. Whatever else you can say about me, you can't say I used you and you can't say I used my baby's memory to get you."

And that, David realized, was to a certain degree, the truth.

The jury deliberated for four hours. *One hour for every year I was away,* David mused. The jury returned its verdict in late afternoon. As the twelve men filed in and sat down, David noticed that they avoided looking his way. They looked at anything, anyone other than him. His chest tightened. Nevin touched him on the elbow. They rose to hear the decision.

"In the death of Jameson Sweet, we, the jury, find the defendant, David McKay, guilty of murder in the first degree."

Guilty.

The word echoed within him. He closed his eyes and bowed his head. Mayhem exploded behind him. He heard cheers and whistles, catcalls and boos. Amid the uproar, he barely heard Nevin's whispered promise: "I'll get it reversed on appeal." There was the bang of Richter's gavel and a stern demand for quiet. The order was ignored. Richter banged his gavel again and again. David forced himself to take a deep breath and straightened up. He glanced behind him and saw that a fistfight had broken out in one corner of the room. Guards pulled the men apart. Richter was furious. He declared a twenty-four-hour cooling-off period and said he would postpone sentencing until the next day.

David listened with half an ear as the judge ordered his return to the Tombs. Annie, Nella, and Snyder had rushed to his side. Nella's sapphire eyes glittered with what looked suspiciously like tears. Snyder squeezed him by the shoulders. Toby's mother stood by her chair, afraid to approach. Roy shook his head sadly, his eyes watery.

David felt numb. All around him was pandemonium. People wagged their tongues and slapped hands as if settling bets. Others looked sadly at David and shook their heads. Reporters pushed and shoved and finally climbed over one another in a mad dash to file updates.

David caught Canfield's eye. The aristocratic lawyer sat stock-still, his back ramrod straight. His disapproving face seemed as hard as chiseled stone. He rose and approached David. Nella and Snyder dropped back. Canfield looked David in the eye.

"I never thought I'd rejoice to see twelve white men put one black man behind bars. But men like you shame us all." His rigid demeanor momentarily softened. "Thank God your father isn't here to see this."

David's jaw hardened. He held himself still. Nevin smiled grimly. Granting a glance to the little group at David's side, Canfield gave a curt bow, clicked his polished heels, and turned away. David watched him blend into the crowd and disappear. Then he saw Rachel. There, in a corner. Their eyes locked. He felt himself grow pale. He saw her relief at the verdict and he remembered her words, *If you're waiting to hear me say I'm sorry, you'll be waiting a long, long time.* He acknowledged her with a courteous nod. Her eyes narrowed and a feline smile bowed her lips. She blew him a kiss, then turned and sashayed out the door.

On Tuesday, April 27, Richter sentenced David to die in the electric chair. The execution was set to take place in two weeks, on May 11, 1926.

Nevin had begun work on an appeal even before the jury presented a verdict. Within days, he laid it on Richter's desk, claiming several points of error in the trial.

Nevin maintained that the jury was biased against David from the beginning. At least two of the jurors had been heard to make racist remarks, he wrote. One man named Jack Dawson had said, "[It] does my heart good to see a nigger go down. If they choose me for the jury, ain't no way I'm gonna let that nigger go." A number of people had overheard the second juror, "Sling" Monahan, say it was a shame the state was "gonna waste 'lectricity frying a spade. Just string him up and get it done with." In response, Baker produced formal statements by each jury member about their utter neutrality and lack of racial prejudice.

Nevin also contended that the virulent news coverage and raucous crowds gathered outside the courthouse had poisoned the atmosphere and intimidated the jury, excluding any possibility of a fair trial.

He maintained that Nyman's gossipy testimony about David's alleged sexual adventures should have been excluded. The testimony was inflammatory and unsupported, he said.

He concluded his appeal with the customary refrain that the prosecution's evidence as a whole was weak, circumstantial, and "of questionable taste."

Richter commended Nevin on his eloquence and surprisingly said that he himself was not fully convinced of David's culpability. But the jury was convinced "beyond a shadow of a doubt." If Nevin wanted a new trial, he'd have to go to the New York State Supreme Court. Richter handed down his decision on Friday, May 7. David McKay had four days left to live.

He rubbed his forehead. "I'll be filing the appeal tomorrow. If we could get a new trial—"

"A new trial ain't good enough. It could end the same way. We gotta trap her, fix her. Show that she's the one done done it."

"You think she killed Sweet?"

"I know she did."

Uptown that evening, Annie sank to her knees and leaned heavily on the edge of her bed. Putting her hands together, she closed her eyes and prayed fervently, paraphrasing the eighty-ninth Psalm.

"You have exalted the right hand of David's adversaries; you have made all his enemies rejoice . . . and covered him with shame. Selah. How long, Lord? How long? Will you hide yourself forever?"

Downtown, David tossed on his hard mattress. He could hear Rachel's voice as though she were in the room.

"You understand why I had to do it. It would've been so different if you people had been nice to me."

"We people? We took you into our home. We shared our lives—"

"You kept me around as a 'social case.' Someone you could point to. Look down on. Feel sorry for. Daddy McKay couldn't stand me. I wasn't good enough, smart enough, fine enough. Now I've got everything he built. His name, his money, his house. I fought for it. I earned it. And I'm gonna keep it."

The next morning, Annie walked into her kitchen and found Rachel going through the cupboards. Annie halted in midstride. Her mouth sagged open. Rachel turned around, saw Annie, and put her hands on her hips.

"This kitchen is a mess. It has to be redone."

"'Scuse me?"

"This kitchen," repeated Rachel bitingly, "is a mess. I'll show you how I want it—"

"But I've got my kitchen just the way it should be."

"This is not your kitchen. It's my house and my kitchen."

"I done run this kitchen for years. I cooked your meals here when you was a young visitor. And I did it just fine—"

"Well, I'm not a visitor anymore. I'm mistress of this house and I want changes."

"But Miss Rachel, Mr. David don't like it when someone else is in this kitchen—"

"Mr. David isn't here. He's gone and he's not coming back. This is the beginning of a new day—my day—and you'll do what I say."

Annie crossed her arms across her chest. Her dark eyes swept over Rachel.

"All right, I'll take my orders from you. But first, tell me one thing."

Rachel waited.

"How could you say you loved him?"

Rachel's eyes widened. Her hand flashed out to slap Annie, but Annie caught Rachel's arm in midair. Her strong, callused hands closed around Rachel's bony wrist and forced it down. Rachel tried to yank herself free, but Annie held tight.

"*Miss* Rachel, I done watched over Mr. David since his mother died, so I got the right t'ask a mother's question. One mo' time: How could you say you loved him?"

Annie's eyes were hard. Rachel stared back at her, defiant, but she couldn't hold out against the old woman's strength. Rachel's gaze faltered. Her angry pride buckled and a shadow of shame flitted across her face. She looked down, struck silent, and Annie, with a look of contempt and pity, released her. Rubbing her wrist, Rachel stumbled to the doorway. She halted on the threshold and turned. Her face was drawn and haunted; her voice hoarse.

"You ask a mother's question; I'll give you a mother's answer. I used to love David. But that love died long ago. It got buried with a baby in a D.C. graveyard."

Annie gasped. Rachel flung herself from the room.

"Lord, help us," Annie cried. "What's she gonna do now?"

Rachel had run upstairs to David's bedroom. Annie found Rachel hastily packing her few things. Rachel looked up. "I'm taking over the master bedroom."

"But Mr. David don't want nobody in there."

Rachel slammed the lid of her second suitcase shut. "Old woman, you better learn to listen to me." She pointed to her two bags. "Take this stuff for me."

"No, ma'am. You wanna move in there, you gotta do it by yourself."

Seething, Rachel grabbed her bags and dragged them out of the room. Annie followed her to what had been Lilian's room. She watched Rachel from the doorway. "Mr. David—"

Rachel spun around. Fury contorted her pretty face. "Get out!" She shoved Annie out of the room and slammed the door. Rachel's narrow chest heaved. Spying Lilian's brushes on the dressing table, she crossed the room and raked them all into a trash can.

That afternoon, she quit her job at Harlem Hospital and went on a Fifth Avenue spending spree. Later, she stood before the mirror in the master bedroom, admiring herself in her new mink coat. *Suits me just fine.*

She heard the downstairs doorbell ring. *Who could that be? Probably another one of them damn reporters.* They had constantly pestered her since David's conviction. *Will there be an appeal, Mrs. McKay? Do you still believe in your husband? Hell, no,* she wanted to say. It had taken all of her self-control to bite her lip modestly, to do her best to look shy and smile sadly.

"Miss Rachel?"

She swung around. Annie stood in the doorway. Rachel decided that she hated her. She would replace her as soon as possible. "What is it?" she snapped. "I told you I don't want to be disturbed. If it's one of those newspaper people—"

"It's Mr. Canfield. Mr. Byron Canfield."

Rachel raised an eyebrow. Now this was a surprise. What could *he* want? She should refuse to see him. That would be best. After all, it was his fault that David was behind bars. "Tell him to go away."

Rachel turned her back on Annie and returned to admiring her reflection. *I look mighty fine in this fur coat, mighty fine.*

"Miss Rachel, I knows you don't wanna hear no advice from me, but when a man like Byron Canfield says he wants t'talk t'you, it's best t'hear him out."

Rachel swung back, a sharp rebuke on the tip of her tongue. But something stopped her. She wondered. Maybe Canfield's visit didn't have nothing to do with David at all. She'd heard that the old geezer had an eye for the ladies. Maybe with David gone, he was looking to give her a little company? A nasty little smile played about her lips. She almost giggled. Everybody knew he was one of the most important Negro men in all America, a real big shot with the Movement. He knew just about everybody. If she got in good with him, her life was made. But better not be too nice to him at first. Got to play the hurt wife, mourning for her wronged man. Oh, yes, she could do that well.

"All right. Show him into the parlor. I'll be down in a minute."

A Man of the Superior Sort

Byron Canfield prided himself on being a realist. He knew that no one was perfect, himself included. But he preferred to believe that he was of the superior sort—the kind of man who rarely made mistakes and when he did, moved quickly to correct them. That afternoon, he found himself at the McKay house on a mission he would've never foreseen. Nonetheless, he was looking forward to it with relish.

Rachel entered the room. She was exactly as he remembered her: lovely to the eye, with an air of fragile delicacy that would evoke the protective instincts of any warm-blooded man. Coming forward, she shook his hand. "You're an unexpected guest." Her smile was charming but restrained.

"Lovely home you have here. Exquisitely done."

Rachel's smile warmed. "Thank you," she said. "I enjoy decorating."

He was quite aware that it was Lila McKay, not Rachel, who had decorated the house, but he was of the opinion that most people gladly accept even the most blatantly undeserved compliments.

They chatted amiably over this and that, and then he came to the apparent point of his visit.

"I hope there are no hard feelings, Mrs. McKay. Of course, I was very upset at the death of Jameson Sweet and I only thought it right to inform the police of what he had told me. But you must believe that it was done without any personal animosity."

Rachel accepted this pretty little speech with a polite murmur.

"I won't take up much of your time," he said. "But there was one other small matter."

Rachel regarded him steadily, expectantly. He had to admire her poise, her self-possession, and the hypnotic effect of those emerald eyes.

"And what would that matter be?"

"Simply this."

He went into his jacket pocket and withdrew a thin envelope, which he handed to her. Opening it, she found a ticket bearing her name for an ocean liner to Italy. Her eyes widened with puzzlement and suspicion. She looked up at him sharply. "What's this?"

"The other ticket, in Jameson's name, is in my office safe. I didn't learn of the tickets until yesterday. They were forgotten in the confusion over his death. Apparently, he intended to go away." Canfield paused. "And he expected you to go with him."

"That can't be. You're mistaken."

She said it mildly enough, but something unpleasant flickered in her eyes.

"My dear, you needn't deny it. The evening he died, he messaged his secretary and asked her to make travel arrangements—for two. He gave her your name."

"Really, Mr. Canfield, I—"

"Jameson was like a son to me. And like a father, I suspected certain things but lacked the courage to confront him. There were opportunities, but I missed them and I'll always regret it. He was distracted. His work had begun to suffer. I thought it was his wife's illness. Now I know there was another reason."

"You've overstayed your welcome. Please leave."

"David McKay's statement that he accused Jameson of killing Gem is part of the public record. It's a fairly complicated story and the newspapers botched most of the details. I didn't see any point in learning them myself—not until I heard of Jameson's travel plans. Then I sat down with Nevin Caruthers. He related every detail of the whole indelicate tale. He also showed me an analysis of the so-called medicine Jameson was giving Lilian. I made a call to Harlem Hospital and had a very interesting conversation with your former superior. It seems there's been an unexplained shortage of the very same drugs—"

"You can't believe—"

"I'm afraid I do. Jameson was a tough attorney, but a weak man. I can't blame him. Seeing you, my dear, I can well understand how you got him to do your bidding."

"Leave!"

"The ticket is still valid. If I were you, I'd use it. At least, I'd try."

"I am staying here." She arched her small head regally. "You have nothing against me. Nothing. You're just trying to intimidate me."

"Of course I am." He said it almost kindly. "My dear, have you any idea what will happen to you if you do stay? You will be arrested. Caruthers and

I will work to the bitter end to see you convicted. Should we fail and you retain your freedom, then you may of course spend your life in this house. But no one will visit you. No one will open his door to you. I'll see to it that you are socially dead to everyone who matters. When I'm done, you'll be buried alive, grateful for the company of jail-house prisoners."

Fear had crept into her eyes. "Why are you doing this?"

"Because you destroyed a wonderful young man. Jameson had his failings. He was perhaps too ambitious. Too bitter. But he had pride—in himself and in his people. He had vision. You betrayed him. Worse, you made him betray himself. And for that, I will never forgive you."

"But—"

"I was too late to save Jameson, but I owe it to myself—and to the Movement—to save David. He's a good man. I underestimated him. Now he's behind bars for a crime he didn't commit, and you and I are to blame. I intend to make amends. And I intend to *make sure* that you do, too."

The doorbell rang. Rachel gasped. Her frightened gaze flew from Canfield to the parlor doors, then back to him. She heard the murmur of official voices. The parlor doors slid open and David stood there. Two escorting police officers, Detective Peters, Nevin Caruthers, Adrian Snyder, and Annie stood behind him.

Said Canfield: "You see, my dear, you did it all for nothing."

Rachel ran to David and flung her arms around him. "David, please! You don't know what this man's been saying to me. He's threatened me. He's—"

David gently but firmly disengaged himself. He grasped her by the shoulders and held her away. He gazed down into her panicked face and after a long searching moment, said: "It's over, Rachel. It's really . . . finally . . . indisputably over."

"Please!" she wailed.

Compassion rose in his eyes. He folded her into his arms and she clung to him.

"Baby, baby," he whispered. "Didn't anyone ever tell you to never, ever, burn your bridges 'til you'd crossed safely to the other side? You should've learned that a long time ago."

She hiccupped like a child and looked up at him, confused.

"Now," he said, "it's just too damn late."

He released her. Her eyes widened in fear and shock. The two officers flanked her.

"Oh, God, David, no!"

•   •   •

Days of exhausting celebration followed David's release. Upper-crust Harlem welcomed home its lost son with backslapping, handshaking, and toasts to his good health.

"We believed in you all the time," his neighbors said.

"Sure you did." His smile was good-natured, but his eyes were knowing.

Canfield, backed up by two other leading Movement officials, approached him with offers of reinstatement, but David politely thanked them and turned them down. He preferred to labor outside the established but strife-torn civil rights organization.

Amid all the festivities, he made time to honor his sisters. He saw to it that Lilian's remains were given proper burial. He visited what he now knew to be Gem's grave and whispered words of reconciliation. He also ordered a new headstone and invited Adrian and Nella to a small, very private service in Gem's memory. Afterward, David escorted Nella to her car, then drew Adrian aside. He shook the gangster's hand.

"I want to thank you. Canfield told me how you stepped in and got the D.A. to listen."

"Baker was a tough nut to crack."

"Canfield said you cut a deal. Hope it didn't cost you too much."

"I gave him what he wanted; he gave me what I wanted."

David looked at him.

Adrian smiled. "You don't want to know too much."

"No, but tell me anyway."

"Look, it was a straight exchange. You were a big fish; I tossed him a bigger one."

"Not another race man, I hope?"

"'Course not. A dirty judge."

"Not one of yours?"

Adrian laughed. "Hey, I like you, but not well enough to give up one of my own. No, this was one of the competition's."

Later that afternoon, David approached the door to his father's office. He hesitated, and then reached for the doorknob. Taking a deep breath, he gave the knob a slight twist. In his heart, he still expected it to resist him. He was surprised when the lock clicked and the door swung inward. With his knuckles, he nudged it open and went in. The office was as gloomy and musty as he remembered it, but it had lost its dark magic. It no longer oppressed him. He saw it for what it was: an old room with old things, simply that and nothing more. Walking to his father's desk, he leaned on it. The wood grain felt warm and welcome beneath his hands. He walked behind the desk, swung the wide chair around, and eased down into it.

It felt right.

David stood up. He swept open the curtains and threw up the windows. Light and air streamed in. He inhaled hope.

After the long, stubborn winter, the air had finally gained that balmy touch that signifies spring. The streets were alive with people. Harlemites were bursting out of their cramped apartments, pouring into the streets, searching for life, liberty, and a spark of adventure. The air crackled with vitality and tingled with a steady current of pride. David sensed its strength and felt a part of him reach out for it. Suddenly, Harlem seemed to have so much to offer. That afternoon, it assaulted his eyes with brilliant colors, teased his nose with delicious aromas, and soothed his ears with the rolling notes of jazz careening from radios propped in open windows. David felt nourished by the rich diversity of humanity around him. Bits of conversation floated to him, delicious jokes and improbable tales, his people's words, their idiosyn- cratic phrases—the lyrics to a song he instinctively knew how to sing.

Across the street, an old man pushed a wide broomstick in front of his grocery store and waved his fists at a pair of youngsters who tossed a bread wrapper at his feet. At the next light, two young women ran giggling across the street. A little down the way, three little girls were having a good time with a game of double-dutch, their pigtails flying and skinny legs pumping in time to the dancing rope.

> *Once upon a time*
> *Goose drink wine*
> *Monkey did the Shimmy on the trolley-car line.*
> *Trolley car broke*
> *Monkey choke*
> *And they all went to heaven in an old tin boat.*

On impulse, David made for the Mayfair Diner. Grabbing his favorite waitress by the hand, he took the dirty dishes from her and paid her boss to give her the day off.

"You're crazy," she cried. "Where are we going?"

"Nowhere and everywhere."

Together, they swung down Seventh. They happened to see two men unloading a large refrigerator from a small truck and paused to observe them. David noticed two women standing on the stoop of a building nearby. They were watching the men work.

"I wanted me a new fridge. Wanted it somethin' bad," one said. "Couldn't get it out of my head. But my ol' man, he said we didn't have no money. Well, I knows that was partly true. We did and we didn't. T'tell the truth, these last two winters was so cold, we ain't need no fridge. Just used to set the food out on the windowsill. Still, I had it in my head that I was gonna get one like them rich white ladies got."

The refrigerator's apparent new owner had thrown a cheap coat over her baggy housedress. Perfectly aligned rows of hair clips covered her head. Her legs were bare and she wore flat cloth house slippers. Her upper lip was sunken in as though she'd lost several of her upper teeth. Her attention was fastened on the deliverymen.

"Hey, y'all be careful with that," she yelled, then turned back to her girl-friend. "Anyways, I know the only thing my Joe care about is his beer. So Tuesday last, I up and puts his beer in the oven for a bit, turns the oven on real low. Don't take much. Didn' want it t'explode. Wouldn't you know, by the time Joe comes home, that beer's warm enough t'take a bath in! He took one swig, liked t'gag. Man, don't you know he went out an' bought a new fridge the very next day! Got one of them fine things they had t'order spe-cial. That's why it took so long t'get here."

There was a suspicious noise from the truck. The woman took one look at what the deliverymen were doing, dashed down her steps, and went run-ning across the street, slippers flapping, arms waving, all the time screaming warnings, threats, and advice.

David had to laugh. He hadn't laughed in a long time and it felt good. He felt a flash of exhilaration that stunned him. Yes, Harlem was poor and it was battered, but it never quit. The sense of racial pride that had died at the lynching surged back. These were *his* people and they were a tough lot. He was proud of their creativity, their humor, their endurance and absolute determination to survive.

A great weariness descended upon him and dread rose within him when he thought of the world beyond Harlem's doorstep. He recalled his lonely room in Philadelphia. He was indeed tired of living as a stranger in a strange land. He had learned much and seen even more during his foray into the white world. It wasn't as wonderful to be white as some might think. It was